10 MEN

10 MEN

A REVERSE HAREM ROMANCE

STEPHANIE BROTHER

Independent

COPYRIGHT

10 MEN © Stephanie Brother 2019

ISBN: 978-1-915436-02-3

PROLOGUE

When I was younger, I used to imagine meeting one gorgeous man who'd be absolutely perfect for me. He'd sweep me off my feet and treat me like a princess. I believed that I'd have the happy ever after ending that we all want. Then my dad proved to be a total frog, and mom lost the rose-tint from her glasses. Suddenly, my idea of a fairy tale love life seemed totally unrealistic.

Finding the one used to be something I looked forward to, but after witnessing all the drama and betrayal in my own parent's marriage, I didn't want to dream about something that seemed so unlikely to become a reality.

That was until mom met Roderick McGregor, and he swept her off her feet.

Roderick McGregor is a silver fox, and he's richer than Croesus. I guess you could say mom landed on her feet. I'm sure there are plenty of people who are saying mean things about her being a gold digger, but I'm not going to be one of them.

Mr. McGregor might be rich, but he's arrogant with it. If I wasn't certain that my mom could give as good as she gets, I'd be advising her to walk away. It seems, though, that Roderick might be more than just a little smitten and that mom has him completely wrapped around her little finger.

So, what might all this have to do with my little story?

That is a damn good question.

I used to think that finding the one was going to be impossible.

Then I researched Roderick's ten gorgeous sons on Google, and I became a little more hopeful.

I know they're going to be my stepbrothers, but a girl can fantasize. If you saw them, you'd realize that resisting naughty thoughts about them in all their un-believable gorgeousness is pretty much impossible.

Aaron and Antony, Barret and Blake, Cameron and Casey, Donnie, Elliot, Ford, and Grant. Together they make up the management team for Roderick's huge property business empire.

I'll tell you more about them later and about the twists and turns that my life has taken, but what you need to know right now is that Roderick has one hell of a crazy plan for his sons and his company, and if he has his way, I am going to be a part of it all in a very unexpected way.

Chapter 1

We're moving today. It's been on the cards for a while, but Roderick won't stand for us living in this tiny two-bedroomed place anymore, and mom has finally given in now she has a four-karat rock on her finger.

Roderick isn't messing around. He wants a wife, and he set his sights on mom. I get the feeling that Roderick is used to getting what he wants. If he can't will it, he'll buy it. I'm pretty proud of mom for waiting this long, though. She held her ground and made sure he was not just messing her around.

I know that relationships shouldn't be about game playing, but it seems the more you resist, the more you get pursued. Funny how men want most what is hard to get.

Roderick has sent a truck to collect our stuff. Four large men are packing our things for removal. Mom and I have had to move many times before. We're used to stuffing our possessions into black bags and hoisting them into our rusty old SUV. Now we're standing here watching the men work while we drink coffee in the mugs that mom doesn't want to take with us.

There's a fully equipped kitchen at the mansion we

are moving into. These dollar store specials won't fit there at all.

Mom grins at me. "I have to say that this way of moving beats our usual struggle."

I nod and grin as one of the removal men trudges past with my box of shoes. "It sure does."

"I'm surprised that Roderick didn't come so that he could order everyone around." I glance at her, and she seems to smile as though the thought of him doing that is appealing. I don't understand that at all.

"I'm kinda glad he didn't bother," I say. "They seem to know what they're doing and who needs the stress."

Mum shakes her head. "One day, you'll understand, Laura. Men like to be in charge, and to be honest, if they are capable of leading, it makes life a whole lot easier to follow."

I frown, but she grins. "You remember that film, My Big Fat Greek Wedding?" I nod. "Well, the mom says something like, 'your dad may be the head, but I am the neck, and I can turn the head anyway I want to.' As long as you let them think they're the boss in the relationship, they're happy. What you need to know is how to get them to do what you want them to do and make them think that it's all their idea."

"And you know how to get Roderick to do that?" I ask.

"Sure," she says. "He thinks he's such a tough cookie, but he's really a pussy cat."

I shake my head. Since my first boyfriend, Ollie,

left town, my interest in the opposite sex has all but disappeared. I'm not saying that I don't get horny these days. I do. A lot. It's the looking at guys as relationship material that has waned. My heart was shredded when Ollie's father had to change jobs and move state. I would have tried to keep things going, but Ollie said he couldn't deal with a long-distance relationship. I guess he didn't love me as much as I thought he did because he let me go so easily.

"Well, I hope he's in a pussy cat mood when he sees the chair that you're planning to move into his palace."

Mom grimaces. "It was my dad's favorite chair. I can't just leave it behind."

"It's not me you need to convince," I laugh. Two removal men are eyeing the chair. It's mustard velvet and very bulky. "Where are you planning to put it, anyway?"

"Not sure," she says. "I'd like it in my dressing room, but I reckon Roderick will try and get me to store it."

"Well, I guess he'll have to put up with it because of its sentimental value."

She takes a sip of her coffee and licks the foam from her top lip. "Roderick isn't the most sentimental of men."

"Neither was grandpa," I remind her. Now I'm thinking about it. It's probably why mom loves these domineering men. It's what she grew up with. "If he was still alive, he'd give Mr. McGregor a real run for his money."

Mom seems to shudder. "Yeah, they probably wouldn't like each other at all."

"Either that or there'd be a begrudging kind of respect."

"Maybe." She doesn't sound sure, and I'm kinda glad we don't really need to find out. I hate conflict, especially the family argument variety. It's one of the reasons I've opted not to see my dad for a while. Always too much drama, and I just can't deal with it.

"Are you taking this?" the sexiest removal guy asks. It's our dog's old bed. Neither of us has had the heart to throw it away, and Bongo passed away over a year ago.

I look at mom, and she sighs. "I guess not."

"Okay," he says, gripping it by the soft fabric. "I'll put it in the dumpster."

It feels awful to watch him take it away, but this is it. We have to leave some of the past behind in order to fit into our new future. I lean back against the counter and look around at our place. It's certainly nothing to get sentimental about, and I won't be sad to leave it behind. The only thing that I loved was that it was just mom and me here. We've had fun together, and it's been a real home because of that. Now we're moving, and I know things at Roderick's are going to be very different. For one, mom will be sharing a suite with him, so there'll be no jumping into bed with her on a Saturday morning to watch cheesy re-runs and eat cereal. They have staff quarters, so pretty much all the chores will be handled by someone else. I'm not sure how I feel about that.

And then there are Roderick's sons.

I haven't met them, but as soon as mom mentioned them, I was on Google right away. Well, the McGregors are very well known for their business dealings, but it seems Roderick's sons are known for other things, too. My research has taken me to some interesting places. Newspaper reports about bar fights, magazine articles about paintings, and even some charity stuff for animal rescue. I suppose with ten sons you're bound to get a mixed bag. They sure sound interesting.

There are images of them, too. Images that have kept me awake at night.

I don't know how to sum up the McGregor boys except maybe by saying that I'd be afraid to be in the same room as all of them at the same time for fear my eyes would pop out of my head.

DAMN.

Three sets of identical twins and four unique brothers. Blue eyes, brown eyes, grey eyes, and even some green. Short hair, shaggy hair, beards, blond and brown hair. It's as though all the models from an edition of GQ magazine have decided to take up residence in one house.

One house that I'm about to move into.

OMG.

I'm just hoping that they all have girlfriends and that I can hold my resolve to focusing on my studies and ignoring men, however tempting they might be.

"You know, they're nearly finished," mom says, going to wash her mug in the sink.

"I know." I take her mine too and reach for the cloth to dry them. We may not be taking them with us, but the people moving in might appreciate them. "Are you nervous?"

Mom shakes her head. "You know, Laura. There are no certainties in life, but sometimes you just have to go with your gut. It's been telling me that Roderick is solid from our very first date, but my heart was damaged, and my mind was wary. I told him from the start that I was going to take a long time to trust him, and he's worked hard to earn it."

"Okay," I say, putting my hand on her shoulder. "You're a good judge of character, mom. The trouble is that sometimes people are very good at hiding the reality of who they really are. I don't get the feeling that Roderick is that kind of person at all, though. He strikes me as the kind of person who is just himself, 24/7, maybe to the point of it not being that healthy."

Mom laughs and reaches to pull me into a hug. She smells of a new fragrance that Roderick bought her for no reason other than to see her smile, and that makes me both happy and sad. She doesn't smell like my mom anymore. "I think you're right, baby-girl," she says, smoothing her hand over my shoulder in a way that takes me back at least a decade. "At least, I hope so with all my heart."

We pull away from each other and smile, and I feel a deep sense of relief to see her happy. Beneath that, though, is a sharp layer of fear that Mr. McGregor will turn out to be the biggest douchebag poor mom has ever come across, and we'll be back to square one again.

"Everything going okay in here?" a deep voice booms through the front door.

We both turn to find a gorgeous man leaning against the doorframe as though he owns the place. I recognize him as one of Roderick's sons, but I cannot for the life of me remember which one.

"Elliot," Mom says, moving quickly to place a kiss on his cheek and a pat on his bulging bicep. So that's who it is. Blond spikey hair and a black t-shirt make his green eyes pop. He's in joggers and trainers and looks like he's just coming back from the gym.

"Dad sent me to check on you," he says. It doesn't sound like he's upset about that fact. I guess, when you work for your father, you have to get used to taking orders.

"We're doing good." Mom waves her arm over the almost empty apartment. "He sent enough men to move us out of a mansion. We don't have much stuff."

"Yeah, that truck outside looks half empty." I don't think he's trying to be insulting, but his observation of our lack of possessions still smarts a little.

Mom chuckles. "I told Roddy to send the smaller one, but he insisted."

Elliot rolls his eyes. "Yeah, Dad doesn't do anything by half measures." He glances at me, and I see a spark of interest in the way his head jerks back a little. I guess he didn't notice me before.

Mom must notice, too. "This is my daughter, Laura."

His smile is broad as he steps forward to shake my hand. It's a formal gesture, but the way he grips it between both of his feels intimate or presumptuous. "Nice to finally meet you, Laura. Do you know what you are letting yourself in for?"

Mom chuckles, and I put my head to one side, considering him as he lets my hand go. "Well, Roderick told me that his cook makes the best buttermilk pancakes in the world, so I think I've got the important things covered."

Elliot chuckles and nods. "Dora's cooking is out of this world." He pats his stomach, which is flat as a washboard with nothing to indicate any kind of eating excess. "If it wasn't for her, I'd only have to spend half the time in the gym that I do."

"I'll keep that in mind."

"Is there anything I can do for you while I'm here?" he asks.

"I think everything is covered, honey," Mom croons. She always wanted a son, so I guess I'm going to be witnessing a lot of this.

"Well, that's good. I guess I'll see ya'll up at the house then."

He smiles broadly, his perfect, white megawatt teeth almost sending me dizzy.

Mom beams, too. "You know what. I'm fine here

while the movers finish up. Why don't you take Laura back with you?"

I twist to look at her, wondering what her game is. Mom is definitely hoping that we're all going to get on as one big happy family, but we're pretty much all adults who will be moving on and making our own lives soon. Although all of the McGregor men still live under one roof. Maybe they're going the traditional route and only moving out when they get married. Maybe I'll be the first one to spread my wings and fly. I guess it'll depend on how easy I find it to live with eleven men.

To be honest, the thought fills me with dread.

All those booming voices. All the sexist talk and boring conversations about sport and politics.

I'm even more nostalgic for our little apartment now.

"I want to stay and help," I tell Mom, but she just waves me off.

"There's nothing to do here, sweetie. We're just standing around and watching."

"It's no trouble," Elliot says with yet another grin that has the power to floor me. "It'll be good for us to have a chance to get to know each other."

I guess he could be right. It'll be a little uncomfortable getting in the car with a man who is effectively a stranger, but I guess that we'll all be waking up under the same roof tomorrow, so I might as well dive in at the deep end.

"Okay then, I'll grab my things."

Everything I was going to take myself is piled in a heap by the front door. As I'm picking it all up, Elliot is there to take over. "Let me," he says.

I know he's only trying to be chivalrous, but I can carry my own damn purse. Still, I let him take over because I don't want to look like an ungrateful brat.

"See you later," Mom singsongs from behind us, and then I'm walking away from our home for the last time.

Elliot's car is a sleek SUV, and he sweetly opens the passenger door for me before putting my things on the back seat.

When he gets in, it's awkward for a second until he starts the car, and his music starts blaring. He's listening to some pumping house music which he quickly turns down, and I chuckle.

"I tend to listen to my music too loud," he grins.

"Your car sounds like a gym," I laugh.

He grins. "Yeah, I like my music to motivate me."

"Doesn't it end up making you drive faster?"

"Probably."

He turns out of our street, the car making a soft purring sound. It's an expensive model and not the kind of vehicle I'm used to being driven in.

"So, how are you feeling about moving in with the McGregor's?" he asks. There is definite amusement in his voice, and that makes me like him. "We're a big bunch, so I'm expecting it to feel pretty daunting."

"I guess it is," I admit. "But Mom has assured me that you're all house trained."

He shakes his head. "I think your mom may have been exaggerating a little. I think it's more that my brothers have plenty of people picking up after them."

"I think that'll take me a while to get used to, too."

"The team at the house is great. You hardly know they are there most of the time, but I suppose that's because we're all out at work all day."

"So, what do you do at your dad's business?"

"I'm a site foreman," he says. "I went to college, but I'm not one to sit in an office. I like to be outside and getting my hands dirty, and I like to deal with problems, too."

I nod and gaze out of the window. We're heading towards the outskirts of town where the houses get bigger. I already feel out of place.

"That must be interesting," I say.

"No two days are ever the same."

"So, who's looking after the site today?"

He grins. "Cameron. He's usually doing other things, but Dad wants him to get more involved at a higher level."

I frown. "Other things?"

"He likes to work alongside the laborers, but Dad doesn't like it. He put us all through college so that we could be his management team, but not all of us want to wear suits every day. He sees it as a waste, but we are all contributing, whatever we do."

I'm starting to feel as though Roderick might be a little pretentious. I mean, what is the problem if someone wants to do a manual job?

"Cameron is one of the twins, right?"

Elliot glances at me. "Your mom been filling you in on the family tree?"

I blush, thinking about the hours I spent googling them all. "Sort of."

"It's a lot to take in," he says. "But you'll get to know us all, and then you won't have a problem remembering who we are."

"I think I need a reference manual," I chuckle. "I have the worst memory for names."

"I can arrange that," he says, completely serious. For a moment, I don't know what to say, and then he burst out laughing.

"If in doubt, just shout Mr. McGregor!"

"That'll be one way to get a whole room of men to turn around in one go."

"Exactly."

"So, what do you do, Laura?"

"I'm still in school," I say. "I'm taking Media Studies...I'm kinda hoping to get a job in advertising, but it's ridiculously competitive."

"It is, but you don't need to worry about that," he says.

"Why?"

"Because my dad has so many contacts that he'll be able to secure you out an amazing position somewhere."

I'm silent for a moment. Is that how things work when you're rich? You just decide you want to be something, and Daddy calls up one of his golf buddies to give you a job. No wonder ordinary people are struggling so much. As much as it excites me to think that I could get the kind of job that I've been dreaming about without going through months of groveling and effort, it makes me feel kinda sick, too. I'm a stickler for fairness, and I don't like the idea that I might secure a position I didn't truly deserve just because of somebody else's friendship or influence. The way Elliot speaks would suggest that this is a way of life for them. I guess when you've grown up with Roderick McGregor as your dad, you have an acceptance of the way things work within your world. I suppose he doesn't know any different.

"That won't be necessary," I say. "I've been working really hard, so my grades should speak for themselves."

Elliot glances at me, taking his eyes from the road for just a second. "It's a pretty competitive field."

"I know, but I'm okay with doing it myself."

The car is quiet again, except for the muted beat of Elliot's music and the luxury-quiet hum of the engine.

"I respect that," Elliot says after a time. "But I think you're going to need to accept that things are going to be a bit different for you now that you're a part of our family."

"Is that what I am?"

Elliot chuckles. "You're the daughter my father never had. Trust me. You're going to be sucked into the McGregor family vortex so fast that your feet won't even touch the ground."

"Now I'm scared," I say. I truly am. I'm used to being an only child, and I'm used to having my mom to myself. I'm used to having space, too—maybe not physically but just time to myself. Now I'm going to have to share Mom with ten stepbrothers and a stepfather. I feel like I'm going to get lost amongst all these new people.

"Don't be scared, Laura. We're a bunch of pussycats underneath all the loud voices."

We drive for a while longer, and Elliot tells me about the charity run he's going to be taking part in at the weekend. It sounds like a worthy cause – raising money for a cancer support center. I'm annoyed that I can't join him; I tell him how my injury has stopped me from running for the past six months.

"That kind of injury just needs the right therapy," Elliot says. "I can help you with that."

"You can?"

"Yeah. I'm sure that if we work together on trying to get you better, you'll be joining me on the next half marathon."

I shake my head because I can't imagine it. I'm fine walking, but every time I try and pick up speed, the torn muscle in my left leg screams out in pain.

"Trust me," he says. "You haven't got anything to lose, have you?"

He's right. I don't. "Okay. It's a deal."

He grins so hard his dimples show. I'm pretty sure that Elliot is a really good guy, and I've only been in his company for twenty minutes.

As we pull up outside the gates to the mansion that I'm about to start calling home, I say a small prayer that the rest of the McGregor brothers are going to be just as nice.

Chapter 2

The McGregor mansion is something else. I was expecting it to be big. With ten fully grown sons and a constructions business, there's no way it was going to be anything other than a showpiece. I think it might be the most gorgeous house I've ever seen. A mixture of traditional red brick, with white full height columns and a vast, covered porch to the front, my mouth is hanging open at the sight of it. Forget the amazing, manicured gardens and sweeping driveway. It's like a modern fairy tale.

Elliot drives around to the side, where a large garage door begins to open. Inside it's huge, with enough space to house at least twenty cars. There are some spaces, so I'm assuming that not everyone is home. That would be my nightmare. Being faced with so many new people and not being able to remember anyone's names!

I look down at my hands in my lap. I'm wringing them so tightly that my knuckles are white. Elliot puts his hand on my knee. "It's going to be okay," he says. "My brothers are rowdy, but they all have good hearts. You're going to love them all."

I smile tightly and nod.

"Let's go face the masses," he laughs, getting out

of the car and rounding to open my door before I've gotten my purse from the footwell. "Your new quarters await," he says with a ridiculous bow.

"So gallant," I say.

"My father raised us to be gentlemen," he grins. "We may all be a little rough around the edges, but underneath it all, we know how to treat a lady." He takes my things from the backseat, and we head towards the house. I'm hoping to enter through the spectacular front door. It's at least twice my height. Instead, Elliot puts his thumb on a scanner to open a side entrance. He ushers me through first, and I find myself in a wide hallway. The floors are the most gorgeous soft-colored wood – oak maybe – and the walls are grey. With gilded mirrors and gorgeous brightly colored art, it isn't really what I was expecting. This has been a man-pad for a long time, after all. I guess I had in mind lots of black gloss and leather.

There's the murmur of voices coming from deeper in the house. Elliot closes the door behind us, and I wait for him to pass me so he can lead the way.

"We can head for the den," he says.

They have a den? We follow the hallway around until we enter a huge room with vaulted ceilings. There are giant couches and a cinema-sized TV.

And there are more McGregor brothers.

Three of them.

They're in the middle of laughing at something when one of them spots us. His smile is slow and lazy, and his brothers turn to see what he's looking at.

"This is Laura," Elliot says, his arm sweeping out to indicate me. I smile nervously as they all seem to take their time in looking me over.

The one who saw me first has messy brown wavy hair and the lightest grey eyes I've ever seen. "Donnie," Elliot says, pointing at him. "And these two fuckers are Barret and Blake."

"Nice," Barret says, shaking his head at his brother. They are scarily alike with light brown hair and short trimmed beards, their blue eyes identically intense.

"He meant my brother's choice of words," Blake says.

I blush because for a second, I'd thought he'd meant the word to describe me. "Of course," I say. "Good to meet you."

"She's formal," Barrett says, raising his eyebrows.

"She's pretty," Blake adds, and my cheeks flame.

"And you're being a douche," Elliot says. "Way to make our new sister feel comfortable."

"Sister?" Barret bursts out laughing. "Don't let Dad hear you calling her that."

A look passes between them all, and a few seconds of silence. Doesn't Roderick want them to welcome me into the family? Does he intend to try and keep us distant from each other? Maybe he's not happy about Mom bringing me along as baggage. That isn't the impression I got from Elliot in the car, but who knows.

"I want to paint you," Donnie says, interrupting the moment of discomfort.

Now it's my turn to raise my eyebrows. "He's really

good," Elliot tells me. "But take a look at what he specializes in before you agree!"

"If she does agree, can I observe?" Blake asks. Donnie gives him a withering look, and I feel as though I'm watching an Olympic table tennis match.

"Don't listen to my brothers," Donnie says softly. "I only want to paint your soul."

My soul? This conversation is getting a little weird.

"Anyway." Elliot turns to me and puts his hand on my shoulder. "I'm gonna go and freshen up. I'll leave one of these reprobates to show you to your room." He turns to his brothers. "Be nice."

"Nice?" Blake scoffs. "Better leave it to Barret then."

I see the look that passes between the twins as Elliot retreats into the corridor. I may have done some digging on this family, but nothing has prepared me for the reality of getting to know so many people so quickly.

"You can't paint a soul, Donnie," a deep voice sounds from the corner of the room. A chair swivels around, and yet another brother appears, with a Mac on his knee.

"I can paint anything I want, Antony," Donnie says.

"Twenty bucks says that our little sister isn't going to let you try." Antony grins, and even from a distance, I get the full hit of a pair of gorgeous dimples and laughter lines that tell me this man likes to smile. Damn. With a shock of dark hair and gorgeous tan skin, I seem to have lost my ability to speak. There is so much testosterone in this room that I have no idea what to do with myself.

He places the laptop on a low table and stands, forming an imposing figure at over six feet for sure. "How about I take you to see your room, Laura," he says. I look at the other brothers, but none of them seems to object. "Dad had his PA arrange for it to be decorated, but I think he may have forgotten to tell her how old you are."

He saunters past me, taking my bags from where Elliot placed them, and I follow like an overwhelmed puppy. It's hard to take in everything around me. More hallways filled with doorways that I glance into quickly but don't get a sense of the rooms beyond —an amazing staircase from the formal hallway that curves and splits in two.

"This is the main staircase, but there are others," Antony says. "It'll take you a while to get your bearings but don't worry about wandering around. There'll always be someone around to help you get to where you need to go."

"Is there a map?" I ask him, and he laughs.

"I guess we could do with one, but it's not often we have new people joining us. Our staff sticks around and, well, there hasn't been anyone serious for Dad in a long time."

"What about you guys. . .girlfriends, I mean?"

He glances back at me. "We don't generally bring anyone here," he says. I don't miss the expression on his face, a flash of somberness before he dials up the Antony charm again. "Can you imagine. . .ten strange women walking about the house?"

I see his point. When there're ten brothers, any kind of socializing is going to end up like a frat party. "It'd be like inviting over the whole cheer squad," I say.

"Now, there's an idea." Antony waggles his eyebrows as we finally finish climbing the stairs. Up here, the hallway is carpeted in soft cream. It's so spongy under my feet I just want to take off my boots and stroll barefoot. "Your room is nearest to mine," he says. "So, if you need someone to fight the monsters under the bed, I'm your man."

I chuckle. "There haven't been any monsters under my bed since I was eight years old."

"Well, a pillow fight partner then."

"I think you've been watching too many teen college movies."

"Maybe something like that." Antony stops outside a door and takes hold of the handle. "You ready?" he asks.

His eyes are dancing with amusement, those dimples and laughter-lines making me feel warm in places that shouldn't be sparking about my new stepbrother. I imagine him in his bedroom somewhere across the hall, shucking off those clothes and sliding naked between his sheets. Damn. This is exactly what I was fearful of, unrequited and completely forbidden feelings for a houseful of sexy men. How the fuck am I supposed to deal with all these raging hormones without combusting?

"I guess so," I say, sounding distracted.

He opens the door slowly and allows me to walk in first. I burst out laughing immediately. It's a pink princess heaven. Every wall and surface is covered with the kind of things that an eleven-year-old would love. Butterflies and flowers hang from the sheer pink canopy that overhangs the bed. There are so many fluffy cushions resting against the headboard that it's going to be some kind of mission to get to sleep each night.

"See what I mean," Antony chuckles.

"It's the princess room I never had," I say softly. Mom always did her best, but there wasn't much spare cash around to indulge in redecorating my room every time I was into something new.

"I'm an architect, so I know some great interior decorators if you want to get it changed."

"That would be so rude," I say. "Your dad went to all this trouble."

"It wasn't any trouble. He asked someone to do it for him."

"All the money," I say, looking around again. I catch sight of an open door in the corner that looks like an en-suite. No sharing bathrooms, at least.

"I don't want to sound like a pretentious dick, but the money really is just a drop in the ocean. Seriously, if you want something a little more appropriate for age and level of sophistication, then let me know. We could sort it out in a weekend. Abbey Rainer is particularly popular at the moment. She has a real eye for space and color."

I get what feels like a pang of jealousy hearing him talk about a woman with so much appreciation. He rests my bags down on a chaise in the corner of the room, and I don't miss the way his back flexes. His hair is shorn close to the skin at the back of his neck, and I get a crazy urge to run my fingers over it, imagining the soft velvety texture. When he turns, I feel my cheeks flaming.

Antony's eyes scan my face, another grin forming. "Little Laura, are you blushing?"

Oh god. How mortifying.

"All those stairs," I say, pressing my hands against my cheeks. "I'm hot."

"Yes, you are." I watch as his eyes drop to my breasts.

We're standing in silence for a few seconds, and it feels so awkward. Is there really sexual tension here between my almost stepbrother and me?

"So..."

"Can I get you anything?" Antony asks, slipping his hand into his pocket.

"I'm good for now," I say.

"Okay then. I guess I'll see you later."

"Sure. . .and thanks for the personal escort. There's no way I would have found my way with directions."

Antony heads towards the door. "You have ten

stepbrothers now," he says. "Ten men to look after you. Better get used to not having to do much on your own."

And with that, he's gone, closing the door behind him.

I take a quick look around, opening drawers and peeking into my new walk-in closet and gorgeous bathroom. My room is four times the size of my old room. I think about what Katelin would think about it. My cousin moved to New York last year. Mom kept things quiet, but I overheard her talking to her sister on the phone about Katelin's harem. I didn't know what it meant until I googled it. It seems she's living with three men.

Three.

As ballsy as she is, I never expected that. And they're not just any men. They're her stepbrothers.

Now here I am with ten stepbrothers of my own. I wonder what she'd think of that.

Amazing opportunity, probably!

I take my laptop out of my bag and sit on the bed with it on my knee. The mattress is so lovely and soft. I pull up the folder I created with pictures of the McGregor brothers. I flick through them again, taking extra time over the ones I've already met. Antony, dimples in full force on the beach. Damn. Elliot sitting outside a café, his stunning eyes bright, sunglasses perched on top of his head. Barret and Blake, one smiling, one serious. Donnie with his ethereal grey eyes and soft wavy hair.

Five down.
Five to go.
This is my life now, for better or worse.
I'm hoping for better.

Chapter 3

My stomach growls.

I've been hiding away in this room for a couple of hours, but my body needs feeding, so I'm going to have to brave it and find the kitchen. I'm guessing that Mom is still at the apartment dealing with the removers because she hasn't come to find me yet. So much for there not being much left to do.

I open the door, step out into the hallway, and look in both directions. There's nobody out here, and I can't hear any voices, so I head back the way Antony bought me until I'm standing at the bottom of the giant staircase. The floor is cool under my bare feet, and I gaze around, feeling as though I've stepped into one of those stupid 'housewives' shows. This place is unbelievable, and it's now my home.

It's going to take me some serious time to get used to this.

I hear voices in the distance, so I decide to follow. At least if I find someone, they can show me where to go to eat.

I get to a door, behind which I can hear loud male voices and the clinking of dishes. I stand for a few seconds, steeling myself to enter. Without knowing who's inside, I feel completely unprepared. It could be all the brothers I haven't met yet. That would be seriously #AWKWARD. I consider running back to my princess room and hiding out but my stomach growls again.

Ugh.

Where the hell is Mom? I should have stayed with her until the removals guys had finished up. Then she could have helped me with orientation around here. I wouldn't be feeling so out of place if she was here, too.

I'm about to put my hand on the handle when I hear my name.

"So Laura's finally here."

"Yep. . .poor girl has no idea what she's getting herself into."

"Well, I think she knows there are ten of us," a voice that sounds like Antony's says.

"Yeah, but not what Roddy has in mind."

"Don't let Dad hear you calling him that," another voice warns.

"Fuck sake. I'm a grown man. I'm not scared of Dad anymore."

"Good for you. But you're still going to have to toe the line on this one, Grant."

"I don't fucking think so, and I can't believe that you're so calm about it. This is fucking unnatural."

"Look, you had to know this was coming. Dad hasn't exactly kept his ideas to himself over the past few years."

"To be honest, I thought he was getting dementia."

"He's as sharp as a tack."

"Yeah, but still bat-shit crazy."

"Crazy or not, if you want your share of the business, you're gonna have to do what he wants."

"It's not like she's ugly," a voice that sounds like Barret's says. "She's fucking gorgeous."

"Yeah?"

"Donnie wants to paint her soul."

"That gorgeous?"

"Exactly."

"She's never going to agree to this."

"It's not like we're ugly, dude. Girls pretty much fall over themselves to get with one of us, let alone ten."

I inhale sharply. Did they just say what I think they said?

"One is a relationship. Ten is a gang bang."

Holy fuck. They did. My heart begins to race as I lean in closer, trying to hear better.

"It doesn't have to be like that. It's not a fucking porno!"

"Sure sounds like one to me."

"Well, you always did watch too many dirty movies."

I take a step back, pressing my hand over my mouth with shock.

Shit. Did I really just hear all that?

They want to share me like I'm a piece of meat. Like I'm one of those women with big plastic-looking tits and blown-up lips.

Ten of them.

I'll admit to having some naughty little fantasies over their pictures and for having a bit of a thing about Reverse Harem romance novels since I found out about Katelin, but this is real life. They're talking about this shit in the open with each other, not just imagining it in their heads.

And not only that, but their Dad is also in on it, too. Is that why he wants my mom? To get to me. I feel ridiculous for even thinking that because I'm a nobody from nowheresville. If Roderick wanted to snag a potential wife for his sons, I'm sure there'd be plenty of eligible girls out there from the State's top families to consider.

"It's not like any of this is a done deal," a voice I think is Antony's says. "We still have to win her over. . .we still need to make her want it."

"She'll fall in line when she hears what's on offer. Who's going to pass up a marriage proposal that comes with all this?" another voice says. It sounds like Antony's, but the tone is harder.

"I don't think that you should assume that," a laid-back voice that I think is Donnie warns. "We all need to treat her carefully. Laura isn't the kind of girl who'll respond well to being told what to do."

"Most women love a bit of domination," the harsher voice says.

"Most women who put up with you."

There's a scoffing noise. "At least I've got a woman."

"Not for long. Not when Dad sets this whole thing in motion."

I don't get any of this. They're all gorgeous. Surely

their father should want them to all find nice girls and live their spectacular lives in relative normality. What the hell has he got to gain to try and get them to share me? I remember someone mentioning a share of the business. Is that what this is about? I don't get it.

I can't go in there now. How can I face them with the taint of this conversation in the air? I need to get out of here and clear my head. I need Mom to get here so I can ask her what the hell is going on.

I stumble further down the hall towards what I think is the back of the house. I come to a door that is open to the gardens. The fresh air hits me like a welcome balm, and I draw it deep into my lungs, scanning for somewhere that I can hide. There's a seating area that's sheltered with large bushes, and I make my way over, perching on the dark wooden seat. I exhale, my hands clenched tightly in my lap, my mind rushing over the conversation I just heard.

It would be easy to convince myself that I made it all up because it's so obscure and so hard for me to get my head around as a result. These men are strangers to me and yet they have such assumptions about how I'm going to be involved in their lives. Add to that my stepfather's involvement, and I have no idea what to make of any of it. All I can think is that I'm not going to be able to live here. All the planning my mom has done has been in vain, but we no longer have our apartment. I have nowhere else to go, and could I really snatch this all away from Mom? She's had it so tough and has finally met a man who treats her well and has the capability to be able to look after her for the rest of her life.

I think about my friends. Would any of them be willing to let me stay? Maybe for a day or two but longer than that would be tough. I could move into accommodation at college if there was any free, but I'm deep into the semester so it's doubtful. I'm just starting to think about excuses for Mom when I hear voices.

"The new contractor that Dad has brought in is gonna cause us a lot of ball ache…"

Their conversation comes to a halt when they see me.

"Hey," one of them says. They're identical twins with sandy blond hair and sparkling blue eyes. Their faces, although similar, have something different about them. . .I know I'm staring, but it's like looking at one of those spot-the-differences puzzles. It's their noses. Maybe they've been broken.

"Laura?"

"Course it's Laura. Who the hell else would it be?"

They shove at each other like naughty kids. "Hi," I say, offering a pathetic little wave. I'd smile, but I'm still thinking about what I just heard.

"Hey," they say in unison. "I'm Casey," one adds. "And I'm Cameron," the other says. "What are you doing out here?"

"I'm just getting some fresh air."

"Oh yeah," Cameron says. "And the bare feet?"

I look down, embarrassed, and have no way to explain that bit.

"They say something to frighten you off already?" Casey asks. It sounds like a joke, but maybe it isn't.

I blush, wondering if he's referring to the conversation I overheard. I don't think they were in the room because they've come from another direction, but I can't be sure. I don't know this place well enough to find my way back to my own bedroom.

I shrug. "I'm an only child. I'm not used to living with this many people."

"This many strangers," Casey says.

I nod.

"Well, we won't be strangers for long," Cameron says, running his fingers through his hair.

"So I've heard," I can't help mumbling.

They glance at each other and then back at me.

"What did you hear, Laura?"

I say nothing, and that must be enough to confirm their thinking. "They told you about the plan?" they say together. It's said with a whole lot of disbelief.

I nod. "I overheard some stuff I probably wasn't meant to."

"That you definitely weren't meant to."

"Not yet anyway."

They shift from foot to foot.

I blink, shocked that they're not denying anything. Although I know what I heard, I was half hoping that maybe my listening-through-door skills weren't great. It's stupid, but my throat starts to burn, and I blink, fearing that I might be about to cry. It's not like me to get emotional but this is just too much on a day when I thought that things were going to be so different. This isn't the kind of different I was expecting, and I need to get them away from me before I make a fool of myself.

"If you don't mind, I think I'd like to be alone," I tell them.

"Okay," Casey says, looking worried. They don't hesitate, so at least that's good, but I can't get my head around how they seemed so casual about the idea of stripping me bare and taking turns with me. I watch them go, and when they're out of sight, my shaky hand goes for my back jean pocket, and I pull out my cell phone. I think about messaging my mom. She needs to know what's going on here, but I'm worried that she won't believe me. I mean, Katelin was a real shock for both of us, and her future happiness is so wrapped up in this family.

How do I deal with this without causing a whole heap of drama?

No matter how I run things through in my head, I just can't find a way.

Mom has been my rock for so long. I trust her. I guess I just have to be honest and see what her reaction will be.

I quickly tap out a message to my mom. *Mom, I need to talk to you? Where are you?*

Seconds later, my phone chimes. *What is wrong? I'm gonna be there soon. Just gotta finish up here.*

Can it wait? I guess so, but what do I do? Skulk back to my ridiculous cotton candy room and hide until she gets here? I don't even know how to get there without asking for help, and that is something I just don't feel comfortable doing.

I message again. *I just overheard something, Mom. Something not good. I need you to get here quick.*

There is no answer, and my heart kicks up a notch.

My phone rings. It's Mom. I guess messaging wasn't really working for this kind of discussion.

"Laura, are you okay? What's going on?"

My heart thuds in my chest. "I don't know how to say this, Mom. I know how you feel about Roderick, and we've just moved all our stuff and let our place go. . .but, I don't think I can stay here."

"What are you talking about, honey. What's happened? Have the boys been unwelcoming?"

"No, not exactly?"

"What did you overhear?"

I take a deep breath. My mind rushes through all the different ways to say this, and there is no perfect solution. "I know how this is gonna sound," I start. "I know you're going to think I'm crazy, but I think that Roderick is blackmailing his sons...to..." I pause be-cause what were they really saying? The sex talk was only half of it. The business and the marriage part seem more important to mention. "Marry me."

There's a pause on the other end of the phone, and I start to doubt myself. This is ridiculous. Surely, I'm mistaken. Mom is going to call me out and tell me

I'm losing my mind, but then I remember how clearly I heard the McGregor boys talking in the dining room and how Cameron and Casey didn't deny anything. I know I'm not making this up.

"What did you hear, honey?" Her voice is calm. Strangely calm. No laughing or accusations about the level of my insanity.

"I heard them talking about a plan for them to share me, Mom. They've created a ridiculous pink princess bedroom for me like I'm five years old, and now they're talking about passing me around ten of them like I'm. . .a piece of meat. There's something wrong going on here, Mom. Something very wrong. This isn't what I signed up for."

The end of the line is silent, and I'm imagining Mom trying to get her head around what I've said and thinking about how it's going to impact all her plans.

"Where are you right now?" she asks.

"I'm on a side patio. I'm alone and safe. What do you want me to do? Should I just call a cab?"

"Just stay where you are," she says.

"What?" I'm flabbergasted that there isn't an ounce of shock in her voice or even any denial of the information I've just given her.

"I'll be there soon. We can talk about it when I get there."

"Talk about it."

She sighs, and I pull my phone away from my ear and look at it as though it's malfunctioning. "Did you not hear what I said?"

"I heard," she says. "You weren't supposed to find out this way."

"What?"

"Let me finish up here, and I'll tell you more later."

"Are you serious?" My voice sounds frantic. "You knew about this?"

"It isn't what you think, honey," she says.

"I know what I heard, Mom. And to be honest, I don't even know what I think," I say, and without waiting to hear another word, I disconnect the call.

She knew. Mom knew about this, and she still moved us in here. Is that the deal? Roderick gets Mom, and I come as part of a weird package deal? I feel sick.

So sick, I actually consider calling my father. For a fraction of a second, I really consider dialing his number and ordering him to come and pick me up. And take me where, I think?

That's really not an option.

He's been about as present in my life as a dead person since he moved away, and I know that all I'm going to hear is insinuations about my mom's mental state and how she's been stealing his money, AKA child support. I can do without that particular pile of shit right now.

I'm stuck. Stuck waiting for Mom to get here and explain herself. Stuck with nowhere else to go. I stand, but I have no idea what to do next. Rubbing my throbbing head, I look around. How can Mom even have considered moving me in here with these ten men?

I'm her only daughter, and this is what she sees as best for my future. I mean, I know we've had it hard the past few years. Since Dad left, Mom's really struggled to keep us afloat. Is that what this is? Her way of ensuring that neither of us ever have to struggle again.

"Hello," a soft voice sounds from near the doorway.

I jump backward, startled out of my internal struggling.

"I want to be on my own right now," I say when I find Donnie coming towards me. His eyes are soft, his hair flopping gently. I wonder if his brothers chose him as the least threatening of the lot of them. I hope he's not going to try and deny things. Instead, he puts his hands up and tries to smooth things over.

"We aren't going to hurt you, you know."

I scowl. "No, you've got other things planned for me." He seems to flinch at what I'm suggesting.

"Most of us aren't any happier about this than you are, in case you were wondering." He looks as miserable as I am.

I glance behind me, worried I'm about to get ambushed by them all, but we're alone.

"I just feel as though..." I trail off, not really knowing what to say.

"That you've been brought here under false pretenses."

I nod. "I don't get how this is even something that anyone in this household would consider."

Donnie nods. "I get that, but you're an only child, right?"

"Yeah."

"So you don't get how close a person can be with their siblings."

I frown. What is he suggesting? "Sharing toys is one thing, Donnie. Sharing women is something else."

He shrugs. "It happens, though."

"Maybe in your weird world of the rich and fucked up. Is this what goes on behind closed doors where there is money involved?"

He runs his hands through his hair and looks contrite. "It's not like that, Laura. My brothers and I would treat you as you deserve."

Oh my god. Is he serious about this? "You can't actually think it's a good idea."

"My dad has his reasons," he says with another shrug.

"And you all just follow on like eager little puppies."

He shakes his head. "We all have an opinion, Laura, but none of this is new to us. It's something that Dad has been talking about for a really long time. We're all probably desensitized to it."

"I don't think there is any 'probably' about it."

He takes a step closer, and I put my hands up. I don't think he's trying to get into my space, but he notices and adjusts his position. "I get how it must sound to you, but maybe you'll feel different once you get to know us. Maybe it won't all seem so bad.

Maybe you might like us." The hopeful tone of his voice makes me feel sad. How can anyone be hopeful about a situation like this? It's so far removed from the reality of what life is supposed to be.

I shake my head because I can't imagine ever getting to that place. "You make it sound like some sort of cult, Donnie."

He laughs, but it's self-conscious. "Maybe it is a bit like that, living as a McGregor. It's us against the world. It always has been, and if Dad has anything to do with it, it always will be. Loyalty isn't a sin, though, is it?"

"Depends on if it's blind," I say.

He shakes his head this time. "None of us are stupid, Laura. We've all seen what it's like in the world. We've dated. We have friends who aren't part of our family."

"And none of that has made you see this as freaky?"

"Not really. There's good and bad in everything," he says. His expression is distant, as though he's thinking about something from another time and place.

"It doesn't matter what you say about this. I still can't get my head around it," I say. "I'd like to be alone for a while."

"Sure. Do you want something to eat or drink? This is your home now. Just help yourself to whatever you need."

Home.

How could it ever feel that way now?

I had these hopes. Silly dreams about what it would

be like to live in a big family and not have to worry about Mom. Feeling like we were in a place where we could settle down.

All of it has been shattered.

This home is built on false pretenses.

Mom has let me down in a way I would never have thought possible.

As I think through the reality of what my next steps will need to be – dropping out of college, getting a job, leaving Mom behind – a sob escapes my throat.

Chapter 4

I don't want Donnie or any of Roderick's other sons to see me crying. I haven't even met half of them, and this wouldn't be the way I'd want to be introduced. I'm ashamed to be this weak and pathetic and don't really understand why I'm responding this way. I guess that I didn't realize how much of a picture I had built of what our new life with the McGregors was going to be like, and now that fantasy has been shattered, it has left me feeling totally empty and disappointed.

And Mom knew about their sick plan and wasn't opposed to it.

I feel sick.

Standing, I turn my face away from Donnie and start to hurry away, holding in the sob that is fighting to leave my lips. He starts to call after me, but I don't turn back, and he doesn't follow. I'm grateful that he seems to understand that I don't need his comfort, not after what I heard.

I need to find somewhere to hide for a while. Somewhere I can wash my face and let the redness from my eyes recede before I face anyone.

I begin to make my way across the estate, scanning for a way into the house that's away from where I assume the McGregor boys are all still hanging out. I'm so desperate that I'm practically jogging, something I haven't done in six months. A sharp pain surges down my left leg, reminding me of my injury, the one I can't seem to stop aggravating long enough for it to heal properly. Forcing myself to slow down, I curse. I don't need pain on top of everything else. I wish I had taken the time to put on shoes because the soles of my feet are already tender. The pain in my leg worsens and I know that if I don't stop for a while, I'm going to be out of action for ages. I can't risk taking more time out of college. Stopping, I ease myself down to the ground, brush the dirt from my feet, and lay back in the thick green grass. The sky is beautifully clear, but its beauty does nothing to make me feel better.

I groan loudly.

For fuck sake! I can't believe my bad luck.

I groan again, aggravated, frustrated and furious and disappointed, and to be honest, a little bit embarrassed. I mean, they were all talking about fucking me. I mean, I know that men's minds work in different ways to women, and I know that I have had some seriously X-rated thoughts about them over Google research, but that was in my own private fantasy time, not being discussed casually over food.

There's a rustle in the foliage to my left, and as I turn, a man emerges. "I thought an animal was dying out here," he says, resting his hands on his hips. "But it turns out it's just a groaning woman."

I scan his features, trying to recognize him. Damn, he's hot. Is he one of the McGregor's or one of the staff? I'm trying to scan through my mental recollection of all my Google pictures, but I've not been stalker enough, and I can't match the face to a name. He has dark eyes that aren't brown or grey in this light, but something in between, and straight dark hair cropped short.

"Humans are animals. You do know that don't you? And I'm in pain, here!" I say with a tiny spark of joy that I can still pull out the snark, even when I'm down. I wipe the tears from my face and try to pull myself together.

His expression softens a bit. "Why are you holding your leg like that? Did you hurt yourself?"

Unwilling to let the good-looking man get the better of me, I lift my chin slightly. "No. I'm just groaning and clutching at myself for the sheer pleasure of it."

His curious gaze sparkles with a hint of amusement.

"Groaning and clutching do tend to go hand in hand with pleasure."

Well, he's got me there, but I'm not going to let him see even a hint of a smile. "Are you one of the five brothers I haven't met yet or the lawn guy?"

He splutters with laughter. "I'm Grant, so I guess that just leaves four brothers you haven't met yet."

"Might never meet at this rate," I mumble, trying to sit up a little.

"Let me help you stand." He holds out his strong, manly hand, and I grasp it, pulling myself onto my good leg and tentatively resting a little pressure on the bad. I wince, and he grimaces sympathetically. "Have they managed to make such a terrible impression already?"

"Let's just say the choice of conversation topic was the problem," I say.

His eyes flash for a moment, and he nods. "Yeah. I can see how that might be the case. I mean, anyone would have thought you'd be desperate for ten millionaire husbands."

For a moment, I think he's seriously suggesting I'm crazy, then I see the laughter dancing in his eyes and remember it was him that didn't sound all that happy about the prospect either. He takes my hand and rests it around his neck, putting his arm around me to support my weight. He begins to move in the wrong direction.

"I don't want to go this way," I tell him. "I need to..." I trail off, looking around. In reality, I have no idea where I want to go.

"You need to rest for a little while," he says firmly. "You definitely need to take the weight of that leg as soon as possible."

"What, are you a doctor now?" I wince again from the pain as we continue to shuffle forward.

Grant stops, looks me over, then scoops me up until I'm resting in his arms like an inappropriately dressed bride about to be carried over a threshold.

"I wanted to be a vet," he says softly, eyes fixed ahead.

I'm about to remind him that I'm a woman, not an animal but something about the way he mentioned it like it was a wistful dream stops me in my tracks. Wanted. As in, past tense. "You work for your father, right?"

"It's the only way," he says with a bit more grit in his tone. "Roddy is the king of the castle here, and we are just his minions."

"I know what minions look like, and none of you are short and yellow."

"Might as well be," he mumbles.

"But you're the only one not falling into line over this plural relationship, bullshit."

He shakes his head. "How do you know that?"

"I overheard you talking."

He adjusts me in his arms. "Work is one thing, but my dick and my heart are my business." I find myself blushing like a virgin at his casual mention of his dick. Things warm up quickly between my legs, too. I don't think I'd be reacting like this if I wasn't pressed up against his chest with the scent of his alpine-fresh cologne all around me. Or if he looked less like something off the cover of a magazine.

"Am I that much of a horrible prospect?" I ask, trying to keep things light. His mouth quirks up on one side, morphing into a lopsided smile.

I notice that he seems to be taking me back to the house, and I really don't want to be facing anyone else right now. "Don't take me back into that house," I say.

He doesn't look at me when he says, "I'm taking you to my place." His voice seems lower and just a little laced with smooth caramel. I think that it must be my imagination because I suddenly remember my Google search that said he's the one who already has a girlfriend he's wild about, so he's not likely going to put the moves on me. Plus, he seems like a genuinely good guy.

"Your place?" I'm confused. I thought they all lived together. "You don't live with your family?"

"I've not earned a room in the mansion."

"So I guess you're the one I need to talk to about finding a way out of that place."

"Sorry, princess. That kind of information is on a need-to-know basis only."

I flinch at the use of the term princess until I remember my monstrosity of a room and realize he must be referring to that.

"So you've seen Roddy's idea of décor for the modern woman."

Grant laughs, and I feel the vibrations of it right through me. "Roddy wouldn't know a modern woman if one hit him in the face."

"I guess I need to tell my mom to get on that one then," I say as he stomps up the steps of a tiny brick home that looks like it might have been built for staff.

"I'll just bet you're desperate to get thrown out of that ridiculous confection of a room," he teases.

"You got kicked out?" I ask.

He shakes his head, looking slightly embarrassed, then resituates me in his arms in order to open the door. "Truth be told, having my own space apart from the pack gives me a basic degree of privacy from an environment where everyone seems intent on prying into my business."

"That proves you're the smartest one of the bunch."

He only grunts, sitting me down in a comfortable armchair with a plaid spread thrown over the back of it. Taking a look around, I decide that I love the small, tidy place that Grant calls home. It's decorated in a lodge style with heavy, dark wood and brown leather furniture and walls covered with pictures of animals. One large, framed print shows him bandaging a beautiful thoroughbred's leg. Catching me staring, Grant explains. "Donnie took that picture of me patching up the racehorse my father invested in after he took a tumble. He recovered enough to walk again, but he wasn't up to speed after that."

Smiling at Grant, who is now kneeling beside my chair, I'm suddenly shy. "If you can patch his leg up, maybe you can do the same for mine."

"What happened to yours?" he asks, looking up at me with smoky gray eyes framed by thick dark lashes. My heart skips.

"I tore my hamstring sprinting about six months ago," I tell him. "Every time I think it's healed enough for me to give it some serious use, it craps out on me again."

There's a low whine from the corner of the room. A huge Doberman has been sitting watching us, and I didn't even notice. He seems to be staring at my leg. If a dog could look empathetic, this one does. Out comes his tongue, and he licks the exact spot that's hurting on his own front leg. It seems like magic at first, and then I notice a small spasm is making the muscle jerk.

"Killer, fetch." Grant's voice is so commanding that it startles me. The dog rushes off to another room and comes back, dragging a black duffel bag. When Grant says, "Good dog" in his deep rumbling voice, the dog wags its tail. I think if I had a tail, I'd wag it for Grant, too.

Grant paws through his bag, pulling out a cold compress. He squeezes the white bag, mixing the chemicals inside, and then presses to my leg. Cool soothing relief soaks into the muscle, and slowly the tiny contracting movements stop.

"Is that helping?" he asks.

"Yeah, it is."

"What you said before is true." Pausing to look up at me, he's so handsome it takes my breath away. "In a world where there is only animal, vegetable and mineral; humans are animals. Most people are just too self-important to see that."

I find myself nodding in agreement. "People like to feel powerful. To feel superior. We tell ourselves that we're smarter than animals, so hurting them and killing them doesn't seem so bad."

Sitting back on his heels, Grant gives Killer a scratch behind the ear, and when the animal drops its huge head into his lap he nods.

"I read an article on chimpanzees learning sign language and how to follow voice-prompts from humans, and it got me to thinking," I say. "We're not smart enough to know what they are saying to each other when they vocalize, but they somehow learned enough of our language to understand what we're asking them to do. Sign Language is considered a real language, and those chimps picked it up."

Grant's face lights up. "I never thought about it that way."

I spy a small silver frame over his shoulder with a woman's smiling face looking back at me. She's really pretty. Blonde hair and perfect teeth. The all-American cheerleader type. I can see what he sees in her from the outside, but Grant seems like a deep person, and I'm nosey enough to want to find out more. "Does your girlfriend love animals, too?" I ask him.

Instead of the nod and smile I expect from him, I see his eyes go cold, and his expression turns vacant. It's as though he's closed himself off. Without saying a word, he rummages through his duffel again and pulls out a flexible wrap, which he expertly uses to apply gentle pressure to my injured calf. I feel the silence like it's a physical pressure, and I want to apologize for saying something wrong, but I'm not sure what I did.

Coming swiftly to his feet, he turns on his heel and strides across the room to the front door. I'm not sure what's happening. Is he going to just leave me here, injured and currently unable and unwilling to return to the main house?

When he jerks it open, I get my answer. He steps out and walks away, leaving the door ajar behind him.

Killer whines again, his eyes also trained on the door. It's as though all the light just left the room. It seems as though this McGregor brother is well and truly closed off.

I look back at the smiling woman in the frame and wonder what the hell happened to turn Grant from smiling eyes to stone with just one question.

Chapter 5

Within moments my mom knocks gently on the door. I recognize her knock even before she pokes her head through the doorway. "Little piggy, little piggy, let me in."

I can't believe she's seriously going with that approach in this situation.

When I was a kid, that was my nickname, but it seems completely wrong for her to use it now. Her face falls a little when she sees my expression, but she still comes into the room and takes a seat on the masculine sofa across from me. "This day went sideways real fast, didn't it, pumpkin."

I don't even know what to say. Is she expecting me to be fine with her? Sideways doesn't come anywhere close to covering what this day has become.

Devastating.

Strange.

Part of a parallel universe where my mom has lost all her morals and joined some kind of cult.

"Mom, you knew about this?"

She nods. "But it isn't like you said, honey."

"So, how the hell is it?"

She lifts her shoulders in a half-hearted shrug. Crossing her legs, Mom wraps her arms around her knee and laces her fingers together. "What I know is that Roderick is intent on finding one woman to be with his sons. They've always done everything together. They share the same house, swap clothing, and just take whatever vehicle they feel like every day. They operate as a unit, love spending time palling around together, and are open to considering one 'wife'." She does air quotes when she says wife. At least she's aware that polygamy isn't a legal reality. "As far as I know, the plan was to offer you first dibs on the wife slot."

I make a scoffing noise. "Dibs. I don't think dibs is really the right word, Mom. This isn't school, you know. And so nice that I get a choice in the matter."

"Of course, you get a choice. You know I'd never force you to do anything you didn't want to do, but I know these are good boys, and I know Roderick." Sighing, my mom reaches out to put her hand on my knee. "I didn't want you to find out like this. Of course, it seems weird to you. You've only been here for a few hours. You don't know these people or anything about how they live their lives, but when you do, you'll see why I'm not shocked or horrified about the prospect. You know there are lots of benefits to having more than one man. You know how happy Katelin is."

An article I read floats through my mind. It was about a group of friends who had all ended up in polyamorous relationships. They explained the difficulties they faced, not only because those around them found it difficult to accept but also because of their own preconceived ideas. They also went on to explain how well it works. More money for the family. More strong men about the place to work and take care of the manly jobs. More strong men to meet the needs of their woman. I remember feeling warm between my legs at the thought of having more than one lover at the same time—that feeling of being shared, of being overwhelmed by the physical strength of more than one man.

I remember feeling that maybe two might be a good number. Three would be tougher to manage. Four. . .well, I didn't even know what to do with that number.

Now Mom is talking about ten. Even if I fell in love with every single one of them, and the prospect of that is remoter than is worth even considering, ten men are just too many for one woman.

That's ten men who'd need their emotional and physical needs meeting. . .EVERY DAY!

I'm not sure if that would even be possible.

None of the McGregor boys that I've met so far has been small. They are all strapping at over six feet. I can't imagine that any of them would be lacking in the trouser department. Ten big cocks for one woman just seems greedy. Or foolish. Foolish would seem a better word. I'd never be able to sit down!

I just don't get how Roderick thinks that it's even a possibility. One divided by ten just doesn't feel like something that would meet anyone's needs. At least, not for the boys. For me, it'd be too much. Way too much.

"So how come I get a choice, but the boys are getting pushed into this? I'd never want to be with anyone who didn't want me one hundred percent. You know, some of them don't even want this."

"They don't?" Mom says, sounding surprised.

"You didn't know that?"

"No. Roddy told me they were all on board with giving it a try."

I shake my head. "Sounds like Roddy has been over-egging the pudding a bit."

"Mmm." Mom gives me a small smile. "I know all of this seems totally farfetched, but I just want to make sure you're happy and looked after, poppet. I don't want you to ever have to go through what I went through." She rests her hand on my knee, and I feel tears burning my throat. I know things have been hard for her. They've been hard for me, too. The rejection. The money worries. I've shared it all with her.

Now Mom has met Roddy, and things are changing for her. I guess she doesn't want me to get left behind. She's trying to find a way to solidify our security and position once and for all.

"But it's not right for Roderick to hold their inheritance to ransom over this, is it?"

Mom shakes her head. "No. That isn't something he's told me he's going to do."

"And even if I did happen to be on board with

giving this crazy idea a shot, how would I ever know if they really cared about me now that Roddy's put such a high price on my head?"

"It has complicated things."

"Maybe some women would be happy that the money is central to all of this, but you know I'm not like that."

Mom smiles in a way that makes me think she's proud of my independent streak. "Money isn't the be-all and end-all, but there is certainly something to be said for a man who can provide financial security."

"A man..." I emphasize.

"Or ten," she says with a wink.

"Ten men," I say softly, then I burst out laughing. I know I must look a little manic, but I can't help myself. This is loopy. Off the charts, cuckoo!

"Ten good men," she says. "Good looking, intelligent, funny, and all with good prospects."

For a moment, I wonder what is driving what here. "Is that why you're marrying Roderick?"

"What do you mean?" she asks, looking confused.

"You're not marrying him so that I have a shot at this crazy plan, are you?"

"No." She shakes her head and puts her hand over her heart. "I love him. It seems I've been lucky enough to find someone who has it all, and I want that for you, too."

"I'm not going to let Roderick's wealth turn me into a puppet on a string, Mom. I've heard what his iron-handed tactics have done to his sons. These people are all strangers to me, and I will not be drawn into the crazy." Even as I'm saying the words, my mind is flitting over another potential angle. What if Roderick is marrying Mom to get to me? I'm not a big-headed person by any stretch, but I just can't work it all out.

"I'm worried, Mom," I say. "What if I refuse and Roderick isn't happy? What if he puts pressure on you to force me, and you won't do it? I don't want to mess up your new life. I don't want to cause you any heartache."

She takes my hand in hers and squeezes it. "Don't you worry about me. I'm a big girl, and I'm not scared of Roddy. I'll talk to him and get to the bottom of what is going on here. There is bound to be an explanation for what you overheard."

"I hope so, Mom. Maybe this whole thing is an April Fools gag! Make a fool of the new girl."

"It's not April, sweetie," she says. "Do you want to walk back with me now?"

I look down at my leg, and for the first time since she got here, she registers how I'm sitting.

"Did you hurt yourself?"

I nod. "My bad leg is playing up."

"Oh honey," she croons. "I'll get your new insurance details from Roddy. We can go and see a specialist."

"I have new insurance?"

"Of course," she says, looking very pleased with herself. "Only the best now, honey."

Grant's deep voice sounds off from the doorway. "I'll be happy to walk her back when she's had time to rest her leg."

We both look up to see his serious face fixed on us. I wonder how long he's been standing there. How much did he hear? The last thing I want is for him to think that we're gold diggers. It couldn't be further from the truth, but Mom's last comment about 'the best' doesn't sound great.

"Is that okay?" she asks me.

I nod, almost unable to keep a smile from my face at the prospect of more time away from the masses and another chance to spend some time with Grant.

"That would be good of you, Grant," she says, getting to her feet. "You look after my baby girl."

Closing the distance between us, she drops a kiss on my forehead and smooths back my hair. "Call me if you need anything, okay?"

"I will."

"I'll see you later, sweetie." With a small smile, she heads out the door, giving Grant a nod on the way past. He quietly shuts the door behind her and then locks it.

It seems like a strange thing to do, but I kind of understand why he'd want to. This place is just crawling with McGregor's. It's probably his only way of securing a little privacy.

I like the idea of being locked away from all the crazy that's waiting for me outside these walls.

"I can't believe you talked to your mom that way," he says.

I'm confused. Did he think I was rude? "What way?"

"I don't know. . .you just told her what you thought, and she listened."

"That is kind of how conversations work," I say, but I'm guessing from his expression that it's not how things work in Casa McGregor.

"Not 'round here," he says. "If I was honest with my dad like that, he'd threaten me with something. He'd find a way to get his way. I mean, what's stopping your mom from tossing you out on your ear and refusing to finish paying for college?"

Tilting my head, I gazed up into his worried eyes. "Nothing other than we don't really work that way. And anyway, if she did, I could probably couch surf with a few friends. My mom's not paying for my college. I get financial aid for that. And I haven't had an allowance since I was fourteen."

"Wow," he says. "You really are Miss Independent."

I shrug. "Mom doesn't have a lot of extra money, and I like to be able to choose what I want without worrying about anyone else thinking badly of me."

"That's fair enough. Roddy doesn't like his family working for other companies. Everything I have has come from him. It's not exactly the most mature way to live."

"But that's okay. You guys are so successful. It would seem silly to work to benefit someone else's business."

He takes a deep breath and sighs. "I guess it would be okay if construction was my thing, but it isn't. I've just had to forget about what I want to fit in with the family."

"That's a shame," I say. "I work for myself. It's not exactly glamourous, but I get to choose what I do and don't do."

"Choice can't be underestimated." Grant runs his fingers through his hair and glances over at Killer who is watching us from the corner of the room.

As soon as he sees Grant is giving him some attention, the dog raises up and trots over, easing his bottom back onto the edge of the sofa like a person. It makes me smile.

"I don't know whether he thinks he's human or we're dogs," Grant says, giving Killer a pat.

"Either way, he isn't far off from the truth. He's really well behaved, unlike most of the animals I know."

"Unlike most of the humans that I know."

We laugh, but the silence after stretches tight.

I like Grant. He's easy to talk to and honest. It's an important quality. One I haven't experienced in men much. He finds it hard to hide his emotions. That's how I can tell. I think back to his face when I mentioned the woman. I don't want to upset him again, but I also don't want to ignore what happened.

"I upset you earlier," I say gently. "I didn't mean to pry."

Again his eyes seem to shutter. He turns away, staring out of the window.

"She died," he says simply.

I wasn't expecting that at all and immediately felt terrible. It's a stupid thing to think, but in the picture, the woman looks vital and alive, and I didn't see anything about it when I was researching the boys. "I'm so sorry. What happened?"

"Cancer." His voice is a little gravelly, and I can almost feel the pain that's radiating from him.

"That must have been so hard to go through."

He nods, looking pensive. "We were together all through college. I thought we would be together forever. She was..." he pauses, stroking Killer. I can see it's a kind of therapy for him. "She was perfect."

I look over at the photo again, at the smiling girl who is no more.

"I'm sorry," I say again, feeling a little lost for words in the face of such obvious grief.

"You don't need to be," he says. "Life gives, and it takes. I've accepted that. I had all that time with her. I knew love. Some people never have that in a whole lifetime of trying."

His words stab at my heart. I know I'm still young, but I'm one of the people he's talking about. I've had relationships, but none of them have ever felt deep enough to be described as love. Crushes, maybe. Infatuation. Someone to pass the time with. Not exactly fairytale romance material. I feel a pang of jealousy and then feel ridiculous for envying a dead girl her true love experience. She deserved to have happiness with Grant, even if it was for a short time before she died.

"Do you think that it's possible to love someone again?" I ask him. "I'm trying to understand why you're so against your father's plan."

Leaning forward with his brow furrowed, I worry that I've said something that'll hurt him again. Or worse, that he'll be angry.

"I don't know, Laura. All I know is that I can't hope to be lucky twice when some people haven't been lucky once."

I give him a small smile. "I don't think that's how it works, Grant. There isn't a quota of luck or love."

"I hope you're right."

"You seem like a good man. I'm sure there are plenty of other girls out there who'd snap you up in a heartbeat."

Even as I say the words, I feel a pang in my heart. I've read stories about women who say they fell in love within seconds and always thought they were made-up tales for trashy magazines. I tell myself I'm being stupid for thinking that I'm having feelings for a man I've exchanged a few dozen sentences with, but I can't help how I feel.

Yes, Grant is one of the most gorgeous men I've ever seen. Calvin Klein models have nothing on his chiseled face and smooth tan skin, but it's more than what I can see on the surface. Grant has a good heart and a set of moral values that I respect. He's treated me gently, even in difficult circumstances. He's observant and kind.

"I'm damaged goods, Laura. Who wants to walk in the shadow of grief?"

"Someone who cares for you. Someone who can see that you're worth it. Grief doesn't last forever."

Killer makes a low whining noise as though he agrees with me and Grant shakes his head.

"How did you get so wise?" he asks me.

I laugh, and I'm sure my cheeks turn beet red. "I'm not wise, Grant. I just believe that good things come to good people."

"You should have a lot of good coming your way then."

I laugh again. "I do if your dad has anything to do with it."

"Maybe my dad has the right idea," Grant says, his eyes flashing mischief.

If my face wasn't beet red before, it sure is now. "Your dad sounds madder than a hatter," I say. "But I'm flattered."

Again the silence stretches, tense as a coiled spring. Killer looks between us as though he can feel it, too. I know animals are supposed to have more intuition than humans, so maybe he can. I have an urge to reach out and take Grant's hand in mine. For the first time since my loser ex-boyfriend Ollie left town, I feel like

I want to connect with a man, but this isn't a good time. Not with everything bubbling away back in the main house.

As if Grant can read my mind, he asks me why I've not been snapped up yet. "I guess I just haven't had my allocation of luck," I tell him. "My last boyfriend made me lots of promises but didn't deliver. I didn't listen to my gut telling me that I shouldn't trust him. I didn't listen to my heart either. It's weird how you can feel lonely even when you're with someone. Maybe lonelier than you would if you were by yourself."

He nods. "That's how you know you're with the wrong one. With the right person, you should feel at peace."

"Peace," I say softly as I contemplate what he said. I don't think I've ever seen a relationship that looked peaceful. There always seems to be some kind of drama or a level of power-play that just looks plain uncomfortable.

I never thought that peace should be something I should be searching for, but sitting here with Grant and Killer, and nothing but the quiet hum of the refrigerator in the background, I understand the appeal. Something about Grant's presence quiets my inner voice. She tends to overthink, but here, she seems to like it.

He rests his hand gently on my left leg, and I jump, not expecting the contact, even as I find myself craving his touch. "How's it feeling?" he asks.

"Still sore," I say. In reality, it's feeling better, but

I know if I say that, he'll take me back to my vomit-pink room and the harem of men who I'm supposed to be getting to know.

"Well, how about I make us something to eat," he says. "You must be hungry. And then, I'll give it a rub and see if we can get you back on your feet again."

"That sounds amazing," I say.

Killer agrees with a bark, and we both dissolve into fits of laughter.

Chapter 6

I'm imagining that Grant is going to rustle up something quick. Pasta, maybe. Or a grilled cheese sandwich. Instead, he emerges from the kitchen with an amazing-looking chicken and avocado salad. No wonder he's so trim if this is the way he eats. Killer has to go to the kitchen to get his food, and I can hear the crunching and slobbering from down the hallway.

We eat on our knees, which is fine, and Grant flicks on the TV, asking me if I'm happy to watch a nature program, before settling back and tucking in. His choice of program doesn't surprise me. The food is delicious, and again, I wonder at how completely comfortable I feel relaxing in this stranger's house with my leg up and now a full belly. When I'm done, I groan in appreciation, and Grant laughs, looking pleased with himself. He takes our plates and then flops back next to me on the sofa.

"How's the leg feeling now?" he asks.

"Still sore," I say. "I think it's going to take time to heal again, at least until the point that there's no pain."

"Maybe," he says. "Can I try something?" He shuffles closer to me, and my traitorous heart does a little flutter.

"Sure," I say. Grant's strong hands wrap around my thigh, and his fingers test out the muscle carefully. He watches my face, looking for areas where the sensitivity is high enough for me to flinch. It's as though he's mapping my muscle.

"Okay," he says. "I'm going to try and help it." His fingers begin to knead, taking care to avoid the really tender spots. I'm tense, expecting pain, but it doesn't come. What he does is actually really soothing, and I end up lying back and closing my eyes. The really sore spot is close to my knee, but he concentrates his attention on the whole muscle, sometimes coming high up onto where it meets my hip. The sensation is amazing, awakening parts of my body that really should be asleep right now. He nudges my legs to open a little so he has more room, and my pussy flushes hot in a second.

What is my body doing? This is crazy. Grant's being kind, and here I am getting turned on by his therapeutic massage. If he knew what kind of effect he was having on me, I'm pretty sure he wouldn't be comfortable carrying on.

"Try to relax," he says softly. Does he know how this is making me feel? For a second, I wish he'd move his hands higher. I wish he'd lean forward and kiss my lips with his gorgeous mouth.

He continues his ministrations, the press of his fingers coming tantalizingly close to the top of my thigh, and I stifle a sigh. Oh god.

This feels too good.

And Grant looks too good and smells too good.

And my mind is whirring on all the bad things he could do to me if I just...

I'm watching him, his brow lined with concentration, the muscles of his shoulders and biceps working with the effort of trying to relieve my discomfort, and it's as though he can feel my eyes on him. When he turns, I can't look away. I'm trapped in the intensity of his gaze, and the electricity between us sends a shiver up my spine.

"Is it working?" he asks with a voice that sounds a little huskier than it did before.

I nod, seemingly unable to formulate a sentence. My mouth is so dry.

"That's good." His hands have stopped moving. They're just there, wrapped around my upper thigh, their warmth seeping through the fabric of jeans and onto my skin.

I nod again, feeling ridiculous. He chews his bottom lip, his eyes focused on my mouth, and I think he must be feeling what I'm feeling. You'd have to be dead not to notice this energy. . .this connection.

"Laura," he says softly. My traitorous hand seems to move of its own volition and gently touches his fingers. His eyes flick down, and his chest heaves. Then, before I have a chance to think any more about how wrong this is, how stupid, his lips are on mine.

My heart surges at the kiss. It's slow and sensual for a second, but then it's as though everything between us ignites. He feels so good. The slide of his tongue against mine is so explicit it makes me moan.

I take hold of his shirt as my mind scrambles to process what is going on between us.

Am I really doing this? After telling my mom that the plan is ridiculous and that these men are off-limits because they're going to be my stepbrothers. After stressing and crying at the situation. After hearing how Grant isn't interested in the plan at all.

Yes, I am because at the moment, nothing else seems to matter enough to stop.

Grant's hand finds my breast and squeezes with the perfect amount of pressure. My bra is thin, and so is my shirt, so his thumb easily finds the bump of my nipple and gently strokes it. Oh god. He's really good at that. Really good. I don't know what to concentrate on, the delicious slide of his tongue or the pressure of that thumb. I want to moan, but I'm so conscious of what we're doing and how fast it is.

As if he can feel my uncertainty, he pulls back and cups my cheek.

"I wasn't expecting that," he says. His eyes are filled with intensity, and I just don't want to break the moment. If I start talking now, I'm going to start thinking, and then I'm going to acknowledge what a terrible idea this is, so instead, I lean forward and kiss him again, and it's all the encouragement that he needs.

What started slowly progresses a whole lot faster when I let my hands roam Grant's chest until they find their way under the hem of his gray sweat-shirt and make contact with his hot, smooth skin. He doesn't waste any time doing the same until his hand is filled with my naked breast, bra tugged down in the roughest, rudest way I've ever been unclothed.

Oh god, the heat of him is too much. My leg is hurting, but it doesn't prevent me from shifting forward so that I can get closer to him. I'm eager and greedy, and I want to see the amazing body that I can feel under his sweater.

"Take it off," I tell him, and he removes his shirt in the best way. You know the way guys in films just yank with one hand in a way that says S. E. X.

And that's when I get to see my first McGregor brother up close and personal.

He's tan and perfectly defined, as though he works out on the regular and eats really clean. It's the kind of body that gets featured on all my favorite kinds of books; chiseled and sexy as hell. I just gawk at him as he looks down at me like I'm a feast he wants to devour.

Damn, I want him to eat me.

Those lips would feel so soft. That tongue would slide and flick perfectly against my clit. It's been way too long since I had an orgasm, and that's probably half of why I'm acting so foolishly and with so little care about the consequences.

His smoky gray eyes fix on my belt as though he's thinking exactly the same thing.

"I think we need to head to the bedroom where we don't have an audience," he grins.

Killer whines from the corner, and we both erupt into laughter again. He might only be a dog, but getting sexy in front of him would still be very weird.

"You might have to carry me again," I say, stretching my arms towards him.

"I think it might be a good idea for you to test your leg out. I'd like to make sure I'm not going to hurt you."

Grant stands and puts his hand out to take hold of mine. I shift to the edge of the sofa and put my weight to stand on my good leg, gingerly placing the foot of my injured one on the floor. It still hurts but not as badly as before.

"Think you can walk on it?" he asks me, and I nod.

"Good," he says, sweeping me up into his arms again and laughing.

"I thought I was walking?"

"Nah. I just wanted to check you were in good enough health for what I'm planning to do to you."

My insides turn to jelly at the cheekiness of his grin, and my heart surges. Am I ready for this? Getting frisky on the sofa is one thing, but where we're going is now layered with more intention.

He carries me as though I weigh nothing and, in his bedroom, he rests me down on the bed carefully, and I gaze around at this place that Grant calls home. It's decorated in the same style as the den, with dark wood and manly fabrics. It's warm and rugged, exactly like the man who sleeps here every night, and it smells good of him, too.

"I think it's time you lost some clothes," he says softly, beginning to unthread his belt and unbutton his jeans. I swear my heart almost stops beating as he strips away the layers until he's standing before me in just his boxers. Damn, he's turned on, and I'm still almost completely dressed. His hand goes to his cock, taking hold of it and squeezing.

I start to unbutton my blouse, watching his hand move ever so slightly. He's teasing himself while I get undressed, eyes watching for every new bit of skin I reveal.

"And the jeans," he says with a demanding edge to his voice. I do as he did and unfasten my belt. I take my time, and he's too impatient to wait. In a flash, he's there, rough fingers, tugging down the zipper and then the jeans until I'm left in my simple bra and panties. He buries his face between my breasts, inhaling deeply, then he presses a soft trail of kisses from down my stomach to the top of my panties. The heat of his breath warms my clit.

"You smell so good," he says, breathing in deeply again. I'm not used to hearing that kind of thing. Ollie wasn't exactly the most vocal during sex, and it was always pretty much the same silent routine. I can tell already that Grant is so much more experienced.

His fingers hook into the edges of the pink fabric,

and his eyes find mine, a final check that I'm okay with him getting me naked.

I know how impetuous and stupid this is, but I'm too damn horny to turn back, and, in a way, it seems funny as hell to me that I'm about to get physical with the one brother who wasn't interested in auditioning me for marriage!

I unhook the clips of my bra just to let him know exactly how ready I am for him and his eyelids immediately go heavy at the sight of my breasts.

I know I'm being stupid. Having sex with Grant should not be top of my to-do list right now, but he looks so good, the muscles of his shoulders rippling as he settles between my legs. I hold my breath, waiting to feel his tongue, but instead, he takes hold of my ankles and forces my legs up, spreading me open even more.

"That's better," he says. I rise, resting on my elbows, and he looks up at me with a grin. "I like to see what I'm working with."

"Is it work?"

"The best kind," he laughs. He slides his hand over my stomach to the middle of my breasts and presses down. "Lay back. Relax."

"Don't work so well with an audience?"

"I work well in any circumstance when it comes to eating pussy, but I think you'll enjoy it better if you close your eyes and trust me."

Trust.

That's a big thing to give over when you've known someone for such a short space of time. Would I trust someone to drive my car after spending three hours with them? Would I trust them to hold my credit cards? No. But for some reason, we can find it easier to trust them with our bodies, and maybe with our hearts.

I know what I'm like. I don't generally do casual sex because my heart always ends up invested. I think that's where men and women differ the most.

I lay back, taking a deep breath, and try to let the tension leave my body. I let my legs go slack, and it's then that Grant takes his first lick.

Oh.

The sensation is toe-curling. It's gentle, tiny little flicks that set all my nerve endings on fire. My hips rise, seeking more, and he places his hand on my stomach to still me.

"Slowly," he murmurs against my pussy. "There's no rushing here."

And he's right. There's no one waiting on me—nothing I need to do today. No reason to hurry, so I let him take his time. I let him eat me as though he's savoring the most delicious food at a Michelin Star restaurant. I let my mind wander as he strokes his tongue between my legs uses his fingers to bring me so close to orgasm that my whole body twitches.

This man knows women, that much I can tell. He doesn't need to ask me what feels good, he just does it, and he's in no hurry. He takes me close three times before I'm begging.

"Please..." I gasp. "Don't stop. Let me..."

I don't have time to say the word 'come' before I do. I think he was waiting for me to plead with him before he tapped my clit with his finger and turned me into a moaning, writhing wreck of a woman. I think I leave my body because I don't remember him climbing up and over me. When I come around, his face is buried in my neck, his hand on my breast, his cock resting heavily against my pussy.

"That's my girl," he says, and I can tell he's smiling. Grant has a right to be cocky. He's pretty damn spectacular at that.

"I...I.."

"Speechless," he laughs. "My work here is done."

Grant starts to roll away from me as though he's going to leave the bed, and I grab hold of him, holding him tight, even though I know he's only joking.

"You're going nowhere!"

"You want more?" he gasps. "So greedy!"

I scowl because what happens next is more about him than it is about me. I've never found it easy to come during sex, but I want him to feel the pleasure he's already given me. I want to make him a quivering, pleading wreck, too, so I don't correct him.

He doesn't put up any further resistance, though. His hand darts out to his nightstand, and he rummages around for a condom.

"I'm on the pill," I tell him. "And clean." I know because I got checked out after Ollie.

"Better safe than sorry," he says, holding the foil pack and smiling. "For a moment, I thought I was going to come up empty-handed. It's been a while since I needed these."

There's a moment between us where Grant gazes down at me, and I'm worried he's going to pull back. Is he remembering the last time he was with his girlfriend? Is this going to get awkward? I don't want it to. I really want the more that comes next, and I know he needs it, probably a whole lot more than me.

"You going to wrap it then?" I smile and look down at his cock, taking in the size of it. Damn! He has a whole lot to wrap.

"Yes, ma'am!" He kneels between my legs, tearing open the condom with his teeth and rolling the latex down the tower of his cock with a speed that I marvel at. This point in proceedings is often not that sexy – an interruption to the main event – but watching Grant get himself ready for me is arousing enough for my eyes to widen. His thighs are thick, and his abs crunched into a six-pack that would have most men weeping in jealousy over. His hair flops forward a little, and I get an urge to ruffle it like he's a little boy. In the low light of the room, he looks almost black and white, like a photography model in a coffee table book. I don't know what I've done to deserve this, but I'm going to relish every moment.

When he's done, his eyes meet mine. "I wasn't

expecting this," he says, resting his hand on my right thigh. Even this aroused, he's still conscious of my pain.

"I know," I say. "Me either."

"But it feels right."

I nod because it does. There's no awkwardness at all.

"You want this?" he asks me. He's holding his cock, stroking it slowly.

"I do," I say, and he grins, climbing back over me and kissing me deeply. There's a sweetness to Grant that has my heart swelling. An emotional vulnerability that makes me feel connected to him more than I should. His hand smooths my hair, thumbs grazing my cheekbones. We move as one, with a synchronicity that makes this whole thing feel so right.

His legs nudge mine wider, the hardness of his cock grinding against my clit. I want to feel him push inside me, but he's still in no hurry.

"You feel good," he says, squeezing my breast and leaning down to take my nipple into his mouth. He sucks gently at first, nibbling and flicking until I'm writhing.

"Now, Grant," I say, not caring that I sound desperate. His eyes find mine, and they are filled with laughter and emotion.

"Am I making you wait too long?"

"Just a little bit."

"I don't like to be rushed, baby," he says. "I like to take my time."

"You can take your time when you're inside me," I

say, tugging at his hips. His ass is like a rock beneath my palm, and it flexes as he adjusts. The pressure of his cock at my entrance has my heart skipping. This is it. The moment before. When we've done this, there is no going back.

Grant is going to be my stepbrother in a few months, and this is going to change how we see each other forever.

For a fraction of a second, I want to ask him if he's worried about it, too. I know he doesn't agree with his father's plan, so maybe this is about rebellion for him. I think there is a hint of rebellion in me, too.

Rebellion can be a dangerous activity, but I can't regret this when it feels so good. . .so right. He nudges inside me just a little, and I gasp. His cock is so thick and the stretching so good that I open my legs wider, wanting him deeper. He really doesn't like to be rushed, though. He enters me so slowly that I'm dripping by the time he's all the way inside, dripping and quivering.

"Oh god," I gasp as he takes hold of my hands and holds them above my head.

"You like a man to be in charge," he says, nibbling on my lip. "You've got a bit of a sass mouth, but this is what you really like."

Grant starts to move, and it's slow and steady. He grips my wrists just tight enough that I can't let go, and he's right. I do love feeling powerless. I love knowing he is completely in control. It's when I feel safest. I wonder if his animal-whisper ways are what gives him that extra perception around people. It's a bit unnerving for someone to know something about you that you haven't told them directly and within such a short space of time.

He kisses my lips, sliding his tongue over mine in the same rhythm as his cock, and it's bliss to be so overwhelmed with sensation. I move my hips, grinding against him until I'm panting. I didn't know sex could be like this. I didn't know it was possible for me to feel frantic and desperate and possessed, and it's an awakening of sorts. I let go of all my inhibitions and get lost in the moment; the smell of him, the taste of him, the low rumbling groan he makes as he gets closer. I notice the swell of his cock, too, the increased pace of his hips as he chases his pleasure. I feel my hips straining for more contact because I'm close, closer than I've ever been to coming during penetrative sex.

Is it possible? Could I come this way?

"Fuck," Grant hisses. "Your pussy feels so..."

I don't hear him finish his sentence, though. There's a loud moan that obliterates his words—a loud moan coming from my mouth. I'm coming. It's like the crack of a whip in its speed and intensity. My mind seems to stop as my body takes over, going completely rigid. Grant doesn't stop moving, his hips pounding into me, his eyes squeezed tightly closed. I watch his face as he comes, the release relaxing all his facial features until he looks completely serene. His cheeks flush with pleasure. His chest heaves with exertion. There's so much beauty in his surrender that I want to cry.

What would it be like to love Grant and be loved by him?

Passionate. All-consuming. Yes. Gentle and kind. Definitely.

He has everything a woman could want, and I've gotten to see it all so fast.

I lay beneath him, reveling in what has been but already yearning for what will never be.

This is it for us—a stolen night between two souls who needed what the other could give in the moment.

When the sun comes up, I have to leave the warmth of Grant's arms and face what the world is about to throw in my direction.

A ridiculous plan.

Ten men.

It's so stupid, but it's enough to make me run.

One night in the McGregor mansion. One night with an amazing man.

One night that I'll remember for the rest of my life.

A life that's about to take a whole new and un-expected path.

Chapter 7

I don't have to do the walk of shame because it's 5 am by the time I find some sense in my head, and I'm prepared to tell Grant I need to get back to my own room. I can just imagine what Mom would think if she saw me now. All my protestations about the 'plan' would seem kind of hollow at this point. I slide on my clothes, perching on the edge of his bed, listening to his soft breathing. In the low light, with a sheet tangled over his hips and legs, he looks almost ethereal. I can't help but smile goofily because I know what my friends would do if they could see me now. They'd be squealing like crazy!

I feel awkward waking him, but the alternative is to risk going back to the house with my rumpled hair in yesterday's clothes and a beet-red face. I pat his arm gently and whisper his name, and he stirs, opening his eyes that are still dreamy with sleep.

"Hey," I say.

He smiles slowly, the realization that I'm in his bedroom and what we did showing in his satisfied expression.

"What time is it?" he asks.

"The crack of dawn."

"You thinking about leaving me?"

"Yeah," I say. "Before the rest of the house wakes up."

"You think they don't know that you didn't go back to your room?" he says. "Nothing goes unnoticed in that house."

"Well, I guess I can say I went to see a friend."

He shakes his head. "Mmm. . .that could work, I guess."

"Only thing is, I need you to show me where to go."

He chuckles, reaching out and laying a big warm hand on my knee. "Is the McGregor mansion causing you navigation issues?"

I nod. "Something like that. I wasn't in there long enough to explore."

"Before my idiot brothers scared the bejesus out of you."

"Exactly!"

His hand slides up my thighs, and I'm immediately warm between my legs. Those eyes, watching my reactions, make me shiver. "Well, I hope I restored your faith in the McGregor men just a little."

I smile. "Quite a lot. I don't think I'm going to be able to sit down for a week."

"So I take it you're not up for some more fun," he asks, looking hopeful.

"No..." I say a little too quickly. "I mean that I don't think my lady could take it."

"She just needs a little more training," he says, sitting up so he can kiss me. His lips are so warm and soft, and the way they move so mesmerizing that I think he could ask me to do anything, and I'd say yes.

He draws back, cupping my cheek. "Let me get some pants on, and I'll help you back."

I watch him dress, finding soft, dark blue sweats and tugging them onto the gorgeous body that gave me so much pleasure. It feels like, with every layer he adds, there's more distance between us. When he's dressed, he helps me up, and I test my left leg by placing my foot on the floor and gently resting my weight on it. It's still sore but better than it was. Even so, Grant can tell I'm in some pain, and he insists on carrying me back to the house.

I'm not sure what we look like, padding through the garden like a groom with his new bride. The morning is warm and damp, the air so fresh with the scent of the garden that I inhale deeply.

This is my favorite time of the day, and just as I'm thinking it, Grant says, "Isn't it beautiful."

"It is. So tranquil."

He smiles. "Some of my brothers like to party late, but there are a few of us who like to rise early. We're lucky that we haven't bumped into Donnie painting or Elliot working out."

"We are," I say. I like Grant a lot, but I'm certainly not ready to complicate an already ridiculously com-plicated situation by letting everyone know what hap-pened between us. If we can keep this amazing night a secret, it will be best for everyone.

At the back door, Grant presses his finger against a flat black pad, and the door unlocks. It's all so high-tech. "You're gonna need to speak to Jackson about getting access sorted to the house," Grant says.

"That's if I'm staying."

"You want to leave?" Grant asks. I can't miss the disappointment in his expression and feel instantly terrible.

"I think it will be the best for everyone," I say.

Grant shakes his head. "Your mom will be devastated."

"Maybe." Grant gently lowers me until I'm standing in the hallway, and I can rest my hand against the wall for support.

"You shouldn't let my dad bully you out of here. You know he can't make you do anything you don't want to do."

"He bullies the rest of you!"

Grant shrugs. "That's different. We're his flesh and blood and we've seen the sacrifices he's made for us. We have a duty to put the family first."

We start to shuffle slowly in the direction of my room. Grant keeps looking over to check I'm okay.

I have so much to consider, and with so little sleep, I know that my capacity for rational and logical thought is very diminished.

How can I stay? There is always going to be a feeling of awkwardness, no matter what I say or do. But can I leave? How will that affect Mom's relationship with Roderick? I don't want to do anything to damage her happiness. I owe her so much.

We slowly climb the stairs, and I grip the handrail and Grant's arm for stability. "Nearly there," he whispers.

I know where we are now. The door to my silly pink powder puff room is closed, and I rest my weight on the handle. The door swings open, and I'm momentarily stunned again at the ridiculousness of it.

"It really is pretty special, isn't it," Grant whispers, shaking his head.

"Special is a very good word for it."

A few seconds pass as we look at each other, the realization that we're parting hitting me in the gut in a way that shocks me. "So..."

"I didn't expect this," he whispers.

"Me either..."

More seconds pass, his eyes flicking over my face like he's trying to commit my features to memory.

I have no idea what I want him to say next. I loved our time together, but this is all too much. The implications of us starting something are huge. By doing that I'm either admitting that I'm taking a step towards Roderick's ridiculous plan or that I'm rejecting it in favor of just one son. Either way, it's going to cause trouble. And I know Grant has a lot of unresolved issues. Do I want to get tied up in that, too?

I really need to keep my life as simple as possible. I may need to disengage from this household at a moment's notice, depending on what happens next, and having even a little bit of my heart invested in Grant is just too much of a risk.

"I had a great time," he whispers.

I nod and smile. "Me, too. . .this all kinda took me by surprise."

He nods and smiles back.

"I should get some sleep," I say, looking over my shoulder at the bed behind me.

"Guess I'll see you at breakfast," Grant grins. There's no awkwardness now, and I'm so grateful—my stomach rumbles right on time.

"I would say that's a pretty good assumption to make."

"Sweet dreams, beautiful," he whispers, leaning in to press a soft kiss to the corner of my mouth. My knees almost buckle, and everything in me is screaming to tug him into this room and not let him go. Then he starts to walk away, and my heart clenches.

I wish I wasn't this way. I wish that my heart were harder and didn't get tangled up in feeling things it has no business rushing into after a nice afternoon and the best sex I've ever had. My heart would be choosing wedding dresses and picking cake flavors if she had half the chance.

I watch Grant walk away, and my heart tells me that I shouldn't have let him go, but my mind, in her boring, sensible voice, tells me I did the right thing.

Gah.

Life is too complicated.

I turn and close the door, facing into this space that is supposed to be my new home.

I'm too beat to even take off my clothes, but I still make it into the bathroom to clean my teeth before flaking out onto the bed.

My final thought before I fall into an ocean-deep sleep is of Grant's eyes and the way he looked at me when we were fucking.

In a few months, he's going to be my stepbrother, and everything we did last night will sit awkwardly between us.

But all my memories of Grant will be amazing ones.

I think I'm ruined for life.

Chapter 8

It feels like I've only been asleep for a minute when I'm roused by a knock on the door. For a second, I'm confused about where I am, imagining that Mom's voice will be calling me to get up and ready for whatever it is I'm supposed to be doing today. But it's not Mom's voice I hear.

"Laura."

The voice is deep and definitely male. Elliot?

I sit up with a jolt, eyes opening to find I've been sleeping in a raging sea of candy floss.

I'm at the McGregor mansion. Holy fuck.

"Yeah," I call back. My voice is husky with sleep, and my eyes are practically glued together with dry-tiredness.

"You decent?"

I actually have no idea, but when I look down, I remember crashing out in my clothes. "Yeah," I call again.

The handle turns, and a freshly showered Elliot enters the room slowly, hair still a little wet and cheeks pink.

I know I look like absolute shit, and I know I should care, but I'm too damn tired to find a fuck to give.

"You always sleep fully dressed?" he asks, grinning.

"Not usually," I say with a shake of my head.

"Feel like coming down for breakfast?"

I look down at myself as though it should be obvious that I'm in no state to be entering the land of the living at this point. "Think I could do with freshening up," I say.

"You look pretty good to me." Elliot grins again, his megawatt smile practically laying me out cold.

"You're obviously way too easily pleased," I say, rolling my eyes.

He shakes his head and leans against the door frame as though he's settling in for a long conversation. Why is he not seeing how much I need to get out of these clothes and into the shower?

"You fancy hitting the gym with me instead?" he asks. "I need to do some stretching."

As hideous as I currently feel, that sounds like it might be a good idea. I attempt to move my bad leg, and an ache of pain moves through the tissue. Stretching is a necessary evil.

"My leg is bad." I rub my hand over it gingerly to illustrate the point.

"Well, I can help you with that."

"Can you give me five?" I ask, looking towards the bathroom.

"Sure. I'll go and grab some things, and I'll come back." Elliott leaves and closes my door quietly behind him.

It takes me all of five minutes to shower, scrape my hair up into a messy bun and tug on my gym gear.

Elliot gives me a little more time than I need, which shows he's a patient guy. I'm limping when I open the door, still not able to put my foot on the ground without wincing. Elliot's face is immediately concerned. "Wow, you've really hurt yourself."

"Something like that," I say.

"Running away from someone?" I guess he must have heard about yesterday from his brothers.

"Are there no secrets in this house?" I ask, blushing a little. If he knew I was running, he must also know what I overheard and my reaction.

"Not very often." He shrugs apologetically, but his smile tells me he's not that bothered. I guess he must be used to having zero privacy living in a house like this. "You ready to go?"

"Yeah," I say, grabbing my phone and stuffing it into my purse.

We make our way through the house, taking a different hallway and set of stairs. Elliot fills me in on the routine in the house. Generally, the boys are up early for breakfast and out the door by 8.30 am, but it's Saturday today, so things will be a little more relaxed. We reach a set of large walnut doors, and Elliot tugs at the handle and leads me into a sprawling fitness area. There are machines for cardio and weight training and a large soft-floored area for stretching and other floor work. Through glass doors, I take in the gorgeous indoor pool and what looks like a spa area. I've only seen this kind of thing in magazines before and can't help feeling completely overwhelmed at the luxury of it all. If I stay here, I'm going to get to use this every day if I want to. This is a lifestyle I never imagined would be mine. Even as I think it, I hate myself for being impressed by material things. I'm no Stepford Wife. The last thing I'd ever want to be accused of would be that I was a gold-digger.

I catch Elliot looking at me as I'm gazing around, and I'm mortified.

"It's nice, isn't it?" he says softly as though he knows what's going on inside my head.

"Yeah. No wonder you're in such good shape. The college sports facilities are nothing compared to this."

"Sweaty changing rooms and hundred-year-old equipment?"

"They smell like feet," I say, and he chuckles.

"So, you wanna sit over there so I can look at that leg?"

For a second, I remember Grant's hands on my thigh and how amazing it felt and my cheeks heat. Does it feel right to have Elliot touch me under the circumstances? I'm not sure. I've made no commitments to Grant, but that doesn't mean I don't feel a sense of loyalty to him because of what happened between us. Elliot is only thinking about helping me, though, I rationalize. This isn't about anything else.

"Sure," I say, making my way over to the soft floor and dropping my purse. I struggle to lower myself because of the pain, and when I'm sitting, the matting is cold through the fabric of my workout pants.

Elliot kneels next to me, his eyes trained on my

thigh, and he reaches out to gently feel his way around my problem. His hands are big and strong, but his touch is gentle. Even so, the pain still makes me gasp.

"Sorry," he mutters, pressing a little lower where it doesn't hurt quite as much. "Can you try and relax it a bit. The muscle is in a state of spasm. I want to see if I can ease it for you a little."

I take a deep breath and try to relax, letting my leg go as loose as I can without wincing. Elliot shifts a little closer. "Breathe in," he says. "Then let it out slowly."

I do as he says, and as I start to exhale, he begins to stretch and knead my thigh. It hurts but in a good way. I can tell he knows what he's doing. "Okay?" he asks as he releases me.

"Yeah, I think so."

"Can you take it if I do some more?"

"Sure." I inhale and then exhale as he has instructed, and each time he stretches and massages, I can feel my leg relaxing a little more. I watch him, his face serious with concentration, and I notice some slight similarities between him and Grant. There is something around their brow and the straightness of their noses that hints at their family connection. Their coloring is so different, though.

The early morning sunshine casts a bright beam of warm yellow light across the space, illuminating Elliot's blond hair and fair lashes. Before I can look away, Elliot's blue eyes flick up and catch me. There's a moment of intensity there before he breaks into a smile.

"How does that feel now?" he asks.

"Much better," I say.

He leans back a little. "Do you think you could put some weight on it?"

"Maybe."

Elliot gets to his feet and holds out his hand to help me up. I initially take all the weight on my right leg and try slowly to press my left foot against the floor, testing the injury. It's not perfect, but I can straighten my leg so much more now.

"You have magic fingers," I say. There is just nothing worse than being physically incapable, and Elliot has managed to help a lot.

"You have no idea," he says with a wink, and I can't help but chuckle.

"Easy, tiger. I'm your soon-to-be-stepsister."

"Is that what you said to Grant last night?" he asks with a knowing grin, and my heart skitters. Has Grant said something? That would feel like a serious betrayal. Elliot's jade eyes are sparkling with amusement at my obvious discomfort. I am certainly not going to confirm or deny anything at this point.

"What did you hear?" I ask, figuring that I might as well know where I stand.

"I heard that you were hiding out at Grant's, and someone may have heard some interesting noises after dark which definitely wasn't you discussing your soon-to-be familial position."

My face feels like it's on fire, but I'm not going to give him the satisfaction of being embarrassed. "Didn't your father tell you about listening behind closed doors? You never hear anything you want to."

"On the contrary," Elliot says, linking his hands behind his back and widening his stance. "What was heard was very interesting and definitely what some of us want."

"Some of us?"

He grins but doesn't answer straight away. Standing like that, in his gym gear, I can see the contour of his muscles and the bulge of something very substantial. I guess size may run in families, and despite being indignant and angry and this conversation, I get a little shiver down my spine.

"I'm not going to beat around the bush with you, Laura. You're my kind of girl in so many ways, and this is something I know is going to make my father very happy. I know I can make you very happy. I guess the missing link here is whether you're interested in me the way you were interested in my reclusive brother."

Holy shit. I was not expecting that. Elliot has cut through all the crap and just laid it out there. I guess maybe I've been naïve. After the conversation with Mom, I should have realized that this subject was not going to be covered up anymore. They all know that I know. They might also know that I've expressed reservations, but I guess the more confident ones are still going to try and convince me, especially now they know that I've given in to Grant.

I feel like I'm standing at the precipice. One more step forward, and I'm going to be tumbling into oblivion. The thing is that oblivion is looking good right now. That oblivion is over six feet of some of the best-looking man I've ever seen in my life.

And he's interested in me.

To be his wife.

I have to stifle a nervous giggle.

Forget this being a precipice. I feel like I'm in a parallel universe.

"I...I don't think I know what to say," I stutter.

Elliot smiles wider. "It's a lot to take on board," he says. "I get that."

"That's a bit of an understatement."

"But is it something you're considering, Laura? I mean, you told your mom that you thought all this was crazy and pretty much immediately got involved with Grant. And I know my brother. He's not exactly a Casanova, especially since he lost his girlfriend."

"Are you suggesting that I seduced him?"

Elliot puts up his hands defensively. "Not at all. I'm saying that I want to understand where you're coming from here. What's going through your mind right now?" He takes a step closer and rests his right palm against my upper arm, gazing down at me. "Do you feel that?" he says softly.

And I do. I do feel the tug between us, the same attraction that I felt from the moment I saw his picture online. It only got stronger when he collected me from the apartment. It's a warm feeling of connection, layered with a hot tug of attraction. I blink, trying to think how best to respond. If I'm honest and tell him what I'm thinking about him, then things are about to get out of control.

He steps closer, and I can smell the scent of his skin and feel his soft breath on my skin.

I'm so torn.

So that's what I say.

"I'm so. . .torn, Elliot." There is pain in my voice, and he gazes down at me seriously.

"Torn?"

I nod, licking my lips. My mouth is so dry.

"I'm. . .I'm attracted to you. Of course, I am. And I think you're a great guy, from what I've seen. . .and I like Grant, too. And I don't know how things went that far last night. I can't explain it."

He exhales. "You regret it?"

I shake my head. "No. I'm not saying that. I'm saying that I'm confused. You must be able to understand. I came here yesterday thinking that I was moving in with my new step-family, not auditioning to be some kind of gang-bang bride."

He snorts and shakes his head. "That's not what this is about, Laura."

"Most women don't sleep with ten men in their lifetimes," I say. "Let alone having to sleep with ten just to perform their marital obligations."

"Sex should never be seen as an obligation."

His smile is broad, and I have to roll my eyes because he's making light of something that I'm struggling with, as though my feelings about all of this are joke worthy. "You know what I mean."

"I get the confusion. I do, but I think that you're overthinking it all."

Now I frown because what is he saying? That marriage isn't a big deal? That this isn't something that I should be thinking about. "This is serious, Elliot. My mom is marrying your dad. We're going to be related when that happens. If I don't take it seriously, I could end up messing this whole thing up. There are feelings involved. The feelings of a lot of people."

"I'm not saying that you shouldn't think about it. I'm saying that maybe if you relax a little and take each situation as it comes, things might be easier."

"You mean that I should be considering each of you individually rather than as a group?"

He nods and rubs his hand up and down my forearm. "That's exactly what I'm saying. It's great that you like Grant, and I'm hoping you like me. And maybe if you take the time to get to know each of my brothers, you'll like them too. Maybe, if you approach it that way, none of this will seem so overwhelming."

I take a step back because I need some space to think, and his manly smell is making me woozy enough to actually consider what he's saying. I must be crazy.

Taking a deep breath, I try to find the right way to respond. "The end result of that, and there are many possible issues in between, will be that I have ten boyfriends, Elliot. Ten. I mean, two would be freaky, but I guess I might just get away with two, but ten." Katelin flashes through my mind again. She's just about getting away with three. Ten is a whole other thing.

"Husbands, Laura."

"Husbands," I whisper, turning the word over in my head. "Yesterday I wasn't even thinking about dating, and now I'm supposed to be thinking about getting married?"

"Life does that sometimes," Elliot says wryly. "It sneaks up on you when you least expect it."

"This isn't sneaking. It's trampling!"

Elliot straightens, looking me over. "Do you trust me?" he asks.

I think for a moment and remember how I felt with Grant. Trust is a many-leveled thing. Do I trust Elliot at this moment? Yes. But I haven't known him long enough to say for sure. He's only treated me with kindness and respect so far, and that's great, but to truly trust, someone has to be tested. It has to be built over time.

"Close your eyes."

I shake my head, and he puts up his hands again. "Trust me," he says softly. "I would never do anything to hurt you."

"Okay." I shut my eyes, standing completely still with my arms hanging by my sides. My bad leg is slightly flexed, and for a moment, the silence in the gym and the darkness behind my eyes feels uncomfortable. Then, before I can react, Elliot's lips are on mine.

It's a ghost of a kiss. Gentle and tentative. It's respectful and hopeful, and instead of pulling away like I know I should, a shiver passes through me, and I kiss him back. My heart pounds, my body and mind warring for control. Oh god. I shouldn't be doing this, but I don't open my eyes because I know that if I did, I'd wake up from this trance that I'm in. His mouth is so soft, his lips yielding and hands gentle as he places them on my hips and pulls me closer. My hands move too, as though they have their own minds, resting on his upper arms, feeling his biceps flex beneath them. The first touch of our tongues is perfect. The hairs rise on the back of my neck and all across my scalp, and I let him kiss me as deeply as his brother did only a few hours before.

Grant.

The memory of his body on top of mine flashes into my mind - his caress. . .the soft murmur of the words he whispered in my ear as he entered me – and I come to my senses. Grant doesn't buy into this whole family marriage idea. When we got together, that wasn't what he was working towards. He wanted to be with me knowing that the plan wasn't what I wanted either. This is a betrayal of that understanding.

I push at Elliot, pulling back from him. His eyes are glazed when they meet mine, his lips slightly parted. "Laura," he says softly.

"Grant..." I say. "...he wouldn't be okay with this."

"You're worried my brother will be jealous?"

"He doesn't want what your father wants."

"This isn't about Grant, right now. This is about you and how you feel."

I take a step back, turning to face the swimming pool. "I can't compartmentalize like that, Elliot."

"I know you liked kissing me," he says, coming to stand beside me.

"I did."

"And I know you liked being with Grant."

"I did, but Grant won't like this."

Elliot turns to me, but I keep staring ahead.

"You don't know my brother so well," he says. "There's a lot of hurt there and a lot of anger, but he loves his family, and he'll come around in the end."

"I don't want to hurt anyone," I tell him. "I don't want to be disloyal. Grant was so kind to me when I really needed someone."

"I'll talk to him."

I shake my head. There is no way that could possibly be the right approach. "No. I don't think that will work."

"So then maybe you need to talk to him."

"And tell him what? That he's not enough man for me, and I'm thinking of sampling his nine brothers, too? I'm sure that will go down a treat."

"You tell him that..." Elliot stops, and the silence stretches uncomfortably.

"Exactly," I say. "There is no way of explaining this without repercussions."

Elliot sighs. He knows I'm right. "So then you have to choose. Between being only with Grant and him being disowned by his dad, or you explaining what's happening here in the hope that we can keep this family together."

His words stab my heart. There is no way I want Grant to lose his family. He may not want to be quite as involved with them as they might want him to be, but that doesn't mean he would fare better alone. This is too much pressure, and it's just not my responsibility.

"I just need to think," I say, and Elliot sighs.

"Thinking can be a dangerous pastime," he says.

I don't disagree, but there's so much at stake here that not thinking could be catastrophic.

Chapter 9

I work out as much as is possible without stressing my leg, concentrating on my arms and abs, avoiding looking at Elliot too much. He's put some music on and has been running for the past thirty minutes. The man is hardly out of breath and is the least sweaty gym-man I've ever seen.

My mind is also running, trying to work out what the hell I should do. I'm attracted to Elliot. That's for damn sure. It's at times like these that I'm grateful that women's arousal isn't as visible as men's. He'd have to put his fingers between my legs to know how wet his kiss made me and how hot I am right now, knowing that he's near.

I'm still tender from fucking his brother, and now I'm wet for him. It seems so wrong on so many levels.

I know I don't want to hurt Grant. He's been through so much, but Elliot is right. There is no easy answer here. Mom always told me that honesty is the best policy. She told me to never leave difficult conversations too long. Time heals but it also has a way of making things worse, too.

After much deliberating, I make a decision. I need to just be honest with Grant as soon as possible. It'll be up to him how he feels about it, and maybe I'm being big-headed to think he'll be bothered in any way. We had a one-night-stand after all. I'm sure he's not viewing it as the start of the world's greatest love story. Then again, it's not like I'm going anywhere. Fucking your stepsister-to-be isn't a decision without potential consequences!

I make my way over to Elliot, and he sees me in the mirror and starts to slow the machine.

"I'm going to go for a shower," I say.

"Do you think you can find the way back to your room?" he asks.

I nod. "Thanks for helping with my leg."

He smiles and steps off the machine. His cheeks are a little pink, and it makes him look so cute. "Have you decided what to do next?" he asks. There's a hint of hope in his voice that I might not immediately be pushing away the prospect of there being more between us.

"I'm going to be honest with Grant."

Elliot smiles. "I'm glad you said that."

"Why?" I ask.

"Because I'm happy to know that you're what I thought you were; an honest and straightforward person."

"Mom always says that honesty is the best policy."

"Your mom sounds like a very sensible woman."

I snort. "That's what I thought until she started professing the virtues of polyamorous marriage. Then I wondered if she might have early-onset dementia."

"She's just had more time to think about it," Elliot

says. "She knows us, and she knows what a good position you would be in, too."

"What position is that? On my back!"

Elliot laughs, his eyes sparkling. "I prefer something a little raunchier, but we can work on that."

When I roll my eyes at him, he laughs some more. "Let's not run before we can walk."

I raise my hand in a wave and walk over to where I left my purse.

"See you at breakfast," Elliot calls as I'm about to disappear through the door. My stomach seems to hear him and grumbles in response. If I wasn't so damn hungry, I'd consider skipping meals in the house just to avoid being faced with all these crazy people.

I'm able to walk faster back to my room, and I'm glad for that. I manage to avoid bumping into anyone else and take a welcome hot shower in my gorgeous en-suite. When I'm dressed, I put on just a little bit of makeup to try and conceal my dark circles and make my cheeks a little pinker.

Who am I kidding? I go all out with mascara and lip gloss, too. As much as I want to pretend that I'm not bothered by what the McGregor brothers think of me, I do care. For all my reticence and fear about this situation, I am intrigued, and I certainly don't want them thinking that their father has made a poor choice in considering me for their future wife.

My anxiety really kicks in as I walk down the stairs. For a second, I think I might have forgotten the way and begin to panic about wandering in an endless maze of rooms and corridors. Then a familiar voice calls out to me.

"There you are, Laura. We were about to send a search party out for you." Spinning around, I come face to face with Roderick himself, the one McGregor man I met before moving into this house, and he's looking at me with interest. "Good morning. I hope you slept well."

I can tell by the fact that his expression is amused that he knows I wasn't in my own bed for most of it. Damn. I don't like them all-knowing my business, and I particularly don't like Mr. McGregor himself regarding me as though I'm a filly for his stable of studs.

Ugh. "Yes, I did, thank you." My voice is colder than I intend it to be, but I don't think it bothers him in any way. Despite the fact that it's the weekend, Roderick is dressed as though he's about to feature on the cover of GQ. I'm not into older guys, but I can certainly see what my mom likes about him and where his sons get their crazy good looks from. He's a cross between George Clooney and Robert Redford.

"Well, that's great. Shall I escort you to breakfast?"

"Please. Lead the way." It's a subtle way of saying I don't want to walk at his side. He seems to understand, and I follow him in the direction I was already heading towards the dining room. As we near, the babble of voices gets louder and louder. By the time we reach the door, I'm wondering how on earth anyone is actually keeping track of anything that's being said. It reminds me of high school recess, the crazy hum of too many frantic and excited voices. I stood outside this door yesterday and heard things I wasn't supposed to. Roderick's hand goes to the handle, and my stomach lurches.

I've got to go in.

"Good morning," Roderick announces loudly as he enters the room, and I follow, more heads turning than I am capable of counting. All eyes are on me.

I blush like a beet and catch a few smiles at my embarrassment.

"Morning," a chorus of voices reply.

"Where would you like to sit?" Roderick moves his arm in a sweeping gesture as though there are innumerable seats to choose from. In reality, there are four empty seats at the main table and a row of stools at the counter. I guess that would be where I'd felt most comfortable, but it would be making a serious negative statement to sit apart from everyone else. I scan and see that Grant is missing, but my mother is holding court at one end of the table, surrounded by her soon-to-be stepsons. She looks at me and smiles, but her eyes are worried. I wish she'd saved me a seat next to her, but she hasn't. I scan the rest of the table, noticing a space next to Elliot. He must have left the gym just after me to make it here before me. I limp slowly down to take my place, watched by way too many interested eyes. It's only then that I notice that no one is eating.

Each place setting is presented beautifully with delicate white plates, sparkling cutlery, and crisp napkins. It's at that point that I realize they are waiting for everyone to be present.

I feel like a kid at Hogwarts, waiting for Dumbledore to announce that dinner is served.

"Ready for a McGregor breakfast?" Elliot teases.

"I have no idea what that means," I whisper back, and the man sitting across from me laughs.

I look up and search my memory for who it might be. One of the two I haven't met yet.

Ford. He's unmistakable with his rugged good looks and huge, bulky frame.

"It means, little lady, that you'd better be ready to eat!" His smile is broad, and the way he's sitting with his arms crossed makes his forearms bulge in a crazy way. Either this guy likes a sunbed, or he's seriously outdoorsy. Tans like that are earned.

"Her stomach's been rumbling for at least an hour," Elliot says, and I find myself punching him on the arm. Where the hell does he get off trying to humiliate me all the time?

"Well, I like a woman who likes to eat," Ford says, and there is a collective snigger from all the brothers at the table.

"That's enough of that," Roderick chimes in.

I catch sight of Grant, who I think is the last to arrive. He does what I did and scans the room, obviously looking for an empty chair and finding me in the process. For a moment, he looks like a rabbit caught in headlights. His eyes widen slightly. It's as though he forgot that I'm now part of the family.

Then he smiles, and my heart speeds. This man was inside me less than six hours ago. I shift in my seat, feeling the tenderness there. There's a cautiousness in the way he approaches, and his brothers all seem to be watching with interest. I guess that Elliot isn't the only one who knows where I was yesterday. I wonder if Grant will choose to sit in one of the other free spots rather than on the chair directly next to me. Maybe he won't want his brothers to catch him looking too enthusiastic.

When he tugs out the chair by my side, I realize that he must not care.

"Laura," he says in greeting as he takes his seat, then squeezes my thigh under the table where prying eyes can't see. I'm as rigid as a post. This is the most hashtag awkward I have ever been in my whole damn life.

Roderick's voice sounds off from the far end of the table where he is sitting with my mom. "We weren't expecting you, Grant."

I'm shocked at the abruptness of his tone, but it doesn't seem to faze Grant at all. "I thought I should show my face at the first breakfast."

"Hope it doesn't end up like the last supper," I mumble and Elliot, Grant, and Ford, who are all close enough to hear, burst out laughing.

"Something amusing," Roderick sneers. "Would you like to share with the rest of us?"

I shake my head and stare down at my plate.

"Well, as Grant has alluded, this is a special morning in the McGregor household. Nora and Laura have now moved in, and our numbers have increased."

There's a murmur of what sounds like appreciation, and I blush.

"Now you all know that I'm expecting you to make them very welcome…"

"Grant's been taking that responsibility very seriously," Ford says, followed by a whole load of snickering from the rest of the table. I mean, seriously, these guys are men, but they are as bad as teens.

My mom places her hand on Roderick's arm in the universal gesture of 'restrain yourself', as though she can tell he's about to lose his shit. I'm glad she's trying to keep everything on an even keel because I can feel the tension brewing.

Grabbing a jug of coffee, I pour myself some as a distraction. I don't even search for the cream because doing so would mean looking around and risking catching eyes with the sea of men I find around me.

"I hope you will all take the responsibility seriously," Roderick eventually says.

"I'm up for that," Antony says.

"Me too," Elliot follows. There are more agreeable murmurs, and I swear my face is so hot it might melt. So much for the shower. My armpits are almost dripping with sweat.

"Thank you, everyone," my mom says. "We are both very happy to be here, and we hope that the transition from an eleven-person all-male family to a thirteen-person mixed family won't be too challenging for anyone."

"As long as no one moans about the toilet seat, we should be fine," Ford laughs.

There are groans all around. "Dude, you still doing that shit?" Grant says disapprovingly. "Don't you know that a flush with the lid up spreads piss and shit all over the place?"

I scrunch my face at the thought.

"Are you boys seriously engaging in toilet talk at the breakfast table," Roderick says, looking disgusted. "I thought I knocked that out of you years ago."

"It was Ford," a voice says. I look across and see Antony's twin, Aaron, who's sitting directly next to his father. There's nothing worse than a tattle-tail, especially a grown man one. I narrow my eyes at him, and he catches me, responding with a smug expression as he crosses his arms defiantly.

Seriously, is he really that guy. I may have had reservations about this plan without really knowing any of the brothers, but Aaron is the first one I've met who I actually don't like. Guess there are only nine contenders, I think and laugh to myself and the ridiculousness of my train of thought.

"Glad to see you're amused," another voice says. I look up, and I'm not sure who it is. Blake or Barret.

"He's Blake," Barret says.

"Maybe you could all wear name badges for a bit," I say, and there is another rumble of laughter.

"Well, this is all very nice," Roderick says, not really sounding like he means it at all.

Then he picks up a little bell that's resting next to his coffee cup and rings it. I feel as though I've entered another century.

Almost immediately, the door to the kitchen opens, and four wait staff enter, carrying silver trays of food. The smell is amazing. As they rest them on the table in front of us, I am blown away. Eggs, deliciously crispy bacon, and hash browns. Waffles, pancakes, and French toast. Fresh berries, yogurt, and granola. Toast piled high with real butter and various expensive-looking preserves. Is this how they eat every day?

I'm going to be the size of a house if I'm constantly presented with this much choice. I don't even know where to start.

"This is a weekend tradition," Elliot says as he reaches for the eggs. "We don't all have to sit together for meals during the week."

"If Dad has his way, we would." I don't miss the edge of resentment in Grant's voice. I'm starting to understand a bit clearer why he's chosen to live so separately from his family.

"I'm glad," I say. "I think my body will be craving a protein shake by the end of all this."

"Plenty of protein here," Ford says, forking a huge bunch of crispy bacon.

"Plenty of fat, too," Elliot says. He's more cautiously heaping scrambled eggs onto his plate, along with some seeded toast.

"Nothing wrong with curves on a woman," Ford says, grinning at me like a Cheshire cat.

I roll my eyes and focus on sorting out a not-too-large plate. There is loud chatter and plenty of clinking of cutlery against plates. It's an odd feeling to be part of this. In a way, it shines a spotlight on my life with mom and the solitariness of it. For a second, I get an ache in my heart, thinking about how things will never be the same. I'll never be her sole focus again, and I know I'm going to miss that mother-daughter time a lot. Now I'm a single fish in a very big pond filled with larger and more boisterous fish. I'm going to be lucky if I get noticed at all.

As everyone begins eating, there is a clink of a knife on a glass and the rooms chatter slows so that Roderick can speak.

He stands, looming large over the rest of us who are seated at the table, his grey hair and piercing blue eyes making him look severe. "My boys all know that I'm not a person to mince his words. I did not build McGregor Corps by compromising. I had a plan, and I followed it. I knocked any obstacles out of my way, and I paved the path to your prosperous futures by carrying out exactly what I knew would be in all of our best interests."

He pauses, gazing over his offspring much like I imagine a shepherd would survey his sheep. There is ownership in that expression, and it makes me feel seriously damn uncomfortable.

"I know that Laura is aware of the next stage of the

plan and that this has happened in a rather unfortunate way." He's looking at me, and I feel as though I might be sick. What is he trying to do? Humiliate me? This is mortifying. My mom looks over at me worriedly. I can tell she's uncomfortable about what's happening. The boys all seem to be either looking at the table or looking at their father.

Grant's hand finds mine under the table, and he squeezes it gently.

"Don't do this," Grant says to his father. "It's not the time or the place."

"Don't tell me what to do, Grant," Roderick says menacingly. "Now Laura knows, there is no point in you all trying to win her over privately and individually. Laura, I offer you my ten sons, and I hope you will consider them and consider what this offer will mean for your future."

Elliot's hand finds my knee under the table, but even with his and Grant's reassurance, I still feel completely out of my depth.

"Laura?" Roderick says, as though he's waiting for me to stand and deliver a grateful acceptance speech. I get a flash of me dressed in a red-carpet gown, holding a golden award. Ugh. I wonder if he has ever experienced anyone telling him no. Probably not.

"This isn't the way to go about this," Elliot tells his father. "You're scaring the poor girl half to death."

"She has already accepted your brother," Roderick says. "Why should I assume that she will not accept the rest of you?"

"Because it's weird," Grant says. "Because Laura hasn't grown up in this freak show of a family and has realistic expectations for her future which don't include marrying more than one man."

"Ah, so that's what this is," Roderick says. "You've claimed her, and you want to keep her for yourself. Is that it?"

"I have not claimed her. She isn't a prize or a trophy, and we are not in some third-world country where women are treated this way."

Roderick goes to reply, but instead, it's Aaron who speaks.

"Grant, you know why Dad wants it this way. One woman to keep us all together. If we all go and get married ourselves, we'll have ten women to deal with. Ten small parts of the business. Ten reasons to fall out and everything will be weaker as a result."

"And you think we're not going to fall out now? Look at us. This is a recipe for disaster."

"You're just slow to realize that this is for the best," Aaron says. "You're always the one who wants to be separate. Maybe you should just do what you always wanted to and leave. Get that vet job you're always going on about with the filthy animals and leave the rest of us to get on with it."

"Oh, you'd love that, wouldn't you?" Grant says, shaking his head. "Look at you. On the one hand, you're willing to go to these ridiculous lengths to keep the business together, and on the other hand, you're the first to try and split up this family."

"Is any of this necessary right now?" Elliot says. "To be frank, I feel like we are all displaying some very poor manners when it comes to our new guests."

There is what feels like a ripple of silence, then Antony speaks.

"Laura, I promise it isn't always like this. Just know that we are all really happy you're here, and whether you're willing to consider this proposition or not, we'll always be family."

"Well said," Donnie agrees. He smiles at me, dimples out in full force, but I don't really know how to react.

"I think we need to let Laura be," another voice says. It's Casey, I think.

"Give her a chance to settle in," Barrett says.

"Yeah, let's all leave Grant to be her welcoming committee," Aaron says. I don't miss the sarcasm, which feels a lot like malice in his voice.

Roderick's face is almost as red as a tomato at this point. "You will take this seriously," he booms. "You will all take this seriously." His eyes are on Grant, fierce and unyielding, but Grant doesn't look away. This time, it's me squeezing his hand for reassurance.

"We're not living in India, you know. Arranged marriages are outdated," Grant says.

"I would say, son, that it seems like you are appreciating the arrangement more than anyone else at this point in time."

Grant goes to stand, but I press down on his leg. I need him in the room as my strongest ally. There is no way I'm going to let him storm off. "What I do in the privacy of my own room is my business. Laura is not a broodmare. She's an intelligent young woman who can make her own choices."

"I've heard that she might be willing to choose Elliot, too," Aaron says with a smirk.

I look at Elliot with a frown, but he keeps looking at the plate in front of him. For fuck sake. We had a conversation about an hour ago, and it's already common knowledge. That is not how I operate or what I would expect of anyone else. I snatch my hand away from him beneath the table. There's no way I'd consider such a snitch.

"Laura is free to do whatever she wants," Grant says. His throat sounds tight, and I feel terrible that he might be hurt by what he's heard.

"So you say," Roderick says.

I look at my food which has gone cold while all this has been going on. What looked so appetizing is now rubbery and stale. I take the napkin from my knee, take two blueberry muffins from the platter in front of me and wrap them carefully, then I stand.

"The first breakfast wasn't exactly what I hoped it might be," I say softly. I'm cold inside with a calm fury that I almost don't recognize. "I'll be leaving today. All of this has made it impossible for me to stay." And with that, I push my chair back and stride out of the room.

"Laura," I hear my mom gasping. Another chair scrapes, and I hear footsteps behind me, but I don't turn. I break into a hobbling jog, suffering the pain from my thigh because I don't want to speak to anyone right now. I just need to get back to my room and start packing. I'll call Danna. She'll be able to put me up for a couple of nights while I sort myself out something more permanent.

I'm almost in my room when a strong hand grabs my elbow.

Chapter 10

"Calm down, little lady," Ford says as I spin around and try to pull out of his grasp.

"You need to leave me alone," I hiss. "You all need to leave me alone."

He puts his hands up defensively. "You don't need to bark at me, sweetheart. I'm just here to make a suggestion that might be helpful."

Helpful? Sure. I'm sure being a girl scout is the first thing on Ford's mind. All his suggestive comments at breakfast are still at the forefront of my mind.

"Oh yeah. And what is that?"

"I have this cabin about two hours from here. I was planning on heading up there now to spend the weekend, do some hiking, fishing, you know. . .chill."

"And?"

"Why don't you come? It would get you away from all this, and maybe it would give you some time to work out how you feel about it all."

Ah. . .my feelings are what Ford is worried about. Of course.

"Give you a chance to try and get into my pants, you mean," I snap, and he roars with laughter.

"I'm sure what's in your pants is very nice, but I

only like to fuck girls who are really into me, and I don't usually have to try very hard."

Wow. This guy has a huge head to match his huge biceps. Arrogance is not an attractive quality in a man.

"I think I'll pass," I say. "I'm going to stay with my friend."

Ford cocks his head to one side and looks me up and down. "Well, you could do that, but I'm sure that's the first place Roderick will send a search party to. He'd never suspect you came with me after your little tantrum back there."

"It was not a tantrum...it was...ahhh," I hiss in frustration. "I am perfectly justified in being pissed off here. Can't you see that?"

"I can, Laura. It's why I'm here." Ford holds up his big hands, his face now more serious than I've seen it. "Let me help you, okay. A couple of days away, and you can work out what you want to do next."

I look him over, mind scanning over my options. Maybe he's right. Maybe going to Danna's wouldn't be the best idea. Mom will call her for sure, and I don't want to put her in an awkward position. I'm going to need her for sure when the weekend's over.

But I'm reticent to go anywhere with this flirty, cocky man. I can already tell deep in my bones that Ford is trouble with a capital T, and I don't need any more o that in my life right now. The problem is that I'm already neck-deep in trouble right here. Maybe I'm just going to have to accept Ford's level of hazard to escape from this mansions-worth.

"You have to promise me that you're just gonna leave me be," I say.

He raises his eyebrows. "What kind of man do you think I am?" He shakes his head. "I can promise that okay. I go there to get away from it all. I'm happy with my solitude. You can be happy with yours, but we need to hurry before the cavalry start coming to drag you back into discussions."

I know this is crazy, but staying in this pink vomit room with Roderick breathing down my neck and Mom worrying all over me is definitely not an option, and I don't really feel like I can be honest with Danna about any of this. Not after I've been here for a day. I guess Ford's cabin is my only option. I mentally promise to keep him at arms-length for the entire trip.

"Okay. I'll be ready in five."

I open the door to my room and start the process of gathering just enough for a rural weekend. Sturdy boots, jeans and a couple of shirts, slouchy stuff to wear in bed, a jacket, and toiletries all packed into my knapsack. I grab my purse and cellphone charger and my laptop, too. We may be trying to escape, but that doesn't mean I want to be completely cut off from the world.

When I'm done, Ford is at the door with his own bag, looking even more rough and ready than he did minutes before.

"Gimme that," he says, tugging my bag from me.

"Wow, a gentleman," I joke, and he scowls.

"Not really," he says. "But I know how to look after a woman."

I don't miss the level of suggestion within that statement. I'm starting to wonder if there is something in the air in this place. It's not normal to feel so much electricity for so many men at the same time. For the past few months, I've struggled to feel any electricity for anyone.

"My truck's outside," he says as we start to descend the stairs. I hobble as fast as I can because I'm so desperate to avoid bumping into the rest of the McGregors. I'll lump my mom into that group, too. She might have tried to stick up for me, but in the end, it's all lip service. I know where she stands on this, and it's not really in my corner. Roderick is too important to her and too influential. Maybe dogmatic might be a better descriptor.

We're just about to close the front door when there's a shout from behind us.

Elliot

"Hey," he calls. "Where are you going?"

"I'm taking her to the cabin," Ford says.

"You're leaving?" he asks me. I nod tersely, not trusting myself to speak to him after he let me down so much.

"But you're coming back?"

Ford nods, and I'm grateful he's taking over. "I'll bring her back tomorrow night. Hopefully, things will have calmed down a bit by then. I think Laura needs some time away from all of this crazy."

Elliot nods his eyes on me intently. "I'm sorry," he says. "I shouldn't have said anything."

"You broke my trust," I tell him. "You knew that it wasn't the right thing to do, but you told him anyway."

He nods again. "It's always been that way around here. Secrets aren't acceptable in this family, but I get why you're upset, and I'm sorry."

As much as I want to stay angry with him, I understand where he's coming from. I've been at this house for less than twenty-four hours, but I'm pretty clear that it's not a typical family. Roderick is like a puppet master, and the boys have never known any difference. "I'll be back tomorrow," I say, and he smiles a small smile. "Don't tell Roderick or Mom, okay?"

Elliot looks reluctant but nods when I frown. He's already betrayed my trust once. He better know that doing it again won't be tolerated.

"See you later, bro," Ford booms and starts striding down the stairs towards the biggest vehicle I've ever seen. I guess a big muscular man like Ford would look ridiculous in anything smaller. He opens the rear door and tosses our luggage in with no consideration. I make my way around to the passenger door and struggle to get inside because it's so tall. Once I'm settled, and Ford has belted himself in, he starts the noisy engine, and we're off.

The radio station is set to play country, which fits Ford down to the ground. It's not something I'd choose to listen to, but I still find myself humming along a little.

"So..." Ford says.

"Yeah?"

"Grant, eh? He'd be the last of us that I would have bet on being your first."

I snort. "He wasn't my first, Ford."

Ford chuckles. "Okay, woman-of-the-world. I wasn't suggesting Grant popped your cherry, although the thought is making me as horny as fuck."

Shaking my head, I study his strong profile. The windows are down, and his dark-blond hair is getting ruffled by the wind. He's wearing aviators but is still frowning into the sunshine. In his tight green tee, he looks like he should be in the marines. "You need to keep your horny to yourself, Ford."

He grins, and his dimples come out in full force. "Don't worry, lady. My dick is tucked safely away, at least until you beg me for it. Then I'll happily give it to you good."

My traitorous body is aroused immediately. What is it about a confident man and some dirty talk that sets me melting between my legs?

"That's not going to happen, Ford. I've already made enough of a mess of things that I'm thinking I'm going to need to get my own place. Adding more drama to pie is not a good idea."

"My dick has never been referred to as 'drama' before," he laughs. "Huge, maybe. Massive, sometimes. One of my ex-girlfriends used to call him Monster, but in an affectionate way."

"Bragging, much?" I laugh, but my eyes find their

way to his crotch area, and I can see what he's talking about. Damn.

I need to get my mind out of the gutter, so I do a one-eighty and start asking Ford about where we're going. Ford describes the cabin he bought as an escape from the family mansion. It sounds idyllic, buried in the woods with only the basic comforts. I'm hoping they include a hot shower and a soft, warm bed, or me and Ford will definitely not be friends by the end of the weekend.

"There's a lake nearby. You like fishing?" he asks me.

"Never been," I say. "Only child with a flaky father."

Ford raises his eyebrows. "It's a father's duty to teach his kids survival skills. People these days struggle to boil an egg without a YouTube tutorial."

"You going to teach me to fish?"

"Only if you call me Daddy," Ford grins.

I punch him on the shoulder. "Oh my god, Ford. Don't you ever stop?"

He takes his eyes off the road and grins at me, flashing a perfect set of pearly white teeth. "I can go on and on and on, baby," he says.

I bet he can, too.

"What else is there to do at the cabin?" I ask.

"Well, there's a hot tub," he says.

"A hot tub." I'm starting to think that this cabin is less about time away from it all in the outdoors and more a place for Ford to seduce a stream of women. "Since when is a hot tub a basic comfort?"

Ford chuckles. "Okay, maybe basic was a bit of an overstatement."

"How many women have you gotten in that hot tub, Ford?" I ask. To be honest, I'm not sure if I want to know.

"Unlike my brother, I'm pretty good at keeping things to myself," he says, but I don't miss the smug grin on his face.

"I didn't bring a suit," I say.

"I never wear one," he says. "It's better that way."

I shake my head. "Well, when you're planning on going skinny dipping, just let me know so that I can give you some privacy."

"Not going to happen, baby girl," he laughs. "I'm used to being free up here, and that means not worrying about clothes very much."

"Ford, I think you need to take me home."

"Worried you won't be able to keep your hands off me," he laughs.

"I'm more worried I might end up tripping over Monster," I say and jump half out of my seat when Ford roars with laughter.

"You know something, Laura," he says. "When Roders suggested this shared-woman thing, I was very dubious. I mean, it's pretty damn hard to find a decent woman out there, and what kind of woman would ever buy into settling down with ten men. But I'm kinda hoping that you're going to give it some very serious thought because I think you might just be the perfect girl for me."

I blush so hard at this rough compliment because I know it's from the heart. I don't think that Ford has it in him to construct sweet talk for seduction. Everything he says seems to be exactly what he's thinking with no sugar-coating, and I like him for that. "You hardly know me," I say.

"But I know me pretty damn well," he says. "You know what's on my list of requirements?"

I shake my head. "You have a list of requirements?"

"Pretty smile," he grins. "Check. Nice tits," he glances at my chest. "Double check."

"Ford," I say in a warning tone.

"Let me finish. Sassy mouth. Definite check. And a sense of humor."

"You're pretty easy to please if you only have four things."

"On the contrary. Smiles and tits are easy to come by, but sass and humor don't seem to have been on the top of God's ingredients list when it comes to most women."

"And that didn't sound one bit chauvinistic," I scowl.

"On the contrary, darling. I'm pretty damn certain that women are the finer sex."

"It doesn't always have to be a competition. Sometimes it'd be nice to find a man who was just happy to be an equal."

Ford nods, and he's quiet for a while. I gaze out of the window, watching civilization disappear, and nature take its place.

It's been such a long time since I had a few days away from it all. My injury and then college have been swamping me, and even though it's taken a weird set of circumstances to get me here, I'm grateful for this chance to decompress. I close my eyes for a while, concentrating on my breathing and the dulcet tones of the country singers on the radio. I'm don't intend to fall asleep, but I'm dog tired after my night with Grant, and I slip into an easy slumber. The next thing I know, I'm woken by Ford's huge hand on my arm.

"Time to wake up, sleeping beauty," he says. "Your castle awaits."

Chapter 11

It's not a castle. If we are going to talk fairytales, I'd say it's more like the woodcutter's cottage from Little Red Riding Hood. I can see Ford as a woodcutter, too. He has the biceps for it and the strong shoulders and back required to swing an ax.

For all my protestations about keeping this trip neutral, I think I'd like to see that!

The cabin is really nestled into the woods. It looks as though it grew with the trees. Thick timbers that still appear connected to the trees they were sawn from make up the walls and steps leading up to the gorgeous, covered porch. Ford has parked his truck on a paved track and is looking at me expectantly.

"It's so pretty," I say.

"Pretty?" He scoffs. "It's not pretty. It's a manly, rustic cabin."

I put my hand over my mouth to stifle my giggle. "Am I damaging your macho image, Ford?"

"That'd take a lot to do," he says. "Come on. I'll show you around."

He jumps out of the truck and grabs our bags while I make my way around to meet him. The damp smell of the forest is so strong, and I inhale deeply, relishing the freshness of the natural scent. There is a coolness too that comes with the shade of the branches. I'm eager to see the lake that Ford has talked about. I imagine rolling up my jeans and trailing my feet in the water.

The cabin steps are rough and uneven in a perfect way. I love the fact that it's all so unmanicured.

Ford unlocks the front door and throws it open, ushering me to go in first. When I do, I'm stunned.

Inside it is stunning. Like, Hello Magazine, 'I've had my ranch designed by a top designer' style. The whole place is paneled in gorgeous, lacquered wood. A large stone fireplace dominates the room. There are huge comfortable-looking sofas in soft cord-style material that I just want to flop onto. As he gives me the tour, Ford shows me the kitchen, which completely fits with the rustic theme. Copper pans hang from the ceiling, and I wonder if anyone uses them. I can imagine Ford grilling meat outside, not rustling up gourmet food in designer cook wear.

The whole place smells amazing, of something woodsy and alpine.

"This is stunning, Ford."

"I know," he grins. "When I saw it, I knew I had to have it. If I could live up here, I would for sure."

"I can see that. The locals would call you Mountain Man or something equally mysterious."

"I like that," he says. "So, shall I show you to your room?"

"Okay."

I follow Ford through to the back of the cabin. We

pass a large, closed-door, and Ford drops his bag outside. I'm assuming that's where he'll be sleeping. Then he leads me to a door a little further down.

Inside is a ridiculously large wooden bed complete with a plaid-style comforter and way too many pillows for any one person's needs. There's a carved wooden wardrobe in the corner and a matching chest, too. The window is wide, and the view out into the forest is so stunning it almost takes my breath away.

"Wow, Ford."

"Sure you're not going to get lonely in this big bed?" he asks with a suggestive wink.

I roll my eyes, and he chuckles. "I think I'll be fine."

"You sure? There are bears in these here woods. They'd love a little Goldilocks like you."

I shake my head. "What's with all the fairytale references? You a closet Hans Christian Anderson fan?"

His face falls a little, but he nods. "I had a book when I was a kid."

"Me too," I say, wondering why he suddenly looks so sad but not feeling as though I can ask. Funny how almost strangers can sex talk but not deal with emotions and sadness. Humans are just way too complicated for me to understand sometimes.

"Wanna freshen up for a bit, and we can head out?"

I nod. "Sure."

He leaves me for a while, and I look around the room, quickly unpacking my bag. There's no bathroom attached to the room, so I peek my head out of the door and look left and right. There's another door a little further down, so I wander in that direction. I'm in the right place, but again, I am blown away at how gorgeous it is—there's a walk-in shower with rainfall head and a bath that is big enough for two. Thick, clean towels rest in the shelving units, begging to be used. Does Ford have housekeeping up here, too? I lock the door and use the facilities, taking time to splash my cheeks with water and brush my fingers through my hair.

When I'm done, I head back towards the living area of the house and find Ford chilling at the counter.

"I'm ready to experience the great outdoors," I tell him, and he grins.

"I'm gonna give you your own rod, Laura. I expect all my guests to catch their own supper!"

"Are you serious? I don't think I can deal with killing something to eat it." Ford rolls his eyes. "I know that might sound stupid to you, Mr. Outdoors, but I've never done it before."

"Don't fuss, girl," he laughs. "I'm not expecting you to beat it over the head. And I'll do the gutting and filleting."

I scowl but reluctantly agree. "As long as I don't have to get any blood on my hands."

We head out the back door to a small outhouse where Ford gathers the rods and other items we need. This may be a rustic retreat, but I get the impression that everything in this shed is top quality. We even have folding chairs for extra comfort. Ford carries everything, leaving me hands-free.

The walk to the lake is short and pretty. I stop to snap a few photos, noticing that my phone has no service up here. For a second, I get a flash of panic. I'm not good at being cut off from the rest of the world. What if there's an emergency back home? Then I find myself feeling relieved. This really will be some time away from it all. No worried phone calls from Mom. No interruptions from the rest of the McGregor brothers. No inquiring messages from my friends. They must be desperate to hear how my first day has gone at Mansion-McGregor, but what the hell can I tell them at this point?

The woods are so tranquil; only the sound of birds and the rustle of the leaves underfoot disturb the silence. Ford seems to have entered his 'wildman' zone and isn't interrupting with his usual flirty banter. Maybe he's run out of innuendo. I follow behind him, watching the ripple of the muscles in his back like a stalker. I can practically feel the solid muscle on my fingers tips just from imagining.

I need to stop imagining.

We settle down at a spot where Ford has had the most success in the past. He starts bragging about the size of his biggest catch, and I roll my eyes. I find myself doing that a lot with Ford but not in a horrible way. There's already a feeling of affection between us, and we've only been hanging out a few hours.

"It's not all about size, you know," I tell him.

"Errr...yes it is. Fish and dicks. It's all about size."

"Dicks again, Ford."

He shrugs. "God must have known that to preserve the future of the human race, man would need to be obsessed with sex."

"What about, woman?"

"Well, it's definitely a bonus to find a woman who's obsessed with sex, but it's a lot less frequent."

"Even with Monster?" I laugh.

"To be honest, Monster can be a bit of a mixed blessing. Some girls love it. Some girls look terrified."

I snigger, taking a seat on my chair while Ford fiddles around with the rods and bait. "You're not exactly selling it to me, you know."

He shrugs again. "I figure that it's always better to be prepared in whatever you're going to do in life."

"I told you that I'm not doing anything with you, Ford. I just slept with your brother. Wouldn't that be weird."

Ford roars with laughter. "You think that we're all considering embarking on a polyamorous relationship without having shared girls in the past. I've fucked more girls with Grant than I have with any of my other brothers."

My eyebrows practically hit my hairline. I hadn't even considered that they might be used to sharing already or that Grant might have experience of ménage type sexual relationships. He just didn't seem the type. "Isn't that weird?" I ask. "He's your brother."

"Hey, watching other people fucking is sexy as hell,

and if you wanna do that kind of thing, you have to be able to trust the other guy. I'm not up for any surprises, if you know what I mean."

I do know what he means. I've read a few romance novels where threesomes with two guys and a girl have involved the men having sex too, but I get how it might not be right for every guy.

"So what you're saying is that you're used to going where your brothers have already been. That sure makes me feel good."

"Why should it not? It's just sex, Laura. You don't need to have so many hang-ups about it. Nobody's thinking anything bad about it, and nobody would."

"Maybe not in your family, but in the outside world, things might be perceived to be a little different."

He casts out my rod, the whip of the line, hook and bait cutting through the tranquility, and hands it to me. I hold it gingerly because I have no idea what I need to do, but he seems content that I'm okay as he begins to sort out his equipment.

"I don't think you need to worry yourself about what other people think, pretty girl. Other people don't walk in your shoes. Other people won't know your pleasure or your pain."

"I didn't take you for such a philosopher," I say.

"Didn't anyone ever tell you to never judge a book by its cover?"

I smile and am just about to quip back when I feel a tug on my line. "I've... I've got something," I shout.

"Shhh," Ford says. "You don't want to scare it away."

"I don't think my voice is the thing that fish needs to be worried about," I say. "The metal hook embedded in its mouth is its biggest problem."

"Just turn to reel him in slowly," he says. "That's it. Gently."

I do as he says, feeling the resistance of the fish struggling but still managing to keep it coming towards me. Then Ford is up with his bucket. When the fish first comes into sight, I'm shocked at its size. I'm certainly not going to be able to eat it without some help. Ford handles it expertly, taking it off the hook and getting it into the bucket with confident efficiency. It doesn't matter what this man does. He always seems to be able to handle it without a fuss.

"Well, it looks as though we can go home," he laughs. "You sure you haven't done this before."

I grin, feeling pleased with myself, forgetting in the moment any worries about fishing. "Beginners luck!"

"Well, I think I need to bring you out with me every time I come," he says, slumping back into his seat, legs spread wide.

"Hopefully, I won't need to escape much after this weekend. I should get myself sorted pretty quickly."

"We all need to escape reality now and then." There's a wistfulness about Ford's tone, which catches me by surprise. He's such a quandary of overconfident cockiness and thoughtfulness. "Nothing wrong with needing to get away. We'd probably all be a whole lot healthier if this was our day-to-day reality anyway."

I agree with him in a way, but I can't imagine such

a basic life. "Wouldn't you get bored?" I ask him. As much as I'm having fun, I'm not sure I'd be cut out for a life of rural solitude.

"Nah," he says. "Not with all of this on my doorstep."

I've never been into outdoorsy guys particularly, but I like Ford's laidback character and his no-nonsense approach to life. I try and cast the line back out and get everything all tangled up. Ford laughs but helps me get it all sorted out, and then we settle in for a quiet afternoon of fishing.

The conversation is flirty and fun, and I find myself smiling a whole lot more than I've done in a long time. By the time we're ready to pack things up, we've caught ten fish of varying sizes, and Ford looks exceptionally pleased with us.

"Plenty for the freezer," he says.

The walk back to the cabin seems to take longer. The fresh air and relaxation have made me sleepy. Ford carries everything and sorts it all out while I take a seat on the comfy couch. I snuggle in and close my eyes, intending to just rest a little, but I must fall asleep because when I open my eyes, the room is filled with the low light of dusk mixed with a few candles dotted on the coffee table and hearth, and Ford is sitting at the end of the couch with my feet in his lap.

"Sleeping beauty is awake, and I didn't even need to resort to a kiss," he says.

I pull my feet away from him and struggle to sit up. "Shit, sorry. I...have I been sleeping long?"

"A couple of hours," he says.

"Ugh. And you've been sitting there for how long?"

"Long enough to hear you were murmuring my name in your sleep," he laughs.

"I did not," I say, blushing like a beet and with absolutely no certainty that my denial is the truth. How fucking embarrassing would that be?

"Errr. . .you did, little Laura. There was even some moaning involved. I would have given my right arm to slide into that dream of yours."

"Ford," I shout. "You gotta stop this."

He moves closer on the sofa, resting his huge arm over the back and leaning in. "Why, baby girl. We're both adults, and we're in this beautiful cabin, all alone. There's nothing wrong with a little flirting."

"A little flirting has a tendency to lead elsewhere," I say.

"Exactly." Ford's eyes sparkle wickedly as he smiles.

"But we can't," I say with as much resistance as I can muster. "We shouldn't."

"No one has to know, Laura. Is that what you're worried about? I'm not like my brothers. I don't feel the need to constantly report on my personal life to my father. Roderick might think he's the boss, but I'm a free spirit outside of the company." He reaches out to tuck my hair behind my ear, and I can't stop my whole body from shivering. "You see," he says. "There's something pretty damn magical going on here. Something that we'd be stupid to ignore."

"Ford..." I whisper as he moves nearer. I can smell

the clean scent of his skin and feel his warm breath against my cheek as he leans in to kiss my neck. Oh god, that feels so good. It's been less than twenty-four hours since I had sex with Grant, but I'm still horny. My mind skitters over what Ford said. No one has to know. He would keep it a secret. It'd be like scratching an itch for both of us. We could burn off this sexual tension, and tomorrow I'll go back to my original plan of moving out of Casa McGregor and leaving all of this crazy behind.

I feel like I'm in a position where I'll regret saying no as much as I will regret saying yes. Does that sound stupid? With Grant, I felt an immediate emotional connection, and I don't understand how I can feel that same strength of connection with Ford. They are just so different. His lips travel slowly up my neck to just under my ear, and I shiver again. "You smell so good," he murmurs. "Like strawberries and cream."

His hand moves to my waist, traveling slowly up to just below my breast. I'm expecting him to move in to squeeze, but he doesn't. I want his hands on me. I want him to be frantic and dominant, to use his size to make me feel small and overpowered. He could do it so easily, but he doesn't. Instead, he moves to un-button my shirt, parting the fabric so slowly I want to scream. All the time, he's looking at me as though he wants to gobble me up.

Ford is the Big Bad Wolf. He's the Beast, but the way he's acting, I could mistake him for Prince Charming.

I'm not wearing sexy underwear. It's my plain cream

cotton set, but Ford doesn't seem to mind. He traces a finger along the edge of my bra, right down into my cleavage, then up the other side. He slides his finger just underneath the seam and does the same thing again. It's slow torture as he gradually moves closer and closer to brushing my nipple.

"Are you getting wet between those pretty little legs?" he asks me, looking me right in the eyes. I can't speak. My throat is desert dry, so I nod instead.

"Good," he says hoarsely. "Good. You're going to need to be."

I remember what he said about 'Monster,' and my pussy squeezes in response. I've never really thought too much about the size of a man's cock before. My previous boyfriends had all been average, so it was fine. Grant is the biggest I've had, but if what Ford has said about his is true, I'm going to get to feel what all the fuss is about. Does size really matter? Is huge really better?

Maybe it's the thought of me getting wet that makes Ford lose a little of his composure. His thumb tugs the fabric of my bra down, and suddenly my nipple is bare and on show.

"Fuck," he says, brushing it gently. "So pink and pretty."

His lips close around it, and he sucks, gently at first and then harder, making me moan. I don't understand the physical connection between my nipple and my pussy, but it's there. A buzz of nerve endings that make me feel crazy.

His hand searches out my other breast and squeezes, and I'm lost in the sensation. My eyes are closed, legs falling open, ready for anything and everything Ford has to throw at me. I'm not expecting him to pull back and scoop me up as though I weigh nothing, though.

"Ford," I squeal as he strides towards the bedrooms. It seems Ford and Grant do have things in common.

"You want me to do you on the couch?" he asks, laughing.

"Who said anything about 'doing' anyone, and maybe you could just give me a little bit of notice."

"What do you want me to say? Laura, just sucking your nipple has my dick pretty much bursting out of my pants. If I don't pick you up and carry you to my room, I think I'm gonna go crazy."

He smiles down at me warmly as he says it, and my heart melts. So cocky, matter-of-fact, Ford is getting as frantic as I'm feeling. I love the fact that he's strong enough to carry me. The feel of his hard body against mine is just too much.

Outside his door, he has no trouble turning the handle, and he sweeps into a gorgeous, rustic-style bedroom. He lays me down on the comforter and tugs his shirt off over his head in one movement. My eyes feast on a body so amazing that I can't even process my thoughts in words. Everything about him is so bulky; thick arms, heavy pecs, abs that look like they need their own time zone. His skin is tan and smooth, and I know just how warm it will feel under my palm. I'm itching to touch him, but he's not coming closer.

Instead, he strips off his jeans and socks and comes to kneel between my legs.

"Laura, Laura," he says, bending down to nuzzle my breasts. "You look good enough to eat."

His tongue slips across my skin, leaving a wake of coolness. It's only then that I realize that he hasn't kissed me yet.

I don't know how I feel about that. Kissing is intimate. In a way, it can be more intimate than sex itself. He looks up at me, smiling. "Can I eat you, Laura girl?"

Oh god. The way he says it is so sexy, and all possible resistance washes away. "Yeah," I say softly.

He tugs at the button to my jeans, unzipping them and pulling them from my legs in a motion so fast my ass is lifted from the bed. Ford buries his face between my legs and inhales through the fabric of my panties. "Damn, you smell fucking amazing," he says.

I'm not sure how true that is. It's been hours since I had a shower but maybe that's the way he likes it. I'm sure my panties must be damp. He tugs them aside and moans when he sees my pussy. Stroking a finger over my clit, he smiles when I squirm. "Little Laura is getting desperate. Don't worry, baby. I'll give you what you need."

What I need is his tongue on my clit, and he gives me that. He gives me that good. His mouth is so warm, and I'm so swollen. He eats me like his life depends on giving me pleasure, holding my legs when I get wriggly, and reaching up to squeeze my nipple when I'm close. Each slide of his tongue pushes me higher. He takes me to the brink until I'm begging and begging...telling him not to stop...telling him I'm gonna...

Then he stops. I look down at him, and he's grinning so hard. "What..." I gasp.

"Listen, little lady, I wanna feel you come when I'm inside you. I wanna get you over the edge with my cock. You don't gotta get impatient. We got all night."

As though he wants to illustrate the point, he fists his cock through his boxers, and I forget all about how I was almost on the precipice of a delicious orgasm. Oh. My. Goodness.

When he said it was called Monster, I thought there might be some element of bravado in the name. He said his ex-girlfriend gave it that title, and I thought that maybe she was just trying to boost his ego.

But no.

Monster is right.

His hands are huge, and they struggle to accommodate its length and girth.

"You ready to see it," he says, gazing at me through heavy-lidded eyes.

I don't think I really am, but I nod anyway. I'm not going to admit that there's a thrill of fear running up my spine.

He pulls just the front of his boxers down, and I'm fucking speechless. Monster is an understatement.

Ford should be working in adult movies. He has the kind of cock that could take on the world. I swear he could club someone to death with it.

I never worried about the size of a man's cock and

the effect it could have on my insides before. I wonder about the woman who named it Monster. Was that before or after he fucked her?

"You seriously think that you're going to come near me with that thing?" I say. My eyes are stretched wide, and he grins his signature sexy, laid-back smile.

"I do, baby. I do. Trust me. I've got you slippery enough. All you've got to do now is relax."

Relax.

How the hell am I supposed to do that?

"I don't think I can," I say.

"Trust me, Laura. If you can fit a baby out of it, you can definitely take what I've got to give."

"Ugh," I say, picturing my little lady stretching in labor. "That is not a good image to plant in my head right now!"

He laughs, shifting his body so it's stretched over mine and letting the heavyweight of his cock flop onto my belly. Gazing into my eyes, he nuzzles my nose with his. "You fuss too much. Sometimes you just gotta lay back and take life as it comes."

"Take Ford as he cums, you mean!"

"That too."

I'm staring at his lips now, wanting his kiss so badly it's almost a physical pain, but I'm not going to beg him to kiss me.

Thankfully I don't have to.

The first brush of his lips is like the slip of satin over mine. I'm so hungry for him, but I let him control the pace. I want to feel him in charge, and I expect him to be demanding, but his lips are soft and teasing, and by the time I feel the slide of his tongue over mine I'm half drunk and shivering.

I'm so enthralled by his kiss that I don't notice him searching the nightstand for a condom. He manages to get it on with one hand and the finesse of a pro. Then he's shifting his hips until the wide, blunt head of his cock nudges my entrance. I tense, which is completely the wrong thing to do, and Ford must notice because he strokes my face and runs his fingers through my hair until I'm relaxing again. Then he starts to push.

The stretch is there almost immediately. I widen my legs, raising them just enough to give him a bit more room. By the time he's in an inch, I'm panting.

"That's it," he croons. "That's perfect."

"Fuck," I mumble, digging my nails into his bicep. It's not an intentional effort to make him feel some discomfort but rather my need to have something to grasp while he pushes deeper in.

Ford's raised up on his arms, hips pressing slowly forward. He's obviously used to this approach because he looks completely relaxed. I gaze between our bodies at the explicitness of his giant cock surging forward into my soft pink folds. It's something to behold. A phenomenon I never thought I'd witness outside of porn. I'll admit to having watched some huge-size clips out of general curiosity.

"You're taking it so well," he says, with a breathless edge to his voice that wasn't there before. He's almost all the way in, and it's the first sign that his restraint is testing him in any way.

"I don't think there's more room," I say.

"Trust me," he pants. I wiggle my hips, and he rests his weight on me, and suddenly there is. He's in so deep I don't feel like I can move. I'm impaled, and he has total control.

"Fuck," I grunt, panting as I absorb the sensations.

He grins down at me. "I intend to."

And he does. Oh, he does.

Every thrust is ecstasy, the stretch just adding to the amazing sensation as he grinds against my clit. My mind empties of everything, and, as I gaze up at Ford's gorgeous face, I let my body go. He's in control now, his hands grasping my breast then stroking down my side to grab hold of my ass. The press of his fingers sends me higher, his dominance perfect in the moment.

I'm fucking Ford.

Everything I made him promise would not happen.

Oh my god. If he wasn't inside me, he'd be getting a roasting. And if I wasn't starting to feel my orgasm climbing again, I'd be disappointed with myself. As it is, all I can be is fucking ecstatic. "Oh," I gasp, grabbing his arm and digging my nails into his flesh.

"You're so fucking beautiful, princess," he grunts. Then he's swooping his arm beneath me and pulling me, so I'm sitting in his lap, my legs clutched around his big body, pussy stretched to capacity by his monster cock. "Does it feel good?" he asks, and I moan, clutching at him as he grabs me by the hips and moves me up and down in a punishing rhythm. "Mmm..." I moan because it does, it does, and I'm so close that I scrunch up my eyes and pinch my nipples between my fingers, and I then I'm coming and coming and coming around his thick cock.

"That's it, Laura," Ford rumbles as I go limp in his arms and let him use my body like a rag doll. "Told you I'd make you come," he says, but his voice is sounding strained, and I can tell, for all his bravado, that he's about to come himself. He tugs me forward, burying his face in my neck and taking hold of a huge handful of my hair as his cock empties inside me. The way his body shudders is about the sexiest thing I've ever felt, and I reach around, holding him against me.

My mind is scrambled, my body wrung out and limp, but I don't want this moment to end. I want to relish the feeling of him softening inside me. I pant, trying to take in enough air to sate my depleted body. Ford is panting, too, a thin sheen of sweat covering his smooth back.

Even soft, his cock still feels like it's touching my internal organs. I'm hoping it might be easier for him to pull out than it was for him to push in.

I wish I could say that I immediately start to question my actions in the aftermath of some of the best sex I've ever had, but I don't. Moral values are out of the window. I'm a sweaty, breathless wreck, probably ruined for any man who comes after Ford, and all my inhibitions have been fucked right out of me. Ford starts to laugh breathlessly, licking my earlobe and telling me I'm perfect, and I want to tell him that he's perfect too, but I don't get the chance.

There's no time to relish this moment with Ford because there's a noise by the open door, and when we both turn to see what's made it, we find we have an audience.

Chapter 12

What the fuck are they all doing here?

I look to Ford, immediately thinking the worst. Did he plan this? Take me away to seduce me, then tell his brothers to come later so that they could join in. Was this part of Roderick's plan? A ploy to get in another McGregor into my panties?

Just as our eyes meet, he tugs the comforter up over my body and rolls himself so that his body is between me and the door.

"You need to get the fuck out of here," he says in a low, warning voice. If I hadn't just experienced the gentleness of Ford's touch, I'd be fearful of him now. He's seriously pissed off and that tells me that he definitely didn't know.

"Are you planning to keep her all to yourself?" a voice asks. If I was to guess by the tone, I'd say it was Aaron. "Don't think that will go down too well with Dad."

"Aaron, don't start with me right now."

"What are you going to do, Ford? Hit me with your cock!"

"Don't push me, Aaron. You might be my brother, but that doesn't mean I won't deal with you if I have to."

"Come on," another voice says. It's softer. Donnie, I think. "This was a bad idea."

"We'll be in the den." That's definitely Elliot. What the hell is he doing here? Doesn't he listen to anything I say?

The sound of footsteps gets gradually quieter as the McGregor brothers retreat. Ford, whose body was coiled so tightly, relaxes. He looks down at me, worried. "You okay, Laura girl?"

He strokes my cheek, and I feel the burn of tears in my throat. I shake my head, not trusting myself to speak.

"They shouldn't have come. They certainly weren't invited. I need you to believe that."

"I guess our secret isn't going to be a secret for very long. I bet Aaron's already put a call into headquarters to let your dad know that brother number two has scored a home run."

"It's not like that, baby," he says. "It wasn't like that for Grant, and it certainly isn't like that for me."

"So, what's it like for you?" I ask.

"I saw a girl who has everything I look for, and I wanted to know what it felt like to get close to her. If you like me enough for this to be more than a one-night thing, then I'd be fucking made up, but if not, there're no hard feelings. Life's too short to stress about everything all the time."

"But what about your father's plan? Are you up for that. . .sharing me with all your brothers?"

"Well..." Ford pauses for a little, resting his head

on his hand, stroking his finger over my collar bone. "I'd be lying if I said that it's something I've always wanted. We might be an unusual family, but I still grew up reading all the same books as you and seeing all the same TV shows. I know what life is supposed to be like; one man, one woman, a couple of kids, and a dog. I get the fantasy behind all the fairytales."

"But you're prepared to compromise?" I ask, cupping his cheek with my palm, wondering at this strong and sensitive man. He's so much more than I initially thought.

"I hadn't made my mind up one way or another. Everything hinges on the girl, you see. I told myself that I'd wait and see. . .reserve judgment, so to speak."

"And now it's me?"

"Now it's you. I want you all to myself. I'm a greedy fucker, but I'd be prepared to share you if that's what you want. I don't want to hurt you or my family."

"And what about you? How do you feel about all your brothers being with me like this?"

He chuckles lowly. "Half of me wants to rip their dicks off, and the other half of me wants to see you fuck them all."

I don't even know what to say to that. I can't imagine the situation in reverse. If I had nine sisters, would I be happy to watch them all take their pleasure from Ford? Fuck no. I'd want him all to myself. I'd want to know that his mind, body, and heart were all mine. I don't understand how he can be okay with me sharing anything with anyone else.

"You think that's fucked up, don't you?"

I nod. "I just. . .I keep coming back to just not getting how you can all be so cool with the idea."

He smiles ruefully. "It's a McGregor thing. From the outside, I think our family must look like some kind of weird cult."

"It does," I tell him. That's exactly what it feels like. These boys have been brainwashed.

"But that's not how it is, Laura. We just understand what it takes for a big family like ours to stay together. It's not as simple as when there are a couple of kids. To keep ten men together is going to take something a bit special. Something a bit out of the ordinary."

"And you think that's me?" I ask. I've never felt anything but ordinary.

"I think if anyone has a chance of doing it, it's you."

"But you don't know me," I say, feeling exasperated.

"I'm a pretty good judge of character," Ford tells me. "It comes from growing up with a lot of money and having to weed out the people who were motivated to be our friends because of that."

I try to imagine a teenage Ford having to deal with fake friends and girlfriends who just wanted to be part of the McGregor clan. It must have been tough.

It's funny how when you have no money, you imagine that rich people have it easy. You think that money is going to solve all your problems, but in reality, it just brings along a whole host of different issues.

He leans down to kiss me again, his warm lips a soothing balm against the raging confusion. When

Ford touches me, it's as though everything inside me goes still. "There's no rush to decide on all this, Laura. You just take your time."

"You think Roderick is going to be happy with that."

"I don't think Roderick is ever happy about much," he says. "And who gives a fuck about his timeline. This isn't something that you can rush into. You need to spend enough time with each of us to know if there is chemistry and trust there. Then you'll have to spend time with all of us to see what the dynamic is going to be like. I mean, we're all used to living with each other, but not having one girl between us. I'm not sure how it'll work."

"You mean the physical side?"

"Yeah."

In a way, I'm glad that Ford seems to be as uncertain about that part as me. It boggles my mind every time I consider it.

"And how would you like it to work?" I ask. I might as well get some idea of what might be involved.

"Well, I'm not a guy who can go ten days without sex, so I'm not really into the idea of a one-on-one schedule."

"So, what does that mean?"

"I guess I'm saying that waiting to have you all to myself won't be an option."

"And what's the alternative?" I ask.

"Well, we could all just leave it fluid, but I think that might cause issues."

"Or..."

"We could all just be together."

"Ten of you?" I gasp. "At once."

He grins, the Big Bad Wolf back again.

"You worried you won't be able to take us all."

"Hell yeah. Of course, I am. My pussy feels pretty sore now, Ford. And that was just sex with you. How the fuck would I be able to do that ten times?"

"You'd be surprised what you can get used to," he says. "Don't forget, it's our first time together. You'll adjust."

"I think I'd have to," I say.

"We'd take it slow."

"You'd have to."

He snakes his hand between my legs and strokes over my opening. "Did I really hurt you?" he asks, looking regretful.

"A little," I tell him. "But it all felt good."

"That's good," he says. "How about I draw you a nice warm bath with some healing salts, and I'll go and deal with my brothers while you relax."

That sounds amazing. The last thing I want to do right now is face the hordes, and the fact that Ford is so concerned about my wellbeing has me feeling all gooey. Whoever is out there has now seen me naked in a very compromising position. They've intruded into my privacy, and I don't think I could find it in me to be polite right now.

"Okay," I say. "That sounds good."

Ford is up and off the bed, and I take my chance to admire his gorgeous ass and the masculine v of his back and shoulders. He looks like he could be a heavy-weight boxer, all solid muscle packed over strong bones. He grabs his boxers and heads out the door. I hear the plumbing groan as the bath taps are turned on. Then he's back with a soft white robe in hand.

"Here, put this on," he says. "I'll keep the boys in the den. If you want to go straight to bed after, you can – in here or in the room I showed you. You decide. I can bring you supper. Or if you want to come and join us, then that would be cool, too."

I nod, not really sure what I feel comfortable doing yet.

When Ford has retreated, I slide the robe on and make my way to the bathroom. The water is already halfway up the side of the bath, and it's steaming perfectly. It also smells amazing; something sweet with lavender. I tentatively put my hand in and find the temperature fine so I shed the robe and get into the water, sinking low and letting my whole body relax. In the cocoon of the water, I exhale a deep breath.

I don't even know what to think of what's happened over the past forty-eight hours. I've slept with two different men, two different men who are brothers. And kissed a third.

Who am I? This Laura isn't anything like the Laura who used to live in a small apartment in a building in the less desirable part of town. It's nothing like the Laura whose heart was broken and pined for a guy who wasn't a quarter of the man that Grant or Ford have turned out to be. I feel like I've woken up from a dull and boring dream into a vivid and colorful reality. Could I explain any of this to my friends without sounding like a complete freak?

No. Absolutely not.

Am I seriously thinking about what Ford was saying? I don't know. I guess at this point, I could see myself with Grant and Ford. I like Antony, too. And Elliot was on my nice list until he opened his big mouth. I'm not sure how I feel about trusting him. As for the rest of them, I just don't know.

They're all good-looking enough for sure, but looks aren't everything. I mean, Antony and Aaron are identical twins, but I find Aaron's personality really off-putting. All that sucking up to his father makes me cringe.

I giggle nervously, thinking about a book I read recently. It was about a girl who had a one-night stand with twin brothers and then discovered they had another set of twin brothers. She'd ended up falling in love with them all. It was pure fantasy and hot as hell, but here I am with ten brothers on offer. My pussy clenches, remembering some of the sex scenes when all the brothers were involved. Some held her down while others touched her. I'd loved the fact that they were all focused on her pleasure. Would that be what it could be like for me?

I think that's what Ford is suggesting.

I'd be like a sultan with a harem.

Ten men who could satisfy me on demand.

I'd never need to use a vibrator again.

I take my time washing, churning everything that has happened over and over in my head. By the time I'm dry, and back in my robe, I'm even more confused than I was before.

But I have to make a decision. Do I hide out in my room, or do I brave it and hold my head up high?

That is the question.

Chapter 13

As I get dressed into something less revealing than a bathrobe, I decide I'm no chicken.

I'm not going to let this situation overwhelm me, and I'm certainly not going to let Aaron think he's getting one over on me.

So they saw me naked.

So what.

It's not like I'm built differently from any other girl. Between the lot of them, they've probably seen more tits than I have, and I own a pair!

I scrape my hair back and check my appearance in the mirror. My cheeks are pink from the warmth of the bath, and my eyes are bright. It's amazing what good sex can do.

As I open the door to my room, I can hear voices in the main part of the cabin. They don't sound like they're arguing, so that's good. I could see how pissed Ford was at their behavior, but I guess he must have made his point while I was bathing.

The discussion pretty much halts as I enter the room. There are five of them lounging in the den; Aaron and Antony, Donnie, Elliot, and one of the B twins. I can never tell who is Blake and who is Barrett.

There's a moment of awkward silence before Ford emerges from the kitchen carrying plates.

"There she is," he says warmly. He places the plates on the dining table and heads in my direction. "You all good?" he asks.

I nod, and he grins down at me. "Wanna help me with that fish you caught?"

"Sure," I say and follow him into the kitchen. The silence follows us for a few more seconds then the boys are chatting again.

"They're sorry," Ford says.

"Yeah?" I'm not sure I believe it.

"They were getting ahead of themselves. . .assuming you were further along in your thinking than you actually are."

"Well, I guess they need to remember that being brothers doesn't qualify you all for the same privileges."

He nods. "That's what I told them. They need to take the time to get to know you and show you what they are all about. If, and only if you like them, things can progress."

"I guess," I say. "But it feels weird."

"What do you mean?" Ford takes four trays of fish from the oven. There's a huge salad on the counter and some rice, too.

"I mean that with you and Grant, it just felt natural. It wasn't like you were auditioning. This feels way too stilted and forced."

He nods. "I get what you're saying. . .you gonna

sleep in with me tonight?" I nod, thinking about how good it'll feel to sleep wrapped up in Ford's big, strong arms. At least with him, I'll feel safe. The woods outside the cabin are deep, dark, and spooky.

"I take it the rest of them are sleeping over."

He nods, beginning to put the fish onto a large platter. "There's no driving back this late. It's too dangerous."

"Are there enough beds?" I guess he must not have shown me all the rooms. "A couple of them will need to sleep in the den," he smiles. "Unless, of course, you decide to share my bed with more than just me."

"Ford," I say with a warning voice.

He raises his hands. "You were pretty sure this morning that nothing was going to happen between us, weren't you? Now, look at us! Who's to say that you won't have the same kind of reaction to another one of my brothers out there."

"That's making a bit of a bigger leap, Ford. Group sex might be a regular for you, but I'm a one-man girl."

He puts his serving spoon down and rounds the counter, grabbing me by the hip and tugging me against him. Monster stirs against my belly. Damn. "We're not defined by our past, sugar plum. We're masters of our future. You could be a one-man girl for the rest of your life if you want to be, but that would be because you were making a decision not to do anything different. And just because you opt to try something different doesn't mean you will have to continue that way forever." He kisses me on the nose.

"You don't need to be so rigid about yourself and what you can and can't and will and won't do. You're a young, beautiful, intelligent woman, and you get to make your own choices."

I scan his face, not really believing that a man like Ford could be a real person. Surely, he must be putting this on. This gorgeous man is so physically handsome, but his internal beauty is so much more. I've always seen men as people who restrict my life. My dad was overbearing with my mom and me. My past boyfriends have always had a tinge of jealousy wrapped up in their characters. I never expected to find a man who would be promoting my right to choose how I live my life and the person I want to be.

"Where did you come from, Ford McGregor?" I ask him, reaching up to stroke his cheek.

"Pretty sure I was squeezed out of my mama's coochie," he laughs.

I swat his shoulder. "Ugh, Ford. Not a good image."

"I'd rather be talking about squeezing into your coochie." He puts his hand between my legs and cups my pussy, putting just the right amount of pressure against my clit to make me moan.

"Are we ever gonna eat?" a voice shouts from the den.

"Yeah," a chorus of voices agrees.

"Coming right up," Ford shouts back. "Will you help me grab those bowls?" He indicates the rice and salad as he grabs the trays of fish.

"Sure."

I follow Ford out of the kitchen, and we place all the food on the big table. "Come and serve yourselves, you bunch of lazy assholes!" Ford shouts.

There's a rumble of objection but they all haul their butts off the sofas and head on over to where the food is standing.

"Laura caught the big one," Ford says proudly, pointing at my prize catch.

"We saw," Antony jokes, giving me a wink. The heat that spreads on my cheeks annoys the hell out of me. Why can't I just deal with their rude humor without getting so ridiculously embarrassed?

Donnie hands me a plate. "Well done!" he says. "I didn't catch shit the last time I came up here fishing with Ford."

"That's because you were trying to sketch at the same time," Ford laughs.

"The lake is beautiful," I say. "If I was a drawer, I'd be pretty inspired to do the same."

"I'd like to sketch you," Donnie says. He stares at me, scanning my face and body as though imagining the art he would create from my silhouette. It's kind of weird and sexy at the same time.

"I think you should let the girl eat," Ford says, slapping Donnie's shoulder.

"I didn't mean right now. . .maybe later, though?" he asks hopefully.

"I'm not sure," I say. "What will I need to do?"

"Donnie specializes in nudes," Antony laughs.

"Oh." I don't do a good job of hiding the shock

from my face. Is he seriously suggesting that he wants me to model without my clothes on? That would be a whole lot awkward.

"You up for that?" Donnie asks. There's nothing suggestive about how he's approaching this, which makes me feel a little more comfortable. "You could cover up with a piece of fabric. I love painting fabric."

"I'm not sure," I say. "Not tonight anyway. I'm too sleepy."

"Leave the girl alone," Ford says. "Let's eat."

We all serve ourselves, the boys plating mountains of food. I take a seat on the couch, and Ford and Donnie join me. The rest pull out chairs and eat at the table. It's quiet while everyone fills their bellies. These boys take their eating seriously. The fish is so fresh and delicious that I'm focused on tucking in, too. I guess that an afternoon of fresh air and an exhausting bout of sex is enough to generate a healthy appetite. I had looked at the bowls, wondering if there would be heaps of leftovers, but as it turns out, there is only just enough.

"My goodness," I chuckle. "You guys are acting like this is the last meal you're going to have for the week."

"You think we keep these physiques eating small bowls of soup?" Elliot says.

He has a point, but I'm still too mad at him to reply.

When we're done, Ford pulls out a pack of cards from a drawer in the coffee table. Elliott and Antony gather the plates, and I can hear them dealing with the washing up in the kitchen, much to my surprise.

With all the staff at their home, I imagined they'd be too privileged to cope with doing their own chores. I guess Roderick has done a bit of a better job in raising them than I thought!

"Poker," Ford asks after he's shuffled the cards.

I'm secretly really good at poker—one of my dad's useless skills that he passed on to me before he left. "I guess," I say, not wanting to sound too keen. Poker is all about the bluff.

"Shall we make it interesting, Blake?" Ford asks his brother, who's making his way across the room. I hadn't noticed it before, but Blake's got a limp much like mine at the moment.

"What have you got in mind? A little wager?"

"Why not," Ford says, tugging a roll of bills from his pocket. Blake follows suit.

Donnie shakes his head. "Haven't you guys joined the cashless society yet?"

Ford scowls at his brother. "A man needs to carry cash. One day you'll be buying your extra-frothy-mocha-whippy-latte-douchebag-chino from Starbucks, and their card machines will be down, and you'll be fucked."

Blake laughs raucously, leaning back in his chair. "Fucking coffees shops," he scoffs. "When did buying a simple cup of coffee become such an issue."

"You guys are acting like Neanderthals," I tell them.

"You gonna pull out your roll of bills and join us?" Barrett asks.

"I'm a poverty-stricken student," I tell him. "I could offer up some coupons."

"How about you play with your clothes," Blake says, his eyes flashing wickedly. They're bright green and kinda mesmerizing. Combined with his swept-up dark brown hair and beard, he's a mysterious-looking guy. Mysterious looking but damn obvious when it comes to his intentions. Little does he know I've got a good chance of thrashing his ass.

I shrug, trying to appear nonchalant. "I guess I'll have to if I want to join in, won't I?"

Ford eyes me suspiciously. "You sure, princess? We're good. I wouldn't want you getting yourself in too deep."

"I'll take my chances," I say.

"Want us to play for clothes, too?" Blake asks.

"Nah. You guys can stick to the bills if you like."

"Why do I get the feeling that we're about to get hustled?" Ford laughs.

I give them a small smile, still trying to give nothing away.

"What have we missed?" Antony asks as he and Elliot rejoin us in the den.

"Poker night arrangements," Aaron says, over the top of the book he's been reading. It's something very boring looking with businessmen on the cover. I'm as studious as the rest, but I draw the line at reading boring books for pleasure. If he wanted to read, he could have done that at home.

"You got any cash?" Ford asks his brothers.

Elliot pulls out a wallet, and so does Antony.

Aaron doesn't look as though he has any intention of joining us. "I'll sub you," Ford tells Donnie and chucks him a wad. "$200 bucks should keep you going for a while."

Damn. That is a lot of money for a small family game.

"Where's Laura's cash?" Elliot asks, opening his wallet as if to give me some.

"She's playing for her clothes."

"Seriously," Antony says, running his hands through his hair. "My night just got a whole lot more interesting."

I raise my eyebrows. "Wanna deal then, Ford?"

He winks at me and deals the cards. I slide mine off the table, being careful not to show anyone. It's a good hand, but I'm not in it for the short game. I want to take these boys to the cleaners, and I'm only going to do it if I let them think I'm a novice. We play out the game, and I fold prematurely, watching the way the boys play, looking for little tells that will help me in later rounds. I take off my shirt, grateful that I put a tank on underneath. Eyes widen.

We continue this way. I'm down to my tank and jeans by the time I start to play properly, choosing to lose my socks, earrings, and watch first. I love watching their eyes widen when I win my first round. By the third, Ford is shaking his head, and Blake looks pissed. I'm $400 up and still decent. The night is going very well.

The next round is a little more complicated, and I lose to Elliot. I've used up all the easily sacrificial items already, so the only thing I have left to play with is my jeans or my tank. Either way, I'm getting a little more undressed than I planned. All eyes are on me. I contemplate pulling out of the game, but I know that Blake wouldn't let me live that down. His eyes are challenging me, waiting to see if I'm going to have the guts to continue. I'm thinking that getting down to my bra is going to give me even more of an advantage. There is no way these boys will be able to concentrate as well as they have been with my boobs on show. Add to the fact that the bra I'm wearing is sheer. This could just work in my favor.

I start to take off my top, and the conversation that had been going on between the McGregor brothers dies into silence. I fold it neatly, not meeting any of their eyes, and put it in the middle of the table. "You dealing then?" I ask as I look around. All eyes are on my boobs, and I want to laugh at how easy it is to make men forget what they are supposed to be doing.

"Errr, yeah," Ford says. His hands don't look as sure as they did when I was fully clothed, which is cute because he's already seen these babies bare, and he's still all flustered.

I get my cards, and they are amazing. Three kings, and I'm looking for a fourth. Blake is pretending to look happy, but I can see from the way his nose is a little pinched that he's going to be bluffing if he pushes forward. The round plays out. Elliot folds pretty much immediately. Ford is in, but I don't think that he has much to show for himself. Blake seems determined to go all the way, though. In the end, I'm just up against Blake. All the way, I've tried not to seem overconfident. This game is so much about the way you play it. I have everything inside me crossed because there is a whole heap of money on the table, and I don't want to be sitting here in my panties next round. Even more so because Blake really needs to be taken down a peg or two.

Ford is watching me with a sparkle in his eye. Elliot's gaze flicks between us. When I turn to Donnie, I notice that he's found a pen and a scrappy piece of paper, and he's started to sketch. His dark curls are flopping over his furrowed brow, teeth biting his lip in concentration. I guess the sight of my almost naked body has inspired him so much he's lost interest in the game. It's kind of sweet the way he's so passionate about his art. It's something I've noticed about each of the McGregor brothers that I've gotten to know. They all have something outside of their day jobs that inspire them. For Grant, it's animals, Donnie art, Ford is outdoors pursuits, and Elliot is exercise. I wonder what inspires the other brothers.

I turn my attention back to Blake, who, for a moment, has dropped his cocky façade. I'm wondering what's going to happen, but then he calls. I lay my cards out. Three kings and two tens. Blake groans. He has two pairs, and it isn't enough.

"Damn," Antony laughs when I scoop the pot.

"You're moving," Donnie complains.

I give him the side-eye. "It would have been polite to ask first, Donnie," I tell him, taking my tank and pulling it back on. I gather the cash that I've won and count it out. Across the whole game, I'm eight hundred dollars up. Not a bad result, and I think it's time for me to quit while I'm ahead. This money will come in useful when this weekend is over.

"Hey," Blake complains. "What are you doing?"

"I think it's time I went to bed," I say. "Before I take all your money."

"Or we take all your clothes," Blake replies.

I look down at myself to make a point.

"That isn't looking very likely," Ford laughs. "I think we've been sharked."

"Yeah," Blake grumbles. "Seems like Little-Miss-Innocent isn't that new to poker."

I shrug. "I may have played a few games before."

"You have a very good poker face," Elliot says.

"Not when she's fucking," Ford says.

I grab a pillow and chuck it at him. "What happens in the bedroom stays in the bedroom, Ford. Didn't your dad teach you any manners?"

"We're all friends here," Ford says, hurling the pillow back.

"Can I finish drawing you?" Donnie asks. He turns his paper, and I'm stunned at the likeness he's managed to capture in such a short amount of time. The boy has skills. "It's just a preliminary sketch. I want to take it forward in oils."

"Are you serious?"

"He sells his paintings for a lot of money, you know," Aaron says defensively, as though I'm trying to belittle his brother. He's so prickly, like a grumpy old hedgehog.

"I can believe that," I say, "but I'm not sure how I'd feel about my half-naked body hanging on someone else's wall."

"Would it help if I agreed to keep it?" he asks.

I snort. "I don't know if I like the idea of my almost naked body hanging on your wall either."

"I could give it to you," Donnie says. "It's just that when I find a muse..."

". . .he can't let it go," Antony finishes.

"Remember Casey's girlfriend," Elliot says. "What was her name?"

Ford leans back in his chair and stretches his arms above his head. "You mean Angela?"

"Yeah. That was her name. Angela. Casey caught Donnie sketching her while she was asleep by the pool."

Antony shakes his head. "That was not a pretty show."

"I thought you boys are all about the sharing," I laugh.

"Sometimes, we are," Ford grins, "but it's all about the rules of engagement."

"What do you mean?" I ask.

"Well, there has to be an understanding. You can't

just sidle up to someone's girlfriend and get with her. That's not cool."

"I wasn't trying to get with her," Donnie says. "I just wanted to paint her."

"You still should have asked," Aaron pipes up. Always the one reinforcing the rules. "You know how Casey can get."

"The C twins are into boxing," Elliot explains. I vaguely remember reading about that in a gossip column while I was doing my pre-moving in research stalking. "It's a way of channeling all their excessive aggression."

"Dad hates it," Aaron says.

"He hated it even more when Casey turned it on my face." Donnie winces at the thought.

"You had that black eye for weeks," Antony reminds him.

"It was worth it," Donnie says. "I still have the finished painting in my studio."

Ford begins to pack up the cards. "You just liked it because she had her legs open."

Donnie blushes. "She had good legs."

"Yeah she did."

"Better not go reminding Casey about this," Ford warns. "You know how he gets."

"It's been eight years," Donnie says. "He dumped her seven and a half years ago!"

"Time doesn't heal all wounds," Ford says. "Especially the ones that are driven by jealousy."

Donnie sits forward in his chair, seemingly getting

agitated. "I didn't want to fuck her. I told him that. It's about art."

"Is it about art with Laura?" Antony asks. I've noticed that he has an edge to his cheekiness, as though he enjoys poking people in their sensitive areas to see what kind of a reaction he can get. I don't think Antony is malicious as such. More he enjoys the verbal sparring game.

Donnie blushes, and I actually feel sorry for him. He's definitely the most sensitive of all the brothers I've gotten to know so far, and they all seem to enjoy making him feel uncomfortable.

"Whether he does or he doesn't is pretty irrelevant, wouldn't you say," I tell Antony sternly. "He's not asking to fuck me right now, is he? He's asking to draw me."

"So, what's the big deal?" Antony says. "If it's so innocuous, then let him do it."

The challenge is set. I have two choices, and neither is very appealing. If I say no, then Antony has won in this stupid battle, and if I say yes, I have to let Donnie sketch me in my underwear which I'm not exactly sold on either. Damned if I do and damned if I don't.

But in the end, I think I feel that Donnie needs more of an ally here than Antony does.

"Come on then," I tell him. "You can finish your sketch, but I'm not taking my top off in here again. Let's go to Ford's bedroom."

Ford gives a low whistle of approval, and I give him a withering look. "We're not in kindergarten, Ford."

He puts his hands up. "Okay, okay. I'm being an immature idiot. I get it."

"Don't do anything we wouldn't do," Antony calls after us as I lead Donnie out of the den.

"And that will put absolutely no restrictions on anything," Aaron says, laughing. I'm not sure the laugh suits him. It sounds way too jolly, but I'm pleased to see that he actually has it in him to make a joke.

This could be a huge mistake.

Chapter 14

In the bedroom, I'm uncertain about how this is going to work. "Where do you want me?" I ask.

Donnie pulls a chair from the corner. "Can you sit up on the bed? Try and get as close to the position you were sitting in when I started to sketch you."

I tug my tank over my head, avoiding looking directly at Donnie, who I can see is settling himself on the chair and resting the half-finished drawing on his knee. I take a seat, leaning back against the headboard. I'm conscious of my stomach bulging a little over my jeans, so I suck it in a little.

"Just relax," he says gently.

Our eyes meet as he pulls his pencil from behind his ear.

I sit as still as I can, listening to the scratch of his drawing and the soft sound of his breathing. In the background, there is the occasional rumble of laughter from the den. It sounds like the rest of the boys are enjoying each other's company.

As time passes, I gradually relax. It's funny how shy you can feel when you first reveal yourself to someone, but as time passes, you no longer feel exposed.

The room is a little cold, and I can feel the skin on my arms turning to goose flesh. My nipples harden, too. Donnie clears his throat, and I wonder if he's noticed.

Stupid thought. Of course, he must have noticed. In the den, he'd mostly completed my face and arm, so now I assume he's working on the detail of my torso.

I've never been the kind of person who is comfortable in silence for too long. I feel compelled to fill it in whenever I can.

"How long have you been doing this?" I ask him.

"My dad says I picked up a pencil when I was just over a year old and never wanted to let it go."

"Sounds like it's in your bones," I say.

I can't look at his reaction, which is a little frustrating. There's a long pause. "Do you believe in reincarnation?" he asks me.

"You mean that people die and can be born again as a fly or a donkey or something."

"Well, not so much the fly or the donkey bit. More that we might have been here before."

"Like a past life thing?"

"Yeah."

To be honest, I'd never thought about it, but I know that some people really feel like they can recall living before. I've read a few stories in magazines and always felt a little skeptical. "I don't know. Why?"

"I... I've always felt like art is in my veins. . .like I've lived before and this was my passion. Even from when I was at preschool, I had this instinct for it. I don't know."

"I guess, when you have a talent like you obviously do, it must be hard to try and explain where it comes from. You're searching for an otherworldly answer, but maybe you should just accept that it's all you."

"My dad told me that God tosses out special talents sometimes. I just got lucky."

"I'm not sure I can envisage God tossing anything out, Donnie. If he was responsible for your talent, then it was a gift and one that you should really treasure."

"I do," he says softly. "I just wish I could spend more time doing it."

"Why don't you?" I ask. I guess I assumed that it would be his full-time gig.

"I have to do all the marketing design for the business," he says. "I just do this in my spare time."

"But that's crazy," I say. "With your talent, you could be so successful."

Donnie doesn't reply, and I turn to look at him. His shoulders are slumped as though he's been defeated.

"Have you all had to give up your passions for your father's business?" I ask.

"The business belongs to all of us," Donnie says defensively. "Dad has worked himself to the bone to make a success for us."

"I can see that," I say. "And you guys are lucky to be in such a great position, but the business is your dad's passion. Maybe it wouldn't be such a bad thing for you guys to all have time to indulge your own passions a bit more."

"Maybe," he says. "Don't let Dad hear you talking

like that, though. Not if you're thinking about joining the family in the way that he is hoping you will."

Donnie's eyes meet mine again at this point, the color of them almost dove gray in the low light of the room. There's something so otherworldly about them that I almost get a sense of a person from another era existing within him.

"Don't you think what he wants for you all is crazy?" I ask softly. "Surely you want a woman who can be all your own."

"It's what we know," Donnie says. He leans back in his seat, his drawing temporarily forgotten. "We didn't have the traditional childhood. You know that dad paid for us. . .we were all born from surrogates."

I didn't know that, and suddenly so much of why the McGregor's are the way they are falls into place. "You didn't know your mom?" I ask.

Donnie shakes his head. "I have a photo and a letter. I know that she was an artist, too. Not a very successful one. I think that's why she was a surrogate, for the money."

"She was pretty successful," I say, and Donnie looks confused. "She created you. I'd say that was a pretty huge achievement."

He smiles gently. "Thanks."

"So this plan of your dad's is just like a continuation of what you've been brought up with?"

Donnie nods and looks wistful. "Dad has his own way. He's not constrained by society's expectations."

"And what do you think about me for the choice?"

Donnie's cheeks flush pink immediately. "I don't think Dad could have done any better," he says, looking away as though he's embarrassed. I don't know how to respond. It's seriously flattering that all these gorgeous men are so into the idea of being with me. Seriously hard for me to believe, too.

I know I'm not the perfect woman by any stretch of the imagination. My stomach is rounded, my hips and thighs are too broad. My nose is a little too wide, and my chin a little too pointed. I always look at myself with a critical eye which used to infuriate my mom. She told me that I'm beautiful exactly as I am, but moms are biased.

I know that I can be a little sharp with my tongue, too.

Surely, there are other girls out there who would be better. Sexier girls. Girls from richer families with all the airs and graces that come with a privileged upbringing.

"I'm not special," I tell him. "Not special enough for this." I feel suddenly tearful and overwhelmed. In a way, the pressure of this weighs on me. They all seem so convinced I can be this person. The glue to their future relationships, their way to fulfill their dad's request, but I know I'm not enough.

Donnie slides to the edge of his seat, close enough to reach out and touch my leg. "Don't ever say that, Laura. Don't ever put yourself down. You're an amazing person."

"I'm just Laura," I say. "I'm just ordinary. You guys,

you need someone special. Someone who can be on your arm for the pap shots. And when it all gets out, someone who people will understand exactly why you chose her."

"And why do you think that couldn't be you?"

"I don't know," I say. "Nothing extraordinary has ever happened to me. This is just a giant leap too far."

"Destiny is a funny thing," Donnie says. "But what I know is that we have the power to change our own. Look at my father. He was born into a poor family with a father who liked the bottle more than he liked his wife and kids. He was determined to be bigger and better than his start in life. He was determined to have a big family, but he never met a woman he considered settling down with. He didn't let that stand in his way. He found seven surrogates and paid for the family he wanted. He's always had a strong vision, and he's made his vision a reality."

"But this plan of Roderick's isn't my vision," I say. "My vision was to get myself a good job in a field I enjoy and find one reliable man."

"And that vision sounds good," Donnie says. "You can still get a good job in a field you enjoy. And maybe trade in your one reliable man for ten amazing brothers!"

He smiles at me and reaches out to tuck a lock of my hair behind my ear. His eyes are solemn and beautiful in a way that makes me feel completely calm and at peace. There is tranquility about Donnie. A serenity which I've never experienced in a man before. He's calming like a deep, dark pool, and spending time in his presence is like sliding into the cool water.

"When I paint," he tells me, "only half of it is about the physical appearance of a person. The rest, the important part, is about the light a person exudes. I've always thought of it as their soul."

"You paint people's souls?" I remember Antony joking about that.

"Yes. At least my perception of their soul. It probably sounds crazy, but I see colors in people, and those colors tell me what they are like."

"That's very spiritual," I say. "Very new age."

"I guess. You know we all see the world differently. The way I see that vase over there is not exactly the way you see it. It's about the way our eyes comprehend what's around us and about how that information is processed by our brains. I guess I just comprehend abstract things more visually than most people."

"That's probably what makes you such a great painter," I say.

"Maybe," he nods. "I'm glad we got to spend this bit of time together," he says. "I thought, when you left with Ford, that you were running away from the rest of us. That you were going to leave without giving us a chance."

"I just needed some space to get my head together. I didn't like the way your dad was talking. I didn't like the way that my private information was being shared around."

He nods, and I'm reassured that he understands

how I feel. "Where's your head at, Laura? What are you thinking?"

I sigh. "I don't know, Donnie. I don't. I'm more confused now than I was when I first overheard you guys talking. Then I was sure that the plan was madness. Now I've. . .well. . .you know. . .things aren't so clear."

"Because you like Grant and Ford?"

I nod. "Yeah. And I wasn't expecting it. I wasn't expecting any of this."

"I want you to give me the same chance you gave Grant and Ford," he says. "How did they get you to give them that chance?"

"I don't know, Donnie. It just kind of happened."

He's quiet for a moment, and then he does something I'm not expecting. He leans in to kiss me.

It's the softest, gentlest whisper of a kiss—a ghost across my lips.

My mind skitters. What the hell is going on?

He leans in, kissing me a little deeper. My lips move of their own accord even though my mind is whirring. This is Ford's bed. This isn't right.

All my normal patterns of thought are so contradictory to everything that is happening I just don't know how to be. This is the fourth McGregor brother I've kissed in the past forty-eight hours. I know it's wrong, but it doesn't feel it. It feels totally right. Donnie is gentle and sweet but with an edge of something demanding that has me leaning in for more. It's a strange sensation, as though my whole being is drawn to him. Magnetic. Inexplicable.

Mesmerizing.

That can be the only reason I'm letting him touch me this way.

Donnie has some kind of supernatural power, and I'm putty in his hands.

Or at least that's my excuse for acting completely out of character AGAIN!

His hands are electric, sliding up my arms, grazing the tops of my breasts, fingers moving to slide into my hair and angle my mouth so he can kiss me deeper. I moan as he grips tightly, showing a force I wouldn't expect from a man who is so in touch with his spiritual side. It just shows you shouldn't judge a book by its cover. Donnie is quick to unsnap the front fastening of my bra and faster still to cup my breasts.

"I knew your nipples would be pink," he whispers huskily.

I'm just about to reply when there's a noise in the doorway.

Ford.

We've been caught. How on earth am I going to explain this?

Chapter 15

I feel as though I've been caught cheating.

I pull back from Donnie, using my hands to cover my breasts, even though Ford himself had been sucking on them only a few hours earlier.

"I...I," I stutter, looking anywhere but at Ford.

"Laura, it's okay," Ford says.

Donnie touches my leg, but I recoil, not knowing how to react to any of this.

"Hey..." Donnie shifts back to give me the space that I obviously need.

"It's okay," Ford says again. I hear his footsteps move across the room. "You know how I feel about this, how we all feel about this. Why are you acting as though I've caught you doing something wrong?"

I look up at him, then at Donnie. They both have concerned eyes, and I don't know what to say.

"Because... it's...how can you be okay about it. This... it's all wrong."

I feel like I'm going to cry. I just can't get past my own feelings about this situation. One woman and one man is how it's supposed to be. It's how it's worked for millennia. There has to be a reason for that. Ford and Donnie can pretend they are cool with this but deep down, I just don't know how it's not killing Ford to see me with his brother right now. I'm not suggesting his heart is broken or anything. This is all too new for that. What I mean is that innate flare of jealousy inside us. That need for certain things in our lives to be just for us.

I don't believe it.

My throat burns, and I turn away, trying to find my bra amongst the covers. I need to get decent and go back to the other room where I can be alone. As I'm shuffling across the bed, someone grabs my ankle and hauls me, unceremoniously, back across the bed. I stare up at Ford, who is looking mad.

"You're not hearing me, princess," he says. "There is no problem here. Why are you being this way?"

"Because you can't mean it," I shout. "How can you mean it? How do you not feel like I'm a cheating whore for doing all of this? I feel disgusted with myself."

"Then you're just crazy," Ford says, shaking his head. "Have you seen anyone suggesting anything like that? Have I acted in a way to make you feel like that? I thought I was clear about this. This is what we want. All of us."

"Not Grant," I say. "He was pretty damn clear about that, and now look what I've done. I've let him down."

"Grant," I hear Donnie mumble from where he's standing behind Ford.

Ford rolls his eyes. "Grant is a little slow on the uptake," he says. "He's always been that way. He's got a fierce streak of independence and a whole lot of defiance. The more our dad wants him to do something, the more likely he is to resist. Aaron's told Dad that he needs to change tactics with Grant, but he doesn't listen. The thing is, honey, that you got under his skin right away, and now he's going to need to cut off his nose to spite his face to stand against this."

"I don't want to get between you," I say. "That isn't what this is supposed to be about. This is about unity for all of you."

"No one said it was going to be easy," Donnie says. "But it only has a cat's hell chance of working if you're on board, Laura. I don't like seeing you like this."

"Donnie's right. If we're moving too fast. . .if we're putting too much pressure on you, then you gotta tell us. We'll back off, okay."

His words make me want to cry even more. My emotions feel like clothes in a dryer, tumbling round and round in complete confusion. Two days ago, I was an only child coming out of a bad relationship. Now I have ten stepbrothers who want to be so much more. And for all my feelings of regret and guilt, I really like Grant and Ford and Donnie, and I don't want to push them away. I feel like I should, but my heart doesn't agree.

"I don't know...I..I..."

Ford bends down and kisses the words right out of my mouth, and despite all my protestations, I kiss him back. It just feels so right to be with this man. . .these men. I feel so safe and protected in a way that I never have with any other man before. I feel the bed shift and hands moving to caress my arms. Ford has a hand at my nape so I know it must be Donnie.

Two men touching me.

Lips caress my shoulder.

Two men kissing me.

Hands find my breasts, one from the back and one from the front. Oh god. I don't even know how to feel. My mind is scrambled, but my body knows exactly what it wants.

It wants more. It wants mouths on my nipples, fingers between my legs. It wants pleasure in a way it's never experienced before.

Maybe it's the taboo; I know what I'd have thought of a girl if I heard she slept with two men at the same time. Slut. Whore. Maybe if I was feeling kinder, I'd assume she had emotional problems.

Is that what I am? Is that what I have? Issues leftover from my daddy.

Chasing the taboo of fucking my stepbrothers.

I moan, the feeling of being surrounded by Ford and Donnie almost too much for me to cope with. We're only at the start of things, the first stages of foreplay, so how am I going to deal with the sex? Because that's where this is heading. I can't pretend that I don't want it. I want it so much that my panties are wet against my flesh. My nipples are so hard from where Ford and Donnie are gently tugging on them. Ford's tongue slides across mine, and Donnie's tongue licks up my spine, and I shiver with the sensation.

"Are you okay?" Donnie whispers in my ear. This is my chance - my opportunity to say no. We shouldn't do this. We should stop.

But only a crazy woman would do that.

I can't talk, so I nod, and that's enough for him.

His hands snake around my middle, finding the button and zipper to my pants and getting them open so fast that I don't even have time to respond.

I don't know if Ford and Donnie have done this to-gether before, but they seem to be able to respond to each other's actions fluidly. Ford helps me to lie down while Donnie pulls down my pants and panties.

Ford's mouth latches onto my nipple while Donnie gently parts my legs and settles between them. The first touch of his tongue on my clit is whisper-light, but my body responds so fiercely my hips arch off the bed. He does it again, and my hands find their way into his gorgeous, soft hair, pushing down to seek more contact.

Ford tuts at me. "Impatient, aren't you? Don't worry, princess. We're not going anywhere until you've come like you've never come before."

"Oh..." I gasp as Donnie licks harder. His tongue moves lower, lapping at my entrance, probing in a way that has me widening my legs.

Ford moves to kiss my mouth, keeping his hand on my breast and massaging it in time to his brother's licks. They are like one synchronized person, weaving magic until I'm panting against Ford's lips and writh-ing against Donnie's face. I'm so close, so fast that

I start begging. "Don't...don't stop," I gasp, and they don't. Donnie fingers find my entrance and push just inside me. I'm so slippery that there is no resistance, and as his fingers press against a bundle of nerves that feels so damn good, it's enough to tip me over the edge.

I've never been particularly noisy during sex. I've seen some porn, and I find the way the women shriek and scream to be really embarrassing. I generally keep myself under control, but not tonight. Tonight I lose all my inhibitions and cry out loudly.

The boys don't stop touching me, though. Their hands and lips go from frantic to soothing, helping me to ride my wave for longer and making me feel cherished.

Having sex with multiple partners isn't supposed to be like this, is it? I've seen gang bang porn and it's always all about the men. The woman is treated like a vessel for them to use, but it's not like that with Donnie and Ford. I'm waiting for them to strip off too so that they can take their pleasure, but they don't immediately. It takes me coming around and reaching the waistband of Ford's boxers for them to realize where I want to go next.

"You sure?" Ford asks, grabbing my wrist to slow me down.

I nod and continue, tugging them down. His cock is so hard that it's out and ready in seconds. Donnie moves to kneel between my legs, watching me stroke his brother's cock, his eyes heavy with arousal.

"That feels good," Ford says softly. He rests back on his haunches, watching my hand working him. His abs tense with every stroke and I think it might be one of the sexiest things I've ever seen.

"You got condoms, Ford," Donnie asks.

Ford nods and reaches into the nightstand drawer, pulling out two. He tosses one to his brother, who stripped himself down to nothing while I've been focused on Ford.

Damn. These McGregor boys are seriously hot and seriously hung. Donnie's cock isn't quite as long as Ford's, but it looks thicker. He rolls the condom down slowly, eyes fixed on mine. There's a dark line of hair between his navel and his cock, and I get the urge to nuzzle into it. I want to smell his arousal feel the softness of his skin against my lips, but I'm still too boneless from my orgasm to move. Ford is closer, so I tell him to move higher on the bed. I think that sucking Ford's cock might be one of my life's greatest challenges, but I'm a trier.

"You sure," he says as I go to take him in my mouth. "It's not easy."

I smile up at him, warmed by the uncertainty in his voice. For such a big, tough man, he really does have a very considerate side.

The first lick of my tongue against the head of his cock has him gasping. Maybe he doesn't get this much. Maybe Monster is too much for most girls?

I run my tongue gently around, all the time keeping eye contact with him. I can feel his legs shaking.

Donnie moves between my legs, widening to give himself space. He takes his cock and rubs the head of it over my clit and further down, dipping just inside my entrance, enough to make me moan. Ford seems to like the way that feels because he moans too.

Donnie continues the slow stroke until I can feel the wetness of my arousal leaking between the cheeks of my ass. I want to beg him – *fuck me, give me that big cock, fill me up* – but I can't because Ford's cock is keeping my mouth busy. His hand has found its way into my hair, and I love the gentle tugs he's giving, pushing himself just slightly deeper into my mouth. The taste of him is so masculine. It's making me light-headed. "That's it, baby," he says softly, just as Donnie pushes deep inside me.

"Oh," I grunt as my pussy stretches wide. There's a burn there from where Ford had fucked me sore earlier in the evening, but it's not enough for me to want him to stop. I'm so wet that he slides in easily, holding my legs apart and thrusting slowly at first, getting faster as he gets deeper.

"That feel good?" Ford asks me, taking hold of the root of his cock and running it across my lips. "Yeah," I gasp.

"Keep it up, bro," Ford says, watching his brother fuck me good. "The lady approves."

"Her aura has gone red," Donnie says breathlessly.

Ford laughs. "I forgot you had an eye into her soul."

Donnie's cock feels so good I can't concentrate on sucking Ford's cock anymore. I take hold of it in my hand and stroke him in his brother's rhythm while Ford reaches between my legs to rub my clit.

"Oh..." I gasp, getting another reminder of how much better it can be with two men. Donnie's hands are gripping my ass, but Ford can play with me too. I've never come twice in such quick succession, but I can feel it building again. It's not as fiery in its intensity but like a deep rolling wave, heading towards the shore with the power to obliterate everything in its path.

"Don't stop," I find myself gasping again.

"We got you," Donnie says, beginning to pick up his pace. His hips are like a machine, cock so big and swollen that I feel stuffed in the best possible way. Ford keeps pace, his finger stroking me with a matching tempo.

"That's it, baby," Ford says, leaning down to suck on my nipple. At least, that's what I think he's going to do but instead, he bites, and the wicked feeling tips me over the edge. Oh, I come, and I come, and I come, and Donnie's cock thickens as he reaches the precipice and empties inside me. There's sweat running between his pecs and a flush across his cheeks. His fingers dig into my flesh as though he wants to hold me close to him for as long as he can.

"Fuck," Ford murmurs. "That was sexy as hell."

Ford. My mind starts to come back to itself, and I feel the wetness of his pre-cum in my palm. He must be desperate to release, too.

Donnie starts to pull out, patting my thigh as he retreats.

"It's your turn," I tell Ford.

"You sure you can take it?" he asks.

"Yeah, if you go a bit easy," I say with an embarrassed smile. I'm just not used to the size of them or the amount of sex.

Ford rolls me onto my side and takes his position behind me. Donnie lies in front of me, stroking my face with his fingertips, kissing my lips while I listen to the sound of Ford unwrapping the condom. He's gentle when he starts to enter me, using the tip of his cock as Donnie did to gently open my pussy. It's wet, so it doesn't take much, and it feels so damn good.

Ford fucks me slowly, his hips drawing away and pushing back against my ass in a tantalizing rhythm. I want to move too, but his hand is gripping my hip so firmly I'm fixed in place.

Donnie's crazy-light-eyes find mine. "You can come again, you know," he says. "You think you can't, but you can."

"It... it's not that easy," I pant.

"Your aura has calmed, but it's not going to stay that way for long."

His fingers find my clit and press gently and slowly. His eyes stay on mine, the intimacy almost too overwhelming for me to bear. "Keep thinking about Ford's cock," he tells me. "How good it feels; how big he is."

"I..."

"He's fucking you good, isn't he? Stretching your little pussy so wide. I know you love it, don't you? Your pussy was dripping for my cock, too."

Donnie's other hand finds my nipple, and he presses it in a matching way to my clit.

"Fuck," Ford says. "You feel good, girl."

His pace is getting faster, each thrust of his hips more demanding.

"She's getting close," Donnie says.

How does he know? Can he feel my clit swelling or see it in the flush on my cheeks or is he really looking at my aura? I don't know how to feel about that. I've always thought that stuff was a load of new-age bullshit propagated by a sixty-something hippie con artist. Not exactly anything like Donnie.

Ford keeps working, the press of his fingers getting hard, the pounding of his hips even more demanding, but it's Donnie's finger that finishes me off, and the look in his eyes as he does is transfixing. I don't think I've ever had an orgasm with my eyes open. To be honest, I wasn't even sure it was a possibility, a bit like sneezing, but I can't look away from him. It's as though he's feeling my pleasure like we're connected on a higher plane.

It's strange and wonderful all at the same time and made even more wonderful, but the swell of Ford's cock inside me, a sure sign he's on his way to coming too.

"Fuck," he bellows, followed by a pained groan that would be more fitting with an injured bear. His breathing is fast and hot against my ear, and his hand moves to grasp my breast as though he needs something more to anchor him as he rides his wave.

All the while, Donnie is watching me.

And it's beautiful. All of this is beautiful.

Not sordid.

Not wrong.

Not abusive or brutal. I don't feel in any way taken advantage of or marginalized.

I feel worshipped and treasured. I feel pampered and important.

These men have shown me that sex with more than one partner doesn't have to be about taking. It can be about giving, too. Just because there is one of me and two of them doesn't make me the passive party here.

My mind is officially blown because many of my worries about the plan were based on what this would be like.

The sex.

How could it work?

I couldn't see a way for me to feel the way I wanted to about physical relationships with more than one man. I couldn't find a way to believe that there would be any intimacy, but there was.

The sex with Ford and Donnie was more intense and connective than any of my previous sexual experiences.

But where does that leave me?

I'm now three feet deep into a ten-foot hole.

Grant, Ford, and Donnie. There are seven more feet

for me to fall, and before tonight, that felt too daunting to consider.

But now I'm not so sure.

Chapter 16

I wake feeling way too hot, with a mouth that is desert-dry. It's so dark in the room I can't see in front of my face but almost immediately I realize where I am; sandwiched between two of the most gorgeous men I have ever laid my eyes on. Their breathing is soft, their arms, which are slung over my naked body heavy and warm.

Oh god, it's real. It really happened.

I feel like squealing because this isn't me. This isn't the Laura I thought I was a few days ago. This is the stuff of my private fantasies. The stuff previously reserved for the characters in the books on my kindle.

I lay as still as I can for long as I can, not wanting to disturb these sleeping men. I enjoy the feeling of safety and protection, marveling at how amazing I feel. I desperately need to pee, though, so eventually, I have to try and move out from between them. It takes a lot of careful maneuvering, but I manage to sit up and shuffle to the end of the bed. Ford's shirt is tossed on the floor, so I grab it and tug it over my head. It smells so much of him that it leaves me woozy.

There must be a serious pheromone thing going on.

I tiptoe out of the room and towards the bathroom. The house is silent, but I strain my ears in case the other boys are still up. I use the bathroom as quickly and quietly as I can and begin to tiptoe back to Ford's room. I'm just wondering how I'm going to slip back into bed between Donnie and Ford without waking them when a person steps out in front of me.

"Oh..." I clutch my heart with the shock and hear a whispered laugh in response.

"Caught wandering the halls after dark," Antony says. "That would get you detention at Hogwarts."

"Harry Potter, Antony?" I would never have taken him for a JK Rowling fan, but I suppose all these strapping, good looking men were little boys at one time.

"My favorite character is Neville," he chuckles.

I have a soft spot for Neville, too. "What are you doing wandering around in the middle of the night?" I ask him.

"Blake is snoring," he tells me. "And I'm a light sleeper. I was going to grab some blankets from the closet and try and get some sleep in Ford's truck."

"You're going outside?"

He shrugs as though it's nothing at all. "It's a big and quiet truck."

"And this is a cabin with plenty of space. There's a sofa in Ford's room. Why don't you crash there?"

"Well, I didn't really want to intrude," he says with a wink.

He has a point. Less than five minutes ago I was butt naked.

"You could have tried knocking," I say, blushing.

"And wake up Ford. You don't know that man very

well yet but let me tell you that he's not a pretty sight when his sleep's disturbed."

"Noted," I say feeling a little chastened. He's right that I don't know any of them very well yet. I scan his face for any sign that he is being judgmental, but I don't see it. Instead, my gaze is met with eyes that are sparkling with what looks like amusement.

"So, little Laura. You seem to have taken the Mc-Gregor family by storm." He leans against the wall as though he is settling in for a long conversation rather than a quick middle of the night chat.

"It wasn't my intention," I say.

"I'm sure it wasn't, but we have a way of getting under people's skin."

His comment prickles just a little but I don't want to show it. "I don't know if any of you have gotten under my skin," I say. "Between my legs maybe."

He laughs a little louder than he should, given that most of the house is sleeping. "Well, some have been luckier than others," he says.

"Is that what it is? I'll have to keep an eye out for the leprechaun," I say sharply.

"Maybe he should keep an eye out for you," Antony says. "I bet you've got no panties under that shirt and a little man would be the perfect height to get a look up there."

He makes a small subtle move forward, reducing the space between us just a little.

Part of me thinks I should just smile and get back to bed as quickly as possible. Am I seriously starting to have a flirty chat with yet another McGregor? On my prior actions this past couple of days, the answer should definitely be no.

"My lack of panties is not for discussion, Antony," I say with as much disapproval as I can muster.

He groans. "I was just guessing about that but now you've confirmed it, how am I gonna sleep knowing how close I came to your bare pussy?"

"I'm sure you'll sleep fine," I say, but the blush on my cheeks must be showing Antony that his sex-talk is getting to me.

He shakes his head, looking down at my legs. "I'd sleep even better with my face just there." He slowly moves his eyes up and holds my gaze.

"Antony," I say with a warning tone.

He puts his hand over his heart. "What is it, lovely Laura? Aren't you attracted to me? Not as valiant as Grant, or rugged as Ford? Not as arty and sensitive as Donnie?"

"You searching for compliments now?" I ask.

"That's not my style," he says. "I'm just curious about what you look for in a man."

"Integrity," I say almost immediately.

"I have integrity," he says.

"Honesty."

"Your hair is a mess," he says. "Honest enough?"

I quickly reach up to smooth what I discover is a terrible case of bedhead.

"Maybe too honest!" I laugh.

"What else?"

"Kindness," I say quickly.

"I rescued a puppy last week. It was tethered at the side of the freeway. Check to kindness?"

I nod, not able to hide my growing smile. "Good teeth," I joke.

He grins wide and his pearly whites glow in the darkness.

"Looks like you've got it all," I say.

"Sure you don't want to add some more requirements? Good body? Good job? Good family?"

From anyone else, it might sound like a horrible boasting exercise, but Antony isn't like that. The 'good family' party he says with an eye roll.

"Your family is interesting," I say.

"I've got a bunch of amazing brothers and one very difficult father. If you can put up with him, the rest are golden."

"What about Aaron?" I ask.

He shrugs. "I can see that you haven't really warmed to him. He's my twin but we're only alike in looks. Aaron is much more like my dad than any of the rest of us."

"Why do you think that is?" I ask.

Antony looks uncomfortable for a moment, as though my question has hit on a nerve. "He's the oldest. Maybe that has something to do with it," he says in an offhanded way that doesn't fit at all with his expression. What am I missing here? This family has so much strange history that it's hard to fathom why all the relationships are as complicated as they are.

"So, we should probably hit the sack," I say. "Before Ford wakes up and sends out a search party for me."

"There's about as much chance of that happening as me getting lucky tonight," Antony laughs. "Ford sleeps like the dead."

"Come on," I say, ignoring his comment. I get the feeling that Antony covers a lot with his flirtatious and cavalier façade. I walk carefully and quietly until I'm back by the door to Ford's room and Antony follows closely behind me.

It's so dark in the room but I can make out the shapes of Donnie and Ford who are both still sleeping soundly. There was just enough space for me to get back in between them.

Antony looks at the couch. "I'll get a blanket," he says and disappears. I start to hunt for my panties because there is no way I want to be flashing my lady-garden at Antony in the middle of the night. Also, I'm hoping it will help me resist any further moves from Donnie or Ford.

My mind is officially blown, and I need to spend some time away from all these men to fathom whether I've been dragged into some sort of weird amazing sex vortex!

I think it's safe to say that I don't trust myself at all.

As I've just finished pulling on my panties, Antony reappears clutching his bedcovers.

I smile at him but just as I'm about to climb back onto the bed, Ford rolls onto is back and effectively obliterates the space I was going to fill between the boys. With his arms and legs spread, there is now no room for me to get back into bed without waking them.

Ugh. Now I need the sofa.

"Fuck," I mutter.

"You know this is a pull-out," Antony says. He lifts a cushion on the sofa and pulls a lever. Suddenly a whole section of bed unfolds.

A whole section of double bed.

"I don't know..." I say. What the hell is it going to look like when Ford and Donnie wake up and find me in bed with Antony. This is getting ridiculous.

To be really honest, they probably won't think anything at all. Maybe they'll be happy. They all seem to get happier as more of them seduce me.

"It's just to sleep," Antony says. "I think you're sexy as hell but that doesn't mean I'm going to try and get your clothes off in this situation. That would just be creepy!"

Antony starts to make the bed and I watch him tuck the sheet neatly around the mattress and settle the covers into place. Again, these boys seem to know what they're doing when it comes to household chores. Not sure why I find this so sexy, but I do. When he's done, he jumps in and pats the empty side. I carefully peel up the corner of the blanket and sit on the edge of the bed gingerly.

"I promise I'm not going to bite," Antony says, putting his hands behind his head and grinning at me.

It's so weird to lie next to someone you don't know

well and who you're not being intimate with. It's like a complete invasion of personal space but, true to his word, Antony closes his eyes and keeps to his side of the bed. I curl up, facing away from him and try to relax enough to sleep. After about five minutes, Antony whispers, "One day I hope we'll be doing this differently."

I smile but I don't reply.

I guess the one thing I've learned over these past few days is that anything can happen.

I don't know how long I've been sleeping for when I come to and find myself wrapped around a man's warm body. For a moment I'm confused. Who am I in bed with?

Then I remember.

Antony.

After everything that I said to him it's me who's invaded his personal space. How fucking embarrassing. I start to try and lift my arm away, but his hand quickly grasps my wrist and holds me in place.

"I was enjoying that," he whispers with a smile in his voice. "You're very good at spooning."

"I was sleeping," I whisper back. "I didn't know what I was doing."

"Liar. I could tell you wanted to get your hands on my body all this time. You've just been in denial."

"Oh my god." I try to pull away again, but he holds me firmly in place.

"Laura, Laura, Laura. You know I could make you very happy."

I scoff. "You're pretty sure of yourself."

Antony rolls, keeping hold of my hand and putting it around his waist. We're so close, pillow to pillow and under the quilt like two lovers. Even with hardly any light, I can see how gorgeous he is. I don't even know what to do with myself. If Antony had spoken to me in a bar I would have been lost for words. In this situation, I'm a total goner.

"I can be sure of myself. Confidence isn't necessarily a bad thing, is it?"

I shake my head.

"But you know what, Laura. This isn't about me. It's about you. You need to find yourself and accept what an amazing situation this could be. Can't you see how good it would be to have all of us?"

I close my eyes because I don't want to hear it again. How can they all be so certain? I just don't get it.

Antony seems to take it as an opportunity. He presses a soft kiss to my forehead, then to my cheek, then to the corner of my mouth. I try to pull back, but he holds me firmly, moving back to my forehead.

He's so gentle that I start to soften.

It's only then that I notice that he's let go of my hand and I'm still holding on to him like I'm scared he's going to run away.

I should try to escape now. I could jump out of this bed and back into bed with Donnie and Ford, but his kisses are so soft and even with my eyes closed I can picture the laughter in his eyes and want to smile at the way he's managed to make me laugh.

They say that laughter is the best medicine and I have to agree with that. Happiness that radiates from within is a beautiful thing to see and feel and I know that is what attracts me to Antony.

It's why, when he presses his lips to mine, that I kiss him back.

I can feel the smile on his lips when I do.

I get lost in the sweet, sliding kisses and the feeling of his warm skin against mine. It's so slow and soft that I feel any residual resistance melting away, so when his hand moves from my waist to caress my breast, I don't tell him to stop, and when his fingers slide between my legs, slick with my wetness, I let my knees drop open. Like his brothers, he seems to own a map to my body. Two fingers pressing inside and his thumb on my clit is bliss. I should be pulling away. I should be telling each of these men that this is a terrible idea, but I don't. Instead, I grip onto him as he rubs and rubs and fucks me with his fingers and, like he has a key to unlocking all the mysteries of my pussy, he makes me come and come and come in waves of completely absorbing ecstasy.

While I'm still coming down from oblivion Antony gently rolls me over. His cock is hard and hot between my thighs and he presses forward until he enters me from behind. My pussy clamps down, still pulsing from my orgasm and he groans in my ear, holding my hip and angling my pelvis so that he can get deeper.

"You're so wet," he whispers. "So fucking hot and wet."

I groan, the thickness of his cock making my legs tremble. He thrusts in an even pace, hand moving to my breast to tug at my nipple. My nerve endings come alive with every touch.

I know that Donnie and Ford are just feet away and that makes this even hotter. They could wake up and find us. I'm not worried about what they would think, though. Instead, I imagine they are watching and it's like a trigger, increasing my arousal ten-fold.

Who knew that being watched was my kink? With every new experience I have with the McGregor's I seem to find out more about myself.

Antony's finger finds the hot bud of my clit and taps in the rhythm of his thrusts. I'm so desperate to come again that I arch my back, forcing him in deeper.

I think he must like that because he takes hold of my hair and pulls my head until my back is a crescent. God, I love it when men take control. The edge of roughness and the fierce pounding of his cock in my pussy sets me alight all over again.

My mouth is a soundless O, conscious of the rest of the sleeping people in the cabin.

Antony's cock swells and he pulls out sharply, his hand moving between us. I feel the shudder of his orgasm, I'm assuming his come spilling into his palm. He cleans himself on a tissue from the dresser and kisses my neck, settling behind me and gathering me into his arms.

I'm so tired and sex drunk that I don't have a chance to regret a thing. I'm asleep in seconds.

Chapter 17

When I stir, I have no idea what time it is. I'm still for a moment, listening out for any breathing but not hearing anything. I turn my head slowly, finding the bed beside me empty.

Phew.

Then I look over at Ford's bed, and that's empty, too.

Shit.

Did he and Donnie wake up and find me in bed with Antony?

I can't believe that I missed out on that conversation.

I roll onto my back and stretch my arms into the air. Parts of my body feel deliciously sore. Flashes of Ford's fingers pressing into my skin, of Antony's kisses, and Donnie's tongue between my legs makes me hot all over again.

If nothing comes of this crazy situation with my soon-to-be stepbrothers, then at least the memories will keep me going in my dark and dry days. Or maybe my days with another man who doesn't quite get me as hot as these boys do.

I've been in what I thought was a loving relationship and put up with mediocre sex because I didn't feel like I had a way of asking for what I needed without hurting his feelings. I know how easy it can be to push my wants and needs aside because the rest of the relationship was okay. I don't think I realized how important it is to have that physical connection, or at least to be with someone who is completely focused on trying hard enough with you.

Just as I'm about to get up, there's a knock on the door.

"Come in," I call, pulling the covers around my neck even though I'm pretty decently covered in Ford's man-size shirt.

It's Antony, and he's holding a steaming mug. I feel my cheeks heating, the intimacy of last night feeling awkward in the light of the morning.

"There she is. Sleeping beauty."

"Don't you start with the fairytale reference!" I say. "Your brother has that one down."

Antony looks confused.

"Is coffee good?" he asks, walking across the room to hand me the cup.

"Coffee's perfect," I say.

"Elliot, Blake, and Aaron have left already today. Apparently, there is something happening at one of the sites that needed some attention."

"Oh, okay," I say. "They didn't need you?"

"Not this time," he says with a grin. "Lucky me."

"Yeah, working on a Sunday sucks," I say, trying to keep the conversation away from any mention of sex. "So Ford and Donnie are still here?"

"Yep. Ford is out doing some clearing around the cabin. He likes getting his hands dirty."

"And what about Donnie?"

"He's meditating on the porch."

I chuckle, and so does Antony. "I know they are my brothers, but sometimes even I can't figure out how different we all are."

"Differences are good," I say.

"Sometimes, they are the source of a whole heap of frustration and confusion," he admits.

"So how come you're not rolling your sleeves up and helping Ford with the graft?"

"Because I am on breakfast duty. Ford may be able to rustle up something passable out of his river catches, but he's less successful at making things that take some finesse."

"And you have that finesse?" I ask, sipping my coffee. It is delicious, and if this drink is anything to go by, then I can believe that Antony is going to cook up something pretty spectacular.

"My mom was an amazing cook, apparently," he says softly.

"Did you meet her?"

He shakes his head but doesn't elaborate. "I'm happy to take that skill from her. Dad is useless in the kitchen, but at least he knows how to choose a good chef!"

"Yeah. That's definitely lucky."

"We would have grown up on grilled cheese sandwiches and ramen if he didn't make his fortune."

I've eaten a fair few of those in my time, especially after Dad left, but I don't say anything. I don't need to share my tales of woe with Antony. It's not that I'm embarrassed but more that I already feel on a completely different footing from them all. I really don't want to make that any worse.

"So, what are you cooking?"

He smiles and takes a bow. "For my lady, there will be buttermilk pancakes with bacon, blueberries, and maple syrup if that pleases you."

"That sounds amazing," I say. It also sounds extremely fattening, but I'm past the point of caring. I burned off so many calories last night, and my belly is growling.

"You wanna come and watch the master in action," he asks, running his fingers through his floppy dark hair. Dressed in gray sweats and a tight tee, he looks mind-blowing.

"I might have a shower first."

"I think we all prefer you dirty," he laughs.

Ugh. What is it with guys? "I'll see you in the kitchen," I say with an eye roll.

Antony chuckles and leaves, and not watching his ass as he retreats is an impossibility. Damn. Those are some serious glutes. Glutes that drove a cock that made me come hard enough to weep.

I sip my coffee a little more, then get up and head to the room where I left all my stuff. The covers are rumpled from where the others crashed in there last night, but at least my things look untouched.

I shower and drag on some leggings and a slouchy top. I go to apply some make-up but find I can't be bothered. If I'm going to be sharing a house with these men, they are going to see me in all my glory. Guess I should start as I mean to go on.

When I get to the kitchen, Antony is there whisking something in a large bowl. It must be the batter for those unbelievable-sounding buttermilk pancakes. "Just in time," he says. "Can you chop those strawberries and add them to the bowl?"

There is a bowl of blueberries and raspberries on the counter and a box of the hugest strawberries I've ever seen next to them. "Sure," I say and pad over to do as he's asked. I have to pop a berry in my mouth before I get started because it would be wrong not to, and Antony catches me, telling me not to eat everything before we get to the table. He's just so cheeky.

As I'm halfway through removing the stalks, Donnie comes in; barefooted and very relaxed looking.

"There she is," he says, strolling to where I'm standing. He strokes my hair, holding my gaze with those eyes that seem to stab my heart. "It looked like you were sleeping really well next to Antony." He smiles. "Were Ford and me moving around too much?"

I shake my head. "I got up to pee, and when I came back, there wasn't any space for me to squeeze back in."

"Damn," he says. "I was looking forward to a good morning cuddle, but it looks like Antony had all the fun."

I blush furiously, and Donnie laughs.

"He was wrapped around you like a tortilla in a burrito."

"I told him to keep his hands to himself, but he doesn't seem to take instructions," I say.

Antony laughs. "I take instructions fine."

"I warned you to keep your hands to yourself," I say. "That didn't go so well.

Donnie laughs. "Seems like you've lost your magic touch, dude."

Antony shrugs. "Some women just take a little longer than others to see perfection."

I pretend to gag. "Perfection might be an overstatement!"

"I didn't hear you complaining," Antony laughs, putting his hand over his heart as though I've wounded him.

"When you've eaten his pancakes, you're going to agree that he's perfection," Donnie smiles.

The sound of feet being wiped vigorously at the backdoor causes me to turn. Ford throws the door open, looking around the kitchen. "Well, isn't this all very cozy?"

"I don't think you need a wife when you've got Antony around," I say.

"Antony is alright in the kitchen, but there are other rooms where he's lacking certain bodily features."

"And we're related, dude," Antony laughs. "Incest is not cool."

"Ugh," Ford and Donnie say at the same time.

"Looks like you need to get yourself cleaned up," I laugh. Ford is sweaty and dusty, with bits of woodchip in his hair and a smear of dirt on his cheek. In his checked shirt, jeans, and boots, he's the very picture of a lumberjack. In fact, I'm sure I have a few novels with men on the covers who look just like him.

"You don't like me dirty," he asks, stalking across the room and grabbing me around the waist with just one of his big arms. I'm hauled up against him until we're nose to nose.

"Ford!" I swipe at him, but he's not letting me go.

"Didn't your momma tell you that dirty men are a whole lot more fun?"

I shake my head. "You know what my momma looks for in a man," I say. "She's chosen your dad."

"Fair point," Ford says, planting a hard kiss on my lips.

"Get in the shower," I tell him. "We'll have breakfast ready for you by the time you've finished."

He tugs me harder against him, the press of his very hard cock almost painful against my hip. "Did anyone ever tell you that you're pretty damn close to perfection?" I burst out laughing, and so does Donnie. Looking smugly at Antony, I say, "Looks like I'm giving you a run for your money."

Ford lets me go, looking between us, confused.

Antony puts down the bowl, which looks fluffier than I've ever seen a pancake batter. "He said 'close', Laura. Close."

I glare at him, and Donnie chucks a cloth at his brother. "Just make the damn pancakes, bro," he says.

Ford shakes his head at us and disappears towards the bathroom. Donnie takes a seat at the table, where he's left some paper and pencils. He starts sketching almost immediately, the pencil moving so fast I can barely comprehend how he's controlling it.

Antony begins to pour the batter into two pans on the stove. The sizzle is immediate, and the smell makes my mouth water. I take a seat at the table, watching Donnie sketch. I wasn't aware that he was drawing me again until I saw my profile on the page. He's captured me in a way that is disconcerting. Maybe more than a photograph would.

"Why are you drawing me again?" I ask.

"You don't like it?" Donnie looks a little crestfallen, like a kid who just had his new toy snatched away by his brother.

"I'm just asking," I tell him.

"I'm getting another angle. I like to have lots of sketches completed before I start to transfer it into a larger painting."

"Will you need me to pose for the painting, too?"

His light eyes flick up and fix on mine. "I can work from the drawings, but I prefer to have my subject present. Would you do that for me?"

I shrug. Yesterday it would have been a daunting prospect, but after last night, I feel a whole lot more comfortable in Donnie's presence. "Sure. As long as it doesn't interfere with college or cause any issues."

"What kind of issues?" he asks. His attention has drifted back to his work, but his eyes keep flicking to observe bits of my physical appearance.

"I don't know. . .with your dad."

Donnie chews the end of his pencil. "Roderick doesn't really like what I do, but as long as I keep it in my own time, he doesn't really have a say in it."

"Okay. Just let me know when."

Donnie nods and continues, but at a slower pace. I guess he's not so worried about capturing everything now he knows I'm willing to pose while he works.

Antony is bustling around the kitchen like a crazy person, flipping pancakes and assembling plates with berries and bacon. By the time he's done, Ford is back, washed and dressed in clean clothes.

We all sit down to tuck into the fantastic breakfast feast. I'm given the food first before the boys take theirs; yet another good sign that these men have been raised well. It's nice, eating and chatting away. The boys discuss the work Ford has done and future improvements he wishes to make to the cabin and surrounding land. They move on to chatting about a work project they are all engaged in, and I listen with interest. It feels natural to sit with my soon-to-be stepbrothers this way, but I remind myself, there are only three of them. I remember what it was like at the first breakfast back at the mansion. So much loud chatter. It was really overwhelming.

I enjoy the morning for what it is, fun with friends, or more accurately, friends with benefits.

In an hour or so, we're going to have to pack up our things and head back to reality, and I have no idea what the future holds.

This weekend in the woods hasn't exactly had the mind-clearing effect I hoped it was going to have. When I left the mansion, I was convinced I needed to leave for good. Now I'm not so sure.

Walking away from all this is so much harder now I'm getting to know the McGregor brothers.

Grant, Ford, Donnie, and Antony are all so amazing.

Now, I'm more confused than ever!

Chapter 18

We ride back to the mansion together, and the journey is filled with loud, tuneless singing to more of Ford's cheesy country classics. We arrive back at the mansion late in the evening, and I successfully manage to keep out of everyone's way that evening. In the morning, Donnie, who agreed to drop me off at college, makes good on his word.

It's weird to be chauffeured rather than having to get the bus, but I have to admit that it has some perks. Donnie has good taste in music, and we sing along together for most of the journey. When we're outside, he asks me if I'll model for him later.

"Sure," I say. "Providing I can complete any work that's required for tomorrow."

He nods, smiling. "I was quite a good student in my time, so let me know if there is anything I can help you with."

"See ya," I call as I exit the car.

The campus is bustling, and I get a familiar rush of happiness. It took a lot to get here, and I love the atmosphere. I'm close to the building where my first lecture is taking place when I see Danna.

"Hey," she calls, waving and weaving between the throngs of hurrying students.

I'm happy to see her, don't get me wrong, but I'm also worried about the questions I know she's going to ask me about my weekend with the McGregors. Danna has known me since I was eight years old, and she can spot bullshit a mile off. "Hey," I say.

"Don't hey me," she says. "Where the fuck have you been? I've been calling your cell all weekend, and nothing. You move into the McGregor mansion with ten of the hottest, most eligible bachelors in the Northern Hemisphere, and all I get is a hey! Hey isn't going to cut it."

I keep walking, smiling at her drama but panicking, too. "I was just really busy," I say.

She pulls her bag, which is bulging with folders, higher on her shoulder. "Busy doing what? That's the point here, Laura."

"Just family stuff," I say.

"Really. Family stuff? What the hell does that mean?"

"Just having meals and hanging out."

She grabs my arm to stop me before we reach the doorway. "Don't make me harm you," she jokes. "If I have to use torture to extract information, I will. You spent weeks gushing about these guys and what it was going to be like to share a house with them, and now you're acting too cool to tell me anything. What are they like? What happened?"

"They're really nice," I say.

"Nice. Nice is all you have."

I shrug. "What do you want me to say? They're all

just normal guys who look like sex gods? They're my stepbrothers," I say. Even as I'm avoiding telling the truth, my insides are creeping with guilt. Danna is my bestie. Besties shouldn't lie to each other. She'd be devastated if she found out I kept something of this size a secret from her. I know this because I'd feel the same way.

"They're not your stepbrothers yet," she says, punching my arm. "And why the hell should that make a difference? You're not blood-related. Just because your mom decided to bone their dad doesn't mean they're off limits to you. You should be thinking of this as an opportunity. Under other circumstances, you'd never have a chance to spend time with men like that. You've got a chance to bag yourself a very eligible bachelor."

Little does she know!

"I'm still at college," I say. "I'm not really looking to bag anyone."

"I don't mean that you need to marry one of them, but you could have some very serious fun with any of them. I mean, damn. If you're not going to, you need to invite me over so I can have a chance."

"No," I spit out before I have a chance to tame my mouth.

Danna narrows her eyes at me. "No...? Mmm...very interesting!"

"What I mean is..." I stutter, trying to think of a good reason for saying what I said. ". . .it's a bit early on for me to be bringing people back to their house.

I still don't know my way around. Maybe after a few weeks."

"I smell bullshit," she says. Ugh. This is just what I feared. "You want to keep them all for yourself."

"Don't be ridiculous."

"Mmm..." she murmurs again suspiciously.

"Look, we better get to class." I glance at my watch to emphasize the point. If we don't get moving, the lecturer is going to be pissed. I start to try and join the throng of students walking into the building, and Danna sticks by my side.

"This isn't over, Laura," she says with a mock threat. "If I have to pull your teeth out to get you to talk, I will. Didn't your mom ever tell you that sharing is caring?"

"We'd be happy to share you," a voice shouts from behind. I turn and see the most obnoxious boy in my classes laughing with his mate.

"Fuck off, Connor," I shout, which is followed by a 'wooo' sound from all the students around us.

"You know you need some cock, Laura," he shouts. "Wipe that sour look off your face."

"Yeah, well. I've heard you're pretty small in that department," Danna says, wiggling her pinky in the air like a maggot.

The 'wooos' are now peppered with laughter.

Connor's friend is laughing, and Connor's face is burning red. "Want me to show you what I got, bitch?" he says, his teeth gritted.

"No thanks," Danna responds. "I don't have my magnifying glass with me."

We're outside the lecture hall by this point, so we hurry in and take our usual seats, quickly unpacking and avoiding looking at where Connor goes to sit. As long as he isn't behind me, I'm okay.

"That guy is such a dick," Danna says.

"Yeah, he is, but you don't want to make him angry," I say. "You don't know what he's capable of."

Danna rolls her eyes. "Connor is a pussy."

"That's what people think about a lot of serial killers before they find out that they chopped up twenty women and fed them to pigs." I look around and spot Connor on the other side of the hall with his eyes narrowed in our direction. "Enemies are hard to shake, you know. Especially ones like Connor who like everybody to think they are something special."

"Fuck Connor and his small dick. Guys like that need to be taken down a peg or two, so they get to understand that they aren't anything special."

I've known Danna for long enough to understand that I just need to shut up now. There's no convincing her once she's gotten something like this into her head. I just hope she takes some of what I've said on board. The last thing I'd want to see is her getting hurt by a douchebag like Connor, and there are many ways a man can hurt a woman.

The lecturer appears, and we get through the next hour, frantically typing our notes out. I'm so glad I don't have to write much. My handwriting is atrocious when I need to go fast, and there is no point in having notes if you can't read them yourself!

As we're packing up, Danna gives me the side-eye. "You need to tell me what's going on, girl. I know there's something. You're so damned clammed up."

"It's nothing. Seriously."

"You fucked one of them, didn't you?"

I turn to her, shocked that her mind would go that far. "What?" I stutter.

"Your cheeks are turning red, Laura. You did, didn't you? Which one was it? Casey? Blake? Ford?"

"Stop it," I say quickly.

"Ford. That's it. You think you can hide this kind of thing from me but what you're forgetting is that I've been with you on this fucked up journey called life for long enough to know all of your tells. Why didn't you want to say anything? Was it bad? Did something happen?"

"No," I say quickly. The last thing I want her to think is that Ford is a bad guy. That is so far from the truth that it almost hurts to think it.

"So it was good?"

"Danna..." I pause because I just don't know what to say next.

"Yes. That's my name, don't wear it out. You don't have to tell me the details, Laura. I've seen that guy shirtless in pictures on the internet. He has a body to die for and a face that would make angels weep. If you got him to stick his dick in you, I'm surprised you're even able to walk today. But I want you to know

I'm hurt. I'm very hurt that you got to do something so fucking amazing, and you don't want to share the details with your bestie."

"It's not that," I say. "It's... The guilt is eating me up. She's right. I should be sharing everything with her. The joy and the pain of life. That's what our trusted friends are for. It's just my own anxious feelings of shame that are holding me back. "I did. . .okay."

"Well, excuse me while my head explodes. Is that why your phone was off? You were so busy fucking your new stepbrother that you didn't even have the energy to take a call."

"No...well, kind of."

"Shit. I can't even look at you the same. It's like you just told me you climbed Everest or something. Ford McGregor is a god."

I burst out laughing, imagining what Ford would say if he heard Danna's comments. "He's just a man, Danna. A really nice, very sexy man."

"Is he hung?" she asks. "I bet he is. I bet he's got the dick Connor wishes he had."

"TMI," I laugh.

"No such thing as TMI, baby," she says, sliding her laptop into her bag and packing up her folder. "The stuff you call TMI is the stuff we'll be laughing about together when we're in our forties."

"Women in their forties don't laugh about dirty sex," I say, thinking about my mom with her friends and getting grossed out.

Danna put's her hands on her hips. "Of course they

do. What do you think they talk about? Botox and recipes?"

"Pretty much," I say, shuddering at the alternative. Are Mom's friends asking her for details on the size of Roderick's cock? If his sons are anything to go by, I'd say there is a pretty good chance that my mom struck lucky, but that very thought makes me vomit a little in my mouth. "Can we stop talking about this? Our moms are in their forties."

"Oh my god. My mom talks sex to her friends all the time. Stop being such a prude, Laura."

Damn. If only she knew just how unprudish I became this weekend, I think her head might explode.

"You got another class?" I ask her.

"Nah. I'm gonna head over to the library. I'm thinking about getting ahead on this essay so that I don't have to do anything tonight."

"That's a good idea," I say. "I'll come with you." If I'm going to be posing for Donnie later, it'll be good for me to get a bit more organized.

We stroll across to the building which houses the library. It's one of my favorite places; the quiet stops my head spinning, and the musty smell of books reminds me of fun times with my mom, sitting in the reading corner of our local library.

There's a study area on the second floor, so we head up there. All the while, Danna is probing for more details. I end up telling her quite a lot because not sharing the details is starting to make me look more suspicious. She shrieks at my fishing story and then even more when I let slip that Ford's cock has a nickname all its own.

"Was it really that big?" she whispers really loudly. A few heads at adjacent tables turn slightly, ears straining.

"He has a reputation for good reason. That's all I'm saying."

"Spoilsport," she says, shaking her head as though she considers me to be a huge disappointment.

I look at her over the screen of my laptop. "What do you want me to do? Show you using my hands?"

"Yes," she nods furiously. "I want to see full-on visual descriptions."

I roll my eyes but can't help laughing. She looks like an over-enthusiastic puppy. "That's not very classy," I say. "I could end up marrying him, and then you'd know the size of my husband's manhood."

"Marriage? Who said anything about getting married? Oh yeah, that's right. You!" Danna points at me with wide eyes. "Damn, that man must have some magic in his boxers to get you talking marriage after one fuck."

"Can you just concentrate on your work?" I hiss. "What's the point of coming to the library so we can have a conversation in a place we aren't even supposed to be talking?"

Danna narrows her eyes at me again. Wagging her finger, she says, "Don't you think you're getting out of this that easily. We will work now and gossip later.

I'm going to drop you back to the McMansion after last class, and I want to hear it all."

I turn my attention back to my assignment, but my mind isn't focusing. I've told Danna a tenth of the story, but she's not going to be happy with just that. It's going to take all my resolve to keep my lips fastened shut enough to keep my secrets. I should turn down her ride, but I have no alternative method of getting home other than the bus, and if I opted to get public transport, she'd be even more suspicious. It looks like Danna is coming to the casa McGregor.

I don't know if I should be laughing nervously or bursting into tears.

Chapter 19

The journey back to the McGregor mansion is fraught for me.

Although I'm certain that no one is going to be revealing anything to Danna, I have no idea how they will all react to me having a friend over. I go over the layout of the house in my head, trying to remember which way to go to get to the kitchen.

I also, with a complete rush of mortification, remember what my room looks like. OMG. What is Danna going to say about my pink princess palace? Ugh.

"So, tell me what it's like living there."

"Well, they have a big family breakfast at the weekend."

"Wow, that must take a lot of cooking."

"They have staff," I say. "We just sit our lazy asses down and eat."

"Wow," Danna says. "You need to make the most of that. Unless you snag one of these brothers or meet another rich dude, at some point, you're going to have to get used to living like the rest of us paupers and making your own pancakes."

"Don't be ridiculous, Danna. I've only been living

there for a couple of days. I've hardly lost touch with my ordinary roots."

"You better make sure you don't," she says. "If you start turning up to class with designer bags and a manicure, I'm going to freak out."

"You know that shit isn't me," I say. "I've got my feet firmly on the ground. It just happens to be more expensive ground these days."

Danna pulls the car up to the gate and presses the buzzer. A man's voice answers.

"McGregor residence."

"I'm here with Laura Winters," she says in a faux-British accent, and I practically die with embarrassment.

"Drive right in."

The gates open in a dramatically slow way, and Danna drives the car up to the front of the house.

"I don't even know what to say about this," she says, craning her neck to get a view of the very top. "This place is unbelievable."

"It is pretty awesome," I agree.

"Well done, Mom, is all I can say. She must be really great in bed for Roderick McGregor to have fallen for her. You know he's been single for years."

I shudder at the thought. "Can we stop with mom and sex talk, please?"

I open the car door, step out and grab my bags from the car. "Thanks..." I start to say, hoping that Danna will get the hint that this is a drop-off situation only, but she's already out of the car, chatting away.

"Men are simple creatures," Danna says. "Sex and food are the things that are most important to them. Second comes someone to stroke their ego and make their lives easier. If you give them all of that just the way they like it, then you're in."

"Is that how it works?" a voice says from behind another parked vehicle.

A head pops around and winks. "Hey, Laura." It's one of the C twins. Is it Cameron or Casey? I have no hope of being able to tell them apart. They are seriously identical.

"Hey," I say.

"Who's your friend?"

"This is Danna," I say.

He steps forward and offers his hand. "I'm Casey."

"Well, hello there, Casey," Danna says. She grins at him like a tiger staring at prey, but he seems more amused than intimidated.

"You here to hang out?" Casey asks.

"Well, sure. What are you doing?"

Casey waves at the SUV. "I was just getting something from my truck. Wanna come inside and have a coffee?"

"That was the plan," Danna says, looking over her shoulder at me and winking. Oh lord. This is going to get interesting.

"Come on then." Casey begins to stride towards the entrance, and Danna is right behind him, matching his pace. I'm still struggling to get my bag on my shoulder and shut the car door. It doesn't seem like

Danna is bothered about locking up, but I guess her car is worth around $500 and is next to at least three worth over $50,000, so it's not exactly going to be the first on any thief's list.

"So, how long have you lived here?" Danna asks.

"Over ten years," Casey says. "We moved in when I was 15."

"That must have been quite an experience."

"Yeah," Casey smiles. "It was a good day. I mean, we had a nice house before this, but we were sharing rooms and doing all our own chores. I don't want to sound like a lazy asshole, but it really helps to have people take on some of the work. Dad keeps us pretty busy."

"Then how come you're home so early?" Danna asks. It's only 4 o'clock, so I see her point.

"I was on-site at 5:30 am. Finishing at a reasonable hour is one of the perks of getting up at the ass-crack of dawn."

"I guess," Danna says. "Although 5:30 am sounds a little early for me."

"What about you, Laura? Are you a late riser?"

"Not really," I say. Casey closes the front door behind us, and we all stand awkwardly in the hallway. Danna looks up, taking in the sweeping staircase and amazing light fittings. Thankfully, she doesn't make too much of a big deal about it all. If we were alone, I'm sure she'd be squee-ing right now.

"So, you guys wanna hang out in the den?"

"Laura was going to give me a tour," Danna says,

giving me a look that tells me there is no point in me saying any different.

"That'll be interesting. Do you know your way around yet?" Casey laughs.

"Probably not, but I'll do my best."

"Okay then. I'll leave you guys to it and see you in the den if you can find it."

He strolls off, and Danna looks at me with wide eyes. "Oh. My. God," she gushes. "That is one sexy man."

"There are two of them," I say. "His twin is identical."

"Damn!" She shakes her head. "I'm glad we only bumped into one. I don't think my ovaries would have survived two at once."

"Well, your ovaries had better get prepared because they seem to travel as a pair most of the time, so I'm sure that Cameron is around here somewhere."

Danna puts her hand over her heart. "I'm gonna need a vodka tonic to get through this. Please tell me that you have some stashed in your room."

"I wish," I say. "To be honest, my room is a bit of a mess. I've still got boxes to unpack."

I start to lead Danna up the stairs, and she's full of 'oohs' and 'aahs' at all the artwork we pass on the journey. The house is pretty quiet, but my heart is beating fast as we reach the floor where my bedroom is. Any of the boys could pop out of a doorway, and I'd be like a rabbit in headlights. I know I would be.

I'm almost running down the corridor, and Danna is huffing to keep up. I throw open the door to my room, and Danna burst out laughing behind me. "Oh my god. I think Barbie threw up in your room, Laura."

"Don't start," I say, throwing my bag on the bed. "I want to say that Roderick didn't realize how old I am, but I'm pretty certain he knew I'm an adult woman, and he still thought this bubblegum-freak-show would be appropriate. I'm putting it down to the fact that he has no daughters. I think he indulged all his own fantasies in here."

She spins around, creating a whirly pattern on the soft cream carpet. "Look at that chandelier."

"I know."

She drops her purse on the floor and leaps onto my bed, practically bouncing off the other side. "I think I just died and went to five-year-old heaven."

"I'm not laughing anymore," I say. I sit on the edge of the bed and toss off my sneakers.

Danna turns over and puts her hands behind her head. "So, who's your nearest roommate?"

"I don't know," I say. "I think Elliot's in one of the nearest, and maybe Antony and Ford."

"Well, that would be very handy," she giggles. "You won't have far to go every time you're in the mood for a little booty call."

"We didn't do it here," I whisper. "We went up to his cabin."

"Oh, did you? Very nice. A lovers retreat."

"It wasn't like that. It was supposed to be some time away from all the crazy," I say.

"You've only just moved in, Laura. What crazy

happened on Saturday that you needed to escape on Sunday?"

"Just some stuff with Mom," I say, waving my hand as though it was something stupid. "We should get going before the rest of them get back. I don't want it to look weird that I'm showing people around their house like some kind of realtor-wannabe."

"I'm sure they'll be very understanding of your enthusiasm for your new home. They might have money, but their dad came from nothing. They know what they have."

"Maybe, but I'm hungry, too. We need to hunt down snacks."

Danna wriggles to get off the bed. When she stands, she stretches her arms into the air. "I'm sure that Casey will provide cookies with the coffee. We just need to make our way towards the den."

"Okay. Let's go."

We make our way out of the room, and I'm scanning the corridors like a person in fear of their life. We find our way to a branch in the corridor, and I have no idea which way to go. I hesitate, and Danna starts laughing. "Are you lost already?"

"No, it's this way." I take the turn to the left and start walking. There are the faint sounds of classical music and more doors that are closed, giving absolutely nothing away. The music gets louder, and I'm really tempted to turn around. Am I about to stumble across Roderick's office? Ugh. I don't want to see him right now. I'm still smarting over the breakfast debacle.

There's an open door, and as I come level with it, I turn and am almost blinded by the light streaming in from floor to ceiling windows—amazing canvases of brightly colored nudes' line with walls. I'm considering the fact that this could be Donnie's studio when I see feet poking out from behind a giant canvas. There's some humming going on, too.

"Wow," Danna says from behind me. "That is amazing."

Donnie's head pokes out from behind the canvas. He's clutching a brush, and his hair is a crazy mess. I know from watching him sketch that he has a habit of running his fingers through his curls when he's concentrating. All I can say is that there must have been a lot of concentrating going on this afternoon. "Laura," he says.

"And Danna." Danna leans around me and waves. "Hi."

"Oh, hey."

"This is my friend, Danna," I say, pulling a face that reveals my awkwardness. "We're trying to find our way to the den."

"Ah, well, you need to go back the way you came," Donnie says. "Nice to meet you, Danna. You hanging out with us tonight?"

"Maybe," Danna says, just as I say, "No."

Donnie looks between us and smiles. "Well, either way is cool."

"What are you painting?" Danna asks. She actually has no reservations.

"A female figure," Donnie says. He looks kind of awkward as Danna strides towards him. "It's not finished. I usually don't let people look at my work while it's in progress."

"Oh, it's okay," Danna says. "I'm no expert. Promise I won't judge." She doesn't wait for Donnie to agree. I watch as she strides around him and takes in the painting. From where I'm standing, I have no idea what she's looking at but I see her face break out into a sly smile and her eyes scan the painting and then me. "Well, Donnie. You've captured Laura perfectly."

Fuck. Has he started the painting already? I was sure he'd told me that he was going to wait until I could sit for him properly later. I start to walk around, watching Donnie's face turn from normal tan to beet-red. What the hell is on that canvas that has him so embarrassed?

I round the canvas and can see exactly why Danna looks as though she's stumbled on the juiciest gossip this century. Donnie's painting of me is no simple portrait. It's a rainbow-colored abstract, and I'm fully nude.

Oh. Fuck.

How the hell are we going to explain this one?

He has the shape of my breasts perfect and, most mortifyingly, the butterfly-shaped birthmark I have next to my right nipple. Danna must be able to see how realistic he has me. She's seen me naked plenty of times when we've been getting changed for a night out. We've been friends for such a long time. We're more like family. There's no way he'd know about my birthmark unless he'd seen me naked.

I think that denial is the best course of action here. "Wow, Donnie. That's erm, really good."

"Thanks," he says. He can't meet either of our gazes. He's only been painting but it's as though he's been caught looking at porn by his mom. The painting is so explicit, way more than I thought it would be.

"So, that's a pretty amazing likeness, isn't it, Laura," Danna says. "I mean that Donnie really has captured you in so much detail."

I think Donnie knows what she's getting at, and he glances at me, widening his eyes as if to say sorry.

"It's lovely, Donnie," I say softly. "We should leave you to it. Come on, Danna."

I take her by the arm and tug her towards the door. My cheeks feel hotter than the Sahara sun, and my heart is beating double time. This is exactly what I feared.

I've admitted to Ford, and now she knows about Donnie.

What the hell am I going to say?

We're a few yards down the hallway before she tugs me to stop. "You fucked him, too?" she says with utter glee in her voice. "He knows about your birthmark, so that must mean he's seen you naked."

"No," I say with as much conviction as I can muster.

"LAURA!" Danna puts her hands on her hips. "Are

you seriously going to lie to me like this? I'm your best friend and like the least judgy person in the whole world. Do you think I'd give a fuck if you'd fucked all the McGregor men in one weekend? No. Would I want to hear all the juicy details and giggle like a schoolgirl with you? Yes. Of course, I would because that's what we do. So why are you hiding this shit from me?"

My shoulders slump. I can't look at her. She's my best friend, and I didn't feel as though I could trust her with such a big secret. That doesn't say much about me. Danna has never broken a promise or my trust. She's been my strongest supporter through really tough times, but in the end, I just didn't want her to think badly of me. She might say she's not judgy, but if she was the one telling me she'd fucked four of her stepbrothers in two days, I'd be damn judgy of her. Maybe that's what this is. I'm applying my own standards to her, and that just isn't fair.

"I'm sorry," I say. "You're right. I...we can't talk here, but I promise I'll tell you everything. You just have to promise that it won't go anywhere, okay?"

"Do you even need to say that to me?" she asks, looking half-mad and half wholly intrigued.

"Let's go and get coffee, and we can chat after, okay?"

"Not really. I think if you don't tell me soon, I might combust with the not knowing, but I guess that Casey is waiting for us, and I wouldn't want to keep that man too long."

We start to make our way down the nearby stairs,

and I'm looking around, trying to work out where the hell we are. Danna stops suddenly before we reach the next floor and grabs my arm.

"Wait, did you fuck Casey?"

I shake my head. "No."

"Okay." She looks relieved, as though she's interested in trying to make a move on him. The thought causes a stab of jealousy to hit me in the throat. I love Danna, but Casey is off-limits.

That rush of possessiveness has me reeling. I guess that, despite all my concerns, these boys really have started to get under my skin. We start walking again, coming to the dining room, then further on towards the hallway I think leads to the den. All the while, I'm questioning myself. Why don't I want Danna to be with Casey? He's not mine. I haven't got any claim on him. Yes, his father has plans for him and me, but I'm still thinking that ten is a crazy number. I know my little group of three is good. Ford, Donnie, and Antony work well together. There's no conflict, and I feel comfortable with them all. I like Grant a lot, too. The time we spent together was really special, but he's not into his father's plan at all, so I have no idea where that will leave us.

But there must be a part of me that wants more; otherwise, why would I be feeling jealous at Danna being interested in Casey. The realization is more than a little overwhelming.

We're near the den, and the sound of deep male voices tells me that Casey is not alone. My heart skitters, my palms sweat as I brace myself for what is coming next. I hesitate just outside the room, and Danna is so excited about arriving that she almost knocks me over. We end up practically tumbling into the room, and all eyes turn to see the spectacle we're making of ourselves.

There are so many men in this room.

Casey and Cameron.

Ford.

Elliot.

Blake and Barrett.

And Grant.

I haven't seen him since the family breakfast of doom when Roderick announced that I'd had a little something-something with Elliot. Our eyes meet across the room, and I'm expecting him to be mad, but it doesn't appear as though he is. He gives me a smile, then looks back at the sport that's blaring on the television. He's nonchalant, and I have to admit that I don't like it.

Ford is the first to welcome us. "Well, looks like we have some girls in the house for a change."

He pats the sofa next to him. "Come and sit down and have some coffee. We're talking football, but I'm sure my brothers would be happy to change to something less boring."

"Boring!" Blake bellows. "There is nothing boring about football. Where did your balls disappear to all of a sudden?"

"I'm not saying I find it boring," Ford says. "I'm just

pretty certain that these women here don't want to get drawn into a discussion about the season."

I sit down next to Ford, and Danna sits on my other side. "I have to say I agree with Ford. Football isn't exactly my area of expertise."

"Women only watch it to check out all the bulging thighs and pert asses," Danna announces, and everybody laughs.

"I'll have to remember that," Cameron says. I know it's him because he's wearing different clothes from his brother. Their dirty blond hair even looks a little different today. I wish all the twins would think more about making themselves distinguishable. I mean, it's only fair for newbies like me, but to be honest, each set of twins looks so alike I wonder if the other brothers can tell them apart.

"Yeah. A ball game isn't a good first date," Danna laughs. "You just introduce your potential new girlfriend to a whole team of rugged sportsmen."

"Are you saying that we don't match up to football players," one of the B twins says. He puts his hand on his heart. "I'm mortally wounded by your friend, Laura."

"I wouldn't be," I laugh. "This is Danna, by the way."

"Hi Danna," they all chorus. I don't know why but I find myself blushing again. I still feel really out of place in the house, even though I've been intimate with two of the brothers here and kissed a third. Even though I know what they have planned for me. I look across at Grant, who's still watching the game. It's as though he's purposefully tuning out of the conversation, and I feel bad.

Is he angry with me? Have I made the situation worse for him?

I would never want to cause any problems between these men. Family comes first.

I'm going to need to seek him out and have a conversation with him. I feel as though I've misled him by telling him I was against the plan and then diving into bed with his brothers. I guess if he thought that I was trustworthy, he must be thinking again.

One of the household staff comes in with coffee, soft drinks, and plates of snacks. There are mini-sandwiches and wraps, fries, muffins, and other delicious-looking cakes and cookies. They put it all on the sideboard, and the boys are up like a huge scrum. I guess they're all hungry after a full day of work. If this is what they eat to tide themselves over until dinner, it's a miracle that they're not struggling in the waistline department.

"Hey boys," Elliot says, laughing. "How about we let the ladies go first?"

"Oh yeah," Blake says. He limps back from the table, and his face contorts into a grimace. I sympathize with him so much. Although my leg is feeling better after Grant and Elliot gave it some attention, I know it'll come back. Coping with injuries is so damned tough.

"Come on, girls," Barrett laughs. "You better grab

whatever you want because it's unlikely there will be much left after we're done."

Danna grabs quite a bit, but I'm a little more conservative. I mean, I love my food but eating in front of all these guys isn't my idea of fun, and somehow, I'm anticipating having to step in at some point. I'm not going to be able to do that very effectively if I have a mouth stuffed with a sandwich.

"So, Danna. . .are you at college with Laura?" Barrett asks. He's wearing navy blue sweats, and his feet are bare. It's like a Sunday-morning-themed photoshoot for GQ in here.

"Yeah, but we've known each other for ages. Since we were eight."

"Wow," he says. "So you're the one to come to for embarrassing photos then?"

She laughs, taking a seat on a big recliner, the chair nearest to the food! "Definitely! We both went through some tragic hair stages. And don't get me started on our slogan t-shirt stage. Ugh."

I laugh too, remembering the time Danna's mom agreed to trim her bangs. She ended up with long sections at the sides and a short bit in the center of her forehead. She had to clip it back for weeks while she waited for it to grow out. I don't tell the boys that, though. I'm scared of what she might bring up. Not that I have a lot of skeletons in my closet, but I'm thinking that keeping my embarrassing stories away from these guys would be a good idea.

"And what about boyfriends?" Ford asks, slumping back on the sofa with his overloaded plate.

"Are you asking me to spill secrets on my friend?" Danna asks. "Because if you are, you're going to be sorely disappointed. Besties don't reveal secrets." She looks at me pointedly. "We take them to the grave."

"Wow," Ford says, looking at me. "I think Danna is a keeper."

"I think Laura already decided that, Ford. They've been friends since they were eight!" Barrett puts his feet up on a footstool and pops a chip into his mouth.

"Why? Is Laura going to have lots of secrets for me to keep?" Danna asks, feigning innocence. There is absolutely nothing innocent about that question.

"I don't know, Danna. Laura, are you planning on giving Danna lots of secrets to keep?" His eyes flash with amusement.

I shake my head. "I'm the picture of innocence," I say sarcastically. Grant was taking a swig from a bottle of soda and spits some out at my comment.

Danna looks at him with interest as he finds a napkin to wipe himself.

"You got something to add, Grant?" Ford asks.

"It went down the wrong way," Grant says, turning his attention back to the sport.

"So, is this what you guys do every afternoon?" Danna ask.

"No day is the same in this place," Blake muses. "Sometimes we have to work really long hours. Other days, we get to finish early. It really just depends on where our projects are at and what needs to be done. I guess that's the perks to having your own business."

"It's not our own business yet," Blake says. "We still have one pretty big hurdle to overcome before pop lets go of the reins."

The boys trade glances.

"Oh really," Danna says, licking some mayo from her fingers. "What's that?"

I have a feeling I know exactly what it is, but I'm not going to give her an answer. At least not yet.

Chapter 20

I somehow manage to steer all the conversation between Danna and the boys to subjects that aren't revealing about the plan or our antics over the weekend. I'm not sure how I manage it but by the time we're done eating and drinking, my stomach is in knots with indigestion.

"We should go," I say to her. "I've got some work to do before..." I stop because what I was going to say was *before I pose for Donnie's painting*, but that definitely wouldn't be advisable to reveal.

". . .before dinner."

"Okay, sure." We both stand.

"Thanks for this," I say to the boys generally but looking towards Casey who was the one who had organized for us to join them.

"This is your home now," Casey says firmly. "You don't need to thank people for letting you eat and drink in your own home."

"I think it will take me time to get used to that," I say.

"Well, you have time," Cameron says, "but don't take too long!"

We say our goodbyes in a way that feels way too formal and awkward and then I shuffle out of the room with Danna, trying desperately to remember which way we need to go.

When we're a little way down the hallway, she starts giggling. "For fuck sake, Laura. You really are living the dream. I don't know what you did in a past life to deserve this, but it must have been something deserving of a Nobel prize."

"I think you might be right," I say.

"I mean, if the amazing surroundings weren't enough, there's the luxury of having staff to bring you what you need. You won't have to lift a finger."

"All the boys are capable of looking after themselves, though," I tell her. "It's not like they're a bunch of spoilt assholes."

"I was about to get to the boys. I think I'd be happy to live in a shed if I got to spend time surrounded by those fine specimens," she whispers. "Damn. I don't even know where to start."

"I know," I giggle. She's right. There aren't enough words to describe how amazing my stepbrothers are.

We're making our way down the corridor when a door flies open, and Roderick steps out into our path. Danna practically stumbles into him.

"Oh." She gasps, bringing herself to an abrupt halt.

Roderick looks at us both, drawing himself up to his full height and putting his arms behind his back. "Laura," he booms. "There you are."

"Yes," I say.

"We missed you this weekend. Your mother was particularly disappointed that you chose to disappear."

His tone is condescending and chastising, something that angers me immediately. He might be about to marry my mom, but that doesn't give him any right to treat me as though I'm a naughty child, especially when it was his lack of politeness that sent me running in the first place.

Danna looks at me, waiting for me to respond. Roderick hasn't even had the manners to introduce himself or at least give me time to introduce her. This whole thing is so awkward, and I have no idea what to say to him. Maybe it was a little immature of me to storm off with Ford. It wasn't what I intended at all, but Roderick has put me in this weird situation. He's the one that turned what should have been a really nice breakfast into a horrible and embarrassing public exchange. What did he expect me to do?

"My mom should understand why I didn't feel comfortable staying," I say softly.

"Should your mom also understand why you refused to take or return any of her calls?" he asks. "She was really worried about you."

"I didn't have any service at Ford's cabin. There was nothing I could do about that."

"You could have called to let her know where you were. I don't understand why your trip had to be such a big secret."

Wow. He really is going to keep going with this.

"You know what prompted me wanting to leave. Maybe you should be the one feeling guilty about how things turned out."

Danna is watching our back-and-forth conversation like a game of tennis, her eyes gradually widening with each exchange.

"Well, Laura. I think you are taking a very negative view of everything. There are millions of women who would love to be in your situation. They'd be jumping at the offer rather than treating it as you are. If anything, it is me who should be upset at all this. You are essentially rejecting my family, and for that, I cannot pretend to be unaffected."

Oh. So that's what he thinks. That he offers me his sons and I should be jumping at the chance. He is making me feel so low, as though I am worth nothing compared to the McGregor brothers, a girl who should be grateful for the scraps anyone will chuck at her. I'm devastated.

"Dad, you need to back off," a voice says from down the corridor. Blake is there, making his way slowly because of his limp. He catches my eyes, and his cheeks flush. I get the feeling he doesn't like me seeing him walk.

"Blake," Roderick says in a low warning tone.

"Don't 'Blake' me, Dad," he says, coming to stand by my side. "Laura hasn't been here for five minutes yet, and this isn't how we treat new guests, let alone how we treat new family."

Roderick's head looks like it might explode, but he can't find the words to reply because he knows his son is right. "You need to give her a chance to find her feet here and stop putting so much damn pressure on her."

"Yeah." Casey and Cameron also appear in the corridor, coming to stand behind Blake, now ominous as three against one. "This isn't right, Dad," Casey says. "It's a miracle Laura hasn't completely run away."

I'm waiting for Roderick to tell his sons to mind their own business, but he doesn't. I suppose because the plan is all of their business, the McGregor boys more than their father. Instead, Roderick looks us all over as though he's eyeing meat that has turned. Then he turns and goes back to the room he came from, closing the door noisily.

I start to walk away in the direction we were heading, and Danna, Blake, Casey, and Cameron follow.

"Wow," Danna says. "Looks like you're in someone's bad books."

"Something like that," I mumble. "Thanks," I say to Blake and the twins. "You didn't have to do that."

He shakes his head. "You don't need to thank us," he says. "This wasn't a good thing right here. I think my dad has gotten used to talking to everyone like they are staff. He forgets his manners."

"Well, I appreciate it anyway."

"I should go," Danna says. "I think you need to just get settled, Laura."

I nod. "Okay. I'll see you tomorrow."

She tugs her purse onto her shoulder. "Sure. Coffee shop before lectures?"

I nod, and Blake walks with us toward the front door. Cameron's cell starts to ring, and he and Casey look apologetic and disappear up the stairs, answering the call on the way.

Blake is chivalrous and opens the door for Danna and stands with me while she jogs to her car. She gives us a big wave and a grin, but I can see her eyes are worried for me. I think we both built this move into something very different from what it is turning out to be.

Blake closes the door and looks me over. "You okay?" he asks.

I nod, but I think he can tell that I'm not.

"Look, I was going to take a swim. You wanna come? It'll maybe take your mind off all of this."

I was planning on getting some work done, and then I promised to pose for Donnie, but a swim sounds amazing, and I feel as though I should spend some time with Blake since he was so strong in defending me against his father.

"Sure. That sounds good."

He walks me to my room – it seems everyone in this house knows where it is – and I find my swimsuit and some sandals.

"Everything you need is down there," he tells me. "The changing rooms have towels and all the toiletries you might need."

As we make our way down to the swimming pool, Blake asks me about my leg.

"Is it always like that?" He sounds cautious, as though he knows how difficult it can be to answer awkward personal questions.

"I hope not," I say. "I keep tearing a muscle, and I don't seem to know how to rest it for long enough that it heals permanently."

Blake nods. I debate whether I should ask about his. If I do, he could think I was being rude, but if I don't, he might think I don't care. He's limping next to me, so it seems weird to ignore it.

"How did you hurt yours?" I ask tentatively.

"I was a kid," he says. It's not a matter-of-fact statement of something that happened long ago. There's a rawness to his voice that I wasn't expecting. "Barret was always the messiest, and he left a toy on the stairs. I tripped and fell down. My pelvis shattered, and my femur broke, and part of it came through here." He indicates the place on his thigh where my leg feels the sorest.

"That must have been so painful," I say, wincing at the thought. "How old were you?"

"Eight."

"I hope Barret apologized?" I say, trying to lighten things. I imagine them as cute, tousled little boys hugging on Blake's hospital bed.

Blake looks at me very seriously. "He tried, but..." There's a pause as though he's working out what to say next. ". . .little things can have a big effect. There's no making this better."

That wasn't what I was expecting to hear. It seems

as though Blake is still holding a grudge against his brother for something that happened so many years ago. That must be difficult when the person you are holding a long-term grudge against is your identical twin, especially as they live and work together.

It doesn't take us long to get to the leisure area. There is a loud beat coming from the gym, and as we open the doors, it only gets louder. Elliot is running, and he turns and smiles, pressing buttons to bring the machine to a slower pace.

"Are you coming to train?" he asks me.

"Swim," I say, holding up my suit.

There's a look between the brothers that I don't miss. "I'll come and join you," Elliot says, "when I'm done here."

"Sure," Blake calls. We walk to the right of the gym, and he pauses at a set of doors. "You can change in there, and I'll meet you in the pool."

I nod and head into the women's changing room. It's so sparkling new in here that I wonder if it's ever been used. I suppose the male changing rooms must get way more use in a family with this many men. I find a bench to rest my things on and take a seat to change. It doesn't take me long to slip on my simple navy swimsuit and sandals. There's a mirror on the far wall with a walnut vanity unit that looks like something from a high-end hotel. I gaze at my body, taking in my thighs which have always been thicker than I would have liked, and the roundness of my belly. I have a womanly shape despite all the training I've done. It's not a bad shape. I try not to look at myself with a critical eye which can be hard with the amount of airbrushed photography on show in the media. I guess I have a traditional woman's shape from before high-intensity training and lean muscle became the look. Grant, Ford, Donnie, and Antony all seemed pleased with it, too. I turn so I can get a view of my ass which is round and wide. I know there's a little cellulite there but there doesn't seem to be much I can do about that. I eat well and exercise. It's just a part of my body's design. I pull my hair up into a high ponytail and exhale a deep breath. This is about relaxation, not self-assessment.

When I exit the changing room, I'm immediately hit by the heat of the pool environment. It's almost tropical in here. Blake is already doing lengths, cutting through the water like a fish. It would seem that his leg works just fine when he's swimming. I head to the shallower end and descend the stairs into the perfectly warm, clear water, allowing the calm of it to wash over me. As Blake turns and heads back, I duck under the water to wet my hair, ready to start swimming. We must pass each other fifteen times as we make our way back and forth, counting off the lengths. My bad leg is holding up but by the end, I can feel some tightness, so I take hold of the wall and have a rest in the deep end. Blake eventually does the same, holding on with one hand and using the other to wipe the water from his face. There are droplets in his beard and the blue of his eyes is identical to the blue of the water around us. I don't know if all the McGregor brothers work out, but he has such amazing shoulders and biceps. It's hard to find a place to look that isn't getting me all in a fluster.

"You swim well," he says. There is nothing flirty about Blake, just simple conversation. It's kind of nice, in a way. Respectful and not my experience of time spent with the rest of them.

"Mom insisted I have lessons from a really young age. She had a cousin who drowned, so safety in the water is a really big thing in our family."

"I'm sorry," he says. "That must have been difficult."

"Before I was born," I shrug, "but I'm glad I learned early."

Blake nods, and there's a moment of what feels like awkward silence. Then I catch him looking at the scar I have on my upper arm. It's from an accident I had on my bicycle when I was young, and I hardly think about it these days. It's only the size of a child's hand, but I suppose it's quite noticeable. He blinks and then looks back at my eyes, realizing he's been caught looking. "I...sorry," he stutters.

"It's okay," I say, moving my shoulder forward so I can look at it. "It doesn't bother me."

"Really?" His voice is filled with surprise. "I mean, that's really good. Not that it should bother you."

"Do you have a scar?" I ask him, remembering the injury he talked about to his leg.

Blake nods. "On my thigh. I hate it."

This is a testy subject. I completely understand

where he's coming from because handling our imperfections can be hard, but I've never wanted to feel that way about myself. My physical and emotional scars tell my story. They make me the person I am today, and without them, I know I'd be completely different. I tell Blake that our scars are part of us, and I feel it's important to embrace everything that makes us who we are. I don't know if it registers, but I hope it does. I hate to think of him being conscious about his body or that his feeling about the way his leg looks might be stopping him from living the life he wants to live.

He nods. "It's just hard when you see a perfect version of yourself walking around every day. It's a constant reminder of what I lost." It's then that it truly hits me just how difficult it must be for Blake. To have a carbon copy of yourself who can walk properly and who has no external imperfections must be a constant reminder of just how damaged Blake has been. I feel sorry for both of them. Blake because he has to live with this and Barret because he was just a kid who made a silly mistake. He can't help being unaffected any more than Blake could have prevented the accident.

"I saw this Facebook video once. It was about a man who developed dysphasia overnight. He went from being perfectly healthy to struggling to talk and use his hands. He became disabled and his whole life changed."

"Shit," Blake says. "Poor guy."

"He wouldn't agree," I say. "He said in the video

that having his disability has made him kinder and more thoughtful. He loves the person he became after he became imperfect in the eyes of society."

Blake raises his eyebrows, and his expression is skeptical. "Sometimes, it's the very thing that could break us that makes us, Blake," I say. Instinctively I find his hand in the water. "Should I feel lesser because of this?" I ask him, bringing his hand to my scar. His fingertips trace the lumpiness of the skin there, a dull sensation since the nerves were damaged. His eyes flick between the scar and my gaze as though he's checking how I feel about him touching me this way.

I wonder if he ever lets anyone see or touch his scar. "It's okay," I say softly.

Blake draws his hand away slowly. His brow is a little furrowed, and his jaw set more firmly than before as though he's intent on making a decision. Then he finds my hand in the water and looks me in the eye.

"Will you feel mine," he says. There's a gruffness in his voice that reveals just how difficult this is for him. I get a lump of emotion in my throat as I realize what a big step this must be for him, and I nod, letting him know that I'm fine with what he's asking me.

He draws my hand deeper in the water, turning my fingers gently until they press against the cool skin of his thigh. I feel the ridge immediately. The skin is thick and bumpier than mine. His legs have a fine dusting of hair, and beneath the scar, I can feel the solid strength of his thigh muscle. I can't look in his eyes while I do this – it feels too intimate – so I fix my gaze on his mouth instead. His lips are slightly parted now, and my stroke of his skin suddenly feels less about scar exploration and more about caressing. The moment is ridiculously intimate, and I barely even know this man. What I do know is that he will stand up for me against his father and do what is right. I know that he's wounded and sensitive and far too self-critical for his own good. When I finally look up to his eyes, he leans in to kiss me.

Was I expecting it?

No.

Do I pull away?

Part of me wants to. He will be the sixth McGregor brother who I've kissed in four days. That sounds crazy in my head, but Blake is so tentative and so gentle. It's as though he doesn't feel worthy of my kiss and that hurts my heart. So I kiss him back, not because I feel sorry for him but because it feels right where it should feel so wrong. I kiss him because I can feel the need in him for acceptance and how tough it must have been to make this move when he is feeling so vulnerable.

And it's a kiss I will never regret. Soft lips caress mine, capturing my lower lip and gently sucking it until the hairs stand up on the back of my neck. His arm goes around my waist, drawing me close to him. He kisses my cheeks, my forehead, my neck, and just when I feel like I might melt in his arms he presses the softest kiss onto my scar.

It's the sweetest thing that anyone has ever done for me. Just that one gesture shows me how sensitive Blake is and how deep his sense of understanding of the damage that life brings to us as we walk its perilous pathways. If we weren't in the water, I'd kiss his, too. I want to show him that the damage he considers to be such an issue for him means nothing to me.

I'm totally focused on Blake, but to my left, I hear a splash and feel a swell of water. Blake stops and turns at the same time as me. There is someone else in the pool, and they must have seen what we were doing. The figure cuts through the water elegantly, and I see Blake narrow his eyes.

"Barret," he mutters as though he wishes it was anyone else.

It's not until the figure reaches the end wall and surfaces that I see that Blake was right.

"Well, well, well. It looks like you beat me to it, bro!" he laughs.

"I didn't know it was a race," I say, raising my eyebrows.

Barret laughs. "Just call it a little harmless twin-rivalry."

"Brothers should be allies, not rivals," I say.

A look passes between them, but neither of them agrees or disagrees. "So, what did my brother say to make you want to kiss him?"

"It's never just one thing, is it?" I say. "It's a feeling that you get from lots of things."

"I'm glad," Barret says. He pats his brother's

shoulder and then squeezes, and I can see that he genuinely means it. For all Blake's resentment, Barret is definitely not a bad guy. "So, shall we swim?"

Blake looks at me with longing. I can see how much he wishes his brother hadn't chosen now to get his lengths in, but continuing to kiss him with others around would be strange. I push off from the end wall and slide quickly into the front crawl which is my favorite stroke. I hear more splashes as I surface to breathe, so I'm pretty sure the boys are swimming, too. I do three lengths, turning underwater. On the third, a hand grabs mine under the water. We come up spluttering, and before I know what's happening, I'm being kissed. My first assumption is that Blake is picking up where we left off while his brother is busy swimming. I kiss back because it's such a cute thing to do.

It's only after a few seconds that I pick up on how different this kiss is. There's more passion here, less tentative care. The slide of his tongue is more urgent. I put my hands on his shoulders and pull back to find Barret grinning like a Cheshire cat. "I've been wanting to do that since you arrived, but my brothers keep getting in there first."

"It's not a competition," I say, but I can't be angry with him because his eyes are sparkling with mischief, and his fingers are entwined with mine beneath the water. There's a playfulness about Barret that makes me smile.

"Oh, it definitely is," Barret laughs. "Do you

seriously think that ten men could be vying for the same woman without there being some rivalry in who wins her over first?"

I shake my head because it sounds so caveman. "You must all be pissed at Grant then," I laugh.

"He's a dark horse, but we won't hold it against him. If he didn't get you to see what a great man he was, I have a feeling you would have bolted this stable on the first night."

"Wow, with the horse analogies."

"You know what I mean." He grins with a perfect white even smile, blue eyes reflecting the swell of the water around us, and I have to agree with what he says. It was Grant's reluctance to be involved in the plan that made him feel safe to me. It was his independence from his family that made me comfortable with him. In a way, I guess that sleeping with him had been a form of rebellion. I didn't realize how quickly his brothers would win me over after, though.

"Maybe," I say.

"So, what would it take for me to convince you that I'm worth a go?"

"Tell me about Blake's accident," I say.

Barret looks over his shoulder at his brother, who is still swimming lengths and heading away from us.

"If I could have swapped places with him, I would have. The guilt of what happened is still here. . .it's like it happened yesterday." Barret puts his hand over his heart, and I can see the true love for his brother and terrible regret that he feels. "I worry about him every day. He's never really trusted a woman before. I think he fears rejection."

"He's never had a girlfriend," I say, completely shocked. Blake is stunning. Like a young David Beckham. I assumed he would have had women falling all over him.

Barret shakes his head. "I've always tried to keep my love life private from him because I didn't want to make him feel bad."

Blake turns in the water and starts to swim towards us. I don't know if he's realized we're talking. I know he definitely didn't see us kissing. Barret turns to watch him, and I see pure love in his eyes. I just hate to see so much hurt wedged between these two brothers. It all seems so pointless.

When Blake surfaces, he looks between us with hurt and uncertainty in his eyes. For a second, it seems like there is a horrible possibility of Blake getting angry with Barret, and I couldn't stand it if it was me who put yet another wedge between them. Before he gets a chance to speak, I lean forward and kiss him. He seems to freeze, obviously uncomfortable at being this way with me when his brother is so close, but then, as I stroke my hand over his wet chest, he seems to relax. I draw back and look into his eyes which are heavy-lidded with arousal. There's so much hope there that I know what I'm about to do next is really risky. I cup his cheek, and then I turn to Barret and do the same. The twins look at each other, neither really knowing how to react. Then I lean in and kiss Barret, too.

I hear Blake's quick inhale of breath, but I keep holding his cheek. I turn back to him and kiss him again with his brother's kiss still hot on my lips. It's mesmerizing to move between them this way and hot as hell. Even in the gently warm water of the pool, I can feel my pussy heating.

As I'm kissing Blake, Barret moves behind me, sliding his lips over my neck and running his hands over my hips and ass. Blake must sense what is happening and tentatively places his hands just beneath my breasts. I draw back and look him in the eyes, nodding my head to let me know this is okay.

It's more than okay.

It's amazing. It's perfect.

I know that I can help these twins find each other again. I hope, by sharing me, that Blake can recover from the injury he is still feeling and regain trust in his brother.

Blake slides the strap of my swimsuit down, tugging it until my right breast is revealed. He inhales sharply at the sight of it. I take his hand and press it against my breast, and instinctively he tugs at my nipple in exactly the way I love.

"Fuck," he says softly, and with so much awe in his voice, I want to take him into my arms and hug him. I've never wondered about what it might be like to be a man's first and find that I like the idea way more than I would have thought.

Barret isn't slow to push things forward. He has the other strap of my swimsuit down and over my arm before I realize what is happening. It only takes a few more seconds before he's pushed it over my thighs.

Damn, this boy is keen, but it's good.

Good for Blake not to have to make each new step forward. Good for me to feel their desire.

Blake's eyes shift downwards, taking in the sight of my naked body through the undulating, reflective surface of the water. His hands move over my breast, down my sides to the dip of my waist, and around to my ass. Each new point of exploration brings new heat to his eyes. When his fingers stroke the inside of my thighs, I part my legs to let him know it's okay. I want him to touch me. I need it for my own pleasure and his sexual awakening. His middle finger dips straight to where I'm wet, and he sighs softly.

"It feels good, doesn't it," Barret says to his brother.

Blake nods, his eyes still looking down.

"Find her clit," Barret orders.

Blake's finger slides forward until he feels the hard nub at the front of my pussy. He circles it softly, and I moan to let him know how good it feels. "That's it," Barret says, moving his hands to squeeze my breasts and pinch my nipples, the rhythms matching perfectly.

Blake leans in to kiss me again, his tongue sliding over mine in a way that makes me shiver. I've never been a girl who's been quick to come. It's always taken a lot, even when I touch myself, so I'm not sure why I'm so close to coming so soon, but I think that it might be because there are two of them.

Everything is better with two; four hands to caress, two mouths to kiss. The prospect of two cocks straining to fuck me is more arousing to me than I would ever admit to anyone.

No wonder Katelin was prepared to wreck her reputation to live with her three stepbrothers. No wonder she risked angering her mom and stepfather to follow her heart.

Now I've had more than one man, the prospect of going back to a single monogamous relationship seems so unappealing. My previous dreams of one man who would become my husband seem trivial and boring. I know people say that men are ruled by their cocks, but I think that my pussy definitely has a very vocal opinion in this. When combined with my heart, that seems to know that these boys aren't just out to use me and abuse me but really want to make a future as one big happy family. It's a heady mix.

I'm so close that my legs start to shake. Blake never slows his tempo, keeping it maddeningly even. Barret seems to feel just how near I am, and he slides his hand between my legs from behind. I think he pushes his thumb inside me because whatever it is feels big and blunt. I rise up on my toes, and he pulses his thumb against my g-spot. It's such an intense feeling that I cry out. Blake's eyes widen, the effect they are having on me seeming to be fascinating to him.

"Mmm..." I moan, grabbing onto his arm as I come

in wave upon wave of pleasure. I'm so weakened that I slump into Blake's arms, and he holds me tight, stroking my hair, telling me that I'm beautiful and perfect and everything he ever wanted.

Barret's hands caress my back, my ass, my thighs.

When I've come back to myself, I feel totally relaxed. It's so strange to find that the person I was less than a week ago, filled with inhibitions and worries, has faded away so completely. We're in a pool, with no privacy from the household who might decide to take a swim or do maintenance. I'm with two men who, up until a few days ago, I'd only seen on Google, and I just feel so comfortable.

"Can we take you up there?" Barret asks, pointing to a large double lounger that's covered with towels and pillows. It looks like heaven.

I nod and duck under the water to retrieve my suit. Blake and Barret wade to the nearest steps, and I'm practically drooling watching them get out of the pool. Water pours off their ripped bodies, leaving their tan skin glistening. Wet swim-shorts leave next to nothing to the imagination at the best of times, and Blake and Barret's erections are very obvious. Lord. Are all these men so identically hung? It would seem that I've hit the jackpot.

As I pull myself out of the pool, the cooler air hardens my nipples. Blake is already making his way over with a towel. I can see him trying not to show his limp, and my heart bleeds again. I just wish he could see that it doesn't affect his sex appeal in any way. If anything, I seem to have a real warmth for his wounded-puppy persona.

"Thanks," I say, pulling the plush, cream towel around myself.

My eyes fall to his crotch and then back to his face, and immediately he's blushing. I lean in to kiss him, placing my hand around the cool tented fabric of his shorts and finding the hard, long cock beneath. His breath hisses as he inhales sharply, eyes focused on my hand.

I've always wondered if men feel vulnerable when a woman has their hand wrapped around their cock this way. I know that I feel powerful. There's a rush in taking control some of the time, especially with Blake because all of this is so new to him.

"You're so hard," I tell him. He makes a gruff sound, closing his eyes as I run my hand back and forth. "Where do you want to put this?"

His sapphire eyes flick to mine, filled with yearning and passion. His fingers go between my legs, two pushing right up inside my pussy until I'm standing on my tiptoes.

"Here," he says. Then he pulls his fingers out, takes my hand, and walks me to the bed.

Barret is waiting, his hand on his still-clothed cock and a wide smile on his face. "Your bed awaits." He pats the bed next to where he's sitting, and I take my place next to him, shuffling back until I'm lying in the middle. Blake gazes at me as I draw my feet up, leaving my legs open and slack. He eyes my pussy as though it's a feast and he's starving. Then he's kneeling between my legs and pressing his mouth on my clit.

The rush is unbelievable. To know that my pussy is the first he's ever tasted is overwhelming. He makes a hungry sound, his tongue tracing all the soft, slick pinkness. I rest on my elbows, gazing down at his angelic expression. There's a wonder there, wonder about a woman's body that I've never really seen in another man. He's on a voyage of discovery, and I'm happy to lead him. I put my hand on his cheek and make him look up at me.

"Later," I tell him. "I want you to fuck me now."

Oh god. His expression is so fiercely primal that I almost come again. He might be inexperienced, but that doesn't mean he doesn't know exactly what he wants. Blake tugs his shorts down, throwing them on the tiled floor next to the bed. His hand goes over his scar for a moment, but when his eyes find mine, I shake my head to let him know that's not okay. I want to see him. All of him.

We are not just the parts of us that make us perfect.

We are all the good and bad, the perfect and imperfect, the beautiful and the ugly and everything in between.

Instead of concealing himself, he fists his cock, gazing at my pussy while he does it, a pink flush spreading across his cheeks. I wonder how fast his heart is beating. Mine is racing as though I've just done a half marathon.

I don't tell him to put a condom on. I'm on the

pill, so I know we're good. I want him to enjoy this the way it's supposed to be. Bare. Raw. Skin to skin. I want him to feel that moment of letting go inside of me and watch his cum spill from my entrance as he pulls out.

These are things that condoms take away from sex, and I have to say that I miss them.

"I'm on the pill," I tell him.

Barret groans from behind Blake. "You gonna let us come in your pussy?" he asks.

I nod, my clit swelling at his words, and his smile spreads wider.

It seems that I'm not the only one who likes it bareback.

I look at the scene before me.

Two men wait to fuck me.

Two cocks wait to spread me open.

And after, two loads of cum will drip from inside me.

I don't know what I did to deserve this.

As Danna said, it must have been something Nobel Prize-winning.

I grab Blake's wrist, needing him to move faster. His cock is dripping pre-cum, and I want him to spread it over my pussy to lubricate the way.

Fuck. He rests himself over me, his cock falling heavy and hard onto my clit. I take hold of it, rubbing it through my folds, feeling the slickness of both our arousals mingling.

Blake moans, his hips moving to nudge the head

of his cock inside me, just a little. His eyes find mine. "Do it," I tell him, spreading my legs wider. I bring my heels behind his ass, urging him forward.

Blake closes his eyes and thrusts steadily, allowing me to open up to accept him. I watch him with awe, feeling the significance of this moment for him.

This is huge.

Bigger for him than for me.

He's the fifth McGregor brother that I've welcomed between my legs. I'm actually completely overwhelmed by that realization. Before I came to this house, I was a relatively conservative girl with ordinary fantasies about what my future would bring. Now, here I am, living a completely different life.

"Fuck," Blake groans as he moves with a punishingly good rhythm. His cock is so wide and long that my pussy is straining to take him. His mouth claims mine in a searing kiss as his hand grasps my left breast and squeezes.

The way he's rotating his hips has my pussy straining for more contact. The rough brush of pubic hair stimulates my clit. I undulate beneath him, moaning and not caring that his brother is a foot away, waiting his turn or that anyone could be watching from the corners of this room.

Elliot said he was going to join us for a swim. He could be here right now, looking at his brother fucking me raw.

It's the thought of being watched, combined with Blake's increasingly hard thrusts, that tips me over the edge. I see stars claw at his back, clasping his body to mine with my legs riding wave upon wave of pleasure, and Blake groans too, his cock swelling as my pussy milks him to orgasm.

"Wow," Barret says. "That was fucking hot."

Blake sputters with laughter against my neck. "I wasn't expecting marks out of ten, you asshole!"

"And there's my brother, back to his usual self."

I smile up at Blake, stroking his still wet, light brown hair back from his brow. "That was perfect," I say softly, and he beams like I just gave him the best gift ever.

He'll always remember this. I know because it's inevitable.

Your first is always etched into your brain, whether it's a good or bad experience. Mine was lackluster, to be honest. I thought I loved him and that he loved me, but after we had sex, I knew that neither was really true.

Blake adjusts himself as though he's worried about crushing me. As he kneels up and draws his cock out of my pussy, I feel that amazing sensation of cum trickling out. He's watching it, and so is Barret.

"Isn't that the horniest fucking thing ever?" Barret says. Blake's fingers find my entrance, and he slicks the cum up and over my clit. It's slippery and warm, and I'm turned on all over again.

"Are you gonna get the fuck out of the way?" Barret laughs.

Blake scowls. "You wanna stop butting in like a back seat driver. I'm not done."

"You look pretty done to me."

I hold up my hand. "Boys, the bickering isn't sexy." I laugh, and they look suitably embarrassed. They probably hadn't even noticed they were doing it. Without having a sibling, I'm not experienced in these kinds of relationships.

Blake leans over me to kiss my mouth, then he moves aside to let his brother in, too. I wonder how Barret will feel about going where his brother has just been but that doesn't seem to be anything other than a turn-on. He climbs on top of me, leaning in to suck my nipples, taking each tip into his hot mouth and tugging just the way I like it.

"You have the sexiest breasts," he says. "Just more than a handful, and these nipples." He shakes his head as though he has no idea how to describe them that would do them justice. "But you know, what? I wanna see that ass of yours. I noticed it that first day you came sauntering into our house. Flip yourself over."

I grin at his cheekiness and do as he asks, getting myself onto my hands and knees. He runs his hand over my body, from my shoulders, and along my waist, then over the curve of my hip. He touches me as his brother's seed drips from inside me. Blake is watching it all, his cock already hard again.

I feel the press of Barret's dick against my messy entrance and moan. I shouldn't be horny again this quickly, but since I moved into this house, my pussy seems to be misbehaving in the best possible way. He surges forward, using the lubrication Blake left behind to smooth his path, and it feels amazing.

Slick.

Hot.

Hard.

I push back to get him deeper, and he reaches around to rub my clit in the rhythm of his thrusts.

"Fuck," he groans, gripping onto my hip hard enough to bruise. "You're fucking amazing," he gasps.

Blake moves forward to stroke my breasts, squeezing and tugging at my nipples. I watch the motion of his hand stroking his huge cock. Slow and steady, like he wants to prolong the pleasure as much as he can. I'm about to tell him that I'll lick it for him when a door bangs.

There's someone coming.

Chapter 21

We all freeze.

I crane my neck in the direction of the noise, panicking. It could be Mom. What the hell would she think? Or Roderick; how embarrassing would that be.

No one wants to be caught having normal, missionary sex, let alone hot group doggy-style sex. This is about as compromising of a position as anyone could put themselves in.

It's not Mom or Roderick, though.

It's Elliot.

Oh. My. God.

I can't move. Barret's hands are holding me right where I am. Neither boys say a thing as their brother makes his way around the pool.

Then, as Elliot is just twenty feet away, Barret starts to thrust again.

Fuck.

He's acting like nothing is happening. Like we're just relaxing by the pool with a book and a cocktail. Elliot is dressed in swim shorts, his erection already visible.

No one says anything. Elliot's eyes burn into mine, his long eyelashes making him look angelic even as his eyes flash dark as a devil.

I don't move to cover myself, even though I could. The deepness of Barret's thrust makes my eyes roll, and Blake's hand is fiercer on my breast. It's as though they've amped up the passion now we have an audience.

Is this what makes group sex so intense? It's not just the extra cocks, hands, or mouths; it's the extra eyes that are watching that make me vibrate with lust.

Elliot is right beside us now, and he leans in to kiss me. I remember how amazing his lips felt on mine from that first kiss in the gym. I was uncertain then. I am worried about what Grant would think and what this would mean for my life with the McGregors. I feel light years away from that point now.

I kiss him back, and the moan that comes from his throat when I do is mind-blowing.

He's pushing his swim shorts down, and damn. His thighs are phenomenal, but his cock is something else. Perfectly proportioned and hard as a baton.

"Let her lick it," Barret says. His voice is hoarse with lust, his cock swelling inside me as he utters the words.

"You want to?" Elliot asks.

I nod because what else can I do.

It's like being in a restaurant, faced with the dessert menu and wanting everything on it.

Elliot kneels in front of me, holding his cock tantalizingly near. He's shower fresh and stunning, every muscle of his abs perfectly toned.

"You ready?" he asks, running the head of his cock

over my lips. I lick out. The skin there is hot and silky smooth. He's not pushy like I thought he might be. He lets me set the pace, which I like. I start slow, licking down the length, nuzzling into the small patch of trimmed hair at the root. He moans when I inhale the scent of him, that primal need to involve all the senses, setting the hairs rising on the back of my neck. Barret's going slow, obviously enjoying the view.

It's only when I take Elliot deep into my mouth that they both start moving faster.

I know I'm being spit-roasted. That term is one that boys in high school used to throw around when they were trying to one-up each other about the porn they had watched. It's a term that has always disgusted me. I imagined it being an abusive situation where the woman was being forced to take two men into her body. I couldn't ever imagine wanting this, but I do. I want it so badly.

I can taste when Elliot is getting close, the salty-sweet evidence slickening my tongue. Barret feels huge inside me, every thrust taking me closer. Blake is holding my hair back from my face and watching his brothers fucking me. It's crazy that this is his first time. I hope it doesn't screw him up for life.

I know I'm close to coming. I just need something more to get me over the edge. It's as though Barret reads my mind just at that moment, and he slaps my ass hard. It's such a shockingly good feeling that I can't hold it back. I come and come and come, my pussy clamping down on Barret's cock and my mouth moaning around Elliot's.

Barret is there with me, thrusting a few more times before he unloads inside me.

Then it's just Elliot left. He goes very still, his ab muscles contracting, his thighs flexing, then I feel him spill over my tongue.

I swallow, and he groans, low and loud, as though he can't hold himself together anymore.

My arms are like jelly, so I collapse onto the bed, rolling onto my side. Barret slips from inside me as I do, and my pussy is leaking cum all over the lounger. I'm wrung out and totally overwhelmed.

I never imagined I would do these things.

This was for other more adventurous people than me. In my more judgmental moments, it was just for girls who didn't give a shit about their reputations.

I never imagined that would be me.

Now I can't imagine ever going back.

Chapter 22

I'm late to pose for Donnie. After I recovered my senses by the pool, I made my excuses and went for a shower. The boys were all so sweet, hugging me, kissing me, telling me that they're so fucking happy that I'm here and want to be with them.

It was all perfect until I shuffled away to the shower, cum still dripping down the inside of my thighs, and I realized I'm seven brothers in.

Seven.

As I showered myself clean, running my hands over my swollen sex, my mind started with its stream of doubts.

I tried to push them away, but heart and mind don't always sing from the same hymn sheet, and I'm not very good at knowing which one to trust.

I don't feel used.

I should, but none of the boys have made me feel anything other than desirable.

They've all been so welcoming.

It's just me with my own preconceptions.

I knock at Donnie's door – he's shut it this time, maybe conscious of Danna being in the house – and he opens it with a flourish.

"I was about to come and find you," he says.

"And here I am." I curtsy, and he laughs, leaning in to kiss me softly. It's such a tender and familiar gesture, but my heart feels guilty. I've just been kissing, sucking, and fucking his brothers, and he has no idea. Or maybe he does. Gossip travels like wildfire in this house.

And he probably wouldn't care. I get the feeling Donnie is chill through and through.

"I'm all ready for you," he says, waving his hand over to a low bed area that is draped in fabric.

I've worn leggings and a slouchy top, but I'm not sure if this is suitable attire. "How do you want me?" I pull at my top, and he grins.

"Naked?" His silver eyes sparkle, and his perfect white teeth flash a grin. He's cheeky but very cute with it.

Naked.

I supposed I should have expected it. The picture I saw earlier was very sexually explicit as far as art goes.

And it's not like he hasn't seen me without clothes before.

I don't want to look like I'm nervous about it, so I go over to the bed, slip my leggings and panties down, then tug off my top.

Donnie inhales sharply, maybe at my faux confidence. There is something clinical about this.

I turn, and his eyes are on my body. My nipples harden in the cool room.

There're a few seconds of silence that feels like an eternity.

"How shall I lay?"

"On your back. Can you put one arm over your head and your other hand on your belly?"

I do as he's asked, keeping my legs flat and straight. My top half feels sexy and relaxed, my bottom half not so much.

Donnie arranges me, moving my hand further across the pillow, relaxing my fingers. He tips my head a little, so I'm looking at where a fresh canvas has been set up. He moves my other hand closer to my pussy. "Can I move your legs?" he asks.

"Sure," I say, thinking what the hell is he going to do with them. He takes my right leg and lifts the knee so that it's bent and raised. Then he does the same with the left. My pussy is on show like this, spread open like a rose in full bloom. His eyes flick there, but he's professional today.

"That okay?" he asks.

I'm not sure what he wants me to say. My clit feels hot, the exposure to his eyes enough to turn me on. I wonder if he can see that I've just had sex. Is my pussy pinker and more engorged? It certainly feels that way.

"If it's good for you."

"It's perfect," he says.

He practically runs to the canvas, and I can hear him preparing. Every so often, his face appears around the side as he takes in my form to transfer it to a two-dimensional representation.

I don't know how long I've been in this position,

but it feels like an eternity. Trapped in my own head with no distraction is not a good place to be right now, and trying to keep my thoughts away from sexy times is way too hard. I'm just about to ask for a break when there's a loud knock at the door. Donnie freezes, and then the door burst open, and Casey and Cameron appear.

"Hey Don, you wanna come..."

Casey trails off, staring at me with flaming eyes. I'm so damned embarrassed, but I don't want to move in case I fuck things up for Donnie.

"I'm busy," Donnie says, moving to stand between his brothers and me.

"So we can see," Cameron says. Neither of them moves, and their eyes move over my naked flesh like real physical strokes. There are only three brothers I haven't had sex with, and two of them look like they want to ravish me where I lay. Wonder if Donnie would want to paint that?

I almost laugh, but I manage to hold it in. The whole situation in this house is ridiculous.

"So, you wanna leave us to it?" Donnie asks, looking pointedly at the door.

"Not really, but I guess that four's company today," Casey laughs.

"That's not what I've heard," Cameron laughs. "Four's pretty magic, isn't it, Laura?"

What do they want me to say? 'Yeah, fucking three of your brothers at a time is pretty damned fantastic.' It'd be the truth.

"Well, we're busy right now, and I don't want to mess this up."

The twins walk over to look at the canvas. There are whistles of appreciation. "This is fucking amazing," one of them says. "One of your best," the other adds. It's hard to work out who is who just from their voices.

Casey comes back into view. "How much do you want for this?" he asks Donnie.

"It's not finished yet."

"When it is?"

"I don't know. . .I'm not sure I'm going to sell it."

"Planning on keeping it for yourself," Cameron asks. "I can understand why you would."

"I don't think I'd get any work done if that was on my wall," Casey says.

"It's not porn." Donnie sounds deflated, and I look at him worriedly.

Cameron slaps him on the back. "No, it isn't, brother. It's amazing."

"We'll get out of your hair then," Casey says.

Donnie turns to me, I assume to check I'm still in position, and when he does, his eyes widen.

"Stay where you are," he says to his brothers.

Casey and Cameron look confused. "What is it?"

"Her aura. It's changed since you came into the room. I've never seen anything like it."

"You want us to stay so you can paint her aura?"

Donnie nods and waves them to a sofa that's close

to where I'm lying. I'll have a good view of them both if they sit there, and they'll have front seat tickets to the show between my legs. I close my eyes, my pussy clamping down as though it's hungry. My clit is burning again, hot and begging to be touched. There is no way I'm going to be able to pose for this painting with them sitting right there and not start to show signs of arousal. It's impossible.

"I'm not sure that's a good idea," I say quickly.

"Please," Donnie pleads. He looks desperate, as though everything he's ever painted would mean nothing if he didn't get to finish this composition. I don't want to say yes, but I don't think I can say no.

I close my eyes again and take a deep breath. Before I answer, Donnie is thanking me and ushering Cameron and Casey to where he wants them to sit. I keep my eyes closed, trying to hold the position that Donnie arranged me into, legs apart for three sets of eyes to see.

"Open your eyes," Donnie says. "I need to see them."

I do, glancing over at him as his gaze roams over me once more, and he then disappears behind the canvas. My eyes dart to where Casey and Cameron are both sitting like mirror images of each other, legs spread, reclining with matching smiles on their faces.

"Donnie, you're going to owe us, man," Cameron says.

"Yeah," Casey agrees. "I mean, sitting looking at a half-naked woman for a few hours is hard work."

"Shhh." Donnie's brush appears over the top of the canvas as though he's a conductor ordering silence from the orchestra.

Cameron chuckles and nudges his brother in the ribs. "Don't disturb the master."

The room goes silent except for the gentle sounds of breathing and the scratching sliding sounds of Donnie's brushes. I try not to look at the twins, but I can feel their eyes on me. I can feel their gaze between my legs, stroking, stroking, stroking. I feel dizzy, knowing they can see my pussy and imagine what they are thinking. They know what I did with their brothers. They know my pussy's been fucked by seven of their brothers in so few days that I don't feel comfortable even admitting to myself. They know that there are only three brothers to go, and they're sitting close enough that if they reached out, they could caress my skin. They could pinch my nipples and stroke their fingers between my labia. They could get on their knees and put their faces between my legs, taking it in turns to taste me, bringing me closer and closer...

. . .oh god. I shouldn't be thinking these things. My legs have flopped open wider as though my body is searching for the reality of my fantasy. I stay staring ahead until I can't anymore. My eyes flick to Casey, and he's looking directly at me, fire in his eyes and amusement, too. This is all a big game to him.

"This is great," Donnie enthuses, drawing both of our attention. "Just keep as still as you can."

"Most of Laura is really still," Cameron says.

"Just her eyes and her pussy can't stop moving." Casey chuckles darkly, and I can feel the rush of blood to my cheeks and between my legs at his words.

He's right. My pussy clenches again, and I feel it, a trickle of my arousal slipping between the cheeks of my ass.

"Fuck," Casey mutters.

He nudges his brother, who also notices and swears under his breath. Only Donnie seems oblivious to my predicament.

"You nearly done, brother?" Casey asks Donnie.

"Nearly. Why? You hungry?"

"Yeah," Cameron answers. "Fucking starving."

"Me, too," Casey says, and I'm getting the feeling they aren't talking about eating fried chicken.

Fuck. How did I get myself into this situation?

Saying yes to Donnie, that's how.

Art is one thing, but what my body needs has nothing to do with art, and what's on those boys' minds doesn't either.

I'm tired of arguing with myself about the rightness and wrongness of everything that has happened over the past few days. The first night with Grant was a big step, and again with Ford and Donnie, but everything since has felt so natural.

Is it weird to trust a man because you trust his brother?

Apples never fall far from the tree, at least, that's the saying.

I'm not sure any of the McGregor boys are like what I've seen of their father, but they all have a central core of something honorable and good that makes me feel more than comfortable with them. Comfortable enough to imagine Cameron dropping to his knees so that he could press his face between my legs. Comfortable enough to imagine Casey pulling away the slip of fabric that is covering the rest of my body and worshiping me with his mouth too. Comfortable enough to do all this while Donnie watches.

Am I crazy?

I know I couldn't explain any of this to my friends. I couldn't explain any of this to anyone with a hope of them understanding, but I don't know if that matters to me anymore. What we do together in the privacy of this home is no one else's business.

I look up at the two gorgeous men who are currently staring at my pussy as though it holds the secrets of the universe, and I feel womanly and powerful. I feel curvy and sexy, and desirable. Isn't this what every woman wants to feel?

I drop my legs open a little more, giving them a better view of how aroused I am. Casey's eyes flick to mine, and he smiles like a wolf. The crookedness of his boxer's nose gives a roughness to his perfect appearance that I like a lot. His big, strong hands flex in his lap as though he's imagining using them to touch me, and I have to smile back. Maybe he's getting the urge to punch something with frustration.

I look across to Cameron, and he's smiling in a

similar wolfish way. God, these McGregor men drive me crazy.

For a moment, I close my eyes and breathe deeply. I feel as though I should be saying thank you to whatever higher power has sent me all of this joy and pleasure. This whole situation is almost otherworldly in its essence.

When I open my eyes, the twins move, and it's as though they have read my mind. Cameron drops to his knees, his hands going to my ankles. He stares up at me, waiting, I suppose for me to tell him to let me go. It's what I'd say if I didn't want him to touch me, but I don't say it. I want his big hands on me. I want them to slide up the backs of my calves, to take hold of my knees, and push them apart. I want him to cup the insides of my thighs and his thumb to part my labia roughly. I want his brother to drop to his knees next to me, taking my nipple into his mouth while he runs his hand over the warm skin of my belly.

It's Donnie who makes a shocked sound when he next rounds the canvas and sees a whole different pose from what he'd seen before. My eyes meet his, a wanton woman being serviced by these two hungry brothers, and I see him smile. He doesn't do what I'm expecting him to do. He's shared me before with Ford, so I imagined him coming to join us. Instead, his brush scratches the canvas again, painting this new scene; however he's interpreting it into art.

Cameron's tongue touches my clit; hot and warm my hips jump at the sensation.

He licks me as though my taste is as good as his favorite dessert, and his brother matches him stroke for stroke as he kisses me deeply. I don't know what I'm expecting from Casey and Cameron. Each of the McGregor brothers has had his own style when it comes to fucking, and they are no exception. There's a gruffness about their touch that is new; fierce ownership of my body that flicks a switch in my head.

"Don't move," Donnie says.

"You're not gonna direct the sex, Donnie," Cameron says from between my legs.

"Maybe he should," Casey laughs against my nipple. "I'd like to hear how Donnie would get us to transform Laura's aura."

"Mmm." Cameron's lips vibrate against my clit, and I have to moan.

"Fuck her on the sofa," Donnie says. He's already grabbing a large sketch pad, inspiration taking over.

"Now that could be interesting," Casey says. He stands, still fully clothed, and reaches to take my hand. My legs are weak, but I manage to get to my feet at the same time as Cameron.

"Cameron, you sit," Donnie says.

Cameron starts to tug off his clothes, tossing them on the floor and taking a seat on the blue velvet, his cock a tower of arousal between his legs.

"Laura, you sit on Cameron, facing me," Donnie instructs.

Wow. That would be a new position for me, but I'm

interested in trying it. The size of Cameron's cock is daunting, though.

As though seeing my hesitation, Cameron smiles. "Casey will help you."

Casey takes my hand and leads me to his brother, giving me support while I settle myself into Cameron's lap. The head of his cock is so wide, but I'm so wet and open from all the previous sex that it doesn't take a lot for me to slide down on him. God, the stretch is amazing.

"Fuck," Cameron mutters as I bring my feet up to rest on the edge of the sofa, spreading myself open. I look down to see where we are joined, and it looks so explicit that I almost come. Across the room, Donnie is slumped on a chair with the pad on his knee, sketching fast. Casey kneels in front of the sofa, his fingers finding my clit.

Cameron's hands clasp my sides, helping to ease me up and down as Casey teases my pussy. The feeling of so many hands and so many eyes on me sends me into a frenzy. I'm desperate to come. Desperate to let go of all of this tension. I look down at Casey, and he grins at me. "That's it, girl. That's perfect. Just keep moving like that, and we'll make you come."

His finger strokes through my labia, slipping around the outside of my clit, teasing until I'm almost ready to shout at him for it. Then he leans in and licks and I'm finished.

"Fuuckk." My voice is strained, my back arched as

Cameron keeps me moving through my orgasm. I've no control over my legs now. I'm just a wrung-out rag doll being used by the man beneath me. His cock swells, and it's sweet torture to my engorged pussy. I can feel him getting closer, his fingers digging into my flesh harder and his movements more demanding. Then he lifts me off his cock and tugs my body against his. His chest is heaving against my back, skin hot and deliciously sweaty. He groans deeply, and when I look between my legs, his cock is dripping with his come. Fuck, that is sexy as hell.

Casey stands and sits next to his brother. "You gonna come sit on my knee too?" he asks.

I don't think that Cameron will let me go because his grip is so fierce, but after a few seconds, he releases me to scramble over to Casey. This time I sit facing the twin that I'm going to fuck. His eyes are wickedly bright, as though the devil has taken root inside him, driving him to do these things that are so forbidden. His fingers probe between my legs, finding me slippery wet. He takes his cock by the root and runs the slick head of it over my clit and between my labia, teasing at my entrance but never pushing inside. I lean down to kiss his mouth and relish the slip of his tongue over mine. When he's teased me until I'm trembling, he grabs my hips and pulls me onto his cock, stretching me open again. He's so deep inside me that I can grind my clit against him with every roll of my hips. Cameron's hand comes out to stroke my nipple, worrying it between his thumb and forefinger so that my head drops back with the sensation.

I'm lost in what we're doing—a different woman from the girl who came to this house a few days ago. The pleasure of being with these amazing men has transformed me, and it's glorious. I let go of all my worries, all my inhibitions, and ride Casey like he's the last man in the world. Gripping the back of the sofa, I lean into him, resting my face against his neck and inhaling his scent. He smells so good, like the ocean on a summer's day. His hand comes up to grip my hair, the other hand tugging my hips against him in a punishing rhythm. I want to let go again, but I don't think I can. My body is wrung out, my mind frazzled from what's come before.

"You're so fucking sexy," Casey groans in my ear. "Your pussy feels so damn good."

"Mmm..." I moan, his words sending shivers through my body.

Cameron's hands slide down my back, cupping my ass and gripping hard. "That's it, Laura. Fuck my brother. Make him come in that tight, wet pussy."

I move faster, grinding harder, rolling my hips until I'm a panting, sweaty mess of a girl.

"Shit," Casey gasps, his grip on my hair tightening so that I have to arch my back. There's a second where I think he's going to come inside me, his cock swelling and pulsing with arousal, but then he lifts me and tugs me against his body, just as his twin did, groaning with his orgasm.

Damn.

That. Was. Hot.

"Fuck," Donnie mutters from the other side of the room.

"You get all that?" Cameron laughs. "Or was doll-face here moving too fast for your pencil."

"I'm good with moving objects," Donnie says, smiling. "It adds to the dynamics of the composition."

"Glad we added to your dynamics," Casey laughs, kissing my cheek and patting my ass. "Fuck Laura, that was something else."

I blush, closing my eyes and letting Casey and Cameron stroke and pet me while I catch my breath. We're chatting and laughing when there's a sound from outside the room. Casey pulls me against him protectively, just as the door handle begins to turn. Donnie leaps up, but there isn't time to stop whoever is entering the room while we're in such a compromising position.

I don't recognize this man. He's wearing similar smart clothes to the other staff I've seen so I assume he's employed by the family.

"Mr. McGregor," he says, as Donnie finally gets in front of him and grabs the door, trying to force it back.

"This isn't a good time, Brian," he says. "You should have knocked."

"I did, Sir. Maybe you didn't hear," Brian says.

Cameron throws a blanket over us all, but I'm still straddling Casey, and our clothes are strewn all over the place. Brian tilts his head to the side, and our eyes meet, his mouth turning into a grin. There's something horrible about him. Something slimy. I can't quite put my finger on it. It's not his slicked back, black hair, or his slightly crooked nose. It's his demeanor and the fact that Donnie seems not to trust him.

I look away, pretending I'm somewhere else, clutching on Casey.

Brian backs out of the door, in part because Donnie is using his body as a way to usher him out. "You'll have to come back later," Donnie says.

"Of course, Sir."

The click of the door and the slide of the lock let me know it's okay to move.

"Shit," Cameron says. "That asshole shouldn't be bursting into our private rooms like that. I'll speak to Dad about it."

"I'm sure it's nothing," Donnie says. "Brian's been with us for years. I'm sorry about that, Laura. I wasn't expecting anyone. It's usually so quiet up here."

"Just my luck," I say, rolling my eyes.

"I think we should all get dressed," Casey says.

"Yeah. I need to get dinner," Donnie says.

As though it's heard mention of food, my stomach rumbles noisily.

"Think you better take Laura, too," Casey laughs. "Her belly is definitely not happy,"

I stand up, taking the blanket with me. Cameron and Casey are both naked on the sofa, opposite hands cupping their almost identical cocks. It's an image that will keep me warm on my coldest future nights and one that makes me blush despite what we've all just done together.

I find my top first and tug that over my head. My panties are tangled up so I have to work them free from my leggings. I can hear Donnie cleaning his brushes and the twins getting dressed too. When I'm decent, I take a look at what he's painted and sketched.

Wow.

The canvas is stunning. I was not expecting what he's produced and can totally see what Casey and Cameron were saying. It's not just art. There's something primal and sexual about it. The way he's used red and orange and the undulation of the fabric. He's painted my labia in so much detail that I blush.

"It's...very..."

"I know," Donnie says. "Not my usual style, but I have to go where my brush takes me. Sometimes it's to places I wasn't expecting."

"Can you sell this kind of art?" I ask. "Surely no one is comfortable having such explicit pieces hanging in their home or office."

"You'd be surprised. There's a real market for sexualized art, especially among rich, over-fifties men."

"That wouldn't surprise me."

Donnie shakes his head. "But I'm not going to sell it."

"Why?" I ask, feeling more than a little relieved that this will remain in his private collection.

"Because it's you. I just don't like the idea of someone else looking at you like that."

I smile and put my arms around him.

"You're a very sweet man," I tell him. He hugs me back, planting a kiss on my forehead.

"You're a very sweet woman," he says.

"Not so sweet," I say. "Sweet is more innocent than me."

Donnie raises his eyebrows. "Sweetness and innocence don't necessarily go hand in hand."

I'm not sure I agree but I smile anyway and step away so that I don't get drawn into more of this discussion. The sketch pad is propped against the wall, and I pick it up and turn it to see what he's captured. Holy hell. The page is filled with small representations of me, Cameron, and Casey in various positions. They are rough but very clear and beautifully detailed in parts. I get an urge to tear the page away from the pad and fold it. These feel more invasive than the painting somehow. That was just my physical form but this. . .this is all about my actions. These show a woman very different from the one I always believed myself to be.

"I'll keep those to myself too," Donnie says.

"Please. I just. . .it's not something I'd want to leave this house."

"Let's see." Cameron ambles across the room, now fully clothed and gloriously sexy. The thought that I've just had him inside me flushes my cheeks.

"Fuck, Donnie," he says. "You better keep those to yourself. Dad would have a shit fit."

Casey's next to his brother, and he whistles lowly. "Those are..."

"Explicit," I say.

"Fucking sexy," he laughs. "I think I need to keep this. Especially after the last painting that we had a row about."

"Are you still going on about that shit?" Donnie grumbles. "I didn't want to fuck your girlfriend."

"I know that. You just should have asked before you sketched her with her legs open."

Donnie sighs. "You know that I get carried away."

"Enough." Cameron slaps both his brothers on the back. "No point in dwelling in the past when we have the present to enjoy." He throws his arm around my shoulder and tugs me against his chest, planting an enthusiastic kiss on the top of my head. "And we need to go," he says to his twin. "We have to sort out the trucks for tomorrow."

Casey turns and strokes my hair, kissing my lips gently. "Dad was right," he said. "I really think that we can make this work."

"Me, too," Cameron says.

"Me three," Donnie agrees. I blush, and they laugh. "You're blushing now, after all that kinky sex."

I cover my cheeks. "I just. . .it's a lot to take in."

"There's no hurry," Casey says. "You take your time, and we'll be here any time you feel ready to have us again."

The corridor is empty as we head to eat. The twins say goodbye at the foot of the stairs, and then it's just Donnie and me. I think we're going to a dining room, but it turns out that it's not a big family dinner evening. Donnie takes me through to a more relaxed room that reminds me a bit of a sports bar. There's a long wooden table, but it's rustic and chunky. The chairs have plaid cushions, and the walls are wood-paneled. There's a large TV on the wall, and there's only one other person in the room.

Aaron.

My least favorite brother, I think, then I immediately feel guilty. It's not in my nature to be judgmental unless someone has really proven themselves to be bad and Aaron hasn't yet.

He's eating a burger and turns when he hears the door.

"Hey," he says. "I hate eating alone. Don't know where everyone else is."

"It's late. You know those guys always stuff their faces as soon as they can."

"Yeah. And Dad's dragged Ford and some of the others to look at a potential new site."

Donnie pulls up a chair across from Aaron and slumps down. I choose one next to him and take a seat, too. A guy dressed in slacks, a white shirt, and a vest enters the room.

"Hey, Brandon," Donnie says. "I'll take a burger, too. Is that okay with you, Laura?" It looks totally delicious, so I nod.

"Can I have a salad instead of fries, though?"

Brandon nods. "And drinks."

"Water for me," Donnie says.

I agree, and just like that, Brandon disappears.

"How did he know we were here?" I ask.

"There's a sensor on the door that buzzes the kitchen."

"Wow." I seriously don't think I'll ever get used to this new way of living, although I have to say that I'm completely sold on the no cooking and cleaning up for now.

"So," Aaron says, resting his half-eaten burger on the plate and patting his mouth clean. "How did you enjoy the cabin?"

His eyes sparkle as though he knows exactly how much I enjoyed my stay with Ford, Donnie, and his twin. I'm just pondering on whether Antony seems like the kind to kiss and tell when Donnie laughs.

"You're just pissed that Antony beat you to it."

Aaron's cheeks flush pink, and I put up my hand to object.

"It's not a frickin' race," I say. "How many times am I going to have to say that?"

"Probably a lot of times," Donnie says. "Ten brothers means ten times the competitiveness."

"Well, you guys just need to get over yourselves," I say.

I watch as Aaron's eyes flash, getting the distinct feeling that he likes a bit of sass but only in so much as he'd like to crush it out of me. Just like his father, I'm assuming.

"Or maybe you need to get used to it," he says, confirming my suspicions.

"I don't think so," I say. "As I said to your brothers, bickering is not sexy."

Aaron grins. "Yeah, I heard you popped Blake's cherry. Well done you."

Ugh. That is one horrible description of what was actually some seriously intense and caring sex. I don't take kindly to being likened to a dirty man only interested in taking someone's virginity.

Donnie stares at me with interest, making it obvious he hadn't heard yet. It seems Aaron is number one in the gossip brigade.

"Kissing and telling is as childish as bickering. I thought gossiping was reserved for old women."

There's a bang behind me, and Brandon is there with a large tray holding our food. The waft of grilled meat fills the room. I've really worked up an appetite.

Aaron's almost glaring at me now, and I struggle to hold down my glee. There is something really satisfying about poking the bear! He wipes his hands on his napkin and throws it on the table. "I'm sorry you feel that way," he says.

"Are you?" I ask, picking a chip off Donnie's plate and popping it into my mouth. Donnie is watching our conversation like a game of table tennis, head switching back and forth, expression amused.

"Not really," Aaron says. "I'm just fascinated how against all this you were initially but how fast my brothers seem to be bringing you around."

"Some faster than others," I say, taking a big bite of my burger. I know there is relish at the corner of my mouth, but I decide not to rush to wipe it. Aaron eyes it with annoyance. He's always so pristine, so my lack of care about it is probably driving him mad. At least, I hope it is.

"Yes," he says slowly.

"And you're making a very big assumption, Aaron," I say, raising my eyebrows.

He leans back in his chair, folding his arms, the classic defensive move. "And what assumption would that be?"

"That any of my actions have anything to do with your father's ridiculous plan."

I can see he wasn't expecting that at all. It's as though they have some kind of wall chart and are counting themselves down until they hit ten, and it's Christmas. What they haven't considered is that although I find myself liking more of them enough to get intimate, I'm still completely uncertain about where it's all going to lead. Especially as Aaron seems to be impossible to like and me accepting only nine would not suit Roderick at all. It's ten or nothing, and smug-pants over there doesn't seem to realize that it's his arrogance that might fuck it all up for everyone.

"Oh, so you're just passing the time, working through my family." His eyes are filled with a challenge, and his words definitely rile me. I'd rather they didn't. I wish I had tough skin or was more sure of myself and my own actions.

"Aaron," Donnie says in a warning tone. "I don't think this is helping any."

Aaron glances at his brother, a flicker of understanding passing over his face. He turns to his burger, and his nostrils flare.

"I think I'm done here," he says, moving to stand. "Enjoy your food."

And with that, he leaves the room.

Donnie turns to me and shrugs. "I love my brothers, but some of them are easier to get on with than others."

"I know what you mean," I say. "Aaron doesn't seem to like me at all."

Donnie stuffs a chip in his mouth and chews thoughtfully. "I don't think it's that. In fact, I think it might just be the opposite."

I frown, putting my fork down. "What do you mean?"

"Well, you know how at school, sometimes boys are mean to girls."

"Yeah. That was the story of my life."

"Well, some of the time, it's because they like them and want to be friends but just don't know how."

I shake my head. "You're excusing the pigtail pulling, Donnie? The thing is, Aaron isn't a kid, and I don't have pigtails."

"But that doesn't mean he doesn't like you."

"This is so stupid and juvenile," I say. "Society needs to get over excusing men for being mean to women with this shit."

Donnie reaches out and squeezes my arm. "I'm not excusing him. That's why I warned him off. I'm just telling you that I know my brother, and he's just frustrated that he's one of the last."

"The last," I say, realizing that I've actually managed to be with nine out of the ten McGregor brothers in such a short space of time.

"He doesn't know that yet. Look, Aaron's a people pleaser. He's always been that way. He tries the hardest to make my dad happy, and my dad can be a real ass to him. It's like he sees it as weakness."

"Your dad's a real ass," I say to Donnie. "With all due respect."

"He can be," Donnie says. "But he's my dad, and I love him for all his good parts."

I study the man in front of me, feeling such warmth in my heart for all his good parts, too. He's forgiving and open, kind and reassuring. He has all the things I never realized were important to me and so much more.

He smiles at me. "Your aura just went a very pretty pink." My cheeks flush a color that probably matches. "All I'm saying is that you should give Aaron a chance. He's a good man who sometimes forgets himself. I think you'd be good for him because you won't stand for his shit. He needs that."

I shake my head and sigh. "You McGregors are just too much for me to take on board."

"I think you're doing just fine," he says with a grin. "Dad was right."

Chapter 23

I don't see my mom that night. I was expecting her to come and find me for a conversation at least, but she doesn't. After the confrontation with Roderick, I'm worried that she's mad at me. I'm kind of mad at her, too for setting me up into this situation in the first place. I get a pretty decent night's sleep, ignoring a couple of knocks on my door because I was in the bath, trying to soak some sense into myself.

The next morning, Danna is there to pick me up.

Bless her.

I didn't say much over messenger last night, so I think she's ready to explode with curiosity.

"What the hell," Danna says when I've jumped into her car and slammed the door. "What kind of friend are you, keeping me hanging like that. What happened when I left?"

"You don't even want to know," I tell her.

"Oh yes I do," she says. "Of course I do. What did Roderick mean when he said that you're rejecting his family? You've just moved in. You haven't told your mom you don't want her to marry him, have you?"

"No," I say. "Although I am seriously considering asking her what the fuck she sees in him. This is fucking ridiculous. How rude was he? He practically knocked you down and didn't say sorry. Then he leaves you standing there while he tells me off like a five-year-old."

Danna puts the car into drive, and we're off. "Yeah, his tone did leave a lot to be desired."

"I don't think he's picked me out as a special case, though," I say. "He's hideously rude to his sons as well."

"Well, I supposed he's had to get used to keeping them in line. Imagine what it was like raising ten boys. He was probably like an army general just to keep order."

I didn't think of that, but he must see that he needs to tone it down now even if that was the case. I mean, we are all adults. All his sons are qualified and working full time. The days of running this house like a military operation are over. But maybe that's the problem. He's used to being in charge, and now he's struggling to adapt to his new role in this situation. I suppose all parents stay in positions of authority with their kids, but it has to move to adult communication at some point; otherwise, how will his sons ever have the chance to think for themselves. Family might be everything, but sometimes it can be toxic when, instead of helping you to learn to fly, your parents start to try and clip your wings.

"So why does he think you're rejecting his family? Did something happen this weekend? Is that why you went off with Ford?"

"He was just very rude," I say. "And I didn't like it. He made me feel really uncomfortable."

"After he went to all that trouble to decorate your bedroom like a princess palace?"

I shrug. "Yeah."

"And I guess he has no idea about what happened with Ford?"

"I don't know," I say, although I'm guessing he knows everything because his top spy, Aaron, was at the cabin.

"What about Donnie? You have to tell me about Donnie."

Do I? And if I do, where does it stop. Do I tell her the whole truth about the crazy plan?

I can't just sit here like a mute while I decide. Danna is glancing at me, waiting for the gossip. Eventually, she gets sick of waiting.

"Spill, Laura. That boy knew about your birthmark."

"Did you ever think that maybe Ford told him about it?"

"Not really," she says. "And you know why? Because you turned beet-red when you saw that painting. And you ran out of that studio like someone had stuck a red hot poker up your butt."

I guess my bestie knows me too well. If I value my friendship with Danna, which I do, I can't lie. She's my rock, through thick and thin, and I'm just going to have to put aside all my fears of judgment and exposure and face the music. To be honest, I need her counsel. This whole situation has me reeling, and now mom is in Roderick's corner. I don't have anyone else to turn to.

But where to start.

"Roderick wants me to marry all his sons," I blurt out. I might as well start at the beginning. Danna's face is a picture, even from the side.

"What?" She turns to look at me, ignoring the road, and I wave my hands to tell her to focus.

"That's what I was angry about. It's why I went to the cabin with Ford. . .to get away from Roderick's crazy."

She shakes her head in disbelief, and I see it reflected back at me the way I must have looked when I found out about the plan. "What?" she says again, as though she isn't registering anything I'm saying.

"I wasn't supposed to find out this early on. I overheard a conversation on Friday when I moved in and..." I hesitate because there is so much to tell her and I'm wondering how best to go about it. "I hurt my leg, and Grant kind of rescued me. . .and then one thing led to another and..."

"Grant?" Danna squeaks.

"Yeah. . .and then it all got a bit nasty over breakfast, and Ford offered to take me away for the weekend."

"So you went, and one thing led to another?"

"Yeah. . .and Donnie was there and some of the other brothers..."

"Other brothers?"

"And one thing led to another?" Danna's eyes look like they are about to bulge out of her head.

"Kind of."

There's a pause while I recover from discussing one of the most mortifyingly embarrassing things I've ever had to admit to, and Danna recovers from hearing more dirt from me than she's heard since we became friends in total.

"How many, Laura, you lucky bitch?" she asks. The grin that lights up her face is so full of wickedness I burst out laughing. "How many?" she says again.

"Nine," I say.

"NINE!" Her hands start jittering on the steering wheel, unable to contain her glee at my promiscuity! "NINE!"

"Shhh," I hiss even though there's no one around to hear us. We're still on route to campus, so at least I can be sure there are no rogue ears catching this.

"Oh. My. . .at the same time?"

"NO!" I scoff, although I have no idea why I'm being so self-righteous. The multiples are still pretty mind-blowing. I put my hand up to stop any further excla-mations. "I know. It's completely crazy and totally out of character for me. I don't know what's gotten into me."

"Nine McGregor brothers, that's what," she laughs. "How the fuck did you find time to do nine?" I don't say anything, and she punches me in the shoulder. "Spill, Laura. Before I stop this car and extract it all by force."

I grip the handle on the inside of the door needing something to stabilize me while I confess the next bit.

"Ford, Grant, and Antony, I did one-on-one," I say. "But the others…"

"You had a threesome?" she squeals. "I'm so fucking jealous. You know how much I've wanted to do that."

"I do?" I gasp. I'm pretty sure that this isn't a conversation we have ever had out loud. If we had, I never would have been so cautious about telling Danna all my antics.

"Well, you know I love reading those reverse harem books."

"Reading books and having sex with more than one guy are really two completely different things," I say. "One is indulging in a little fantasy without risk, the other is. . .well a whole lot riskier."

"And a whole lot more enjoyable," she laughs.

"Yeah. It definitely had its moments."

"So what the fuck?" Danna says. "You're just working your way around these brothers testing to see if you like them."

"I didn't start out that way," I tell her. "When I overheard what they were thinking, I was shocked and disgusted. I couldn't believe that my mom would go along with something like this."

"I know. It's so weird. I could understand if Roderick wanted his sons to have more than one wife but getting them to share one seems a little stingy. I mean, how on earth will you be able to satisfy all those men. . .no disrespect."

We both burst out laughing.

"I don't know. It's what I've been thinking, too. In

between the bursts of 'this is crazy' and 'I need to get out of this house before I corrupt my mortal soul'."

"Well, I wouldn't worry too much about that," Danna laughs.

"Why not?"

"Well, there was plenty of polygamy in the bible."

"Old Testament," I say. "And always one man with multiple wives."

She waves her hand as though what I'm saying doesn't hold any weight. "Anyway, Roderick is talking marriage."

"Well, that wouldn't even be legal, would it?"

"I guess not in the official sense, but maybe he has an idea of a kind of binding contract."

"I didn't even think about that," I say. "It's all way too crazy."

"Yeah. So crazy you're almost done working your way through them!" I give Danna the side-eye, and she laughs. "Who's the poor bastard you haven't slept with?"

"Aaron," I say. "He's a bit too much like his dad for my liking."

Danna rolls her eyes. "Well, you must be seriously considering Roderick's plan; otherwise, what the hell are you doing?"

I shake my head and sigh. "I don't know. With Grant, it was pure attraction. He was so kind to me, and he wasn't up for going along with what his dad wanted. . .and he's so frickin' gorgeous."

"They all are!"

"I know. That's kind of my problem."

"So Grant isn't going along with this."

I shake my head. "At least, that's what he said."

"Could have just been talking to get into your panties," she laughs. "Guys will say anything."

I stare out of the window, wondering if she's right. I don't think she is. Grant definitely didn't seem like the type to lie, and when we chilled out with him in the den, he just seemed withdrawn. "I don't think so, Danna."

"You sound disappointed. Nine potential men not enough for you?"

"it's not that. It's. . .well. . .I don't know. I like him, and I think it was a be-with-him-and-not-the-rest kind of arrangement. I don't think he'll be interested now."

"Do you think he's angry at what you've done with the other eight?"

"I don't know," I say. "To be honest, he could just think that I'm full of shit. I said all this stuff, and then I've gone and done the complete opposite."

"Maybe, but you won't know until you speak to him, will you?"

"I guess."

We're turning into campus now, and I don't want to carry on this conversation anymore. My heart feels heavy thinking that Grant might be disappointed in me.

"What are you planning, hon?" Danna asks me

gently. "It's not gonna get any less crazy if you stay living there, is it? You seem to have gotten yourself into a bit of a pickle."

"I have," I say. "On Saturday, I was going to call you and ask if I could crash at yours, but I didn't know how to explain what was going on, and then Ford gave me a way out."

Danna pulls the car into the lot and parks up. She turns to me and puts her arm around me. "I wish you had, Laura. You know my parents would welcome you with open arms. I think Ford's way out turned more into a 'shove back in.'"

I nod because she's right. I'm now right smack bang in the middle of this thing, and it seems to have a life of its own. I think back to how I felt on when I heard about the plan, before any of these infuriatingly amazing McGregor brothers had had a chance to get under my skin and between my legs. Getting out of their house was my top priority. It was my first instinct. Maybe it still should be. Staying there isn't going to give me any perspective. I'm only going to spend more time with these boys, and they are going to worm their way into my mind and my heart. I'm going to end up with no choice at all, and that isn't good.

Suppose I give myself some distance. If I let myself get clear on how I'm feeling and more in touch with reality, then I'll be able to trust whatever decision I might make.

"You're seriously thinking about walking away from all this?" she asks, sounding surprised.

I nod, and she pulls away, patting my arm. "You heard Roderick. The way he talks to me is awful. The way he's bullying his sons into this ridiculous situation is terrible. Although most of them seem really keen to go along with the plan, I'm never going to know if they really would have wanted this if they had a choice. I need to know that they are following their own free will rather than being pushed around by their megalomaniac father. I need to know that they'll choose me despite what they will inherit as a result. Things have gotten too crazy, and I'm not happy that this is the right thing for any of us. I really like boys that I've met and had a chance to spend time with but..."

". . .you think this is all too out there for you?"

"Exactly. I feel like I've been pulled into a parallel universe." I run my hands over my face, feeling so unsure. "What would you do?" I ask her.

"Fuck them all," Danna says with a leering grin. "I mean, you've seen them, haven't you? You've practically achieved the unachievable!"

We both laugh, but when that laughter subsides, I ask her the same question again. "Seriously, Danna."

"I think the very fact that you are asking me that question should tell you that you have more reservations about all of this that you should be feeling."

"You're right," I say.

"It happens," she laughs.

"So, I guess I'm gonna need to get some things," I say even as my heart starts to feel blue.

"Yep, and I'll drive you to safety in my beaten-up Toyota for a life of dreary work and marriage to one mediocre dude."

"You're not exactly selling it, Danna," I laugh.

"There might be some chocolate cheesecake thrown into the bargain. My mom was busy making one last night."

I force a tight smile because Danna's mom makes the best desserts. "Well, that seals it," I say even as I feel like I want to cry. "Now, all I've got to do is get through today and find a way to leave with my head held high."

But in my mind, all I can think is that walking away might be the biggest mistake I ever make.

Chapter 24

I make it through my two morning lectures, spending more time thinking about the McGregor brothers than what the lecturers are actually talking about. A complete waste of my time.

This is not good.

I value my education, and I don't need anything or anyone coming along to mess things up for me.

After the second lecture, Danna and I gather up our things so that we can head to the coffee shop. I need caffeine, and Danna's stomach has been rumbling for over thirty minutes because she missed breakfast.

"God, that was dry," Danna says. "I mean, seriously, can they not find someone to teach us who has some life and enthusiasm."

"I know," I say. "That last half hour was awful."

"You looked pretty engrossed," she said.

I shake my head, throwing my bag onto my shoulder. "My mind was elsewhere."

Danna laughs. "I bet it was. My mind would have been there too if I'd had the week that you've had."

I'm blushing as we leave the lecture room, stepping into a hallway that's so busy we are almost pulled over by the throng of students. It's crazy how busy this building gets. We all spill outside, and I wait for

Danna, who's a little behind me. As she emerges, I see another student pointing in my direction and laughing. His friends all look over and laugh, too. I turn around to see if there is someone standing behind me, but there isn't.

Ugh. I hate this kind of thing. I don't know what age you have to get to in life when people can just get past the ridiculous immaturity and just focus on their own shit.

"What is it?" Danna asks, seeing my odd expression.

"Those idiots over there just pointed and laughed at me."

"Ah, just ignore them," she says. "One of them probably likes you, and they are just taking the mickey out of him. You know how lame guys can be."

We begin walking in the direction of the coffee shop, and out of the corner of my eye, I see someone else looking in my direction and then laughing with their friend. I shake my head, feeling like I'm developing some kind of weird paranoia. Then Connor steps in front of us, blocking our way.

"Fuck off, Connor," Danna barks at him. Theirs is definitely a hate/hate relationship, although today I wonder if Connor might actually like Danna. Donnie and his strange ideas about men with crushes.

"You know, I would never have thought it," Connor says with a leering grin. "If I had to guess which of you would be into the dirtiest sex, I'd have said you." He points at Danna, and she grabs his finger as though she wants to snap it off.

"Keep your fucked up opinions to yourself," she says as he snatches his hand away.

"Maybe your friend should have kept her fucking to herself, too." He stares right at me and raises his eyebrows, and immediately, my heart flips with panic. What is he talking about?

"What the fuck are you talking about, Connor?" Danna steps right up to shout in his face, and he takes a step back, holding his hands out by his sides.

"Haven't you seen the news today?" he asks smugly. "There's a sordid sex scandal all over the gossip pages. That family, the McGregors, and your friend here."

"What?" Danna hisses, glancing back at me. I feel as though all the blood has drained from my body. My legs feel like jello.

Sex scandal.

My hands are fumbling as they reach into my purse to seek out my phone, typing McGregor into Google. Surely this is some kind of mistake.

But, as Connor watches with glee, my world comes crashing down.

Chapter 25

I don't know what to do. I read the headline, 'McGregor heirs group-sex scandal', and my stomach clenches as though it wants to bring up everything I've eaten. I swipe down, and there's a shadowy picture of three figures surrounding one woman. They've blurred out the nudity, but it is still blatantly obvious what is going on.

The pool is in the background. The picture was only taken yesterday, and it's already everywhere.

My hand is shaking as I try and scroll through the article, desperate to know what Connor has already read.

A witness has come forward with evidence. It names me and my mom; Nora Winters, the fiancé of Roderick McGregor, and her daughter Laura engaging in orgies.

Orgies.

I can't swallow.

I glance around, taking in a few groups of people who are looking at phone screens and then back at me. I want the ground to swallow me and spit me out somewhere away from all these prying eyes.

As I read further, I can see that the article is not there to expose me but to bring down the McGregor construction empire. I'm really a nobody from a news perspective. Just a vessel for the McGregor boys to use. This is because Roderick built his reputation on family values. Everything about the bolded sublines is hammering the point that the McGregor sons are more interested in sordid sex than the business. Roderick has made an enemy somewhere, or maybe it's his competition who has boosted the story to epic proportions.

I look up at Danna, and she can obviously see that what Connor is saying is true.

"Fuck off," she says, pushing him in the chest and then turning to grab my arm. "Walk," she barks.

I allow her to drag me across campus as I try to read what they've said about me.

NEW STEPSISTER INVOLVED IN GROUP SEX IN PUBLIC SPACES WITHIN THE HOUSE. They mention my college, my father's name. There's a picture of me with Danna at our prom that they must have found on Facebook. Oh my god. This is worse than I could ever have imagined.

Danna doesn't deserve to be bought into this.

There's even an image of Donnie's painting of me, legs spread for the world to see, a blurred area so that it's not too explicit for the news readership.

I want to die.

Tears well in my eyes, but Danna tells me to take a deep breath. "You need to hold it together until we can get you out of here," she says. "You don't want people to see you upset, okay. Hold your head high."

Faces are turning to look at me; people are trying to work out if I'm really the girl they've been reading about, the one who's been used and abused by her stepbrothers like a fuck-toy. Nausea wells again, and I swallow hard, knowing that Danna is right.

"I don't understand," I say, my voice revealing my panic.

"Did anyone see you?" she asks.

"We were in the pool area," I say.

"It's someone on the staff," she says. "A scandal like this. . .they could have sold it for thousands."

"I don't know what to do," I say.

We're almost at the car, and she turns and grabs both of my arms. "You listen to me. You've done nothing wrong. The world might see it differently for a while, but sex isn't bad. It isn't wrong. You had a good time. They had a good time. No one was hurt. You're just going to need to lay low for a while."

"But I'm getting so behind," I say. "All that time that I had off for my leg."

"You can't worry about that now. The college might be able to send you what you need so that you can keep up. I'll give you my notes, but you need to just go home."

Home. I don't even know where that is anymore.

I look over my shoulder at the college I'm unlikely to see again for a while. This is my life being destroyed. Everything I knew is being wiped out in one go.

Roderick and his stupid plan. How did he not consider how this was going to look to the outside world, or was he planning on keeping it all a secret? Maybe he would have married me to one brother, and the rest would have shared my bed only behind closed doors.

But closed doors haven't remained closed.

He must be raging like never before over this. A trusted employee has brought his family to its knees. His precious company is going to be impacted. All his conservative friends will not take kindly to this kind of thing. My life might be damaged, but Roderick has a lot more to lose; the very thing he was trying so hard to protect could be on the verge of implosion.

Danna pulls me into a fierce hug, and I finally cannot hold the tears back anymore. They spill from my closed eyes onto her shoulder as the shame becomes overwhelming. I don't know what to do or where to go. As I draw away and swipe at my eyes, a huge truck pulls into the lot.

"I think we have company," Danna says. "Isn't that Casey's truck?"

Just as she finishes her sentence, Cameron jumps out of the passenger side. "Laura," he calls, jogging over. "You need to come with us."

I look at Danna questioningly, needing to know if she thinks this is what I should do. "You need to go and speak to your mom," she says, taking hold of my hand. "They can protect you."

"Good job they've done so far," I say.

"This isn't something they've done, honey. You can't blame them. Just get out of here and call me soon, okay. Let me know what's happening. I'll keep my mouth shut and blast anyone who dares to ask me anything about any of this."

Cameron reaches us and says hi to Danna. His expression is so worried. "You know?" he asks, seeing my tear-stained cheeks and puffy eyes. I nod, and he pulls me into a fierce hug. "We came to get you. Dad has called us all back home."

"I don't give a fuck about your dad," I say angrily. "This is all his fault."

"He knows," Cameron says. His eyes are regretful and soft, such a contrast to the toughness of his appearance. In work boots and combat pants, he's an imposing figure.

"I just. . .I don't know what to do."

"So let us figure it out," Cameron says. He takes my hand and squeezes it.

"Go," Danna urges. A few people have gathered about ten feet away, and phones are pointing in our direction. That's the last thing we need; frat boys looking to capture footage to sell.

I squeeze her hand and walk hurriedly to the truck. Cameron is close by. He rips the rear door open, and I pile in as fast as I can. Casey is in the front seat, and Aaron is next to me in the back.

Great. Just who I need to be around to see me break into a million pieces.

His face is grave, though. His usual smug expression is nowhere to be seen.

"Laura," Casey says, reaching back to squeeze my knee.

"Oh my god," I say with a quivering voice. I close my eyes, frustrated with myself. I don't want to break in front of them. I hate that this situation is bringing me so low. I feel the same sense of dread I felt when my dad left; let down, broken, humiliated, hurt. I didn't ever want to put myself in a situation like this again where all those same horrible feelings invaded my heart.

I could blame myself. I could believe that I had choices here, and what I've done is made the wrong ones and brought this on myself. I could, but I'm angry, too. Angry at the McGregors who have put me in this situation. They were supposed to take away all of mom's worries and make our lives more stable. Roderick was Mom's knight in shining armor, or at least that's what she told me, but it hasn't turned out that way.

He's the evil villain—the storybook monster. The one who sets out to ruin the princess' life, and I let him. I fell into his trap. I was tempted by his gifts and his promises and now look at me. I'm left with nothing. No honor, no reputation. No home because I can't carry on as though nothing has happened. This is a fucking disaster. I'm going to need to move state to get away from this gossip. As I think all of this, my blood boils. This is terrible, and I'm furious. "I just. . .WHAT IN THE ACTUAL FUCK!" I shout.

Aaron puts his hand out to take hold of mine, and I slap him away. "Don't touch me. How. . .how has this happened?"

"One of our staff members didn't turn up to work today," Aaron says gravely. "We think it was him who sold the story."

"But how did he know. . .?"

"I guess we aren't always as conscious of who is around us as we should be," Casey admits. He puts the truck into gear and swings it out of the lot. I grip onto the edge of the seat and reach for my phone again, starting to read the article in more detail.

"Maybe you shouldn't," Aaron says.

"Why? What are you trying to hide from me?"

"Nothing. It's just. . .I don't want to see you get more upset," he says. His voice is sincere, his eyes pleading almost, and I want to listen to him. I want to trust what he's saying and let these men protect me from whatever is going on in the outside world, but I can't. I have to know. I have to see how bad it is so that I can decide what I need to do next.

"I just need to know," I tell him.

My eyes scan the screen. This article is a little different. There's a paragraph about my time with Grant. The article mentions that Grant was the first and was devastated when I disappeared with his brothers. They paint me as a gold digger who's desperate to get my hands on the McGregor fortune and that I've cast my net wide, trying to ensnare as many brothers as I can. My hand goes to my mouth. The boys don't come off unscathed either. The article talks about past issues, like a bar brawl that Casey and Cameron had that landed them in jail for the night and a sex scandal involving Ford and two call girls in Vegas. There's an insinuation that, although I'm a gold digger, they have taken advantage of such a young girl, making me do sordid things that I could only have been induced to do by drugs or alcohol. The whole piece is filled with judgment and exaggeration.

"I just...I can't..." I say. "Has my mom seen this?"

"Yes," Aaron says. "And your dad has been at the house, too."

My dad.

I don't know whether to laugh or cry. He's been too busy to have anything to do with me, and now he appears out of the woodwork to chastise me. To rub my nose in it. I don't even know.

"Is he still there?"

"No, your mom told him to go. He wasn't exactly helping things."

"Yeah, that sounds just like my dad."

I swallow past the huge lump in my throat, still clutching my phone. The blurry picture of me on my back in the pool area is glaring back at me. "What are we going to do?" I ask. "What are you going to say about all this?"

Cameron turns, his jaw set in a way that makes him look completely determined. "We're going to tell the newspaper to fuck off," he says with so much malice that I get a shiver.

"Maybe not quite in those words, though," Aaron says.

"It's none of anyone else's business, is it?" Casey says with anger that matches his twins.

"That doesn't seem to have stopped it becoming everyone's business, though, does it?" I say. My voice is small and defeated, and Cameron reaches out to put his hand on my leg reassuringly.

"I guess we're used to being the focus of the gossip columns," he says. "There's always been interest in what we're doing because of how high profile our company is, but I understand it must be hard for you to deal with."

"It's not your image that's all over the news today, is it?" I say.

"No, but it's my brothers, and it's yours, and you are all people I care about very much," Casey says. "It hurts me as much to see you guys affected as if it was Cameron or me."

I nod because I appreciate what he's saying and want him to know that. They've immediately come to find me and take me to safety and that means something, even amongst all of this chaos. If they didn't care, it would have been easy for them to leave me at college to face the music alone.

I imagine what that would have been like; all those laughing people. How long before more would have been like Connor and made lewd comments? It would have been hideous.

They've saved me from that humiliation, at least.

It doesn't take long for Casey to drive us all back to the McGregor mansion. Not only are the gates firmly closed, but there are four huge security guards on the inside, and I can see why. There're two vans with reporters and cameras outside. I recognize one from the local news station. Thank goodness the windows are tinted, and I can cower behind the black glass without fear of exposure. As we pull up, the cameras are turned on us. The gates begin to open, and the security guards move to prevent anyone other than Casey's vehicle from passing through. As we draw near to the house, the door to the multi-vehicle garage opens, and we are swallowed into its safety. When Cameron brings the car to a standstill and switches off the ignition, we sit for a moment in the darkened silence.

"It'll be okay," Aaron says softly.

"I don't think so," I reply.

I'm the first to open the door—the first to want to face the music.

There's a determination in me now that comes about only when things are so bad there is no room for deliberation or procrastination.

It's time to deal with the biggest crisis of my life.

Chapter 26

By the time we get into the house, I am angry.

So damn angry that my jaw is pained with clenching, and my breathing is fast.

Before I stepped foot in this house, my life was okay. It might have been a little boring, and there were probably more days when I was short of something I needed than I would have liked, but things were good. Then I moved in with this family, and everything went to shit.

I'm angry with Roderick but especially angry with my mom. What the hell was she thinking with all of this? How could she move us in here knowing what he was planning and the impact it could have on my life.

She's just left me floundering, trying to find my feet and making a whole heap of bad decisions that have led to this.

I know these are good men, but this is wrong. So wrong. And the newspapers have ended up being judge and jury on all of my actions.

Aaron leads the way, and Casey and Cameron follow on.

We reach the den, and everyone is there.

I guess McGregor Corp is running without its management team today.

All eyes turn to us. Mom is there sitting by herself. She's perched on the edge of the sofa as though she feels like she might need to spring into action at any point. Roderick is pacing and the rest of the boys are sitting around looking at their phones or watching whatever is playing silently on the television. There are also some other people in the room who I don't recognize. A man at a desk with a large briefcase next to him and a woman in a purple dress and pink stilettos, scribbling on a pad like crazy.

"There you are," bellows Roderick. "You took your time."

"No, we didn't," Casey says frostily. "We were there and back without any delays."

Roderick glares at him, and that's enough to set me off. How dare he be lashing out right now? How dare he be chastising us for taking the time to get back here when none of this would be happening if it wasn't for him.

I stand in the middle of the room and glare at him. All eyes are on me. It's as though everyone can tell that what happens next isn't going to be pretty.

Ford stands. "Laura..." he says, taking a step towards me. I put my hand out to stop him from coming closer. I don't need his compassion or his platitudes right now. Any kindness will only break my resolve, and crying in this room full of people isn't something I'm prepared to do.

"Why are you having a go at us?" I spit. "This is all your fault."

Roderick puts his hands on his hips, and Mom stands. "This is a DISASTER," he roars. "Do you know what happened to our business today?"

"Your business?" I say incredulously. I can't believe what I'm hearing. "Do you know what's happened to my life?"

Roderick glares back at me but says nothing. I can tell he doesn't give two fucks about anything other than the money and his associated status. His fixation on it is grotesque. "Your life is not my biggest concern." His voice is cold and low. "There are people's jobs on the line here. Our whole future could be rocked because of this."

"Well, you should have thought of that before you pressured your sons into this ridiculous situation. Didn't you consider that it was going to get out sooner or later?"

"It wasn't," Roderick says. "You would have chosen one of my boys to marry officially. You could have been seen in public with just him. Everything else would have been dealt with behind closed doors."

I can't believe the naivety of this man. Everything I did with the boys was within the confines of this home. It's their home that has been infiltrated and exposed.

"Dad. This isn't helping," Aaron says. He comes to stand next to me, and glances in my direction as though he's checking it okay for him to be there. It's a surprisingly considerate gesture from someone I'd previously written off as arrogant.

"What do you want me to do? Pat you all on the back and say don't worry about the damage to everything I've worked for?"

"You've worked for?" Casey says. "What about us? Have we done nothing?"

"You know what I mean," Roderick says and waves his son off as though he's an idiot.

"No, Dad. We don't know what you mean," Ford says firmly. "We've done everything you asked of us, and now you want to scream the house down about something that wasn't in our control. We trusted our staff. Maybe that was foolish, but it's the only way when you're living in such close confines."

"Did you have to fuck out in the open like that? What if her mom had walked in?"

Barret, Blake, and Elliot stand up. "Maybe that wasn't the best choice, but we were doing what you wanted us to do," Blake says. "Sometimes, these things just happen."

"Three of you at the same time just happened," Roderick says. There's a level of disgust in his voice that I wasn't expecting.

"What did you expect?" Grant says. "That we'd be happy spending limited time with Laura one on one? That was never going to work."

"I expected you to be the gentlemen I've raised you to be."

I have to jump in at this point because I'm not prepared to hear him talk shit about his sons. They are the most amazing men who've made me feel so special each and every time. It's not an easy thing to accomplish, given the short time frame and with so many of them involved.

"Your sons are perfect gentlemen," I say. "It's you who seems to be struggling with the concept." There's a sharp intake of breath around the room. Have I stepped too far? Do I care? "Your sons have done as you asked them to do. We are human beings, not puppets. There are eleven people involved here, and you're making out as though it should be as easy as placing eleven dolls into position."

"I am not a stupid man, Laura. I know what's involved. I just expected that you'd all think about what you were doing and how you were doing it a bit more than you have."

The woman with the notepad and the platinum blonde hair puts her hand up but doesn't wait for anyone to give her permission to speak. "I think we need to stop dwelling on what's happened and start working on what needs to be done to rectify this mess."

"Sorry, who are you?" I ask.

"Cassidy Clarke. PR."

"Cassidy is here to draft the press release," Antony explains.

"And him?" I point to the corner to where Mr. Suited and Booted is shuffling papers uninterestedly."

"That's Mr. Lawson. He's the firm's Attorney."

"So, you've got the professionals in to deal with this."

"Yes. Yes, I have," Roderick says.

Cassidy holds up her hand, and everyone goes quiet. I'm secretly impressed at the way she controls the room with very little effort, especially Roderick. She might look likes she's auditioning for Office Barbie, but she's certainly got the respect of this group of challenging men.

"The papers have all positioned this in the same way. Laura's the gold digger, and your sons are the sex-obsessed men who have acted badly."

I put my hands on my hips out of sheer anger at being portrayed that way. "I am not a gold digger. You can stuff all of this. I just want my old life back."

Cassidy waves her hand again. "I am certainly not implying that there is any truth in this gutter journalism. What I'm saying is that we need to explain things in a more palatable way."

"Palatable?" my mom says.

"A way that the average American can understand."

"You think that's possible?" Mom asks.

"Anything's possible."

"Cassidy is very good," Aaron explains. I give him the side-eye because I really don't need him to be justifying her like that. I can see exactly how professional she is.

"So, what is your plan then?"

Cassidy's eyes seem to sparkle at my question. "I think we go with 'Love' at the center of this story." She puts her fingers up to add air quotes to love.

"Love?" Roderick scoffs.

"We release the real story as we create it. Laura

has fallen in love with all the McGregor brothers and them with her. We tell the world they are going to live as one big happy, faithful family."

As Cassidy says those words, my heart jumps in my chest. Love is a big word, and I'm so scared. I look around the room at the men who've become such a big part of my life in such a short space of time, and I know that each and every one of them has a piece of my heart in their hands. I know that if the world was different, I'd be ready to give them everything I am. I'd be willing to rewrite the fantasy happy ending that I had in my mind to include ten perfect men instead of just one. I'd let myself go and drift into the life that I've had a taste of over this past week at the center of this group of brothers who are so different and so perfect for me all at the same time.

But the world is just the way it has always been. Conservative. Judgmental. Built on the ideal of one man and one woman and anything that deviates from that is frowned upon.

I'm just not strong enough to be the person who stands up to challenge society's norms. I have nothing but respect for those that do, but it's too much for me. I'm just one girl, and I know that I'll come out of this the worst. Unfortunately, girls in sex scandals are seen as sluts, but men are seen as studs. It's not fair but that's just how it is.

But I'm torn because I want to be with these men. I want their kindness and their humor, their protectiveness and their affection. I want to know what it is to let my heart burst open with the love that I'm already feeling for them.

I wish that life was simpler, but there's no genie or fairy godmother here. Just a room full of people who can do nothing but try to put a Band-Aid on a gaping wound of a situation.

All eyes are on me to give this plan the go-ahead. It would mean a commitment to following through with Roderick's plan, knowing that I'll never really know if it was me or the prospect of securing their inheritance that had made the McGregor brothers so committed to making this work. I don't even know if they all are, to be honest. Grant is here, but he's not once been vocal about changing his mind.

Eventually, after I've been deliberating for what feels like an eternity, I have to answer. "We can't do that," I say softly. All the boy's eyes turn to me, expressions ranging from hurt to confused.

"Why not?" Cassidy asks.

"Because my life will be over," I say. "I won't be able to go anywhere without being laughed at. The damage to McGregor Corp. could be catastrophic. This is just too much." I put my hands over my face, trying to hide the tears that are threatening to spill.

"But I don't understand," Roderick says. "You were happy to work your way through my sons like a kid through a candy store, but not for anyone to know."

"She's ashamed," Ford says. There's hurt in his voice, and my heart feels like it might shatter into a million pieces.

"You never intended for the world to know what you had planned, did you? You're ashamed, too."

"There are ways of behaving," Roderick hisses.

"Yes, there are," my mom says. She stands and walks to me, taking my hand and holding it tightly. "And you're not behaving well, Roderick. None of this is ideal, but as Cassidy says, we need to look to the future." I stare at my mom, not really knowing what she's getting at. She's been happy to just sit back and watch this situation unfold, to take Roderick's side and standby a ridiculous plan for his sons and me. Now she's chastising him.

"What future?" I say desperately. "What organization is going to want to hire me when all I can bring is a scandal with me?"

"You're a long way from that," Mom says. "You still have to finish college, and anyway, Roderick can offer you a position in his company that would be better than anything you could find on your own."

"You know that isn't how I work," I say. "Nepotism isn't fair."

"Nepotism is part of the world," Roderick says.

I turn to him again, eyes narrowed. "You might be able to bully and blackmail your own kids into doing things, but you can't bully me."

"You think I bully and blackmail my sons?" Roderick laughs. "You think they'd be doing any of this if they didn't want to. They are men."

I shake my head, anger boiling inside me. I remember the defeated way that Donnie and Grant talked about their dreams of being an artist and vet, their passions relegated to part-time hobbies. I know Casey and Cameron wanted to fight professionally, and Elliot wanted to be a sports therapist. The others must have had dreams, too. Dreams that have been squashed by their father's demands and pressures.

I don't want that for them. I don't want to be yet another compromise that they have to make in order to meet their father's expectations.

This stops here.

"Cassidy. You need to find a way to deal with this without me. I have to leave. I'm not going to be yet another thing that Roderick forces on his sons. I'm not going to be bullied into living a life that none of them would have chosen if it wasn't for threats and repercussions."

"Laura, it's not like that. . .we want..." Ford says, but I cut him off mid-sentence with a raised hand.

"Mom, I'm going to stay with Danna for a little while. I need to work out what to do next. Maybe I'll force Dad to take some responsibility for me and transfer to a college there. Hopefully, no one will know anything about this out of state. I can have a fresh start."

"No," Mom says. "You don't have to do that, honey. I don't want you to leave."

"I know, Mom. But I can't stay here," I say. "This is your new life, and that's great. I want you to be happy, but it's not going to work for me."

I look around the room at the men who've come to mean so much to me in such a short time, and I don't know if I can really do this. Walking away is going to break my heart, but staying will ruin everything. Ford takes a step forward, but I take one back. I can't let him touch me because I know that if I do, I'm not going to be able to do what's necessary.

"This was all a big mistake," I say. "I'm sorry for any part I played in ruining your business and reputation."

I turn and walk from the room, my throat burning with tears that I cannot let fall. I can't think about the way my heart feels like it's breaking, or my body craves to be held by their strong arms. I can't think about how safe I felt with them, how worshiped and adored. I can't remember the way my body came alive when they touched me or how much pleasure they gave me. I can't recall my silly fantasies about what our lives would have been like together as one big happy family.

I can't bear the thought of never seeing the McGregor brothers again, but I will have to find a way. I need to be stronger than I've ever been before for all of our benefits.

Chapter 27

I throw what I can of my possessions in a suitcase and scribble a note out to my mom, asking her to send the rest on once I know where I'm going.

A sob catches in my throat. I'm doing this. I'm really walking away.

There's a knock on my door, and I look up from the letter, my heart thudding in my chest.

"Laura." It's a man's voice. Aaron, I think. "Can I come in?"

I don't want him to because I'm wobbly and wavering, and I just can't have him come in here to try and change my mind.

"Go away," I call. "I just need to be on my own."

The handle turns, and I stand, primed to make it very clear that this is completely out of order.

"Will you just hear me out?" he says through the gap in the door.

I grab the handle and yank it forward, finding Aaron standing in the doorway. God, the sight of him sends shivers up my spine. That dark hair and those blue eyes hit me like a sledgehammer, but I can't let those feelings overwhelm me. "There's nothing to say," I tell him.

"Are you sure?"

Honestly, I'm not, and he can tell. A tear trickles over my cheek, leaving a wet trail of despair, and Aaron is there immediately, pulling me against his chest, his big hand wiping away my tear and stroking over my hair. "It's gonna be okay," he says.

"How can you say that?" I say.

"Because we've dealt with scandal before and seen it blow over. Because we want this to work with you more than anything and are prepared to tell the world that we're not just messing around. That this is real."

To hear him say that makes me sob because I just don't know if I believe him.

How can it be real? I mean, I know how I feel in my heart, but I don't trust myself either.

The heart can be so foolish. The heart can be mis-led and corrupted. The heart can stick its head in the sand and ignore all the reasons why the way it feels is just an illusion.

"I can't," I say, pulling away. Aaron takes my hand and pulls me back. His eyes are so fierce that I can't look into them, but he takes hold of my face and forces me.

"You can, Laura. You're brave, and you're strong. Stronger than you know."

I shake my head, closing my eyes and blocking him out. He doesn't know the turmoil I'm feeling. He has no idea of the fear I have in my heart. How can any of this be real? How can I trust these men not to let me down when it's all I've ever known?

Aaron's hand strokes my face, his thumb caressing

my lips, and still, I keep my eyes closed. When his lips find mine, I'm still, but it doesn't stop him from kissing me with tenderness and longing. Tears slip from my eyes, and he kisses those, too.

"I wish I could rewind time and take this all away," he whispers against my ear, holding my head against his broad chest and stroking my hair. "I wish we'd all taken this slower and been more careful. I wish things were different."

"But they're not," I say. "And maybe that's how it's meant to be, Aaron. Maybe this is the universe showing me the way. Maybe all of this is just supposed to be something in my past."

I feel him shake his head. "If every time we faced a barrier, we were supposed to walk away, no one would ever do anything. Sometimes the path gets rocky and treacherous, but there is the greatest reward if you just persevere."

"I don't think this is about perseverance," I say. "I think this is..."

"...a mistake?" Aaron finishes, sounding crestfallen.

"I'm sorry," I tell him. "So sorry."

"No, honey. It's me that's sorry. Sorry that we started off on a bad footing. Sorry that I didn't stand up to my dad when he was acting like an ass. Sorry that I didn't get a chance to show you what we could be like together."

A sob leaves my mouth like a big well of sadness rises up inside me. I had Aaron so wrong. He's not the arrogant man I thought he was. He's so much more, and I'm sad, too. It might sound ridiculous, but I don't want him to feel as though I left him out. He's the only one who didn't get a chance to prove himself, and now it's too late.

"Please," I tell him. "Don't make this harder."

His hand stops stroking my hair. "Okay, Laura," he says softly. "I'll do whatever you need me to do."

I pull away and look up into his gorgeous eyes. "Will you take me to my friend's house?" I ask. "I was going to call a cab, but I...I don't want to spend money I'm going to need."

"Of course," he says. "I don't want you to go, but I'd rather take you than leave you in the hands of a sleazy cab driver."

"I'll meet you downstairs in ten," I say. "I just need to finish up here."

He nods and tucks a stray lock of hair behind my ear. "We could have been good," he says softly. "I know that. Maybe I'll see you next lifetime."

And just like that, my heart breaks into a million shards of sorrow.

Aaron leaves me to pack up the last of the things I'm going to take with me. I hitch my bag onto my shoulder, take hold of the hand of my wheeled suit-case and gaze around my room. It never felt like it was made for me; too young, too pink, too frivolous. A girl I never was and will never be.

My silly fantasies of a happy family, of security, seem so far away.

My hopes for my future have been washed away too.

What has happened over the past few days has the potential to follow me for a lifetime. It could tarnish every future relationship I have, affect every job I apply for, damage my reputation forever.

The internet will make sure of that. Our mistakes are immortalized for all to see.

It's time to leave everything behind.

It's time to become bullet-proof because I won't make it if I let this penetrate me.

I inhale deeply and push out my breath with a sense of defiance.

And with that, I close the door to my fantasy room and descend the stairs.

Aaron isn't alone. All the McGregor brothers are waiting by the huge wooden front door. Solemn-faced, they stand silent; defeated statues.

I didn't want it to be like this. I'm not brave enough to say goodbye, so I freeze where I am. Ten sets of eyes find me halfway down the sprawling staircase, an imposter in this place of luxury and status; Cinderella without her fairy godmother.

"Please don't do this," I say. "This is hard enough without having to say a big goodbye."

"You don't have to go," Ford says.

"Just stay," Blake adds. "We can work through this."

Aaron puts his hand up. "Don't you think I told her all of that and more? She can't, so we just have to respect that. Let her go. Make it easy because making it hard isn't going to change a thing other than hurt Laura even more than this situation has already done."

There's a moment of silence as Aaron's words sink in. I'm so grateful to him for trying to protect me, for respecting everything I've said, no matter how much he might wish things were different.

Grant is the first to raise his hand in a wave. He smiles and brings his hand to his lips, blowing me a kiss. It's so perfectly Grant.

Ford follows, then Donnie. Then there's a sea of hands raised to say goodbye.

My boys.

Ten men who are as beautiful on the inside as they are on the outside.

Ten men who've shown me what it could be like to be treated like a princess.

Ten men who I'm walking away from.

My heart doesn't want this. My heart wants me to run down these stairs and let them surround me with their strong arms and warmth, but instead, I hold my hand up and stifle the sob that is struggling to bubble to the surface.

Grant is the first to walk away, his shoulders bowed. Each of his brothers follows in a parade of men who look as resigned to their reality as I feel.

And then it's just Aaron and me. As I walk down the rest of the stairs, he watches me. When I reach him, he puts his hands into his pockets.

"I know what I just said but are you sure about this, Laura? There's still time to change your mind." I can hear that he's defeated by the flat tone of his voice, but I guess he just can't help asking one more time.

I nod and put my hand out to open the door. My conviction is so thin that I know if he asks me again, it will shatter. I need to get out of here. I need my friend to remind me of the person I was before the McGregors because getting her back is my only hope.

Aaron reaches out to take hold of my case, following me out of the door to a waiting car.

I was expecting him to drive me, but the engine is running, and there's a man in the front seat.

"Gregory is going to drive us," Aaron says, loading my luggage into the trunk, then rounding the car to open the door for me. "Just tell him where you want to go."

I slide across the soft leather seat into the luxury interior of the car, giving him Danna's address. Gregory nods, tapping it into the Sat Nav.

Aaron joins me in the back, slamming the door. The clunk of it is harsh punctuation to my departure. I gaze back at the house, wondering where my mom is. I'm glad she didn't make a scene about this. It would have made things so much harder if she did. I'm imagining that she has enough on her plate trying to deal with Roderick and the fallout from the press coverage. He's demanding enough to keep her head tied up, or maybe I'm just making excuses for her. This is her new life, and I've managed to mess it up about as badly as is possible. What's happened is likely to put a huge cloud over her upcoming wedding.

At least I know that I'm not totally to blame. If Roderick hadn't have come up with this idea and mom hadn't have sanctioned it, there is no way it would have been something I would have come up with myself.

I tap out a message to mom, feeling that the note I've left isn't enough. She responds immediately with a 'sad-face emoji' and a promise to call me later. She tells me she's wired me some money, so I don't have to worry about anything. How things have changed.

It's too little too late but weight off my shoulders nonetheless.

The drive is so smooth, and Aaron doesn't seem to know what to say, so we sit in silence for a while. After about five minutes, he takes hold of my hand, and we sit like that for the rest of the journey. Each mile weakens my conviction. Every stroke of his thumb against my skin makes me want to tell Gregory to turn the car around, but as we pull up outside Danna's house, I know that I'm doing the right thing.

Chapter 28

I've messaged Danna to let her know that I'm on my way, and she's standing in the doorway as we pull up in front of her parent's house. I don't think I could be happier to see her than I am right now. My friend feels like normality. This house that I've spent so much time in growing up feels more like home than anywhere else I could go. It makes saying goodbye to Aaron easier because I catch him glancing at her, so he's conscious that she's there.

"You need anything, you give me a call," he says, slipping a card with his number into my palm and wrapping his hand around my closed fist. "I mean anything, Laura. We can't protect you from the press here. If they find out where you are, you might need some help."

I hadn't even thought about that, and my stomach clenches at the idea that I might bring all this drama into Danna's home. Keeping my head down is going to be a serious priority.

"Thanks," I say. "For everything. I am sorry that it's all turned out like this."

"You have nothing to be sorry for. Please remember that."

He leans in and presses a soft, sweet kiss to my lips

and the lump in my throat that I've been swallowing down for what feels like hours is burning hot again. I turn quickly and open the door, grabbing my purse and rounding to the trunk where I haul out my suitcase as quickly as possible. As I reach Danna's front door and she pulls me into a fierce hug, I finally allow myself to break. The sound of the car turning in the road behind me is enough to cover the sound of my crying, and Danna hustles me into the house, quickly closing the door to the outside world.

I hope that Aaron didn't see or hear that. I don't want him to worry about me any more than he already seems to be.

"Oh my god!" Danna hisses. "My parents have just been talking about the newspaper article."

I drop my luggage and cover my face with my hands. I don't know if I could be more mortified. Mr. and Mrs. Jacobson are regular church-goers. The fact that they now know all about my recent sexplioits is just devastating. The fact that their daughter is pictured with me is mortifying.

"What did they say?" I ask, cringing before she even says anything and worrying that I might need to leave just as I've arrived.

"Let's go upstairs," she says, grabbing the handle of my suitcase. I follow her up, walking past the array of pictures that rise with the staircase. There are some of Danna and me together in her yard, standing amongst the flowers and sitting in a paddling pool. Sweet innocent little girls.

How things have changed.

I'm guessing that Danna's parent's feelings about the little girl that I once was have been completely tarnished under the circumstances.

It's a relief to be here, though. Even though my foundations have been shaken, I feel that I know who I am here. I'm the sensible one against Danna's loud and impetuousness. I'm the Laura who makes good and considered decisions. I'm the girl who knows where she's going; college, work, marriage leading towards a happy ever after that I've had in my mind since I was a little girl.

The fantasy might have become a little bruised when my dad left mom. I mean, I knew he wasn't exactly a model husband. I was old enough to notice the way he'd ogle women a lot younger than him in front of his wife. I knew he didn't appreciate my mom like the princes in fairytales. She would try so hard to make him happy, and nothing ever seemed good enough. It was like she was on a set of downward-moving stairs, trying to climb to the top.

When he left, it was harder for me to believe that there would be a prince for me. If there wasn't one for my mom, and she was pretty great, why on earth would I be any different? But I guess we have that hopeful image of a husband, two children, and a house with a white picket fence drummed into us so hard that there was still a flicker of hope that there might be someone special in my future who would enrich my life.

The past week has done so much to bruise the fantasy. I'd had so many hopes for what life might be like with ten McGregor stepbrothers. I'd started to imagine that Roderick's plan had a chance of working in reality. His sons are amazing; gorgeous, kind, respectful, and strong. All the things that I need in a man multiplied by ten. All my concerns about the sex and the reality of being with so many men had dissolved as well. I'd surprised myself over and over at my capacity and enjoyment of group sex and the loving and caring style the boys have. I'd been astounded at how deeply I felt about each of them in so little time.

Reality has slapped that down in the harshest way.

I couldn't have stayed and been the downfall of the McGregor empire. I couldn't have watched the impact of all of that tear apart everything that the McGregor men have worked for. They have all sacrificed so much of themselves to build a life of security for their family. I have the utmost respect for that.

Danna hustles me into her room and closes the door.

"Holy fuck," she gasps, eyes wide. "You've gone and got yourself into some serious shit."

I dump my bags on the floor and put my hands over my face, feeling completely hopeless. "I don't know, Danna. I really don't know."

"My parents are okay with you staying here, but if the news teams turn up at our door, then things will get complicated."

I remember what Aaron said and feel stupid. Am I the only one who hasn't thought about what might happen now I'm front-page news and outside of the McGregor protection? The prospect of having to face this alone suddenly feels really overwhelming.

"I didn't tell anyone I was coming here. Only Aaron."

"And the driver who brought you?"

I nod.

"And anyone who might have been observant enough to track the car you were traveling in."

I shake my head. "I'm not America's Most Wanted." There's a new level of panic in my voice, and Danna puts her hand on the top of my arm and squeezes reassuringly.

"You're not," she agrees, "But you're pretty hot news right now. There's gonna be people out there who will offer you a lot of money to sell your story. 'Inside the McGregor sex den'." Danna uses her hands to illustrate a huge billboard headline, and my heart sinks.

"I would never do that," I say.

"What would you have to lose?" she asks. "They already have pretty good evidence. It would be your chance to tell your side of the story and maybe enough money to set you up somewhere while this all blows over."

Shaking my head, I take a seat on the fluffy cream throw at the end of her bed. "I could never betray them like that."

Danna sits next to me and puts her arm around me.

"Always thinking about other people. When are you going to start thinking about yourself? What's your mom say about all this?"

"She stood up to Roderick. It's the first time I've seen her do it."

"Well, that's good. What did she say?"

"She wanted me to do what the PR woman was suggesting. Spin the 'real story'." I use my fingers to make air quotes, and Danna looks intrigued.

"What's the real story?"

"That we're all in love."

Her eyebrows practically hit her forehead. "The PR's advice was to admit to everything."

"Yes, with a family values message to try and rescue the company's reputation."

"And the boys were up for that."

"Yes," I say.

"Wow." Danna shakes her head.

"It wasn't real, Danna," I say. "They don't really feel that way. They've been blackmailed into this situation. I'm not saying that they don't like me. I really believe they do, but none of them would have chosen this set of circumstances without Roderick's coercion. Even if the newspaper-reading public bought into the idea that we were all in love, I'd always have a doubt in my mind about how real it is for them."

"But you feel it was real for you?"

I nod. "I know it sounds crazy, but I've never met men like them. The McGregor's aren't anything like any of the men I've met in my life."

Danna smiles. "You've been dazzled by their good looks and amazing bodies."

I nod. "It's hard not to be, but it's more than that. Each of them has proven to me that they were worthy of my..." I pause, trying to think of what word to use. Admitting that I feel love for the McGregor brothers seems crazy. I think that Danna will laugh, but I know it's true.

"Love," she says gently.

I nod. "You know what I'm like. I don't give my heart away easily, but they got under my skin so quickly and effortlessly. Even Aaron at the end."

"I know you, Laura. Probably better than I know myself, I know that you've lost trust in yourself since your dad and Ollie. They let you down, and you blame yourself for allowing them too."

I nod, feeling a little overwhelmed to be seen so clearly. "I just should have seen what was coming."

"Why?" she asks. "It's not a bad thing to want to love and trust, honey. It's perfectly normal. It's the people out there who take that love and trust and toss it in the trash who need to be blamed, not you. Your dad and Ollie were idiots for not seeing you clearly as a person with so much goodness and value."

She takes my hand and squeezes. "And you've taken that distrust and applied it to these men. Is that fair?"

I shake my head. "It's not. I know that everyone deserves to be judged for themselves, and I guess I could imagine doing that if it was just one of them, but it's not. It's ten."

"Ten times the trust," she says gently.

"Exactly. Ten times the risk."

"Or maybe not."

I raise my eyebrows. "What do you mean?"

"There are ten of them, so it's less risk. Each one has a chance of being what you need, Laura."

I consider what she's said, a glimmer of hope flickering in my heart, but I snuff it out immediately. "Roderick has blackmailed them. How can I look past that?"

"Do you think they would do this if they didn't want you? Think about the sacrifice. For you, you're getting a whole lot more man than you ever would have imagined, but they're getting ten percent of a normal relationship. That's a lot to give up."

"I know, and that's why I don't think it's right to expect that of them."

"But it's not your decision to make, is it, Laura? You're deciding something for them that should be something they get to decide for themselves. By walking away, you're treating them like Roderick."

"No," I say, shaking my head. "It's for their own good." Even as I say the words, I realize that Danna is right. That is exactly what Roderick would say about the plan and everything else he's ever decided on behalf of his sons. I hang my head. "You're right," I say eventually. "But I don't know what else to do."

"I think some time away is the right thing," Danna

says softly. "But I really want you to think carefully about what you're walking away from."

An image of the ten brothers standing at the bottom of the stairs waiting for me forms in my mind. I can picture the disappointment in each of their faces. I haven't given them a chance to really prove themselves to me. My ten men are torn between a belligerent father and me, and it's not fair to them at all.

"How did you get so wise?" I ask my friend.

"It's always easier when you're on the outside looking in."

"Maybe," I say. "But I don't think that's it." I reach out to squeeze her hand, and we sit there for a while as I contemplate what to do next.

"Do you wanna take a nice bath?" Danna asks. "A good soak and some thinking space will do you good."

"Yeah. That sounds good," I say.

"I'll get it ready for you. Why don't you sort yourself out a bit here?"

She heads for her bathroom, and I get my stuff organized in her room. I don't unpack much, just get my suitcase open with the things that I need placed on top for easy access. The floral scent of a nice bubble bath begins to fragrance the room, and Danna appears a few minutes later. "It's done, honey. I've left you a towel on the side. I'm going to go downstairs and make sure Mom and Dad haven't imploded."

I grimace, the shame of what they must be thinking of me settling in my stomach like lead.

Danna disappears, and I undress and settle into

the bath, taking a deep breath and dipping my head under the water. The sounds of the house become muted, and I relish the feeling of cocooned safety for a few seconds. There is something so tranquil about being in the water. It can take away the stresses and strains of life, but I think my situation is just too big. I lay back and, instead of relaxing, find myself fretting about everything. My mind chews over everything; Roderick's accusations, Aaron's pleading, Danna's sensible advice, my own jumbled rationale. It's way too much to deal with.

I slip into recalling my time with each of the McGregor brothers. The special moments and the hopes I had allowed me to develop as a result. Tears begin to form in my eyes, and I allow myself to cry. It's cathartic to let all of my pent-up feelings out. The doubt, the dashed hopes, the anger, and embarrassment. I scrub at my skin with frustration, not knowing what to do next.

Then Danna thumps on the door loud enough to make me jump.

"You need to get out right now," she shouts through the door. "The McGregor's are holding a press conference."

Chapter 29

I'm out of the bath and wrapped in a towel in a matter of seconds. The tiled floor is soaking, but I don't try to dry it because I don't want to miss anything.

Danna is waiting outside the door, looking like she might burst from the excitement.

"Come on," she says, waving to where she's got the TV paused. The screen is filled with my boys sitting in two rows. Roderick and Mom are closest to the local news anchor, who is obviously doing the interview. For a moment, I panic, realizing that everyone else who is watching this in real-time already knows what they've said. Pressing the button to start the interview feels like jumping off the highest diving board.

"Ready," Danna says, seemingly understanding my fear.

I nod even though I'm not. This is my life about to be discussed in front of thousands of people, and I have no control over what is being said. Was I stupid to leave when I did? Maybe. I've put myself in this position by doing so.

The interview starts with the anchor summarizing what the viewers already know; that the family has been part of a sex-scandal news story that is everywhere and that they have come forward to share their side of the story.

I think back to what the PR woman was suggesting and wonder what strategy they are going for now. With me not around, the 'falling in love' idea just wouldn't work. Maybe they're going to deny it. Maybe, they've found a way to suggest that the images were photoshopped or that the girl in the images wasn't me. That would still leave them in the lurch, though, and I don't want to be the only one getting away from this scot-free. These are my boys, I think. I need them to be okay.

The camera moves to Roderick. "Yes. The news has been filled with scandal," he says. "They've taken some photos and invented a whole story around it."

"Are you saying the coverage isn't accurate?" the anchor says. "The photographic evidence is pretty damning."

"I'm saying that the coverage isn't an accurate reflection of the situation."

I see my Mom put her hand on Roderick's arm, showing her support for him as she did the day of our first family breakfast. Maybe she can feel how close he is to losing his shit. I'm surprised at how well he's managing to hold it all together.

"And you're all here to tell our viewers what was actually going on in those photos?" the anchor says, unable to conceal his amusement.

"Yes." Roderick looks to his sons, and the camera pans in closer.

Grant shuffles forward in his seat. His face is grave, his shoulders slumped forward, and I want to reach out to him through the screen and lay my hand on his brow. The situation is getting to him, and he has to face the music while I hide out here in my towel like a coward. "Those images..." he shakes his head as though he's disgusted. "They were taken in our home by someone we trusted and sold for personal gain. They might look sordid to viewers, but that isn't an accurate reflection of what was happening." He pauses, and Aaron shifts in his seat.

"It must be hard for your viewers to believe," Aaron says, "but that's not what this is."

The camera pans back to the anchor whose face is a picture. "Laura is your stepsister?" he says.

"We're not married yet," my mom says. "So Laura and the boys are not step-anything."

"But you are intending to marry?"

My Mom smiles. "We were, but things are a little different now."

"Different how?"

Ford leans forward. "Different because we've all fallen for Laura and want to marry her," he says.

There are a few seconds of absolute silence, which you don't often see on TV as the anchor and crew of the news program digest what has just been said. My heart leaps. They've fallen for me and want to marry me. All of them. Even Grant. Even Aaron.

"Marry?" the anchor eventually says with disbelief.

"I know it's not legally possible," Ford continues.

"But we want to pledge ourselves to Laura for life. It might not be a normal thing in our society, but we have found a girl who can make us all very happy, and that's what's important to us. We're all devastated that an employee who we trusted has chosen to profit by exposing a woman who deserves nothing but respect. We're devastated to be judged so quickly. The media have portrayed this as something degrading, but that's not what this is about at all. This is about creating a family unit. This is about bringing our family closer."

"There are how many of you?" the anchor asks, his eyebrows practically disappearing beneath his hairline.

"Ten," Blake says. "There are ten of us."

"And you all want to be with Laura?"

The boys all nod. "Yes," Blake says. "Keeping our family unit closely bonded is important to us all. Family comes first, before anything."

The anchor smirks. "So this is all about family values?"

Donnie leans forward. "When there are ten of you, the chances of you finding partners who are all going to get on well and want to stay as close as we do is very small. Marriage is difficult at the best of times, but throw in the dynamics of a large family, and it can be a recipe for disaster."

The anchor still looks completely skeptical, but he loves the scandal. "Laura must have something pretty special about her." The boys all nod.

"I think our viewers have seen evidence of what

that might be." The anchor turns to the camera and gives a leering grin.

All the boys look as though they want to punch him. Casey and Cameron have balled their fists in their laps, wrapped by their other hands as though they're holding themselves back. Barratt is red in the face, and Ford looks like he's ready to explode.

But it's Roderick that speaks, and it's with a level of calmness that I'm surprised to see.

"I know what it is that you're trying to suggest, and I have to say, Mr. Donovan, that I'm very disappointed. Are women to be defined by sex? Are we to suggest that a person's value and worth is wholly determined by what they will or will not do in the bedroom? I think that is a very shallow and narrow way to look at half of our world. Shallow and unfair."

The McGregor boys are all turned to their father, and the camera catches their surprise.

"Laura is an extremely caring individual who has been a great support to her mother through some very difficult times. She is intelligent, often coming top of her class despite having some physical difficulties that have kept her away from lectures. She's independent, not wanting to rely on handouts or favors. She's strong-minded and will stick up for what she believes is right. She has great friendships and is involved in her local community. She's honest and trustworthy. But I guess, because you've seen some pictures of her engaging in loving physical activity with more than one of my sons, you will judge her to be nothing?"

There's stunned silence.

And my heart feels like it might burst.

I never expected Roderick to defend me like this and to be able to articulate all the good about me so succinctly. . .well, even my own father wouldn't know or value most of what Roderick just said.

"My dad has put it perfectly," Aaron says. "We would do anything to keep Laura safe. Our family and our business mean everything to us, and we are devastated that this exposure has caused damage to something our father has worked so hard for. Laura has left us because she doesn't want to be the cause of any further damage but her not being part of our family is the worst damage that she could inflict."

My hand goes to my heart, where I'm racked with an ache that feels like it might crush me. They are all there fighting to save my reputation, and all I did was walk away to try and save myself. I feel selfish and ashamed. I feel like I let them all down.

"We're faced with impossible choices," Elliot says. "Let Laura go and lose the one woman who can keep us all together. Leave our family business and walk away from everything our father has worked for in order to try and minimize the damage to our company's reputation. And for what? Because we don't love in the standard way. Because we know what is right for us, and we have the courage to choose it?"

The anchor nods. "It seems like you have a whole lot to lose."

"That's an understatement," Antony says. "We've

all given up a lot already. Each of us has chosen to put aside our passions to further our joint interests. I wanted to design houses, but I'm a commercial architect for my father. Donnie wants to paint, but he's the graphical designer for our business. We know what it takes to sacrifice, but this is too much. This isn't for anyone's benefit. All this is going to do is hurt all of us and so a bunch of strangers who know nothing about us or our lives can feel better about themselves and their moral high-horse."

Aaron puts his hand on his brother's arm. "We just want to be able to live our lives in private and for everyone to understand that all our choices are made with love."

Love?

"You love her?" Mr. Donovan asks.

"Yes." It's a chorus of ten voices. The camera pans to my mother, whose face is beaming with happiness.

"And you approve?" he asks my mom.

"How can I not approve? Look at these boys and tell me that my daughter isn't the luckiest girl alive."

At that moment, my phone starts to ring. I glance at the screen and see KATELIN flashing.

My cousin.

I wave at Danna to pause the TV and answer.

"Are you serious?" Katelin screams. "When did this happen, and why the fuck didn't you call me?"

I burst out laughing. "We haven't spoken in five years!" I say.

"Well, I've been busy!" she laughs.

"So I heard," I say. "How are those men of yours?"

"Amazing," she says. "Perfect, blissful, sexy as hell. . .I could go on, but I'm more interested in how you seem to have trumped me."

"Are you watching Dick Donovan's show?"

"Err. . .yeah. My mom just called me to tell me to tune in, and I just didn't get what was going on and then I saw your mom."

"It's been an interesting week."

"A WEEK!" she screeches again. "You got with ten guys in a week?"

"Well, I've only been with nine of them," I laugh, blushing. Danna is shaking her head at our conversation but with the biggest, cheekiest grin on her face.

"Who's the poor sod who didn't get any love?" Katelin asks.

"Aaron."

"Damn. He must be feeling like shit."

"I don't think so," I say. "Things just got real fast."

"Yeah. I didn't think you had it in you cuz."

"I didn't know I had it in me."

Danna scoots closer. "I didn't know she had it in her either," she yells into the phone.

"Is that Danna?" Katelin asks.

"Yeah. I'm hiding at her house while my private life is discussed on live TV."

"Well, you did go and choose some of the highest-profile bachelors in the state. What did you expect? No one is splashing my private life over the front pages."

"Well, they might be when they find out that we're related," I say. "Actually, it'll probably be good if you guys could keep a low profile for a while."

Katelin just laughs. "You know I don't give a fuck about that," she says. "Let them come and try and make me feel shit about loving and being loved by the best three men there are. Let them try to tell me that our committed relationship is anything but perfect, and I'll tell them where to go."

My cousin has always been really feisty, and I can see how having that conviction can go a long way in a situation like this. I wish I was more like her. I wish I had that level of certainty about the choices that I need to make.

"How did you know?" I ask her. "How did you know that your three men were worth the risk?"

"The risk of what? Loving?"

"Getting your heart broken. Having the world think you're a slut. Being judged for just living your life."

"It doesn't sound like those boys want to break your heart, honey. As for the world, people are going to think what they want. You can be living what the majority consider to be a normal life, and people will still be judging you. You've just got to live your life in a way that makes you happy and doesn't fuck anyone else up in the process. That's all we can do."

I take a deep breath and look at the McGregor's all frozen on the screen. "But that's exactly what I've done," I say. "Look at them all sitting there, about to lose everything. What we've done has brought that family to its knees."

"That isn't what I see, Laura. What I see is a family that is standing up to the bigots who are fueling the scandal. I see a family united and supporting you."

Danna nods. "I see that, too."

"You do?"

"Yes," they both answer in unison.

"I can't really do this, can I?" I ask.

"Well, I've got to admit that I didn't think you had it in you?" Katelin laughs. "Little Laura and ten huge men."

"Don't!" I say, cringing with embarrassment.

"You tell me they didn't make you feel like you came so hard the world was going to end."

My silence is a complete admission that she knows what she's talking about.

"Exactly," Katelin says. "And you want to give that up. You want to give those sexy, gorgeous, intelligent, caring men over so some other lucky woman can enjoy them. You crazy girl!"

The thought of another woman fitting into my place with the McGregor's fills my gut with bitter, coiling jealousy, but Katelin is right. If it's not me, then at some point, there will be someone else willing to take a place with my boys. There will be another woman who will have the courage to take these men into her arms and never let them go.

I couldn't bear it.

I couldn't stand by and let that happen.

I can't.

"I want them," I say softly.

"I know you do," Katelin says. Danna smiles broadly. "And they want you."

"I need to tell them," I say.

Danna laughs. "Better finish watching the show," she says.

"You didn't finish watching it yet?" Katelin squeals.

"No," I say. "What happens?"

"Now that would be telling," she laughs. "Just promise me you'll call me at some point next week to fill me in on what happens next."

"I will, I say."

We say our goodbyes quickly, and Danna presses the button that puts the McGregor's back on.

And we watch until I find out exactly why Katelin was squealing.

Chapter 30

They're coming here.

That's what Katelin was screaming about. They told Dick Donovan on live TV that they're not prepared to let me go, and they don't care about the consequences. They are going to follow their hearts and prove to me that this can work.

My heart is beating so fast, and Danna is jumping on her bed like an excited toddler.

This is really happening.

I see it all clearly now. The love these boys feel for their father. The sacrifices they've made for him weren't about them being forced to give up their dreams but them doing it willingly for a man who's raised them to understand that family always needs love and sacrifice to work. I see that the love they feel for me is real, too. For them to put so much on the line to admit to the world that this is what they want and to hell with outside opinion has to be coming from somewhere genuine. I look at them on the screen and am overwhelmed. My ten gorgeous men are coming for me, and I'm happier than I've ever been.

"So are you going to just sit there, or are you going to get dressed so that you're presentable when they arrive?" Danna laughs.

"Oh my god!" I whisper.

"I know, honey. It's pretty overwhelming. Are you okay? Is this what you want?"

"Yes," I say. "It is."

"So, let's get you ready," she says.

As I start to find a suitable outfit for what feels like the most significant reunion I have ever had, I think through everything that has happened. Although I feel guilty for walking away when I did, it wasn't about me having a tantrum. It was about me finding space to think and give me a chance to fully realize what it is that I want for my life. It's also because I truly believed that these amazing boys needed to be free from their father's clutches. They needed to take control of their own lives, not allow themselves to be bullied into something that isn't right for them or just drifting along with the tide because they can't be bothered to choose another direction for themselves. But I see now that what I assumed wasn't correct. Roderick isn't the man I thought he was, and his sons are not being coerced into this situation. That interview has just proven to me that they want this themselves and that their sacrifice isn't forced.

"You know I was convinced that you would have seen the error of your ways and run back to your castle at some point," Danna laughs. "Or that maybe you might have been kidnapped by your wicked step-father and forced into servitude."

"Sexual servitude," I giggle. "He doesn't really seem so wicked anymore, does he?"

She shakes her head. "As long as sexual servitude comes with cake and massages, you know I'd be more than happy with that deal," she says.

"I think cake and massages are on offer. You know, maybe you need to audition for the role of wife," I say.

"I'm not taking your sloppy seconds," she says. "They wouldn't want me, anyway."

It's the first time in a very long time that Danna has said something negative about herself and it's taken me by surprise. "What do you mean?" I ask her.

"I'm not you, am I?" she says. "I'm not the kind of girl that guys want to settle down with."

I look at her seriously. "Why the hell would you think that?"

"You know how I am. Too loud. Too bossy. Too sassy. It's not a winning combination when it comes to guys."

"Maybe not misogynistic douchebags," I say, "but those aren't the kind of guys you want in your life."

"Even the not so misogynistic ones aren't that keen," she says. "I'm strictly in the funny-friend-zone."

"Yes, you are," I say. "In the best possible way. Don't you even think this shit? You're amazing and beautiful and funny as hell. If I was a guy, I'd totally be into you."

"No, you wouldn't," she laughs. "You'd be into Tara Becket."

It's such a left-field comment I don't even know how to reply. Tara Becket is the head of the cheerleading team. Her parents are loaded. I think her father might be high up in local government as well as own-ing half of the factories in the state.

"Why Tara Becket?" I ask.

"Why the McGregor brothers?"

I smart a little bit. Is she suggesting that I'm driven by money and status? "You know their wealth doesn't motivate me. If it did, why would I be here?"

"They're the alphas," she says, elaborating her point. "The ones people notice when they walk into a room. That's what you like about them."

I pull my pretty blue shirt over my head, thinking about how best to reply. Maybe she is right in a way. I do like the way they are self-assured and command-ing. They're successful and motivated. These things are attractive characteristics, but they aren't the only things that attract me. They aren't the reasons why each of the McGregor brothers has found a place of warmth in my heart. It's Donnie's sensitivity and Ford's protectiveness. It's Elliot's considerate nature and Antony's wit. It's Grant's ponderousness and Casey's lightheartedness. It's Cameron's strength and Blake's empathy. It's Barret's kindness and Aaron's fierce loyalty. These are the things that make me be-lieve that they could make me happy.

So I tell Danna that. I tell her that if I could live ten lives and choose each of them to live a single life with me, I'd be happy.

"But we don't get ten lives, sweetie," she says. "We just get one, and you need to understand that it's not your job to decide what's good for those boys or not. By running away from them, you're doing exactly what their dad has been doing; you're limiting their choices because of something that you believe is good for them. They are grown, men. It's important you recognize that they are capable of making their own decisions."

"I know," I say. "I see that now."

"Every choice we make in life has consequences, and they are just never going to want to be free from their family in the way that you would consider healthy because they are siblings and always want to be close. I think you've been struggling to understand them because you're an only child, and you don't know what it would be like to feel bonded in the way that they do, especially the twins. Do you believe what they are saying?"

"I do believe them," I say. "I believe they have feelings for me because I have feelings for them. I know it's all happened so fast, and I suppose that's why I doubted myself and them. It didn't seem like it could be real, but it is, Danna. It really is."

Danna swings her feet off the bed and walks over to join me by the window. She takes my hands and looks at me, smiling. "I know all of this feels crazy to you. We used to talk about kissing a whole heap of frogs until we found our princes. In your case, you seem to have managed to find a whole heap of princes instead." We both giggle, but when the laughter has waned, she looks serious again. "You know I'm not one to tell you how to live your life, but I'm also not one to stand by while you ignore your heart and, as a result, sabotage what could be the best thing that has ever happened to you. Our hearts try to speak to us, but they are quieter than our minds and maybe a little less persuasive. We try to put practical things ahead of the emotional, but that isn't always the right way to be, Laura."

"What would you do if you were in my situation?" I ask her.

"I think you already know," she says with a devilish grin. "I don't think I'm ever really going to forgive you for taking the ten most eligible bachelors within a thousand-mile radius off the market in one swoop."

"You'd give up a chance of having a normal life?" I ask her. A flash of my parent's wedding picture comes into my head. They were so happy on that day, about to start their married life with a whole future of 'normality' ahead of them. It didn't work out so great for them, did it?

"What the hell is normal?" she asks me. "Most of the married couples we know probably never have sex. Most would rather be alone or with someone else, but they don't have the guts to bother getting divorced. You think that normal relationships are some kind of panacea, but they're not. They're as complicated as any other kind of relationship."

"And what about what everyone's going to say about me?"

"Most of the women in this nation will be so green with envy we'll all look like the statue of liberty and who cares about the men. You've ten amazing boy-friends to defend you in any circumstances. It's going to be like having your own personal security firm."

I laugh and pull her in for a hug. Sometimes friends are closer than sisters. I'm never going to know what it's like to have a real sibling, but I feel pretty blessed to have found the next best thing in Danna.

My heart swells with warmth at the thought that they're on their way here. I remember how safe I felt in the arms of each one of them, and I want to cry. I've been so foolish, so driven by my own expectations and limitations that I wasn't willing to see that they might be right. We could do this. We could live happily ever after as one big, amazing family. I'll never have to worry about fending for myself. I'll never again have that insecure feeling that comes with being an only child. My phone beeps and Danna reaches to grab it from the nightstand to hand it to me. As I read the message, a huge smile spreads over my face.

FORD: You better get your things together, baby, because we're on our way to get you, and this time we're not taking no for an answer. We'll do whatever you need us to do to make you happy.

I show it to Danna, and she makes a low whistling sound. "You better get your list together then, girl. Ten men who want to do whatever you need is not something that any woman should be approaching without a big long list."

I shake my head, laughing. "They don't need a list,

Danna. That's just one of the things that makes them so amazing."

I grab my nicest jeans and tug them on, glancing out of the window. Danna's street is quiet, and I'm relieved that I might have time to put on some make-up and deal with my hair. I'm just about finishing up when Danna shrieks.

"There are two huge trucks pulling up outside this house," she says, "and they sure as hell don't belong to my neighbors."

My heart skitters in my chest. This is it. They are here, and I'm going to have to face them. However, this happens, it's going to be awkward. I have so much I need to tell them, and so much I need them to understand, but I won't be able to do all of that outside Danna's house with half her neighbors twitching their curtains.

"I can feel you stressing," Danna says. "You don't need to solve everything right now, hon. Just go and see them, and everything will work itself out over time."

Before I can think about leaving, I grab her and pull her into a fierce hug. I need her to know how much her friendship means to me. Who else would put up with my crazy life? Who else would give me such amazing advice? She's really something else. "You guys are going to be amazing together," she tells me. "And if you get sick of them, you know where I am." We both laugh and hug a little tighter.

When I pull away, I say, "You know they've got cousins."

Danna's eyes light up. "Yeah, how many?"

"Enough," I giggle.

"How do you know how many is enough for me," she says, and I have to shake my head because all I can think is, if I can handle ten, Danna could handle a whole football team.

There are ten amazing men waiting for me. Ten men who are going to change my world forever.

It's time to face the music.

Chapter 31

When we're young, we dream about our futures, the ones we create in our minds from the examples we have from real life and the stories that we're told. Fairy tales are filled with happy-ever-afters and princesses who are swept off their feet by dashing princes.

I'd always hoped to meet my prince, but I didn't want him to save me. That wasn't what my fantasy future was about. I wanted a man who would walk by my side through all of the joy and pain that life has to offer, and I wanted to stand on my own two feet, too.

When I met the McGregor brothers, everything I'd ever imagined for myself was overwhelmed. They had the money to support me so that I'll never need to work. They wanted to take care of me in a way that felt alien. I worried about getting swamped by the sheer number of them and the force of their characters, but in getting to know them, I realized that they didn't want to overpower or overwhelm me. They wanted to support my ideas for how I wanted to live my life. They wanted to find a way that we could all be happy together.

I don't know what I did to deserve these amazing men.

Ten men.

Even as I think it, I can't stifle my smile.

Ten princes, each with his own way of making me feel like the most special woman on earth.

I gather my things and walk with Danna to the front door.

"Don't be scared," she says to me, giving my hand a squeeze. "Every big step we take in life feels like the one that we are going to stumble on, but just remember that you have plenty of arms to catch you now."

I hug her again, and then she opens the door. As soon as they see me, the doors of the trucks fly open, and they all get out. I feel like I'm in a movie, in the final scene where the characters have overcome all their troubles and are now in that sunlit frame where everything is perfect.

Ford is there, plaid shirt stretched tight over those biceps that make me want to melt. Donnie smiles shyly, pushing his floppy curly hair back from his face. Elliot's eyes meet mine and are filled with warmth. Casey and Cameron have opposing thumbs hooked into the pockets of their jeans. Aaron and Antony grin with equally dazzling megawatt smiles. Grant's expression is serious, as though he can sense how overwhelming this must be for me. Barret and Blake are there, standing close, a sign that their bond might have repaired just a little through all of this strife.

And I know I'm doing the right thing.

They are willing to do whatever it takes, and that means everything to me. It means I'm sure that they aren't just complying with their father's wishes, whether to please him or to inherit the business. This is about more than that. It's about each of our individual relationships and their bonds as brothers.

It's about creating one big happy life for all of us.

It's Blake who reaches me first. His brothers seem to fall in behind him, allowing his slower steps to be the pace they all walk at. He pulls me into his arms so fiercely I feel all the breath leave my lungs in a whoosh.

"You can't do that to us again," he says firmly.

"I know," I say, pulling back and putting my hand on his cheek. He steps away, allowing Barrett to take his place, and so each of them takes their turn to fold me into a welcoming and reassuring embrace.

I can't imagine what this must look like to Danna's neighbors. It's early enough that there's no one in their yards yet, and I don't know who's observing from the windows, but do I care? Not really, because this is my life now. These men are more important to me than people's perceptions of me or my reputation.

Ford is last to pull me into an embrace, and by the time he does, I'm in tears. They are tears of relief and happiness, but he still looks so concerned. "Princess," he says. "Why are you crying?"

I pull him to me and breathe in his warm, familiar scent. "I just realized that I found my happily ever after," I say, and he laughs.

"Yeah, you did, baby girl. Yeah, you did."

The boys take me back to McGregor mansion. Mom and Roderick are there to greet us. Mom is so happy to see me back but cautious, too. She wants to know for sure that this is right for me.

"It is, Mom," I tell her.

Roderick's face is darker. "You walked away from my family, Laura. You must promise that you won't do that again."

"Dad," Aaron says in a warning tone. "No one should be asked to make that kind of promise. You need to accept that we're not just plastic figurines that you can place where you want. We're all people who have needed to go through a whole lot to get into this position."

"She almost broke up this family," he says.

"No, she didn't." Casey steps forward. "She tried to keep this family together. She tried to walk away because she didn't want to put herself between you and us. Laura knows what family means to us all. That's part of why this is going to work and exactly why you need to be getting over yourself now."

Roderick nods. "Laura, this is only going to work if you can promise me that you will always try to seek help for any difficulties within the family. Running off doesn't help anyone."

"Danna is family," I tell him. "But I understand what you're saying. I didn't give you all a chance to explain, and that was wrong."

Roderick turns to Mom, and he seems to soften before our eyes. She nods, and his shoulders drop. I didn't realize how much anxiety has been driving Mr. McGregor until this point, but I see it now. He's scared.

Scared that all that he's built – family and business – can be taken away from him. He's just a frightened little boy with his arms wrapped around his toys, terrified to let go and share with anyone else.

He turns back to us all and pauses. I can see him taking the time to choose his words carefully, and that feels like a good sign. In all my dealings with Roderick so far, he's been impetuous. "You know that all I've ever wanted is what's best for you all," he says softly. I can hear the emotion in his voice.

"We know, Dad," Cameron says.

"I'm sorry if anything I've said or done has made you feel like I don't respect the men you've become. You have to understand, I'm just used to things being a certain way, but I'll try." He turns to me. "Laura, I know you've thought that I'm crazy for wanting this for my sons and that maybe I'm more controlling of their lives than I should be. It's been hard to watch you drawing my sons away from me, but I see why you did it, and I hope you can see that in the end, we both have a shared goal here, and that is the happiness of my ten boys." I nod, and Donnie slides his hand into mine. Grant takes my other hand. "All I want is for you to all be happy," he finishes.

"I'm hoping that we will be," I say. "And I will do my best to make this work for all of us."

Roderick nods, seemingly satisfied with my response.

"So you're back, are you?" Mom asks.

"Yes."

"For good," Antony adds, winking at me. He knows what that does to me, and I smile broadly.

Mom steps forward and draws me into a ferocious hug. It seems as though all her plans for us and the McGregor's have come to fruition. "Maybe we should start planning a double ceremony," she laughs.

Roderick's eyes light up, but I put my hand up. "Not so fast," I say. "I'm looking forward to living in sin for a little while before we get onto that, and I wouldn't want to take anything away from your special day, Mom."

"You wouldn't, sweetie," she says, taking my face between her hands and kissing my cheek, "but I know what you mean. You go and have fun with your boys."

I can't believe that Mom just said that, and I blush profusely. I suppose I will have to find a way to be less embarrassed about references to the 'group aspect' now it's going to be part of my normal everyday life.

I let go of Donnie and Grant's hands and turn, finding myself surrounded by my men. Wow. This really is something else. There are plenty of smiles, and that makes me warm inside. I wish I had twenty arms so that I could give them all a hug simultaneously. This will definitely be a frustration, but I'm really going to have to find a way to share myself out.

"Come on then," Aaron calls impatiently. His eyes are twinkling, though. I think he'll always hold that position as organizer of the group.

"Where are we going?" I ask.

"It's a surprise," Ford says, throwing his arm around my shoulders. The boys start walking, and I'm drawn along. There's plenty of chatter and some jostling that is just typical of brothers. We head to an area of the house that I haven't been to before, up more stairs to a higher level.

"Wow," I say as we enter a large room. There are sofas and rows of cupboards. There are also doors on each side. "What is this place?"

"Dad had it designed before he told us about the plan. I guess it was to show us how things could work," Cameron says.

"Come this way," Elliot leads me towards a door at the back. When it opens, I am stunned.

Inside is a massive vaulted-ceilinged room with a huge white crystal chandelier hanging in the center. The walls are painted navy blue with gold accents and in the middle is a bed that must be fifteen-feet square. If it wasn't dressed in sumptuous velvet and covered with pillows,I might have questioned what it was.

"Amazing, isn't it?" Donnie says. He's looking up at the ceiling and I notice for the first time the sky-lights that are creating the amazing warm feeling in the room. It is beautiful.

"Wow," I say, feeling pathetic for not being about to come up with a better word.

"I know. Kind of takes your breath away, doesn't it?" Grant says.

"It's big enough for all of us," Ford says happily. He

really is very cool with all of this and jumps onto the bed as if to illustrate this very fact. "Get your sexy ass over here," he says, laughing.

I know that it's stupid for me to feel shy with them, but I do. I may have had sex with nearly every man in this room, but not all together. Is that what this is going to be? A mass consummation. A sealing of our bond. My pussy clenches at the thought. I walk slowly over to the bed, slipping off my shoes and kneeling to make my way into the center. I lay back, spreading my arms like a starfish, gazing up at the gorgeous blue sky and imagining what it will be like to rest here, looking at the stars, surrounded by these ten amazing men.

The room seems to quiet as each of the brothers slips his shoes off and finds his place around me. I feel like the sun in the middle of a new universe with the planets aligning. Grant is the first to make contact with me, taking my hand and bringing it to his lips. It feels right that he is because he was the first to touch me, the first to kiss me, the first to show me passion and pleasure as I'd never felt before.

"How are you feeling?" he asks.

"Ready," I say because I know that's what he needs to know, what they all need to know.

He rolls closer, placing his lips on mine, sliding his hand over the bare skin of my belly and up under my shirt. There's a murmur of approval in the room. I close my eyes to focus on his touch, but then there's movement on my right and another hand following a similar path. More hands peel away my socks and begin to unbutton my trousers. I don't know who is who, but I find that I don't care. I trust each of these men to put me first, to treat me with respect, and handle me with the gentlest touch.

Fingers unbutton my shirt and peel it away. Hands softly squeeze my breasts and find my nipples through my simple, cotton bra. Lips kiss my ankles and my calves and then the inside of my thighs. I'm so hot between my legs, so desperate and needy that my hips wriggle, seeking more contact.

"She's ready," someone says as fingers press against my damp panties.

"She loves it," Grant whispers against my ear, and I whimper.

"She's going to love it, even more, when I get these panties off." It's Casey, and his voice is gruffer than I've ever heard it. My panties are tugged down so fast I want to laugh, but it's when I feel four hands on each leg tugging them apart my heart skips a beat.

"Damn." There's a chorus of appreciation as they all feast their eyes on my spread pussy. I can imagine what it looks like; soft and pink and wet. I can imagine how it must feel when someone's finger gently strokes from my clit and downwards; hot and slippery. I look down and see Casey kneeling between my legs. Our eyes meet, and it's the hottest thing ever. I gaze around me and find Cameron, Donnie, Elliot, Antony, Grant, and Ford are the ones who've been touching me. The other three brothers are close too, patiently waiting for their turn. Everyone is in varying stages of undress, as though they've rushed to strip whatever they could in the little time they had. Most of them are shirtless, and the sheer amount of amazing, tan, muscled torsos on the show makes my pussy clench. I think I could come from just laying here, looking at them and thinking about their bodies. I think I might spontaneously combust from what is about to happen.

"Lick her," Ford orders. Casey doesn't need telling twice. He grins as he settles between my legs, inhales deeply, and nudges my clit with his nose.

"She smells so damned good," he says.

"I remember," Grant says, nipping at my earlobe. His hot breath sends my pulse racing as Casey's tongue flicks over my swollen clit and down to lap at my entrance.

There's another murmur of appreciation as I moan my approval. I go to move my hand to hold Casey's head, but Grant holds it and pins it to the bed. "No, no," he says. "You don't get to control him. We get to control you."

The thought is horny as hell. Donnie tugs my bra cup down, and his lips latch onto my nipple. Hands stroke my thighs as Casey licks and licks and licks. Ford's lips find mine, and he kisses me as though he wants to slip inside me and never leave; long, languid strokes of his tongue match his brother's rhythm over my clit. I have to shift my hips. I can't take the overwhelming feeling of so many hands, so many fingers, so many tongues.

"She's getting close," Donnie says, pinching my nipple between his fingers. "Her aura is pulsing."

"Her pussy's pulsing, too," Cameron says.

"Fuck," Grant says.

Fingers press into my ass, holding me tight against Casey's face, and I want to wriggle, but I can't.

"That's it," Donnie urges. "Don't hold it back, Laura. Let it go."

I want to. I want to so badly.

"That's it, you dirty girl. You let us fuck you," Ford says. "We're all going to come in that pussy of yours until you can't walk tomorrow."

Oh god. His words are what gets me, my mind tumbling as my body seizes with ecstasy I've never felt before. "That's it," Donnie whispers, stroking my body gently. His brothers follow suit as Casey pulls away, letting me ride the waves of pleasure.

I'm still reeling, eyes closed and body lax. The bed shifts between my legs, his knees nudging me open wider. "Casey's going to fuck you now," Grant whispers. I nod, letting him know it's okay even as I can't speak. I know how Casey will feel; hard, thick, and good. His cock nudges at my opening, taking the slickness and using it to open me up.

"Fuck," someone mutters as he pushes all the way inside. My back arches, and lips find my breasts again. Grant shifts away, and I think someone will take his place, but that isn't what happens. He strips himself naked and kneels next to my head, his cock in hand.

"Suck it, baby," he says. It's not an order as such,

but I imagine it is. He moves closer, and I open my mouth, tasting the salty sweetness of his pre-cum, a sign of how excited he is. He's so big, and the angle is difficult, but he seems to know how to position himself to get as deep into my mouth as he needs to be.

"That's it," Ford says. I think he's the one enjoying watching the action the most. No wonder he was so into the idea of the plan from the beginning if this is how he gets his kicks. I look up at Grant and see the pained pleasure on his face. Casey is fucking me with long, slow strokes that feel so damned good. I can feel the beginnings of another orgasm building, but I know my own body. I don't think I'm going to be able to come so soon. Grant is, though. I can taste his excitement and feel the swell of his cock and the tremble of his thighs. He goes to pull away, but I grab him to let him know I'm okay for him to cum in my mouth. And oh, he does. He does so much that I have to swallow twice.

Casey's hands grip my hips so hard I think I'll have bruises the next day. His slow, languid pace speeds as he gets nearer. A guttural moan builds in his throat, and I know then that he's going to cum, too. The pulse of him inside me feels so good. My pussy is so wet I can feel it trickling between the cheeks of my ass.

"You see how good you make us feel," Cameron says as he watches his brother come undone. "You see how perfect this is."

"She does," Donnie says. "Her aura is peaceful now. Peaceful and contented."

I want to tell him that he needs to stop reading me like an open book, but I know he's not doing it to be intrusive. This is just the way he sees the world, and it must be beautiful. He's right, though. I do feel at peace.

"Who's next?" Aaron asks. Grant and Casey are moving away, and everybody is shifting around.

"Get her on her knees," Cameron suggests. "I want her to ride me."

"That okay, Laura," Ford asks. I nod, and even though I'm feeling boneless, I wait until Cameron is lying down and manage to get myself up and straddled over him. Donnie immediately goes to strip off my bra and shirt. Cameron's cock stands big and thick and proud, so all I have to do is take hold of it and lower myself. I think it should be easy. After all, I've just fucked a man with the exact same cock as him, but it isn't. The new position and angle mean I have to work my way down, stretching and stretching as I go. Elliot comes behind me and grabs my hips, setting a rhythm for my movements. Aaron moves in, taking his place to my right and touching my breast. His cock is grasped in his other hand, and he's working it at the same pace I'm moving. It's hot as hell.

"Do you think you can take us both?" Elliot asks. For a moment, I'm not sure what he's suggesting. I've never had anal sex, and I'm not sure I'd be ready for it now. I'm sure I've read a Cosmo article about how long it can take for a woman to prepare for that.

"I don't know," I say. "I've never done that before."

"In your pussy, baby."

A shiver runs up my spine at the thought. Two of them, moving in me at the same time, sound like heaven, but could I really take them. "Go gently," I tell Elliot. "I'm pretty full already."

He shifts closer, aligning himself. I go still, and so does Cameron. I think about how much concentration it will take to achieve this with men who are sized like the McGregor brothers. My pussy bears down hard as I think about how amazing it might feel to experience two men both moving inside me.

Elliot starts to push, and the stretch is immediate. I lean forward, braced over Cameron. Hands stroke my back and my ass. Cameron raises himself up to kiss me. I find myself relaxing and relaxing, and it's then that Elliot pushes a little harder. The feeling is amazing; the pressure directly on the little bundle of nerves inside me that makes me grunt. Cameron is watching my face, which is screwed up with the intensity of it all. "Go slow," he tells his brother. "Go slow."

So that's what Elliot does. He moves in slow, shallow thrusts, and Cameron closes his eyes, tipping his head back. I can see how amazing this must feel for him, the tightness of my pussy and the taboo of fucking one pussy with two huge cocks.

"Look at our girl," Ford says. "She's taking it like a pro."

"She was made for this," Aaron agrees.

"She was made for us," Blake corrects.

My legs are trembling, my clit grinding against

Cameron from the weight of Elliot behind me. I know I'm going to come soon. It's rising fast, and I don't know what to do. There will be no holding me up when this happens. It's too big. Too all-engulfing.

"She's close," Elliot says, starting to move with more vigor.

"So am I," Cameron says through gritted teeth.

"I'll get us all there," Elliot says with determination. He takes hold of my hair and arches my back, pulling me back into him. It's so damn sexy for him to take control in this way that I come in a second, groaning like a woman possessed. Cameron goes over the edge with me, with his face screwed up like he's in pain.

"Fuck," Elliot gasps. It's got tighter in my pussy as it clamps down with my orgasm and Cameron swells with his. Elliot is there too, pushing into me so deep it burns.

We stay like that, joined like one dozen-limbed creature frozen in time.

I struggle to catch my breath and slump onto Cameron's sweat-slicked chest. Elliot's clutching my hip for stability.

"Damn," someone mutters from my right. I think it's Blake.

"The girl needs a rest," Antony says.

Elliot begins to pull out, and when he does, I feel so empty. I don't like it. I need them inside me. I need more. Even as I think it, I don't recognize myself. Who is this girl with such a voracious appetite for sex? I would never have thought I could be like this. Maybe, if Mom hadn't met Roderick and I hadn't ended up meeting his sons, I never would have discovered this part of myself.

"No," I say. "I need more."

"What do you need, baby?" Ford asks.

"I want to make you all come," I tell him.

"You sure you can take it," he says, sounding a little skeptical. If there's one thing I hate, it's being underestimated.

"I can take four," I say. I have this ridiculously sexy image in my head of being spread out like a starfish, my hands on two of them, my mouth on the third and my pussy on the fourth. I look around at who's left. Antony, Aaron, Blake, Barret, Donnie, and Ford. That's a whole lot of man to satisfy. They are all so big and hard, cocks held in hands like weapons of mass destruction. I've been filled with bravado, but now I'm not so sure. Can I really do this? Ten in one sitting seems like a tall order.

"Four," Aaron says, shaking his head.

I tell them what I'm thinking, blushing like a beet but feeling a sense of belonging with these brothers that spurs me on. I've had sex with all of them already. It's not like this is new intimacy. I guess the fact that I have such an audience to everything is what's making me shy, but I need to get over that pretty quickly. Now I know how amazing it can be to have a harem of men willing to fulfill my every whim. How could I go back to normal one on one sex? I guess it will happen every so often, but this is what I want.

Cameron helps me to roll onto my back, and Barret and Antony move to my sides. Their hands are on my body right away, stroking over my breasts and tugging at my nipples in a way that sends a direct thrill between my legs. I take hold of their cocks, finding them mirror images of each other. There's a collective groan, and both of them thrust into my hands as though they are desperate for the contact. I can't imagine how horny they must be feeling, having stood by and watched so much sex without relief. I clutch them tighter to give them greater pleasure.

I'm wondering who else is going to take place and am overwhelmed to see Aaron moving between my legs. He is the only McGregor brother who hasn't yet been inside me, and the intensity in his eyes shows me how much this moment means to him, too. He slides his hand up my thigh, a gentle caress, and I reach down to take his hand, just for a moment. The room is quiet, as if the other boys can feel the intensity and the significance. When this is done, the full consummation is complete.

Blake makes his way next to Antony for his place, too. If I wasn't feeling so emotional, I would have laughed at the fact that these twins seem to want to do everything together!

I turn my head and look up at Blake. I know it's him because his eyes always seem less certain than his brothers. I find it so sad to see how a childhood accident can still be having such an effect on his confidence. I wish he could see that even with a slight limp and a scar on his thigh, he's still perfect just for being him. I draw my hand away from Aaron and stroke Blake's leg where the scarring is most pronounced. I look up at his beautiful face and ask him to kiss me. I need him to know how much I want him. He does, and it's the sweetest, gentlest kiss I've ever been gifted. The hairs rise on the back of my neck as I take in his tenderness. The angry, sullen Blake who's always barking at his brother has disappeared and I realize that sometimes all we need is to be seen, to be recognized. Sometimes we get stuck in a pattern of behavior that masks the real us. I hope that Blake can begin to find the self he lost on the day of that accident and can forgive his brother for the role he played.

Aaron's fingers slide over my hip, finding my entrance and gently guiding their way inside me. I'm slick and open, and he groans when he feels my heat. There's a pause as each of us takes in each other. I feel like a platter on a buffet, surrounded by hungry men. My eyes meet Aaron's, and I give him the barest hint of a nod. He sees and nods back, shifting closer so that he can begin to push his cock in. I need this to happen first so I can adjust my position.

When he's fully seated inside me, I let out a long sigh. I stroke his chest and the amazing six-pack that makes up his rippling abdomen. His hand finds my thigh, and he gives it a squeeze. These little touches take this from being something soulless and pornographic to being so much more. I take hold of Barret and Antony again and nod to Blake that I'm ready for him, too. He uses his cock to stroke over my lips, and I slowly open my mouth for him.

Aaron begins to move, his thrusts long and slow but punctuated by an urgency when his hips meet mine. My clit is straining for contact, and it gets it when a finger begins to rub it in tight little circles that have me moaning around Blake's cock. He moves slowly, too, using one hand to hold the root and the other to gather my hair behind my head. Barret groans as he thrusts into my hand, his grip on my breast tightening with every movement of my fist.

I don't know who is going to come first and it doesn't really matter. This isn't about speed, it's about us being together and showing each other what it means for us to be a unit. We may not be married, and it will never be possible for us to have the same legal standing as other normal couples, but I don't care.

I know these men are mine, and I will never let anything divide us.

"Laura," Barret groans. His hand grips my wrist as he comes, slowing his thrusts as he milks his own pleasure. Antony isn't far behind.

My mouth is too full for me to verbalize how amazing they are making me feel. Aaron's cock is so big that the stretching feeling between my legs is almost too much. I move my hips in a rhythm to match his, and his grip on my hip becomes tighter.

"That's it," I hear Ford say. His voice seems to be coming from far away, but I know he's close. It's just the pleasure-fog in my mind that is distorting space and time. "You gonna come for us, girl?"

"Mmm," I say, the circling finger on my clit speeding. Oh god, it feels too good.

Blake's hand tightens in my hair, showing me that he's close, and then I taste him, salty-sweet and hot in my mouth. I look up and his back arched, abs flexed, hand splayed over the scar that I know he doesn't like to touch. He's completely lost, and it feels amazing to know I can do that to him.

Now I can turn my attention to Aaron. The others move back, slumping onto their backs around me to enjoy the post-orgasm delirium. Aaron leans over me, kissing my mouth for the first time, totally unbothered that I've just taken his brother there. Hooking his arm beneath me, I'm held tight against his chest. "You feel so damn good," he grunts, his thrusts now tight and deep.

"So do you," I tell him, cupping his stubbly cheek in my palm. Those arctic blue eyes meet mine, and I feel like I might melt under his gaze. I forget that there are nine other people in this room and fully focus on Aaron. He might be one of ten brothers, but he has a unique heart, and it's that kindness and care that he gave to me when I was at my lowest that had my heart surging with love.

The way his hips rub against my clit takes me closer and closer to the release I'm so desperate for. My hips have a rhythm of their own, grinding and straining for contact. "That's it," he says. "Give it to me. I want you to come."

"Don't stop," I gasp, arching my back, eyes squeezed so tightly with concentration that my cheeks hurt.

Aaron speeds his thrusts, and it's just what I need to push me over the edge and tumbling into oblivion. A sound that doesn't sound human leaks from my mouth as my hand clutches his hips, holding him tightly against me while I float away.

Fuck.

I had no idea sex could be like this. The urgency, the desperation, the utter fulfillment. These men have opened my eyes to a new state of being. A place where I don't need to ask for what I need. I'm just given it willingly. It doesn't take long for Aaron to come too; the sound of his release is a deep rumble in my ear.

I feel sweaty and spent, bruised and deliciously used, and still, there are two more of my boys waiting for their turn.

I remember when I first heard about the plan, I was flabbergasted at the idea of ten. How would that work? It would be impossible, I thought, to keep ten men satisfied. I imagined a schedule with each of them only getting one day in ten or three days a month. Even then, I didn't believe I'd want that much sex. It wasn't that I was a prude, but more the sex I'd had was never that inspiring.

How wrong I was.

Ten is more than possible. Ten is amazing. Ten is ideal.

Whoever said three is the magic number obviously hadn't experienced ten.

I take a few minutes to come down from the euphoria, and when I do, I find Ford and Donnie at my sides. It seems fitting that they will be the last. They were my first experience of a ménage, and look where I am now!

"You still got some life in you?" Ford asks with the cheekiest grin on his face. He seems proud of me, and I'm filled with such a deep warmth that I feel like crying. His hand strokes my sweaty brow and then moves lower to cup my breasts and dip between my legs. I nod, but his fingers find my entrance, testing. "You sore here?" he asks. I have to be honest and tell him I am. It's my first time, and I'm not used to so much action. I'm pretty sure that over time I'm going to get used to this and have no problems.

"A little, but I'm okay."

"I don't want to hurt you, girl," he says. "And you know the monster isn't easy to take."

There's a collective groan in the room. "You still using that ridiculous name," Antony laughs.

Ford is unashamed. "I didn't name him myself."

"So you say." Blake rolls his eyes, but he rolls onto his side to get a better view of what's to come.

Casey and Cameron are both stroking themselves, their cocks already hard again. I'm hoping they're just planning to enjoy the view as I definitely won't be able to go a second round with anyone.

"Monster is the perfect name for it," I laugh. "I'll give you all a name if you like."

"I'll pass," Aaron says. "I'm not fifteen anymore."

"You sure?" Grant laughs. "It might explain your lack of chest hair."

"Fuck you," Antony says. "You cuss my twin, you cuss me!"

"All of you need to shut up now," Donnie says. "You're disturbing Laura's aura, and I want it to be just right before me and Ford make her come again."

The room quiets in a way that surprises me. I was expecting more joking around and ribbing, but I guess they respect the fact that they have had their moments of pleasure, and two of their brothers have been patient.

I gaze at Donnie, watching as his pupils widen, the blackness almost obliterating the white-gray of his eyes. "You looking at my soul again?" I ask him.

He smiles. "I can't help myself. It's so beautiful."

"I think you might be a little bit crazy," I say gently, running my hand over his chest. The dusting of hair there is so soft that I get an urge to nuzzle into him and inhale his scent.

"Only crazy for you."

There are some humorous gagging sounds from around us, but it doesn't seem to bother Donnie in the slightest. "How shall we do this?" I ask him. Maybe Donnie and Ford have a little plan. Maybe they liked it how we did it before?

"How about this?" Donnie says. He lays back and encourages me to kneel between his legs. I'm guessing that Ford has an idea of what Donnie is suggesting, and he takes his place behind me. I take Donnie's straining cock in my hands and stroke it up and down, relishing the heat of it. His eyes roll closed, and he puts his hands behind his head. It's a pose of pure relaxation.

Ford pats my ass. "Spread your legs, princess," he says, and my pussy clenches right away. I do as he says and can feel him getting nearer, his finger stroking my clit to get me ready again. I bend down to take Donnie into my mouth, and he groans long and deep.

"Fuck," someone says. It sounds distant, as though I'm immersed in the warm swell of sex feelings and not fully conscious of what is happening around me. Ford presses forward, the head of his immense cock finding my entrance and beginning to spread me wide.

"Damn," he says. I know he's watching the wet, pink lips of my pussy flare around his cock. He strokes over my ass, on the cheek at first and then dipping closer to the place that I never thought I'd allow anyone to touch me. I must stiffen because he tells me to relax. "I'm not going to hurt you, baby. I'm just going to show you how good it can feel."

I think it's his thumb that gently rubs my taint first. It feels big and rough, and it makes me shiver. Even after everything I've done, this still feels really forbidden. His cock pushes deeper, and his thumb presses just a little harder. I take Donnie's cock deep in my throat and wiggle my hips because it all feels too much. I'm too stuffed. Too invaded. Too turned on for my own good.

Is that even that even a thing?

"That's it," Ford says gruffly as his hips press against my ass. I can feel his heavy balls against my labia and clit. He starts to move, using this thumb to press against my ass with each thrust he makes. I use the same tempo to blow Donnie, and his hips start to shift in response.

I make a moaning sound because it feels so damn good. My pussy is so slick that I can hear it each time Ford moves inside me. His thumb never penetrates me, but just the pressure is enough to get me close to coming again in record time.

I'm watching Donnie's face. His eyes are scrunched in concentration, and there are low grunts coming from his mouth. I brace myself as much as I can on my hands as Ford begins to fuck me with more urgency.

Damn. I need to come. I need to come again so badly.

"Mmm," I moan around Donnie's cock, needing Ford to know how close I'm getting. The vibrations must do something extra for Donnie, and he seizes, his abs clenching and torso rising as he curls in on his pleasure. He tastes different from his brother but still salty-sweet and sexy as fuck. I swallow it all down in a way I never thought I would. I'm hungry for these men in every way.

I rise up on my hands, leaving Donnie to come down

from his orgasm. I wish I could see his aura the way he says he can see mine. I bet it would be beautiful.

Ford takes hold of my hips now, pounding into me harder, pulling me towards him with every thrust. I don't know whose finger finds my clit, but I don't care. The pressure is perfect, and it doesn't take long before I'm begging them not to stop.

This final orgasm is different from the rest. It's ferocious and quick, a lightning bolt of pleasure that has me collapsing onto my forearms. Ford must like the new angle because he slaps my ass and speeds even more.

"Fuck," he gasps as his cock swells inside me. The monster is impossibly huge, and I love it. I love it so much that I'd get down on my knees and worship it. When Ford comes, I think the whole house must know it. He bellows and collapses over me, wrapping his arms under my body to hold us together. His breath in my ear is so damn hot I feel like I might melt.

"You fucking blew my mind," he says. "My brains are all over this bed."

I laugh, thinking it's actually his come that is all over the bed; his and his brothers. I'm leaking everywhere, and it feels amazing.

One of his brothers mutters, "smooth" from somewhere in the room.

I want to tell them that I don't need smooth and that all that I'm looking for – all that I'll ever be looking for – is real.

I don't know how long we lay there together. When

Ford regathers his brain, and I find my sense, and Donnie wakes from his sex coma, the brothers all start laughing and joking. It's happy and comfortable, and in this circle of my men, I feel totally content.

My Mom always told me I was going to need to kiss a lot of frogs before I found my prince. It turns out, for me, it was the other way around.

It seemed like such a huge step to leave my ordinary life behind and become part of this crazy-big family. It seemed like an impossible idea that we could all be together as one giant unit. Life has a tendency to throw the strangest curveballs at us, but it's how we respond that counts. The McGregor brothers have shown me that there are many different ways to live life and love. Following the well-trodden path is not always the way to find the greatest happiness.

As I lay between my ten men, I know that loving each of them will bring me ten times the love I was ever expecting in my life.

Ten men.

Ten hearts.

One love.

Forever.

EPILOGUE

Can I tell you that things were perfect after this reunion? Do real happy-ever-afters exist outside of fairytales? I'm not sure things are that simple. I used to try and picture what Cinderella's life was like after she married her prince. Did she have any problems having children or disagreements with her mother-in-law? Did she start to resent the prince because he was free to ride off into the sunset whenever he liked while she had to stay at the castle? Did he not tell her she was beautiful enough after they tied the knot? Did their marriage end up like so many others?

After that first day together, things got worse pretty quickly, not between us but in the outside world. The Dick Donovan show managed to sway some but not all. There were resignations from the business, and a few of the contracts that were in negotiation disappeared. Roderick was like a bear with a sore head for a while, but the boys were good at managing him and I tried to stay out of his way. Mom and I focused on planning their wedding, hoping that by the time the big day came around that things would have settled down. She chose a simple cream suit and insisted that

I wear a gorgeous teal floor-length dress that set off my hair and eyes perfectly. The whole ceremony and reception were going to be held at the mansion. We just had to find a wedding planner who could bring in all of the different suppliers to make it work. I was grateful for that because it meant I could avoid going out for a while.

I'm not a natural hermit, preferring the company of people and the excitement of new environments to staying at home, but for a few months, it was necessary.

The boys were able to deflect any abuse that was thrown their way, but I didn't feel so robust.

The big day came, and it was glorious. Mom looked radiant, and the planner had created the perfect setting on our grounds. An ornate arch woven with flowers provided the backdrop to the Officiant, and white chairs were decorated with beautiful chiffon bows. A quartet played soft, classical music as Mom made her way towards Roderick. We invited only family and close friends, so it was intimate and special. I followed Mom, carrying a posy of wildflowers, my hair set into loose waves.

Roderick's eyes were intense as Mom made her way to the front.

Since the TV interview, my respect for Roderick has grown significantly. He'd not only proven himself to be a man who would defend his sons and me in the most challenging of circumstances but a man who would care for my mom, shielding her from the difficulties the press coverage brought.

Roderick's weren't the only intense eyes.

As I walk behind Mom, I'm watched by ten pairs of eyes that are burning with intensity.

My ten men.

They all stand in matching suits, with gorgeous smiles and looks that almost enflame me with the desire I feel. Roderick had to choose one best man, so he went for Aaron, his oldest son. I know it meant so much to Aaron as their relationship isn't always easy, and he's the son who needs his father's validation the most.

The ceremony is brief and beautiful, the vows personal and heartfelt. The first kiss is sweet and tender, as all first kisses should be, and I look to my boys, imagining what it could be like for us.

Who would have the first kiss when there are ten grooms?

There hasn't been much rivalry since we've been together. Somehow, they have managed to share me with sensitivity and passion rather than competition. It's everything they promised me it would be and more.

I guess they would find a way to decide who'd kiss me first. I know for sure I couldn't decide. Favoritism isn't something I ever want to show.

At the reception, Roderick gave a short speech, telling the crowd of his love for my mom and how she's the first woman to show him what peace truly feels like. I dabbed my eyes as my mom stood.

I wasn't expecting her to give a speech, and she didn't. Instead, she addressed me, telling me that she had something for me. I walked to the top table, and she kissed me, pulling me in for a warm hug that reminded me of years past when I was just a child in her arms.

"This is for you, Laura," she said, handing me her bouquet.

I was momentarily stunned, then, as I turned to walk back to my table, I saw my McGregor boys, each on one knee, with Ford at the front holding a ring in a box.

My hand flew to my mouth.

Was I really surprised? Yes, I was. For all their talk about us spending our lives together, we hadn't formalized the intention in any way.

Their faces were solemn and earnest as though there was a part of each of them that was genuinely worried that I might say no.

"Will you spend the rest of your life with us?" Ford asked. "We love you, Laura."

I didn't hesitate for a second.

Tears filled my eyes as I nodded my yes, then the boys were up and surrounding me, hugging and kissing me and each other in celebration and relief. Applause filled the air as the guests reacted to the surprise with their approval.

Mom and Roderick were there too, congratulating and joining in the hug-fest. Our family, although different from pretty much everyone else's in the world, was so happy.

The ring was a spectacular square sapphire, chosen because of its match to my eyes, surrounded with tiny square diamonds on a thin platinum band. It was Ford who slid it onto my finger, his eyes shining brightly with love.

"There you go, girl. We'll make an honest woman of you."

"I'm already honest," I said.

He nodded and kissed my lips. "Respectable then?" he added cheekily.

"Think it might take more than a ring to do that," I'd laughed.

"I'd tell you not to worry about other people if I thought you still cared," he smiled.

I nodded, glad that he'd realized that I'd gotten over the embarrassment and shame that I felt when I left them all. Instead, I felt pride. I mean, having just one McGregor for a husband would be something to be proud of, but having ten? Well, I had a pretty strong feeling that most women out there would be jealous as hell.

The rest of the wedding passed by in a blur. My cheeks hurt from smiling so hard, and my feet ached from dancing all night. I had ten men to partner with, after all.

After the guests had left, we all retired to our room.

When we were lying in bed, they talked to me about how they wanted things to work if I was in agreement. Their plan was to put their names into a hat and for me to pick one. The chosen brother would be the one I'd officially marry. They wanted it that way to ensure our union was at least partly legal. It would mean that our children would be born into a legal marriage and, if the worst happened, things would be clear. Behind the scenes, there would be other legal contracts to express the finer details of our bond.

My heart was sad that I'd only be able to marry one of my boys officially, but I could see why they wanted to organize things the way they spoke of. One of the legal agreements they wanted to make was that the children would never know who their father was but would be raised with ten. We'd sign to say that no paternity tests would be permitted. I was also happy with this because in the back of my mind, I'd always been concerned that there might be favoritism. It's only natural to feel different about your own child. I'd also worried that I wouldn't be able to give them all a child. This way, it would be pot luck as to who would father a genetic child, and all of them would be able to experience the joy of being a father.

I was the last to fall asleep that night, imagining what our children could look like. Would they have Donnie's soft gray eyes or Elliot's blond hair? Or maybe Ford's build or Antony's dimples. Whoever they looked like, I knew they would be loved from the tips of their toes to the ends of their noses. Ten fathers would make them the luckiest children in the world.

We only waited another six months to marry. It was Barrett's name I pulled from the jar and Barrett who became my official husband. It was my ten men who kissed me when the ceremony was over. My ten men who told me I was the most beautiful bride in the world. My ten men who shared our first dance, who cut our cake into pieces, who made love to me like the world was about to end and they wanted our souls to become one before it was too late.

And nine months later, it was my ten men who drove me to the hospital to witness the birth of our first children.

We didn't find out the sex of the children in advance. I think all of us just expected them to be boys. So when two brown-haired girls with blue eyes made their way into the world, the whole room was completely overwhelmed.

Twins.

That certainly shouldn't have been a surprise.

Hannah and Hope were exactly five pounds each.

Ten pounds of babies born from my love for ten men.

It seemed that ten was my lucky number.

I was overwhelmed as I held my beautiful baby girls, who were sleeping soundly in my arms. What had I done to deserve such joy? My heart felt as though it would burst from all the love.

"Look what you did," Grant said, stroking Hope's soft cheek.

"We did," I corrected. Donnie does the same to Hannah's cheek, and both baby girls stirred, eyes opening as though they are checking who's there. They settled again almost immediately, even though there was a sea of faces around them. I guess they must have gotten used to all the voices that surrounded me.

It hadn't been an easy road.

Life has been full of challenges, but that's what makes it great. How would we know true sweetness if we hadn't tasted its bitter contrast?

I knew for sure that there was never going to be a shortage of arms to hold us or hearts to love us. I was a mom, and I knew for sure that I had done the best for myself, my girls, and the babies I prayed were to come.

These men were going to be everything that we needed for as long as we all had breath in our lungs and beats in our hearts.

Tears started to leak from my eyes, and nine faces switched from happy to worried almost immediately.

"It's okay," Donnie said to his brothers. "Her aura is happy. They are tears of joy."

Ten hands found my arms, my hands, my legs, my ankles. Ten men showed me that they were with me in joy and sorrow, and as I lay between them again, with the future of our family in my arms, I finally felt complete.

ABOUT THE AUTHOR

International bestselling author Stephanie Brother writes high heat love stories with a hint of the forbidden. Since 2015, she's been bringing to life handsome, flawed heroes who know how to treat their women. If you enjoy stories involving multiple lovers, including twins, triplets, stepbrothers, and their friends, you're in the right place. When it comes to books and men, Stephanie truly believes it's the more, the merrier.

She spends most of her day typing, drinking coffee, and interacting with readers.

Her books have been translated into German, French, and Spanish, and she has hit the Amazon bestseller list in seven countries.

Find out more at stephaniebrotherbooks.com